BREAKPOINT

Books by William Brinkley

BREAKPOINT

THE NINETY AND NINE

THE TWO SUSANS

THE FUN HOUSE

DON'T GO NEAR THE WATER

THE DELIVERANCE OF SISTER CECILIA

QUICKSAND

BREAKPOINT

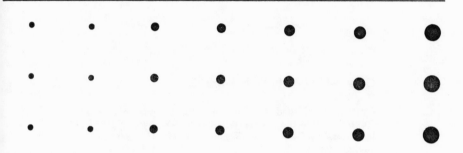

A NOVEL BY

WILLIAM BRINKLEY

WILLIAM MORROW AND COMPANY, INC.
NEW YORK 1978

Grateful acknowledgment is made for permission to quote
from "Brighten the Corner Where You Are," copyright 1913
by Chas. H. Gabriel. © Renewed 1941. The Rodeheaver
Co., Owner.

Library of Congress Cataloging in Publication Data

Brinkley, William (date)
    Breakpoint.

    I. Title.
PZ3.B77155Br   [PS3503.R56175]   813'.5'4   78-1773
ISBN 0-688-03288-5

BOOK DESIGN   CARL WEISS

Printed in the United States of America.

First Edition

1   2   3   4   5   6   7   8   9   10

To

Jean

and

Ralph

CONTENTS

PART I / PALM BEACH

PART II / JEKYLL ISLAND

PART III / THE NEW YORK ISLAND

PART IV / FOREST HILLS

BREAKPOINT

PART I

PALM
BEACH

1

THE BIG CAT

LIKE EVERYONE ELSE WHO HAS EVER BEEN AROUND TENNIS, I had heard of Robert Catlo always. So I suppose I should have been prepared for what I found when my magazine sent me to south Florida. It was a little over three weeks before Forest Hills, and the idea was to do a cover story on Catlo during the U. S. Open as one of the "Living Immortals of Sports." In an age when sports figures are altogether lionized in the press and on television, and when the athletes themselves accordingly cultivate sportswriters, it was typical of Catlo that he refused to be interviewed. When I communicated this information to my editor and prepared, not unhappily, to return to New York—August is not my favorite month in south Florida—I got back a three-word telegram: "So watch him." I canceled my plane reservation and returned to the South Palm Beach Bath and Tennis Club. I was surprised to be hospitably accepted on these terms.

"I suppose even the pimps of journalism," the hospitality went, "have to make a living. You can hang out for a couple of days. Can you hit a tennis ball?"

"If it isn't hit too hard at me."

"You'll pay me two hours of lesson time a day whether we hit or not. That comes to a hundred dollars. There's no reason you and your magazine should get fat off me for free."

"They think it works the other way around."

"But ask me one question and I'll have your ass out of here."

Catlo, of course, was famous for his menacing, faintly dangerous air, on the court and off. One approached him with caution. I had read the old newspaper clips before coming to Florida. The sportswriters had described that aspect of him in their customary florid way:

"There is about him the grand air, the very mystique, of the great champion. He ranges the court like some predatory jaguar, as though that small plot of grass or clay were his own private real estate, to be violated only at peril. This halo of forbidden space seems to follow him everywhere."

Or this, from one of the new lady sportswriters: "His lean, bronzed, Aztec-god body gives off the very aura of maleness. He moves with the fluid grace of a panther stalking the jungle. He has perhaps the loveliest thighs in the sports kingdom." (Catlo was always being compared to the better animals.)

And, from the late fifties, one more sportswriter's paean: "He has no weakness and it is apparent that he is on the threshold of dominating his sport in a way no sport in America has been dominated by one man. The time may be near when no one can be found who consistently belongs on the same court with him. What an awesome arsenal he brings with him. Add to his intimidating air—which has many opponents beaten before a tennis ball is struck—the lethal volley, the shattering overhead, the screaming groundstrokes, the savage backhand, the serve which comes at you like a runaway train bent on head-on collision, all of these executed with the reflexes of a jungle cat, and surely Robert Catlo may be the greatest King Tennis of the long royal line."

There may well never have been a game like Catlo's. His command of the court seemed absolute, as if he held it in his hand. But there was something else. The great game came attended by an equally great style. His game seemed to flow rather than to be played, invested with a grace that made watching him an aesthetic joy, the kind of joy that a great bullfighter gives us. The regal manner, the cocksure maleness, the invincible game—Catlo had it all. If he had been born a short

time later, he would have become the richest and most idol-
ized tennis superstar the game has ever known. But he lost it
all on the eve of the big money and the big fame.

To come upon this figure patting balls across a net to rich
divorcées for fifty dollars an hour was to come upon Bach
teaching "Chopsticks." A caged lion, if I may add one more
beast to the Catlo wild kingdom lexicon. Indeed, the surprising thing was to find Catlo not even more bitter. I discovered
the reason by accident.

I have a habit of losing my billfold when I play tennis. I put
the billfold just inside one of the net posts where it is safely
hidden, so well hidden in fact that I often forget it. When I
got back to the Jolly Roger Hotel after a so-called "playing
lesson" with Catlo—he refrained from mutilating me with
tennis balls only by a conscious effort—I realized it had happened again. I turned the Avis around. It was twilight when
I drove up to the South Palm Beach Bath and Tennis Club.
The courts stood empty, the pro shack dark and locked. Then
I heard a sound like an artillery piece firing. I walked down the
line of twelve courts and came to the last one, where I had
left the billfold and from which the sounds were coming. I
bent and looked through a crescent of the green canvas windscreen.

His back to me, Catlo was receiving serve, one serve after
another. A dozen balls lay around him. I heard that sharp
crack of sound again and saw a tennis ball speed toward Catlo
at a velocity that made me glad the chain-link fence was between me and that serve. Then, a fraction of a second later,
I heard another explosion, of a different timbre from the one
produced by the serve. I could not imagine what this second
explosion came from—Catlo was not hitting the ball back.
Then I saw that the serve was being aimed at a small yellow
ball bucket which Catlo kept moving around to various
places within the service box. The second explosion didn't
come every time but when it did, it sent the basket flying. Then
across the net on the baseline I saw a tall beautiful boy framed

against the Florida evening sky. At that point Catlo, turning to retrieve the bucket from another scattering bull's-eye, saw me and articulated some language that would never end up in my magazine.

"Wait a minute," he said to the tall boy across the net. The tone was ominous.

He walked over and opened the gate. "Step in here," he said.

I found myself experiencing a touch of physical fright. I walked through the gate and stood on the rust-colored clay. Catlo shut the gate behind me.

"What are you doing here?" he said. "You're on private property."

"I came back for my billfold."

"I don't believe you. You're spying."

"Who for? The CIA?"

"Don't be cute with me, Brinkley."

I turned with what I hoped was an air of my own and walked across the court to one of the net posts and retrieved my billfold. Catlo was right behind me.

"For once," he said, "a journalistic pimp has told the truth."

"Well, truth is such a good thing even pimps tell it occasionally," I said. "Speaking of truth . . ."

I glanced at the balls strewn over the court. "Looks like a pretty serious workout. Let me see. Forest Hills is getting close, isn't it?"

Catlo watched me with that cat-look of his that drilled into you to find out how much you knew and how much you were bluffing.

"I hadn't realized it was going to be this year, though," I said. "Very interesting."

"Who said anything about this year?"

"It'll be nice to have the name back," I said. "Don't let me interrupt. Why don't you go ahead. You and Billy Catlo."

Catlo had remarkable eyes, watchful eyes. Large and black, they seemed to be sizing me up. It was as if I were undergoing some kind of secret personal test he had, some code for judging people.

"You're way out of line," he said with that lofty air he had. "But since you're here you can sit down and watch—this time. I may want a word with you later."

Ever since I first went to their country I have thought the Aztec to possess the purest physical beauty that ever existed. No male body in the world is so exquisite: the glistening copper skin, the elegant molded bones, the easy curvatures, the lithe frame, the entire grace. Catlo and his son were classic examples. The son's body was boy-lean, flat-bellied and narrow-hipped. The only difference in the father's was that there was just a little more of him. For the next half hour, in what light remained, Catlo displayed his son's repertory.

I had seen Billy a couple of times, the first as a freshman at last year's national collegiate tournament. He had won that. But instead of dropping out of college and going on the pro tour, as had become the custom since the big new money came to tennis, he had continued in school. He did play the summer tournament circuit in the months following the NCAA victory. He won the "Southerns" at Raleigh without being seriously extended. More importantly, he had reached the third round in one major tournament, the Louisville Classic, and the quarterfinals in another, the U. S. Clay Courts at Indianapolis. In both he beat some pretty fair players. My impression of him had been that he had the gift and that its presence or absence on a given day could fluctuate wildly. But when September came it was back to school. I had speculated at this unexpected turn of events. Maybe Catlo and Billy had decided that education was even more important than being a tennis champion. Or maybe they had coldly decided that Billy, while good, was never going to be good enough to go all the way, and that for a Catlo anything less was not worth going at all. Whatever their reasons, Billy disappeared from the tennis world. Presumably he had been with his books ever since, though evidently, as I watched now, he had also been engaged in these secret sessions with his father. His game had come a great distance since I last saw it.

It was an eerie and almost ghostly sight, in the dimming light of that Florida day and the loneliness of the emptied courts, the two of them on opposite sides of the net, as if Catlo were playing himself twenty years ago. Billy had the same flowing game that had made the father's such a thing of beauty, although with some of the puppy awkwardness of youth. Father and son did not actually play. The father just hit different shots designed to test and stretch and probe the son. Billy had the reflexes, even the Big Cat finding it no easy thing to pass him at net. He had a breathtaking return of serve. The serve possessed by a Robert Catlo, by a Jack Tillotston, is meant to dominate, to overwhelm, even to terrorize. A serve of 140 miles per hour is not expected to be attacked with an eager ferocity and sent screaming back across the net to *itself* become a dominating shot. Billy's return of serve detonated off the racket. As for the kid's own serve, well, Catlo himself had the biggest serve ever clocked in tennis. I saw the father's and saw the son's that twilight afternoon and I agreed with what Catlo said later to me. "It's not as big as mine but it's near enough, and it's growing. It's a little wild but we're working on that. The yellow basket."

Wildness, in fact, was the main problem with the boy's game. He had power and quickness and he had the shots. But too many of these flew out, some by a foot or a yard, most by no more than three or four inches. If someone had asked me at that point if he was ready for Forest Hills, I would have said, "Not yet. Possibly a year from now. Provided something is done about the accuracy—*can* something be done?" If so . . . well, I knew of no player he could not face across the net.

However, nobody asked me. Presently, with my not having said two words to the son, and his not having said one to me or his father, I was dismissed by Catlo. Whatever he wanted to say to me, he had decided to remain silent. When I left they were still hitting, using the last scrap of light to go after . . . what? The deep sweet resonance of the big hitters slamming gut against a tennis ball followed me onto the catwalk that ran along the courts. I drove back to the Jolly Roger in the still and cloudless air that cast a canopy of heat haze along the beach where the colored lights began to glow in the beach hotels and bars. I could see them shimmering in the satin sea. It had always been an odd time of day for me, sad and full of longing, yet fraught with anticipation of something wonderful that might happen with the night, some rare and special girl with fragrance in her garments and light in her eyes.

I always carry a hundred-dollar bill in my billfold. I do not know whether this is my talisman or a childish insecurity in the son of a minister's family where there was never much money around of any denomination. Anyhow when I opened the billfold the hundred was gone. It had never happened before, and I had been in some odd places. Only on Court 12 of the South Palm Beach Bath and Tennis Club. I reminded myself to find a bank tomorrow and get a replacement and to figure some way to amortize the loss in the expense account.

I switched on the news. The weather announcer was saying that a "tropical depression" had been located 100 miles south southwest of Puerto Rico and 1150 miles southeast of Palm Beach. It was carrying thirty-mile winds, moving at seven miles per hour and was being watched by Navy reconnaissance planes as the first potential tropical storm of the hurricane season. This one would be named Agatha, the announcer said with that little human-interest laugh television announcers have for us at such moments. I took a shower and went downstairs to the hotel's "Pirate's Lair" lounge to see what I could stir up.

Next morning after a restless night—no vision of loveliness and desire had materialized beside me in the Pirate's Lair— I drove out to see something called the Lady-Novices Group Lesson. It must have been a strain for Robert Catlo to give those lessons, a man who had known the glory of the Centre Court at Wimbledon and the Stadium at Forest Hills. He stood hour after hour pitty-pattying balls across a net to people whose only tennis qualification was their ability to pay for his services. To Catlo's credit he actually worked at being a good teaching pro. I imagine it was a matter of pride. The ladies, I am sure, would have paid their twenty-five dollars an hour (group lesson rates) merely to *say* they had taken lessons from Robert Catlo, with perhaps a Polaroid shot of him and them standing at the net as proof. He did considerably more.

The twelve Lady-Novices presented a picture of style and correctness—half in tennis dresses, half in shorts and Lacoste sleeveless shirts with the crocodile status emblem about to bite the left breast, all in pure white. They stood ranged in rows of four between the service line and the baseline, watching with docile demeanor the tall, burnished figure across the net, the same sight many a world-class player had gazed upon and felt the terror kindling inside him. The figure now stood quietly before them, immaculate in his Fred Perrys and Converses, holding a tennis racket and at his feet that rosary of the teaching pro, a yellow bucket of balls. I pulled up one of the lawn-green director's chairs with the club's name stenciled on the back and used my restricted hunting license to "watch." The sun burned down from a livid, cloud-free sky in the airless heat that seizes south Florida at that time of year. I was glad to be seated beneath a cabbage palm having my morning Dr. Pepper.

As I watched I sensed that in addition to the magnetism he held for them they also felt some of the menace that Catlo carried with him like part of his body. Though he had to do this to make a living, he was still Robert Catlo and one knew one had best be on good behavior around him. On the ladies' side of the net there was a good deal of humility and a certain feeling of awe at being where they were.

"Some of my methods are a bit unorthodox, Ladies," Catlo was saying. "For instance, I believe one of the first things people should learn is the volley, instead of leaving it to the last. More points are won in tennis with the volley than with any other shot. Why not learn it as quickly as possible?"

His voice fell nicely on the ear. It was quiet and modulated, decidedly on the husky side, almost soothing.

"So the lesson this morning is the volley. One thing I'd like to get straight is the stupid way people use this word. Will you ladies kindly show me you're listening by raising your rackets?"

Eleven rackets went up. "You too, Tish," Catlo said.

"Sorry," and the last racket came aloft.

It was a Davis Classic, probably the most beautiful racket in tennis with its polished spectrum of different-colored woods, and appropriately expensive. This one belonged to a woman I judged to be about thirty-five. The shorts and shirt showed a good figure, rather on the full side, especially the part handled by the shirt. She had dark auburn hair which may have been dyed or at least tinted and she presented a picture of the best grooming that Palm Beach money could buy.

Catlo said, "I want you ladies to master the difference between two words. Nothing identifies you quicker as a greenhorn than to say volley when you mean rally. Rally is what you do when you come out and practice with each other. Volley is something else. Any time you hit a ball in the air instead of off the ground, that's a volley. Never let me hear any one of you ladies say, 'Would you care to volley with me?' "

Catlo paused a moment. His pupils watched him with classroom attention.

"The volley has rightly been called the 'jugular shot' of tennis. Nothing gives you quite so much a feeling of power as a properly-executed volley. You stand at the net and put your arm up high and slam that ball down your opponent's windpipe. The greatest tribute to the volley was uttered only the other day by Billie Jean King. Now Billie Jean can say things *I* can't."

He continued quickly. "One word will always remind you

how to execute a volley. The word is *foot*. Foot as in twelve inches. First"—and Catlo showed them—"the racket is held a *foot* in front and a *foot* to the right of the body. *So.* Also the entire stroke in the volley travels only a *foot. So.* One *foot* for everything. Now here's the other thing to remember. It's the only shot in tennis where you don't swing. You *punch. So.*"

With one hand, Catlo picked up four balls from his yellow basket, as easily as someone else might gather up four walnuts and, demonstrating all this, let them fall off his racket and plop over the net.

"The volley is an especially great stroke for you ladies because it doesn't take much strength. It couldn't since it only has to travel twelve inches. Now let's all practice it together. Raise your rackets!"

The twelve went up like a ragged ballet. "One, *punch* . . . two, *punch* . . . Make it a jabbing stroke like you're punching somebody in the mouth . . . three, *punch* . . . there's nothing like tennis for getting rid of your hostilities . . . *back* . . . four, *punch* . . . five, *punch* . . . not *that* far back . . . Remember, only a *foot*, a *foot*, a *foot* . . . Yes, Lindy?"

Another racket had been raised. "Mr. Catlo, how long do we keep it in the forward position?"

The racket was a Tad Imperial, much less expensive than the Davis Classic, and it was held aloft in the left hand by a girl of about eighteen. Nothing about her was dyed. The figure was coltish, almost on the boyish side, with lean and lithe-looking thighs, small breasts, and a fair complexion made more enticing by a scattering of freckles. She gave the impression, even in that quiet, determined heat, of being exceptionally clean, as if she had just stepped from her bath. Her short, white-blonde hair shimmered in the sun.

"You keep the racket in the forward position," Catlo said dryly, "until you have finished hitting the ball."

He showed them one or two more refinements. "Now, Ladies," he said, "I'm going to leave you. For the next practice hour I want you to divide four to a court, two on each side. I want each team on each side of the net to take turns hitting volleys. Work hard now. It's pretty hot out here and I have to go in where it's air-conditioned and take my morning nap."

He positioned them for the exercise. As I got up from the director's chair, the white-blonde girl with the Tad Imperial was standing no more than six feet from me. Her dress rose and she reached back to her panties so that for a moment I saw the memorable thing fully displayed and clothed only in thin white nylon. I was startled at such boldness until I realized, as she brought forth a yellow tennis ball, that she was wearing the new *bal pockette* panties, a seminal advance in tennis equipment that enables a lady player to hold only one ball while serving. The movement was accomplished so innocently that I had the impression she was entirely unaware of the effect she had on a male bystander. I felt my fingers dig into my palms. I followed Catlo to the pro shack.

"What did Billie Jean say?" I asked.

"She said hitting a volley was like having an orgasm. Right there in the pages of *World Tennis*. If it were true I would never have been able to walk off the court after the first game."

He sighed. I had a glimpse of something I felt he tried to hide, usually with success: frustration. I felt that pride of his would make him do correctly what he had to do, but that nothing could keep him from being, deep inside, revolted by having to do it. I was saddened myself that as great a champion as the game has known should come down to the Lady-Novices Group Lesson. Especially now, when tennis dollars were raining by the millions from the heavens. I looked at him slumped there in the chair. The Catlo physique had been such a measure for grace that it was a mild shock to realize that age was beginning to reach out for him too. The lean brown body was still there. But I could see touches of grey in the thick black hair, the first hints of puffiness along those fine cheekbones.

Maybe the frustration had something to do with it. In any

event he actually suggested, rather curtly of course, that we have a drink that night.

"Right after Billy's workout. I've decided you can interview me, provided I don't find the questions offensive. I'll continue to charge you the same rate I do for lessons."

Fifty dollars an hour for drinking Tanqueray martinis might have seemed on the steep side—for anyone but Robert Catlo. The daily rate was coming to something like $250 already—not your usual summer rate in Florida. Fortunately I worked for a successful magazine that truly liked jocks of all kinds. Especially immortal jocks.

But he made his money where he could find it, scrounging from me, giving lessons, betting with club players $500 a set. The club player won if he took three points. A number of the better-fixed club players in south Florida had tried it. A few had taken two points off Catlo. None, three.

The Pirate's Lair of the Jolly Roger Hotel is reached by crossing a gangplank over a little stream of gurgling water in which a solitary small shark swims silently back and forth. The tables are sea chests and the chairs are rum kegs. The Lair is very dark and conspiratorial, befitting pirates, with the only light coming through portholes no larger than a salad plate. The waitresses are young and foxy. They are costumed in red bandanna kerchiefs, black eyepatches and high black net stockings ascending to red panty-tights with frayed fringes. One of them came over promptly when Catlo and I walked the plank and sat on two of the rum kegs.

"What would *you* like, Long John Silver, oh my," the waitress said, addressing Catlo of course. "How about our 'Gangplank' special for which we are famous, with chunks of pineapple, maraschino cherries, Key limes, and six kinds of rum served in our authentic Pirate's pewter tankard with a stalk of celery sticking out of it?"

Catlo shook his head in disgust. "Bring me a double Tanqueray martini mixed six to one with Noilly Prat, and served straight up in a clean glass. Do you think you can remember that?"

"I can remember just about anything you say, fellow. And how about you, Freddie Bartholomew?"

"A single Tanqueray martini for me, Fanny. I'm cutting back on the hard liquor."

"Oh, we have a wit?" she said. We watched her move brightly away in her net stockings and frayed short-panties.

Catlo had three double Tanqueray martinis, brought by Fanny whose gaze lingered on him more and more. The drinks lightened him only a little. He said I could ask him three questions, no more, and that would be an extra twenty-five dollars for each. I decided that I had best be a reporter for a while and get a little work done on the great cover story.

"Do you feel bitter about it?"

"Things happen. Sometimes, of course, I get a little annoyed at my mother and old man for having me too soon. If they'd waited five years I'd be a millionaire. What the hell. They were both under twenty and they didn't even have the pill."

He shrugged. "*Así es la vida.* Life goes. When I was on the tour we were lucky to get expenses and thirty bucks a day— under the table. I stayed alive by betting on myself. My god, it did happen in a hurry."

None of this was said with self-pity. I never saw a man more free of that condition than Catlo, considering what he missed and how close he came. For it *had* happened overnight. From the thirty bucks for its most lustrous names, tennis had awakened one morning to a state of rosy shock, to the hundred-thousand-dollar tournaments, to the great "tennis explosion" that was to enrich a new generation of child-players beyond the wildest dreams of any of them. It all came very quickly, just after Robert Catlo had passed his peak. The younger pros got him coming down. They were over the Big Cat like eager little hyenas, snapping at him, wounding him. It was Jack Tillotston, then only twenty-two, who finished him off. Tillotston had been King Tennis ever since and he would never have to play pitty-pat tennis across a net with a Lady-Novices Class.

"My missing out on the big bread was nothing personal, of course. Getting screwed seldom is. And maybe things even out. ·The timing couldn't be better for Billy—if he decides to go for it. Do you realize Tillotston's half million dollars a year doesn't even include the endorsements?"

No bitterness showed even when he said Tillotston's name. And yet no one who saw that last match of Catlo and Tillotston, in Wimbledon's quarterfinals on the Centre Court eight years ago, would ever forget it. I know because I was there. If ever a man showed how a champion should go down, Robert Catlo did it on that day in England.

Catlo knew he would have to take the first set if he were to have any chance of winning. I do not know that tennis has seen another like it. The Catlo of old raged across the grass as if this were Agincourt. That body which had brought such grace to the game moved in splendor: the shots exploding from his racket, the huge serve booming ·across the net, the overhead smashes rocketing into the grass; the man racing for unplayable shots and sending them screaming into the chalk on the other side. It was an awesome display of the game and the crowd of 14,000, every last seat filled, had alternately gasped and sat silent in wonder at what was happening before them. Later I came to think that Catlo must have known how it was going to end, but that he wanted to leave behind one set to show what the game was all about. Tillotston, with a youth advantage of thirteen years, had to fight with every shot and tactic he possessed for every point he took, and at the end he won it at 14-12. Tillotston still had to play at the top of his game to take the second set 10-8. But Catlo had put all he had into those two sets.

Soon after the third set began it was obvious that Catlo was playing on nothing but gallantry and pride, and that Tillotston could do as he wished. What he did was rub Catlo's face in the grass. It was the way he took so many points. Some were by massive put-aways or thunderous down-the-line shots and that was all right. But others he won by putting Catlo on exhibition, like some great warrior now grown old and being taunted through a cage. He ran Catlo over the court—hitting a ball to one side, then if Catlo returned that one, hitting to the far other side, and back again, prolonging points that he could have put away for quicker winners. Tillotston performed the ritual not just of burying Catlo for good but humiliating him, never letting up. By no sign, by no gesture, did Catlo ever give way, or ask for less. At the odd-game changeover, that one minute of respite, he would sit in his chair with his back very straight and his feet flat on the grass to let the blood flow down into his legs. When the umpire above him said, "Time, Gentlemen," he got up immediately and walked erect to his side of the net and looked at Tillotston across it, defiant. He tried for every shot, ran for every ball, straining to the furthest limits those once great legs but now, as the third set went on, surely feeling the pain of every step. No one who was there will forget Robert Catlo, lunging gallantly, futilely and at last pathetically over the court, as if to say they would have to come and get him, that nothing would be given away. The last three games Tillotston performed an execution. He ran off twelve straight points while Catlo, summoning something from what source no one could say, fought on to the last point.

Then it was over and Catlo was standing there beneath the umpire's chair, near collapse, his head bowed a little where his hands held to his face a towel on which he had poured a glass of cold water. I have never seen a tennis audience so quiet. Silent, I think, from the knowledge that on that court which had seen so much, they had been witness to something extraordinary and enduring. Then there came a sight great Wimbledon had never seen.

Fourteen thousand people rose to their feet and began to clap and cheer, not the victor but the vanquished. Wave on wave of applause swept down over the plot of grass which had seen every champion the game has ever known, as if to say it had seen none like this. When the applause at last began to die, in some far corner of the stadium a lone voice began to sing.

"For he's a jolly good fellow
For he's a jolly good fellow . . ."

Soon every voice was singing in a gentle, lilting tide that rose into the English sky.

"And so say all of us
And so say all of us
For he's a jolly good fellow,
And so say all of us."

I was in the West Open Stand. I could hear around me a few people crying softly. As a reporter it has always been my rule not to become involved in any emotions that arise in a sports arena, but I would not swear to it, on that summer day at Wimbledon, that I was not among them.

In my experience in tennis, I have not seen a tribute such as that given Robert Catlo. But for all of us that day, the brutal shock of Catlo's execution would remain. Certainly it would remain in Catlo.

"Second question," I said. "Can Billy take him?"

"Billy?" Catlo said his son's name as if it belonged to a stranger. "Are you serious? This year? Not a chance."

"Why not?"

"Too wild. Can't get the ball in enough. You saw that and you claim to be a tennis writer, whatever the fuck that is. Too inexperienced in pressure. In guile. Tillotston would chew him up and spit him out like baby food. Next year or the year after. Maybe."

"Wouldn't you prefer it to be this year?"

That question made Catlo angry. "Well of course I'd *prefer* they gave the fucking title to him without even going to Forest Hills. Any more stupid questions?"

"I think I've spent my seventy-five dollars," I said.

I didn't believe him. Catlo was lying, whatever his reasons. I believed he was working with Billy to make a run at the champion now.

"Did you see that little package in the lesson this morning?" he was saying as though he wanted to get away from the subject. "The one with the tight little ass."

Just on that identification I knew at once.

"Oh, yes. The white-blonde hair. The ball-pocket panties. An important step forward in the game."

"That's Billy's girl. Lindy."

"A splendid choice. He's not wild there."

It came out so suddenly. "The worst thing you can do before a tournament is to do a lot of screwing." Catlo said this soberly, as if it were some unquestioned fiat of tennis, some first principle, like watching the ball or turning your body to the net.

"You can say that again." It was Fanny in the nets and the red panty-tights, bearing drinks. She looked at us out of her one free eye. "I personally never screw before a tournament. Are you playing one tomorrow, fellow?"

She put the drinks down and went away, moving in a gentle, half-moon rhythm. Maybe south Florida in August wasn't so bad.

"Oh, is that what they're doing?" I said.

"What?"

"Are they screwing?"

"Don't be ridiculous. Lindy's a Jesus person."

It was baffling, but I liked the talk. I felt the Tanquerays were beginning to get to Catlo, just slightly, and that tomorrow he might regret, slightly, some of the things he was saying tonight. So I listened. We all have a little pimp in us when it comes to our profession.

"I think she took up tennis just to be able to talk to Billy— and probably convert him. What her people do is convert other people."

"Whatever she does, I think she'll go far in it."

"They have what they call the Jesus Class and Lindy conducts it. She's brighten the corner where you are."

"I'd like her to brighten mine."

"He wants to spend all his time hitting with her instead of me," Catlo went on. "The worst possible thing for his game. Next to doing a lot of screwing, of course."

"You just said she doesn't."

"And won't, ever. Only I'm sure he keeps trying. That's even worse on your game than actually doing it."

Catlo tapped his glass and Fanny was there. "Well, we don't want that to happen," she said. "I guess it's better to do it, big fellow."

"She doesn't realize what she's doing to his game," Catlo said, ignoring her. "Maybe Tish can help."

"Who?" I said.

"The Davis Classic. She should know. She's a shrewd woman. She owns enough natural gas in Oklahoma to heat Delaware for the next fifty years. Maybe she can figure out how to handle Lindy. This is no time for Billy to get mixed up in a big romance."

Fanny set the drinks down. "All right," she said. "This is your last chance."

"Another time," Catlo said with courtesy. He stood up. "You can come watch what we do tomorrow," he said to me. "It's on the beach." He gave me directions and told me to be there at eight. "Look for the sea grapes and a big sand dune."

I followed him over the gangplank, out of the Jolly Roger and into the Florida night. Even at midnight the air was heavy with heat. The Atlantic lay glassy and lifeless before us. We could barely hear it touching shore.

Catlo looked at his watch. "Three hours plus seventy-five," he said. "That comes to two-twenty-five you owe me."

"Put it on the tab," I said.

"Speaking of money." Catlo brought out his wallet and selected a bill. "You're such a baby, Brinkley. When I was coming up in tennis and really scrounging, I checked every net post I saw, the way kids check the coin return in phone booths. One out of every hundred net posts has a billfold somebody forgot. I don't know the odds on phone booths."

He walked off into the sullen night. I put my hundred-dollar bill in my pocket.

2

THE MAGIC WAND

"PLAY SHALL BE CONTINUOUS." THIS RULE 30 OF TENNIS defines the brutal demands on the body of the tournament game. Save for sixty seconds between each two games, on the odd-game change of sides to make certain there are no advantages of wind or sun-angle, a tournament player plays up to five sets and four hours without ceasing to run and hit. It is no light saying that tennis is a game of the two S's, skill and stamina. No one who lacks either ever becomes a champion.

Just north of Palm Beach and beyond the point where A1A curves for a short distance away from the sea, a great sand dune rises from the beach. All alone, huge, uncommonly steep, it commands a view of a small cove where the shoreline indents itself into a lovely U. The dune extends on three sides of the cove, embracing it.

Beneath a clump of sea grape trees set back from the road sat an old, beat-up MG, a Mercury in need of a paint job and a used Datsun. I put my Avis alongside. I could see the dune in the distance, looking from here like the great pyramid at Teualt, which seems to rise out of the sea and where victims were rolled down its stone steps, heads bouncing away, to appease flippant gods. It took a quarter mile of plowing through heavy sand just to reach it but at the end there was a reward. The girl I had seen yesterday wearing the *bal pockette* was sitting on the beach yoga-fashion. Even in a modest, pale blue one-piece bathing suit and an oversized button-down man's oxford shirt, she only reinforced the evaluation I had made then of her inner thighs. She sat just where the water lapped softly in and receded, so that her bottom was getting a rhythmic wash with each movement of the morning tide. It looked refreshing. I took off my trousers—I was wearing bathing trunks underneath, as one always does in Florida—and joined her. There was not a single cloud in the sky to shield the two men from the blazing August sun as they ran up the dune.

We watched them finally crest the dune high above us, pause briefly like successful mountaineers, then plunge back to the bottom where they stood for a minute looking up at it, panting, and paying no attention to us. Then I heard Catlo say, "All right. Only twenty-seven more times." This time when Billy started up, Catlo stayed on the beach, getting his breath back and watching his son. Both men wore bathing trunks, the father the boxer kind, the son Olympic briefs— and heavy shoes. Billy would toil and struggle upward, legs churning, seeing how quickly he could reach the top. Then down the dune he raced, arms flailing. At the bottom he stood gasping. At his father's signal, he repeated the routine. "Only twenty-two more," Catlo was saying.

We sat, Lindy and I, in the water and said little but watched as Billy did the dune again and again. Catlo joined him for the last climb, and Billy beat him to the top. When finally they walked toward us, I looked at my watch and was surprised to see that they had been at it for nearly an hour. Their slick copper bodies poured off sweat like lathered racehorses, and they were gulping air. They stood above us, then Catlo did a curious thing. He knelt in the sand and unlaced and removed his son's shoes. I was struck by how gentle he was, an almost ceremonial act. Billy, freed now, walked to the water and fell into it.

He lay there belly-down on the surface, as if he were a dead floating fish. Then he came back, this time covered not with the wetness of sweat but with the crystalline drops of the sea. I thought again what a startlingly beautiful boy he was. I heard a cry above us, looked up and saw a gull swooping toward the sea's surface in search of a fish. As my eyes came back they happened to fix on Lindy. She had no idea anyone was watching her. Undiverted by the gull's cry or anything else, she was staring at Billy steadily as he came toward us. She seemed to be in a trance, her face filled with an unadulterated and naked look of lust. I was fascinated. It seemed so out of character. The look was there for only a moment. Catlo was saying something and as if startled, she came out of it.

"That bloody dune is the fifth set," he said, looking up at it.

"They don't call it Big Tit for nothing," Billy said.

"Can't you call it something else?" Lindy said.

"You're not going to pretend you never heard that?" Billy said.

"I hear lots of things I don't go around repeating to the big wide world."

I looked up at the dune. "The name does fit," I said.

Catlo and Billy said something to each other in Spanish and both laughed. The language gave them a little private world in which they could be alone when they wished. Our caravan started off single file through the sand to the cars. The sun beat down and the sand burned my feet. I thought of an arena far away, of Forest Hills and September in New York, and of the young princes of tennis raging away at each other across a 36-inch net, for the glory and the raw money and the golden life of sleek cars and sleek-thighed girls. I watched Billy's body in front of me, and his father's in front of him, moving with the ease of their blood, and Lindy's, whose body had that mist-made cream-whiteness of the English girl and seen against theirs was more striking than ever. September. It had always been my favorite month in New York, the city, hammered down by the months of hard heat, beginning to feel autumn's first sweet coolness as it came alive again. If Billy did not plan to be there soon, then I had a couple of masochists ahead of me.

My feet felt blistered when we reached the cars parked under the sea grapes so that I found myself walking quickly, and I saw Lindy doing the same. The two Aztecs, father and son, seemed as unaffected by the hot sand as if they were on a stroll over dewy grass. We got in the cars—Catlo in the Mercury, Billy in the MG, Lindy in the Datsun, me in the Avis—and the convoy started off toward the tennis courts. From my window I could see the stepless pyramid across the sand. Yes, from here, as at Teualt, it seemed to rise out of the sea itself, a marvelous white cone sitting on the blue water. Suddenly, even though I make it a point never to be a participant in the stories I cover, I found myself hoping that the rituals performed upon it by two latter-day Aztecs would be enough, and for sufficiently noble gods, gods that did not require human sacrifices. Then, looking at it, I laughed. The dune did look like a big, wonderful tit.

At the courts, Catlo was waiting for Billy, who apparently had stopped somewhere en route. I tried to probe him, a very difficult undertaking.

"Well," I said, "that's quite a workout for someone who's not going to Forest Hills."

"Tennis requires a player to keep in shape," he said blandly.

"Keep in shape! You don't need that kind of torture to keep in shape."

It was time for the Catlo freeze. "Are you trying to tell me what a tennis player needs?" he said coldly.

At that moment Billy and Lindy walked up, licking ice-cream cones.

When Robert Catlo was twelve years old, his mother bought a tennis racket in a junk shop for fifty cents, the total funds available for a gift for her son's confirmation in Our Lady of Guadalupe Church in Los Angeles. To Catlo's mother tennis was as unknown and esoteric as medieval jousting. The purchase was an act of sheer chance, almost of desperation.

At a playground near their home in the city's Mexican barrio she had seen boys her son's age, running about on dirty asphalt and flinging this instrument at a ball which had once been white but was now black. A little later, she saw a similar instrument in the junk-dealer's shabby window marked a half-dollar. This providential melding of funds available with the price tag on the racket suggests, in view of what the purchase led to, that Our Lady of Guadalupe took a personal hand in the matter.

Until that confirmation day Catlo had never held a tennis racket in his hand. Nor did he ever have a lesson. No money existed for lessons, and even if his mother could have afforded them, he would not, in that time, have been welcome in the tennis and country clubs where lessons were given. He started on that same filthy asphalt court with the same dirty black balls which scarcely bounced. In his hand the fifty-cent racket came alive like a magic wand. For the first time in his life he had found something that was *his* and he embraced the game with a fierce and unyielding love. I do not believe Catlo imagined that with that racket he could become any man's equal, that it would be his ticket through any door. If each of us possesses individual genes that define our specific talents and in some instances genius, then Catlo must have come equipped with one of the largest tennis genes ever installed in the human body. From the dirty asphalt courts he discovered there was something called the "Public Courts," where you could play without money. During the summer he would go there with his half-dollar racket and hit with it eight hours a day. At night he worked as a car washer at the Beverly Hills Racquet Club while the members played the game inside on manicured surfaces. With his earnings he bought better rackets, and at the Public Courts he improved at an extraordinary rate. Catlo had to fight for everything he ever got. His was a life constructed to give him a savage dedication to getting what he went after, by talent, work and craftiness. At thirteen he was beating boys who were fifteen, at fourteen he was beating boys who were seventeen, at fifteen he was beating boys who were eighteen and nineteen. At sixteen he was beating everybody. From that point on most of Catlo's tennis career is recorded in the newspapers and magazines.

There were two things that made Billy's life different from his father's. By the time the son came along there had been changes in the way the currency of copper skin was discounted. The classes that played and owned tennis had been informed that it was no longer "moral" to discriminate against those of differing skin-colors. Also, and perhaps more important, it was no longer "fashionable" to do so. The Ethnic Necessity Rule, sometimes called the House Nigger Rule, became effective. Now it was obligatory not just to admit these people, or at least a few of them, but actually to embrace them, especially in public. Those with copper skin who could use the right fork were suddenly at a premium and were actually sought out, invited, feted. To be fair, some of this welcome was based on honest feelings, for a new generation of the white skin was coming along, many of whose members rejected the concept of copper skin inferiority. The second factor, of course, was that Billy was his father's son. So it was far easier for Billy than it had been for his father.

Beyond all that Catlo had made a proper marriage. In fact, he had married a "Miss Rheingold." Chosen from the ranks of top young models, Miss Rheingold carried the same élan and high tone that an exclusive, top-dollar contract would carry two decades later for such fine bodies as Lauren Hutton and Margaux Hemingway. Catlo met her on the courts at that same Beverly Hills Racquet Club where he no longer washed cars but was now eagerly sought as a playing partner. The beer firm which employed her was using the courts to shoot a sequence showing Miss Rheingold hitting tennis balls. The advertisement conveyed the idea that beer-drinking and athletic good health went together and that the former act could in some osmotic, sudsy fashion lead to a withering tennis game. Catlo happened to be there working out for

Forest Hills. When he saw that she hardly knew which end of the racket to hold, he politely offered to show her. Pretty soon he noticed her legs and they were married.

I never knew Catlo's wife but I have talked with people who did, and I accept their view of her and of their marriage. The marriage was a good one, though punctuated from time to time by conflicting views of the man-woman relationship. Catlo's heritage was the man-directed life, while she had a fine intelligence in addition to legs and had, after all, been a Miss Rheingold. But by all accounts this was a minor motif in a marriage of genuine love and fondness, and pleasure in each other's company. There are pictures of her in New York, Stockholm and Tokyo, sitting at courtside holding a beautiful little half-Aztec boy in her lap, while on the court her husband went about the business of demolishing all Americans, Swedes and Japanese in sight. The photographers often spent more time photographing Miss Rheingold and son than they did the match. There must be hundreds of photographs in the morgues of newspapers and magazines around the world of Billy sitting in his mother's lap watching his father play, or just shaking a rattle or sucking his thumb. Two years after Billy was born she was killed in an airplane crash while en route to New York for another advertising campaign, this one involving former Miss Rheingolds who had gone on to either good marriages or great careers, in which the drinking of beer was presumably the decisive factor.

For a year after that accident Catlo disappeared. He took Billy with him and dropped out of sight—not just from tennis but from the world. I heard a hundred speculations. Some had him on a South Sea island, recuperating from remorse. Others had him spending a secret year teaching the game to the next Emperor of Japan. And some said Catlo and his son were in a monastery in Spain among the cowled monks. Catlo had never told anybody the actual story and it was considered dangerous even to ask him. Only after I had known him for six months did he tell me that he had spent that year living in his mother's modest bungalow in the barrio only twelve miles from the luxurious club where he had first met his wife on a tennis court.

One year later he returned to the only thing he knew how to do. Once again Billy sat alongside a tennis court, this time in a portable playpen, flapping his hands and ogling away while his father gave lessons. When Billy climbed out of the playpen, Catlo started hitting balls with him, but with no idea of selecting his son's career for him. At first this father-son play amounted to little more than baby-sitting. If it turned out that Billy both liked the game and was very good at it, this was a happenstance, and could hardly be blamed on the father. It was just possible the boy had inherited the tennis gene. Counting the lap-time with his mother and the years hitting with his father, Billy Catlo must have spent a higher percentage of his life on or alongside tennis courts than any human being alive. Otherwise Catlo raised Billy in a fairly normal American fashion.

He was a strange boy, as I came to know him. There was a distant quality about him. If I associate the word "menace" with his father, the word "reserved" came to mind when I thought of Billy. Reserved, held back. There was nothing sullen about his aloofness. He was always polite. Rather a feeling of remoteness, as if he did not wish to parcel out what he was to the world.

If you were with Billy, he would not be the one to bring up a subject, any subject. It was as though he did not look upon speech as all that sensational a human attribute. You found yourself wondering what was going on in his mind behind those silences.

I sat at the club with him one day, watching the balls fly back and forth on a dozen courts, and it went this way.

"When does school start?"

"September twentieth."

"Are you going back?"

"I don't know. I've enrolled."

"Is it a question of whether you go back to college or go to Forest Hills?"

"No. It's more a question that if I go to Forest Hills, how I do."

"If you do well, do you drop out of college?"

"I don't know."

"Do you want to go to Forest Hills?"

That took reflection. "If I'm ready I'd like to go."

"When will you know if you're ready?"

"I don't know."

I never knew anyone who used that phrase so frequently. The phrase was his way of keeping the door closed. I waited, then said, "If you come up I'd like to show you New York. It's my town. Have you ever been there?"

"When I was little. With my mother."

That last sentence was all the information he had volunteered.

Of course being the son of a famous father must have shaped Billy in some important ways. He must have felt the burden of the Catlo name, and resentments too—there might be more of these if he followed in his father's footsteps. I never felt Billy's quiet manner had anything to do with a pacific nature. Just the opposite. Something burned in him; something as wild and unpredictable as his game, a hidden fire of intense passions and fierce angers. But there was a certain Catlo quality that held equanimity to be the highest virtue, never to lose your balance. And on the rare occasions when you gave over to anger, you did so for something important to you, and you did it full out without consideration for the odds or the outcome.

Any sculptor would have loved to do his body. There was no grossness, no commonness, anywhere on him. His face was finely modeled, the bone structure clear behind the copper flesh, the features angled and thin, with high cheekbones, a deep brow, an ancient aristocratic face. His body seemed in repose but you felt a quickness there, that his reflexes would act instantly. His movements were without effort, without abruptness. He had that hair that is the blackest black on earth, silky and shining with light. The eyes, wide and remote, were a startling blue, his mother's eyes. He had strong hands with long tapered fingers.

My first and most important character evaluation of a person is whether he interrupts—whether the urgency of hearing his own voice is so unbearable that he must talk. If he doesn't I can stand almost anything from him. If he does I can't stand him at all. By this test Billy Catlo led all others.

Another time, sitting by the courts:

"What happens if you do well at Forest Hills? If you go, that is."

"If I go and if I do well enough, I may go on the tour."

"What is well enough?"

"At least the quarterfinals."

"That's well enough." I waited a moment. "There's a lot of money in tennis today if you make it."

"Yes, I've heard. My father would like that."

"Let me know if you decide to," I said. "I won't tell anyone, if that concerns you."

"Who is there to tell?"

"If I can do anything in New York. Reporters can get theater tickets, things like that."

"I'm not even sure where Forest Hills is," he said.

"You take the subway."

"I was there once when my father played. My mother took me. She held me in her lap while he played. I was very young."

It was the second thing he had volunteered and like the first it was about his mother.

"Do you remember it?" I said.

"Not really. My father has some pictures. Well, if I go back I won't be in anybody's lap this time."

"That's for sure," I said.

I feel sorry for anyone who doesn't play tennis.

I know of no more pleasant place to spend an unscheduled day than a bath and tennis club, even if you're not there to swim or hit one ball. To start with, it is a visually pleasing setting. Catlo's club possessed one of the last complexes of the true clay courts, in this age of instant Sportface, Har-Tru, Laykold, Plexipave and Modsod. Clay, with its lovely Pompeiian-red color, requires too much loving care. These courts were immaculately kept, rolled and manicured in their surrounding garden of palm trees and clipped zoysia grass. The courts were shielded on three sides by files of tall Australian pine to hold back the wind and on the fourth by the blue Atlantic washing in.

The best girl-watching anywhere is surely to be found at tennis courts. Any girl who plays tennis regularly has a good body. As they fling about the court and go for shots in their unfettering garments, they present many pleasing angles. I could sit there for hours, in a director's chair under a friendly cabbage palm, lazy and content, pursuing my belief that the only important hours in life are the hours we waste, watching all the moist young women. Now and then my laziness and contentment would be stimulated to livelier emotions by the sight of one of these fetching creatures as she reached for an overhead, her body held there against the sky with all her girlness showing. Nothing brings out girlness like tennis.

How different from the uninspired greyness of the random country club devoted to golf! The bodies make the essential difference. Whatever else it is, golf is not a game of exercise. Essentially it is a lazy man's and lazy woman's game. Hit the ball, climb into a motorized cart, drive a hundred yards, get out and hit the ball, climb back in the cart. Then finally have six beers. Contrast this with the incessant hitting and racing about the court, the sudden stops and starts that tear at the joints and muscles, strengthening the one and firming up the other. It is not difficult to see why the two bodies are so different from one another. I can tell a tennis body from a golf body at a glance.

So I sat with some of these beatific and redeeming thoughts watching the scenes strung out before me during the "Ladies' Hour" in which they occupied all twelve courts. Catlo still enforced the old tennis customs—all of which will soon be as antique as plus fours and hoop skirts—including white clothing. "Tennis started out white for two good reasons," he told me. "It's nicer than having twenty-eight colors spread out over a dozen courts like it was some bloody Howard Johnson's. And sweat doesn't show through white." Catlo allowed one divergence from the "all-white" rule. Panties of any color were permitted. For some reason, he said, the ladies had agreed readily to the all-white rule except that, in this one area, they stood their ground and insisted an exception be made. "I didn't feel like going to the mat with them," Catlo told me. "The issue seemed too trivial and I decided it did not seriously interfere with the aesthetics of the courts."

Sitting there with the overview (and underview) afforded from my chair and sipping a Tanqueray and tonic, I could only agree about the aesthetics. For a while I played a game of my own, having to wait for the right shots of course, of seeing which color was most popular. Finally I had tallied a score in my reporter's notebook of light blue 3, persimmon 3, ochre 5, black 1, lavender 4 and red 8. Then having surveyed them all, I found more and more my attention lingered on a particular young lady. Lindy, in her *bal pockette* panties, reflected the maximum aesthetics. They were that exotic color, white.

As I watched, I began to feel the need for a hit myself. I went into the pro shack, purchased Fred Perry shorts (size 30) with the laurel wreath on them, a Lacoste shirt (size ½ *patron* with the crocodile, Adidas shoes (size 9) with the three stripes, and a Slazenger Challenge racket with the springing panther on its cover along with a can of Wilsons— and requested a receipt for the expense account. If tennis tack is not a legitimate expense-account item while covering a tennis story I don't know what would be. One could hardly get inside the story otherwise. Having covered many tennis stories, I have a fine tennis wardrobe. I changed and came back to my chair which they would all pass when the Ladies' Hour ended. For bait I pulled up an extra chair alongside. I just had time to complete my drink.

"Do you play or do you just watch? You must play if you're wearing those."

She was standing over me, those sweet thighs on the level of my chin. I stood up.

"I've been known to play if I'm allowed three serves," I said. "Would you care for a Tanqueray and tonic?"

I held out the chair and Lindy sat. I saw that she had blue-green eyes. There was a light line of sweat on her forehead just below her hair, made even more blonde-white from the sun, and the lightest dew of it in the V of her shirt-neck and on the insides of her thighs. Her Tad Imperial rested across her lap.

"What is that?" she asked.

"Well, tonic is quinine water. It's very good for malaria. Tanqueray is a fine brand of gin from England. The British gave us Magna Carta and gin."

"Twelve-fifteen," she said crisply. "I'll have just the tonic please."

"Chief, two Tanquerays and Schweppes," I told the waiter. "With a squeezed whole Key lime in each. And hold the Tanqueray in one," and he brought them.

"They look exactly alike," she said. "Which is the tonic and which is the tank—what's that word?"

"Tanqueray." I sampled one. "This is," I said and handed her the other.

We sat and sipped and talked a little. Lindy told me she was going to college in North Carolina and would be returning in a couple of weeks—about the time, it occurred to me, Forest Hills started.

"Could I ask you something?" she said after a while.

"Anything. Reporters are always flattered to be *asked* questions."

"I don't know a thing about tennis. Is Billy good enough?"

She stopped there but I knew what she meant. I felt the question was important to her so I tried to answer carefully.

"It's hard to say until he gets where they decide that question."

"Where is that?"

"Two places. Wimbledon, which is a suburb of London. And Forest Hills, which is a suburb of Manhattan. You have to have the game, of course, but you must have something else. The ability to play under that pressure. He may have the game. As for Billy standing up under pressure, you'd know more about that than I do." I wanted her to talk about him.

"Don't tell him I told you but he does have a nervous stomach. Sometimes he *throws* after playing real hard."

"Well, that's not really a disqualifying ailment. I sometimes throw myself after I write a story."

"And he does have a temper." She giggled. Then she asked: "If he does have all that, the game and the pressure thing, what happens then?"

"He makes a lot of money."

"A lot like what?"

I was beginning to be surprised at the precision of her questions, as if she wanted a financial printout.

"Well, I'd say about two hundred and fifty thousand dollars the first year, counting the prize money and the endorsements for hairspray and suits at Sears. Maybe more after that if he really has it."

Lindy turned and looked at me. She had an amusing way of cocking her head when she was intent about something. "Are you serious?"

"I wouldn't be anything else with you."

"Two hundred and fifty thousand dollars," she said the

words slowly and in some awe. "That's a quarter of a million dollars. That's a lot if you're nineteen."

"It'll keep you in gut."

She sat for a moment with a concentrated expression, which I found funny and oddly charming, as if she were analyzing what all this really meant. Then, the subject tucked away somewhere for future use, she turned abruptly to another.

"They say poor players aren't supposed to ask good players, and it's bad tennis manners, but here goes. Would you care to volley I mean rally with me?" She giggled again.

"I would love to rally or volley with you," I said. "That rule, like most rules, doesn't apply to extremely pretty girls." She actually blushed. I picked myself up, and my Slazenger Challenge and opened the Wilsons, which let out a fizz like tonic poured over gin.

"I'm not very good," she said. "To be honest I practically don't know anything. But I'm highly motivated. If you see me doing anything wrong will you please tell me. I'd consider that a personal favor."

I looked at her. Yes, she was genuine, or so I believed. "Well, I don't want you to think I'm all that good."

"I'll bet you are," she said. "You *look* like a tennis player."

Coming from her, the words sounded nicer than I would have thought possible. What was more, it sounded truly sweet, not just words you say. I couldn't remember when I had last found a girl "sweet," for that has become a lost adjective as applied to girls.

We went to Court 7. I stood on one end and hit balls to her, not too hard, and watched her move about on the clay with the sea her blue backdrop. What a pretty thing she was to watch! What lovely plumage she had; the light body, small and fine, and that clipped white-blonde hair and those funny freckles which I was beginning to find so charming, the face just emerging from girlhood, and all the fragrance of youth. For some reason I cannot explain, watching a left-handed girl play tennis has always been an endearing thing to me so that even this added to the delight I found in her. She seemed so open to the world, and to life, an eagerness to see what was there, and yet with it a sureness about who she was and what she believed and thought was important. Her naiveté, or innocence, disarmed me so entirely as to induce an old feeling, which was to see that no harm befell her. I understood Billy's attraction to her. I understood mine. And I understood what awesome weapons she possessed, and wondered if she knew. When the hour was gone we returned to the director's chairs.

"Another Tanqueray and tonic?" I asked her while the waiter waited.

"Please."

"With the Tanqueray this time?"

"No, I like just the tonic. For my malaria."

They came and we sipped. "What do you feel about Billy and Forest Hills?" I said.

"How do you mean?"

"If he has to choose between Forest Hills and college, how do you vote?"

"Well, I don't know that I have a vote but . . . "

A bloodcurdling Banshee yell cut off her answer. A tennis racket flew over the fence like a big bird and settled on the zoysia grass, almost hitting me.

"Oh, oh," she said. "Billy's mad again."

Lindy didn't seem at all surprised by the racket's sudden arrival. Racket in hand, she started crisply down the walkway. I followed with my Tanqueray. We opened the gate to the "teaching court." She walked onto the court and handed him the racket.

"Billy," she said. There was reproval in the word.

"All right," Catlo said. "If you're ready, Billy. Only if you're ready."

"I'm ready," Billy said. He re-knotted the handkerchief around his neck. He was grinning.

"You will have to be perfectly quiet if you're going to remain here," Catlo said briskly to us. "Is that clear?"

"Yes, sir," Lindy said.

"Yes, sir," I said.

We took chairs at the side and watched for a while. The play part of my day was to hit with Lindy and to watch her as she consumed a seemingly endless number of Dr. Peppers and for lunch four packets of peanut-butter sandwiches— "I have this thing about Dr. Pepper and those peanut-butter cheese-cracker sandwiches that come in cellophane," she said. The work part was to watch Billy work out. Catlo allowed his son a ten-minute break at the end of each hour. Otherwise they hit all day under a sun that never hid. By mid-afternoon the thermometer on the outside of the pro shack said 101 degrees. The thermometer was in the shade.

The court workout was brutal and unrelenting. One hour each devoted to the serve, return of serve, the volley, the forehand groundstrokes, the backhand groundstrokes, one to lobs, and one hour to overheads and drop shots. As the sun finally gave up and lavender shadows moved over the clay and melded with the Pompeiian-red, Catlo and his son spent the final hour playing each other.

Billy's occasional outbursts were directed at himself. His father met them with a barbed coolness. Once when he hit a ball wildly, Billy launched his racket into the net with a ferocious two-handed forehand. Catlo just looked at him. "Now why do you do that?" he said quietly. "*¿Qué tal?* That only helps your opponent. He probably won't need it."

Billy had a lovely, exciting style to watch, an unusual combination of grace and explosion. Gliding into the ball to take it high on the rise, then with body and racket motionless and cocked, throwing himself against it in one powerful convulsion, exploding the ball off the clay. He covered the court with animal ease, his shots coming off the racket sometimes like gunshot, sometimes in a whisper of touch. Like his father, Billy was in command of the court. Even Catlo had difficulty putting the ball where his son would not find it and fly it back, the boy's body moving over the clay with a grace that would have seemed astonishing for his age had one not known the source. Billy's game remained wild and inaccurate but I thought less so. Catlo kept at him about topspin and with it, subtle and vital changes were beginning to appear. The ball would dip as it cleared the net and touch down instead of sailing out. I watched the individual shots, a familiar *ping* beginning to register in me, that faint, visceral signal, as from some faraway short-wave band, that tells me something of meaning is happening before my eyes. But I could not isolate that special thing Catlo was doing. Then it struck me.

Catlo's game was different. He was playing like Jack Tillotston. It was almost eerie, now that I recognized it, how Catlo copied Tillotston's game. He played Tillotston's famous drop shot, a shot just clearing the net and landing no more than a foot to a yard on the other side of it, sometimes with so much underspin that the ball just stopped and died. Catlo played the shot over and over to his son, sending Billy racing to the net, full out and racket extended. He played Tillotston's "fadeaway" shot, a shot hit deep and low and with tremendous force down the line, with the wrist laid back and the racket pulled toward the body to give it intense sidespin so that when the ball touched on or near the sideline, it traveled away from the opponent. It made for a "heavy" ball, one very difficult to judge, let alone return. Hitting it could turn the racket in your hand.

Catlo had even taken on some of Tillotston's mannerisms, his mock-mincing, swaggering air, his stalling tactics. No one in tennis stalled with the talent of Jack Tillotston. Once I heard Catlo tell Billy, "If you should ever play Tillotston, don't forget he takes every opportunity to violate the rule that play shall be continuous. Expect this to happen like you expect the other parts of his game. When he does it, *you* do it. Walk to your chair and sit down. Get a book out of your kit and read it. Get out a comb and mirror and doll up your pretty hair. Tie and untie your shoelaces. Walk up and measure the net with your racket. Stand and look up at the sky to see if there are any birds there. Also smile at him a lot."

Even more than about his game, I wondered how Billy would be when the high tension invaded him in the Stadium, with thousands watching. When the iron butterflies came. I had seen young players on the odd-game change bend under the umpire's green highchair and throw up into towels—and one miss the towel entirely. It was well and good to stand at the foot of the golden ladder, but the best tennis game in the world would not move you three rungs up it if you could not handle the attacks of nerves as well as the other attacks from across the net.

I went into the pro shack to buy a hat for tomorrow's sun, today's being gone, and also to see if I might bump into Lindy. The shack appeared empty. I was about to leave when I saw that someone was there after all. She was sitting at a desk in the arm of the L-shaped room, studying something so intently that she was unaware I had come in.

"I hear you're pushing Aussie hats today," I said.

She turned. "Hi. I'm sorry. I didn't hear you."

I recognized Tish from the Ladies' Clinic, the one Catlo told me had the natural gas in Oklahoma. Before her was a large, complicated chart. We introduced ourselves.

"If you're wondering, this is the mockup for the big Celebrity Pro-Am this weekend. I'm what the Palm Beach newspapers call the 'chairperson.' How I hate that word."

She had a broad, earthy face. Her body looked diligently and expensively cared for. There was a roundness about her that suggested no sharp bones would get in the way. She was well tanned and in the V of her sleeveless Lacoste tennis shirt I could just see a pencil-line of white across the upper perimeter of her breasts. These were full and looked kindly. She had that air of self-confidence a woman acquires not so much from having money as from having made it, or at least increased it, by her own shrewdness. Her frank brown eyes had smile wrinkles around them. There was a scent of Femme about her and an aura of comfortable bawdiness.

"Who's coming for that important event?" I said. I hated Celebrity Pro-Ams. In all of tennis there is nothing so ludicrous as these rites, in which "names"—movie stars, television stars, even U. S. Senators—play at being jocks, while to make them appear so, the certified members of that profession pat balls soft as Pringle cashmere across the net at them.

"Well, there's Spence Leland." This was a very large movie star and lover.

"And there's Shelly Blaine."

I looked up sharply. Shelly Blaine. Once we had worked on the Washington *Post* at the same time, once we had known each other quite well. So Shelly Blaine was coming here. It had to happen sooner or later. I remembered her telling her television audience she had taken up tennis.

Spence Leland and Shelly Blaine. The club was going first-class.

"I hope you have a young blond boy for Spence," I said. "He likes both."

"Oh, does he? I'm glad you told me. I know just the one. He tends bar at the Patois Pub on Worth Avenue and he'll be thrilled." I was beginning to like her. "There's an even bigger name, aren't we the clever ones? We've got Chester Barney."

"The Green Tongue himself?"

She laughed. "Yes. How does Chester Barney like his?"

Barney was the undisputed king of television tennis. He always opened any tennis match he was covering with a line which had become his trademark: "All you hackers out there! I'm Chester Barney—as if you didn't know!"

"Chester likes it any way he can get it so long as he can continue telling the girl about himself while he's doing it."

"My god, do you realize all these people will be staying in my house? You're a closet full of information."

"Well, I'm jealous. They all make more money than I do. Who else?"

"Jack Tillotston."

I looked at her. "Well," I said. "Well. Now *there* is a name

I wouldn't have expected. What does Catlo think about that?"

"He's glad, I think."

"I can't imagine why."

"He has his reasons. Did you say I could get you something?"

End of subject. "One Aussie hat, please."

"We have them in purple, blue, green, red, orange and terra cotta. Which would you like?"

"White."

"I'll see if we have one."

She got it for me from a box on the shelf. So she helped Catlo by looking after the shop when he was on the courts. She must be one of the more affluent assistants anywhere. A good choice for other reasons too. She struck me as a lady capable of running a pro shack, six natural-gas fields and anything else you wanted to name, including even a Celebrity Pro-Am, which is basically unrunnable.

"You look like the sort of person who would do a lady a favor," she said. "Would you watch the shop for a half hour? Cat will be in then. I have to give the newspapers some photographs of our big wonderful, world-famous stars."

"Well, of course, that's very important, those pictures in the newspapers. I'll watch carefully."

"*Merci* and *gracias*. Oh, incidentally." She had paused at the door. "How does Tillotston like his?"

"He likes just straight fur."

"How nice that there are some left."

"Oh, there are. Me, for instance."

"How nice," she said again, making me feel I had contributed to the general welfare. She was gone with her pictures.

I sat down, put my feet on the desk and picked up the new *World Tennis*. This issue had six pages of text and pictures of Tillotston winning Wimbledon the month before. He was thirty now, but I could see no sign of flab on his big body. He was slower than he used to be but also smarter, more experienced, more cunning, more impossible. Tillotston had a big ass, as they say, and it had never been bigger.

I was still reading the text when Catlo and Billy came in. You could have wrung out their shirts and filled two Tom Collins glasses. Billy groped to a sink at the far end of the counter, stuck his head under the tap and let the water run over it. Catlo got four Cokes out of a small refrigerator. Billy draped a towel over his head and they collapsed into chairs. They emptied two cans, then started to work more slowly on the other two.

"Does this happen every day?" I asked. "I mean the dune and then this?"

"Every day," Catlo said. "Tomorrow and day after tomorrow."

"I was just reading here about the new Wimbledon champion," I said. "Let's see—someone by the name of Tillotston. I'm not sure it's the same name, but I think someone told me he's coming down for the Celebrity Pro-Am. Which is he, a Celebrity or a Pro?"

"He's playing both halves of the draw," Catlo said. "We've got a match set up between himself."

"Tillotston?" Billy said from his towel. He looked like a Bedouin. "I didn't know."

Catlo shrugged. You would think he'd never met the man. "He's a big name. We'll be happy to have him. He'll fill a few of the hundred-dollar seats."

He tilted his Coke and waited a moment. "If he's going around to Celebrity Pro-Ams, he might just be getting a little sure of himself. They serve a lot of gin at Celebrity Pro-Ams. It'll be interesting to see if there's any ripening in that direction. If I were playing Forest Hills I wouldn't be at a Celebrity Pro-Am." Catlo drained his Coke and put the can in a wastebasket. "Also I want him to see Billy's game."

"You what?" I said.

He said no more.

As twilight reached over the empty courts, scarred with the

day's play, we sat talking a little but mostly just listening to the Atlantic washing in. It sounded a bit louder to me, as in a weather-born higher tide. A few small whitecaps dotted the blue. Far out to sea, a two-stack liner pointed southeast. We sat among the flotsam of a pro shack, the boxes and racks of Fred Perry shirts, Adidas shoes, Lacoste sweaters and now even Oleg Cassini tennis dresses, among the stacked packages of jockstraps and panties, and twenty species of rackets arrayed in caddies on the wall, with their glistening wood and now the new glistening steel, aluminum, titanium, tungsten, like medieval weapons.

Billy sipped his Coke. "Dad?"

"*Si?*"

"I want her to go with me to Forest Hills. If I go."

"Are you out of your mind?" Catlo said. "*¿Qué tal?* You'd be finished in the first round. You have no idea what it's like there."

"I may not go unless she goes with me."

Catlo shrugged. "Suit yourself. *No le hace.* In the meantime, let's lock up." He stood. "Oh, Billy."

"Yes, sir." Something about Catlo's voice had made that "sir" obligatory. He looked down at his son.

"Let me know before you go to bed, will you? If you're definitely not going, I can sleep in tomorrow and skip that dune. And all day on Court One."

He said it just like that and there was no question at all what he meant. As we walked out, we could see Lindy coming from the swimming pool. The pool was shaped like a tennis racket.

"I've been wading in the handle," she said. "Are you getting better and better, Billy?"

"I fell apart right after you left. I always play so much better if you're watching." Only with her did he have this sound of banter.

"Billy never tells the truth," she said to me.

She could be so nice and sassy when she wanted. I was

beginning to believe she could take care of herself. She was still wet. Any male over six would have given plenty to dry her off. I still believed she had no real idea of the effect she had.

"Hello, Mr. Catlo," she said. "Will I ever be a tennis player?"

Catlo smiled. "I like Lindy. She's the only person who calls me Mr. Catlo. With your figure, Lindy, you don't have to worry whether you are or not. We're glad to have you around even if you never master the difference between volley and rally."

"Oh, but I have now, Mr. Catlo. Volley is what you hit before it hits the ground."

"I imagine you're going to be a tennis player," Catlo said.

"How could I miss with you as a teacher?"

I began to think she might be a match for him—off the court, I mean.

"Would you like to go with us to the Jesus charisma class tonight?"

For a moment I didn't realize she was speaking to me. Perhaps I was fresh meat.

"I imagine it would be dull for him," Billy said. "A big New York sportswriter."

"It wouldn't be dull at all," I said. "I'd like very much to go."

"Good!" she said. She broke into a bright smile. "I hoped you would and I thought you might. It's at the Neo-Pentecostal Church on the pier. Or better yet, we'll pick you up at a quarter of seven in Billy's MG. He just had it washed."

"That doesn't affect the size of it," Billy said. "It still only holds two."

"I'll sit on the trunk," Lindy said brightly. "I'm smallest. Afterward we'll go to Baskin-Robbins."

It must have been a tradeoff, Billy partaking of Jesus charisma while she partook of tennis. I watched the television news while waiting for them. The weather part mentioned

that the "tropical depression" of yesterday had now gradu-
ated to a "tropical storm" with winds at sixty miles per hour
and so deserved its name, Agatha. Also coordinates, 19′ 04″
North Latitude and 68′ 34″ West Longitude, having just
passed over the northeast corner of the Dominican Republic,
putting her 800 miles southeast of Palm Beach. She was traveling at eight miles per hour. The Navy planes were flying into
the storm to get fresh clockings. "We're keeping an eye on
Agatha for you," the announcer said avuncularly. Suddenly I
had a hunch.

I picked up the phone and rang Pat Hargraves in New
York. Hargraves was tournament referee for Forest Hills.

"Pat," I said, "Brinkley here. Can you tell me just off the
top if Billy Catlo is entered in Forest Hills?"

"Why yes he is. Good to have the name back, isn't it?"

"Yes," I said. "Oh one more thing. Do you know whether
Billy or the Big Cat handled it?"

"Why yes I do. Cat said he was just taking care of the de-
tails for Billy since he'd been through it himself."

"Yes of course," I said. "Just saving Billy the trouble. See
you in the Marquee."

So Billy didn't know he was entered in Forest Hills. What
is that cunning son of a bitch up to?

The South Palm Beach Neo-Pentecostal Church met the
world in an old shed worn smooth by salt spray on an abandoned fishing pier. Somehow it suggested the original Church
to me (the first Apostles being both fishermen and fishers of
men) before it got architectural and forbidding. Throughout
the service I could hear the sea washing in against the pilings
that held it up; softly and yet seeming to my ear to rise, for
in the Navy I had acquired something close to perfect pitch
to the myriad sounds of the sea. There were no more present
than twice the number who had been at the Lord's Supper.

We sang a couple of hymns before Lindy got up to talk.
She was a slight figure standing there, in the first dress in

which I had seen her. She looked as beguiling and fresh as she had on Court 7. I can't recall much of what she said except that her text was 2nd Corinthians 5:17 ("If any man be in Christ, he is a new creature"), but there was no gloom to her words, no dark forebodings; and none, either, of what to me is that other chief put-off of religion as we know it, aggressiveness. Since it would seem religion's purpose to give joy to joyless man, I have never understood why so many religious meetings should sound so sad—or so angry. She made religion seem a nice thing to have. She talked for only about ten minutes and then she said, "Shall we sing 'Brighten the Corner'?"

I held the hymnbook with Billy, who kept shifting his weight from one foot to the other. He even sang a little and I felt it was all for Lindy.

"Brighten the corner where you are!
Brighten the corner where you are!
Someone far from harbor
You may guide across the bar.
Brighten the corner where you are!"

I could hear the sea washing against the pier and then the hymn was over. Everybody hugged everybody else. We went out to the night and to the sea. We stood in the sand and looked out. I thought I heard a roll of thunder, feeble and distant, which seemed strange since stars were strung across an unclouded sky. Then I saw that my ear had been true, that the sea had chopped up and there was white on its black surface. We could feel the southeast wind beginning to whisper along the beach, slight as the rustle of a woman's garments. A taste of wetness hung in the air, from the sky as well as the sea. We stood and watched the wind wash the kelp ashore.

"I was listening to the hurricane report," I said.

"Hurricane?" Billy said. He was watching Lindy watch the sea.

"Well, tropical storm. It's got a name now, Agatha. It's a long way out there."

"I just hope we get to the L's this year," Billy said. "It's named for Lindy so it should bring great things. Of course for me, every day is named Lindy." That uncharacteristic note of banter again. Banter and affection. He was a different person around her.

"You're such a liar, Billy Catlo," she said.

We got into the MG, Billy driving, me in the only other seat, and Lindy perched nicely between us on the retracted top. I could feel a knee just touching my left shoulder, very accidentally I knew. It was crowded there. I hoped the thoughts passing through me didn't send me to some hell where there was no charisma.

"Shall we go walk the plank at the Pirate's Lair?" I said. "They make a sensational 'Gangplank' special. It contains cucumbers, pineapple, celery, maraschino cherries, Key limes —and a touch of rum, of course."

"Well, now," Billy said.

"Let's go to Baskin-Robbins," Lindy said. "I want a triple-scoop banana split with macadamia nuts, marshmallow and chocolate syrup."

So the issue was settled, and so much for the democratic process. Afterward, stuffed with sweetness, I went alone to the Pirate's Lair to clean out my mouth and to see if Fanny was aboard. Just being around Lindy agitated things in me, which I didn't think was quite what Pentecost had in mind, though perhaps charisma did.

"Hi. I'm the pirate from Room Four-eleven."

"I quite remember," she said.

And finally after about three "Gangplanks" . . . Still, Fanny wasn't so available that she couldn't set some terms.

"It depends on whether you want to screw me or lay me," she said.

"Is there a difference?"

"Oh, yes," she said, with a somewhat superior air.

"Which do you prefer?"

"I like screwing. But I love getting laid."

So she taught me the difference that night. It had been a long day and that was a nice way to end it. I always like to learn something. So did she.

"Who's Fanny?" she asked in the night.

"Robert Louis Stevenson's wife."

"How nice. Hold me tight and go to sleep now. Robert Louis."

I woke once to a mild medley of thunder over me and reached sleepily for her. For a moment I thought she was Shelly Blaine.

3

THE GREEN TONGUE

IT WOULD BE A MISTAKE TO TAKE CHESTER BARNEY AS A Boston rube. I have covered numerous stories for my magazine that Chester covered for his network, and besides being colleagues in the high calling of sportswriting, we have become friends, after his fashion. Beneath all that garrulity, that monumental ego which in his telecasts often made it seem that what was happening on the court was of little consequence compared with what was happening in the booth, lay a shrewd, cutting mind. He was a pro.

What I liked best about Chester was that no one impressed him. Of course this is *de rigueur* for sports reporters, who associate daily with Joe Namath or Catfish Hunter or Mean Joe Greene or Jack Tillotston. It is difficult for a man in a jockstrap to be a hero to those around him, particularly those who have to edit his grammar, which all sportswriters do for all athletes in a tradition older than John Peter Zenger. A sports reporter must make it very clear that he is not impressed by Big Names and would not walk across the street to see a personal appearance by Jesus Christ, unless paid to do so on assignment. But Chester Barney carried disdain for greatness to new heights, and not only with sports figures. He took no guff from anyone, and the bigger the name, the less guff he took.

Chester had his own style. At celebrity tournaments he would occasionally descend from his booth to play tennis not only barechested—not so bare, either, since there was enough hair on it to stuff a mattress—but also barefooted. Barney brought a breath of fresh air to a game that for so long belonged to the upper crust, to the country and tennis clubs, and to those privileged few who in the late afternoons sipped their tea-with-lemon or Tanqueray-with-tonic at court-side. People found it strange that he was from Boston, but these were people who saw that city as the Charles River, Harvard, State Street and the Boston Symphony. Barney was the real Boston, idiosyncratic, going his own way, speaking his own mind. Samuel Adams would have loved him.

One look at Barney and the viewer realized that he could not have got his job on appearance, so that he must know what he was talking about. What the viewer saw was something remarkably like a middle-aged Benjamin Franklin. Chester wore half-glass Franklin spectacles and looked over them from eyes, set in a pink, cherubic face, that were preter-naturally large and Wimbledon green. Like his predecessor in communications, the Philadelphia publisher, he was balding on top, but fine curly growths began just above the ears and flowered upward like twin sprays of pubic hair, the color of nails left out in the rain. He had a gorgeous big nose ("my nose for news," Barney boasted), a Mount Rushmore brow, plantation lips and fire-hydrant ears. Even his voice was far from the rounded, resonant register of the normal television Terry Splendid. It was a raspy instrument, its register ranging from twang to honk.

He was a slight man physically. I don't believe Chester weighed more than 135 pounds and by far the greater part of him was located above the waist. His legs, highly visible when he played Celebrity tennis, looked like used toothpicks with reddish foliage. The legs rose to a comfortable stomach which lapped out over the huge silver belt buckle he always wore. Chester claimed the King of Morocco had given him this adornment during a tournament in Rabat. On it was an heraldic symbol in Greek which translated, *Slay not the bearer of bad news.* "Not a bad motto for a journalist," Barney liked to say.

Sartorially he had a style all his own. Chester Barney had one of the world's finest collections of T-shirts. He claimed he wore each only once and then gave it to one of his many girls —"chickies," as he called them. Barney's T-shirts were designed for him especially by René Lacoste, the distinguished French tennis player who became an even greater designer of tennis tack, including the famous shirt with the crocodile (alligator, as they call it, inaccurately, in the U.S.A.). Barney's T-shirts were of Ecuadorean cotton, in all colors of the spectrum and always with a distinguishing mark: the crocodile was reversed so that it looked inward instead of outward, a whimsical touch Barney thought up and which Lacoste did only for him. Chester always wore his reverse-crocodile shirt, on television, in restaurants, and even at black-tie dinners.

"I believe in traveling light," he said. "And ready to go to work."

He used Sniff, the man's cologne manufactured by his principal sponsor, in quantity. Approaching him, you sometimes thought you might be at the factory. "Barney bathes in it," other, less well paid reporters with no sponsors said. "Only on Saturdays!" Barney responded gleefully when someone made the accusation directly to his face. It was impossible to put Chester Barney down. He had a habit of scratching his jewels, but on television this pleasurable habit proved to be no handicap since all shots were made from the waist up. Barney never tried to hide any character trait. I have been in the booth while Chester interviewed me before 35 million people and seen him repeatedly scratch throughout the interview. I had to keep reminding myself that the camera didn't "see" what he was doing. It was an important area of the body to Chester. "One of my ambitions," he once told me, "is to have a chickie give me a blow job while I'm telecasting— preferably in a finals match at a major tournament."

"What's stopping you, Chester?" I asked.

"I haven't yet found the girl," Barney said, "who is worthy of this television first."

And speaking of girls. "The basic choice in life," Chester liked to say, "is whether you go through it first-class or tourist. One is as easy to go as the other. All you need is to decide which. Personally I choose to go first-class all the way, Z to A. Hotels, airplanes, liquor—and chickies."

When Chester traveled to New York, he rode up front in the plane. When he got there he checked in at the Carlyle. When he went in to the Bemelmans Bar he ordered The Glenlivet. At tennis tournaments, he always arrived with a different girl trailing on his arm. The girls had certain traits in common: they were about half Barney's age, they were stunners and they were not pros. They came with him, they stayed with him and, most important of all, they were there the next day. The way they looked up at that homely face with such fondness, even adoration, led me to believe that, for a girl or woman at least, there was more to Chester Barney than met the eye. "Beauty and the Beast, that's the secret, Brinkley," Barney used to explain it.

Before the tennis explosion, Chester had been a sports reporter on the Boston *Sentinel*. He covered tennis during the summer, the only time it was played then, and when the frost came he reported the doings of bowling leagues with team names like "Midas Mufflers" and "Schlitz Beer Belles." Bowling, which he hated, kept him alive until summer when he could cover tennis again. Nearly all of his stories ended up as a stick of type on the sixth page of the sports section, tennis in those days being unable to compete even for the jump space allotted to the three king sports of football, baseball and basketball. But Chester Barney, in his lowly job, never stopped loving tennis in the purest sense—certainly there was no future in it. During those years when tennis was an esoteric sport, Chester came to know everything about the game and everyone in it. For a while he even coached on the side, at Boston College. In academia, too, tennis was then a stepchild sport and the college was happy to have anyone so knowledgeable and proved it by paying him fifteen dollars for each coaching session, twice a week.

The explosion changed all that.

It happened so fast that the television networks were caught unaware and faced a situation unique in their history. In contrast to the pool of talent from which they could pick sportscasters for the big sports, there were scarcely half a dozen professional journalists who really knew tennis. The reason was simple enough. The best sports reporters got themselves assigned to football, baseball and basketball, the hack reporters were given tennis and league bowling. Now that overnight the masses were playing tennis, sponsors with their millions lined up to pay for telecasts of this exotic new sports craze. And no one to report it!

Caught between horror and stupefaction, the networks attacked the problem with panic and stupidity. They picked two or three of their nice-looking young announcers, gave them a crash course in tennis, dressed them in tennis blazers, and sent them forth to telecast tennis matches. The result was a disaster. The blazer lads made goofs that are still recounted with derisive chuckles by tennis fans, who are witheringly articulate. They bombarded the networks with letters venting their scorn for the blazer pups.

The networks immediately became desperate. Especially MBC, whose big commercially-sponsored tennis accounts included the World Championship Tennis tour.

At this time the tour arrived in Boston. During that cold and rainy week matches were continually postponed but there were just enough dry interludes that the nationally televised finals could be broadcast on schedule Sunday at 1 P.M. At 8:30 Sunday morning the regular MBC tennis-blazer announcer awakened in his hotel room with a severe cold. He could scarcely talk. He got his producer on the phone two floors below. The croak that worthy heard was enough to send him bounding up the stairs. When the croak was repeated, it became evident that somebody else would telecast the finals that day.

The producer placed an urgent call to the manager of KBOS, the network's Boston outlet. Did he have any suggestions? It was natural enough for the manager to mention Chester Barney, the *Sentinel*'s tennis reporter, since the newspaper owned the television station. When the producer asked, "Can he talk?" the manager burst out laughing. (This question later became part of the Barney folklore.) "All right, let's get the bugger down here," the producer said. Two hours before air time he saw Barney in the studio and went into shock. But since nothing could be done, Barney was rushed to the Boston Lawn Tennis and Croquet Club where the finals were to be broadcast live.

A shower halted the match during the second set. The tarp went on fast. Although the rain was light, the interruption consumed a total of twenty minutes. Twenty minutes may not be much to you or me but to network television, twenty empty minutes is like the duration of the Pleistocene epoch. Barney just chatted about tennis the whole time. He talked easily and entertainingly. He had hardly begun when the rain stopped. The match continued, Barney picking up the narration smoothly—a precise and perceptive report.

Following that telecast, tennis fans deluged the MBC network offices in New York and its outlets in Boston, Chicago, Phoenix and L.A. with letters, telegrams and phone calls. MBC officials were flabbergasted. After all, Chester Barney violated their most sacred principles: he didn't look right and he had a non-prescription voice. But with nothing to lose, they offered Chester a modest contract to cover three more WCT matches, in Houston, Charlotte and Kansas City. After Houston a volume of mail greater than after Boston followed, and after Charlotte a volume greater than after Houston.

Jack Welker, the acerbic and feared television critic of the New York *Daily News,* watched the last match in Kansas City.

Welker, a club player himself, picked the match to write a column on tennis telecasting. Like the ordinary fans he too had suffered from the blazer boys. His column on the Monday after Kansas City blistered all previous tennis coverage and ended with a paean to Barney. The column concluded:

"It would appear that the golden game of tennis, after some of the most inane, inaccurate, insulting, insufferable television reporting ever inflicted on any sport, has at hand an authentic voice in a man who knows the game and can tell it. He will never win any beauty prizes, but if the networks can overcome this ludicrous *sine qua non*, television tennis has its man. Up with Chester Barney, the Green Tongue!"

Welker later told me he was alluding to the famous radio creature, "The Green Hornet," as well as to Barney's oral fluency. Barney's short-time contract expired with the Kansas City telecast. He was still in his hotel room at the Muehlebach the next morning, getting ready to fly back to Boston, when the phone rang. A lady on the other end identified herself in a no-nonsense voice as the personal secretary of General C. C. Petrov, the legendary chief of MBC. Would it be possible for Mr. Barney to have lunch with the General today? The voice said he would just have time to make TWA Flight 318, which departed Kansas City at 7:50 A.M., provided he left his room that instant and proceeded downstairs to the front of the hotel, where a ticket and limousine from the Kansas City MBC affiliate awaited him. Flight 318 would arrive at 12:32 P.M. in New York, where another limousine would meet him.

That one call, with its outlay of amenities that Barney had heard about but had not personally experienced, pretty much told him how the land lay. Any doubts were resolved on his arrival at La Guardia, where he picked up copies of the New York newspapers and was able to read Welker in the back seat of General Petrov's limousine.

It was a pleasant lunch there in the General's private dining room atop New York, but General Petrov quickly learned that he was not dealing with a Boston hayseed. Worse, the other two networks had been monitoring Barney. They also had read Welker's column that morning and they joined the fray with a will and a cocked checkbook. Barney got the three networks bidding against each other and a frantic auction ensued. The bidding went up, and up. A week later Barney signed with MBC. Chester liked to claim that loyalty played a part in his decision. If so, loyalty is a well-paid virtue: a seven-year contract at a minimum guaranteed salary of $150,000 a year, with increments from sponsors and assorted fringe benefits and perquisites which Barney was able to insist on. It was a nice raise from his $185-a-week salary covering tennis and league bowling for his newspaper. Boston College had to look for a new tennis coach.

Barney himself once told me that it was Welker's "Green Tongue" anointment that turned the trick. "In sports there is nothing like a sobriquet, Brinkley," he said. "Where would the Four Horsemen be if they had never been called the Four Horsemen?"

Maybe so. But Chester Barney knew tennis. He knew its past, its present and, I think, its future as well as anyone alive. And of course he knew how to talk. He could have ad-libbed for twenty-four hours on the game, for he was a library of tennis lore, tennis anecdote and tennis essence. "The thing is, Brinkley," he once said to me, "I'm a hopeless tennis toper. I'd do my job for nothing if I had to. But don't tell Sniff that!"

The name stuck from the first. Barney seized on it as his personal identification and frequently used it in referring to himself. Pretty soon he was opening his telecasts with it: "All you hackers out there—the Green Tongue is with you again! It's *stroking* time!"

In no other sport do so many people who watch the game play it and the fans looked upon Barney as their champion. He felt tennis belonged to the "hackers"—the increasing millions of ordinary players who will never have a Rosewall backhand, a Newcombe forehand, a Gonzalez serve, an Emerson half-volley or the touch shots of John Bromwich but who enjoy the game, mostly on weekends. Chester believed that tennis should be fun. His telecasts were irreverent and often barbed. He came down equally on "the stuffy snobs who run tennis," "the insolent greed that is beginning to overwhelm this great game," and "the prima-donna players who are making millions out of it and yet go into uncouth, childish convulsions when a paying customer in the stands gets up for a leg-stretch." He didn't feel a tennis stadium should be either St. Paul's Cathedral or the Library of Congress reading room. At times he seemed a lone voice trying to keep a little pep, joy and spontaneity in the game. But behind him was an immense and devoted army, the legions of "hopeless hackers, like me," as he called them, "tennis topers." They all loved Chester.

Immense is the "memory factor" of television. No fame can be compared with that of the individual who appears regularly on the tube. Barney was far and away the best-known figure in tennis, better known than Jack Tillotston, Jimmy Connors or Arthur Ashe, though these, too, were recognized on the street, not for their exceptional games but because they played them on television. Even when they did, however, they were seen much less than Chester Barney, who telecast *all* matches. To the television world, Chester Barney was tennis. The game could have found a worse personification.

I was at the airport when Chester arrived in Palm Beach for the Celebrity Pro-Am Weekend. With him on the same aircraft came three other Celebrity tennis players, Senator Orville Thatcher, Shelly Blaine and Spence Leland. But among the welcoming crowd of four hundred there to press the flesh of the famous, perhaps a fourth had come to see Blaine—after all she was on the tube, too; a fourth to see

Leland, the great screen lover; none to see the Senator; and all the rest to see Barney.

Many of the welcomers were children and teenagers. Most wore tennis clothes and a number even carried tennis rackets —a mysterious trait indigenous to tennis. Football fans, for instance, don't go around in shoulder pads and cleated shoes, carrying a football. When the plane set down and the four great ones descended the ramp, several small sub-teen girls dropped their rackets and rushed forward with squeals of "We want Chester!" Crying out, "My fans!" Barney knelt on the tarmac. While the television cameras whirred and the still cameras from local newspapers clicked, he scooped up three or four of these local children into his arms, his chop-teeth all visible in a great smile which was as certain as the weather to appear next day on page 1 of the local newspapers. Barney knew a good "frame" as well as anyone in the business. Then he stood up and scribbled autographs on the tennis balls and racket covers thrust upward at him by the little groupies while the other Celebrities waited with no excess of patience. The Welcoming Committee moved forward.

"Welcome to Palm Beach," its leader said. "I'm Tish Milam, the chairperson."

"You don't look like a person to me, baby," Barney said, looking her up and down. "Well, here we are! Palm Beach will never be the same."

He was decked out in faded blue jeans, Greek thong sandals and T-shirt, this one an off-ochre garment, with the crocodile looking the wrong direction. He leaned forward and graciously kissed Tish's cheek.

"Shall we play a let?" he said and kissed her again.

It was another tennis phrase Barney had put into the language on non-tennis occasions—"let," of course, meaning to replay a point. He took over the introduction chores, as he did reflexively wherever two or more were gathered together.

"Shelly Blaine, Spence Leland and Senator Thatcher, who's running for something as usual, I've forgotten what," he ran the names off smoothly.

There was a lot of hand-shaking and cheek-kissing, and then Chester Barney was back in voice.

"The airline," he said, "tried to talk us into splitting up into at least two flights. They feared the cultural shock if a plane carrying us four should go down in flames. Right, Senator?"

"Well, I don't know about the rest of us, Chester," Senator Thatcher intoned. "But it would surely be a quite irreplaceable loss to the Republic if a plane went down carrying only yourself."

"You're so right, Senator," Chester Barney said. He turned to the chairperson. "Say! I hear you have a hurricane humping this way. Remember I can't afford to get stranded in the boonies."

Only Chester Barney could have called Palm Beach the boonies.

"I'll rush a bill through Congress," the Senator chimed in wittily, "ordering it to stay away until the tournament is concluded." He, too, was eyeing Tish Milam carefully. "Where I come from we believe in the old chivalry of protecting beautiful and charming ladies from all harm. Including hurricanes."

"How gracious you are, sir," Tish murmured.

"If the bill passes," Barney said in a honking voice, "it'll be the first thing Congress has done this year. Isn't that right, Shelly?"

Outside of the tennis world Shelly Blaine's fame was greater even than Chester's. She was the hostess of a daily network talk show which originated in Washington. When she and I were cub reporters on the Washington *Post*, she did paragraphs on capital "personalities." Since then she had shot upward—and she deserved to. She was a brilliant interviewer, in my opinion the best in the business. She was stunningly attractive. I thought she had the best thirty-three-year-old body in America, but then I was prejudiced by the past. She knew everybody in her world of Washington. One of the many rumors about her—so many that it had become almost impossible to separate the true from the manufactured—was that she had slept with two Presidents of the United States while they were in office. Shelly Blaine. It had been four years. From what I felt happening inside me, it could have been yesterday. She wore a perfect beige linen dress. No one in sight was so elegant.

"Chester," she said icily, "do you think we could postpone some of this fascinating conversation and get out of this bloody heat?"

Chester went on beaming. "Nice flight down, eh, Spence? We had some elevating chitchats, didn't we?"

Spence Leland, the rangy movie star, sighed heavily. "Yes, Chester," he said. "We all enjoyed your seminar."

"Good old Spence." Chester Barney erupted into his great laugh, which sounded like an explosion in a gas oven. He reached up and whacked Leland on one of his wide shoulders. "Celebrity tennis is great for the ratings, we hope, eh, Spence? Correct me if I'm wrong but I believe your last flick was down a few points." He turned to the chairperson. "I hope you're not bunking me next to Spence. I haven't gone bi-bi yet. What did you say your name was, baby?"

"Tish, baby."

"Say! I wouldn't mind bunking next to you."

Nothing is like a Celebrity Pro-Am. For instance, Charlton Heston, besides being Ben Hur, Moses and Andrew Jackson, is also a tennis player, so that at one of these affairs you may, if you are a man or a boy, find yourself taking a shower in the stall next to Heston. A true leveler, it binds the great and the lowly.

An outsider is often surprised at how easy it is to get Celebrities for these tournaments. So many Celebrities have only recently taken up the game that they constitute a special branch of the "tennis boom." They are anxious to exhibit themselves playing it. At a Celebrity Pro-Am they can become big jocks hitting balls across a net at the world's top tennis players. In the five years of the South Palm Beach Celebrity Pro-Am, Catlo told me, it had been no problem to line up Johnny Carson, Clint Eastwood, Dinah Shore, Burt Bacharach and of course Heston. This year the tournament committee had come up with its biggest catch ever. Spence Leland was the current Hollywood heartthrob, and Shelly Blaine was so well known that in the annual "most-admired-women" poll she had ranked among the first five for three years running. This year she finished just behind Rosalynn Carter and just ahead of Jackie O.

The format of the Pro-Am rituals is simple. A pro pairs with a Celebrity and they play doubles against another pro paired with another Celebrity. The chief rule, never to be violated under any circumstance, is also simple: the pros hit only cashmere puffs at the Celebrities, shots that any able-bodied grandmother could field. The reasons for this rule are two: first, the Celebrities are supposed to be made to look vaguely like tennis players. Otherwise they won't come back. Second, it would not do if a valuable property like Clint Eastwood, for example, were castrated by an overhead smash coming at him at 125 miles per hour.

In order to accommodate the event, MBC had considerably altered the South Palm Beach Bath and Tennis Club. Court 7 became the Center Court and on the delicate clay of Courts 6 and 8 bleachers had been established, with a seat on a hard plank going for $50. In front of both sets of bleachers were four rows of director's chairs, which retailed for $100 and were known as "touch chairs" because you could reach out and fondle a Celebrity. But of course it was all for charity. The television coverage would go over the waves as a segment of MBC's "Total Immersion in Sports," a five-hour Sunday show in which the network covered every event that could possibly be said to fall under the canopy of "sport," from arm-wrestling to tree-chopping. MBC had installed crudely lettered "spontaneous" signs, carrying such whimsical legends as "Chester Barney is Seeded Number One," and "Love-Six, Love-Six, I'd Love to Make It With You Chester Barney."

Chester Barney himself, with characteristic generosity, had agreed to serve as emcee and commentator not only for the network show, which would carry the matches on Sunday, but also for the untelevised matches on Saturday. Every bleacher seat, director's chair and scrap of standing space was occupied when Barney, holding a microphone, took position front and center at the net. Across the sunny sky a few dark clouds coasted like a flotilla of Goodyear blimps, perhaps silent messengers sent by the still-distant Hurricane Agatha. Today Barney was wearing a Kim-Novak-lavender T-shirt with the wrong-way crocodile.

"Welcome, Hackers, to the demented diversion called tennis," he opened the proceedings. "And just look at all the foxy chickies we have present with us. All riiiight! This is Chester Barney, B-A-R-N-E-Y, the hacker's friend, I fool you never—and it's *stroking* time!" Everybody laughed in appreciation of the self-parody.

"So here we are for the Jelly-Ball Classic!"

"Chester Barney for President!" a little girl's voice piped up from the bleachers.

"Speaking of politics," Barney took his cue, "let us have the introductions, starting with the least important. Our first Celebrity—the pasty chap over there—is said to have presidential aspirations, though having met the man I personally find that hard to believe. Folks, I give you Senator Orville Thatcher."

The Senator acknowledged the restrained round of applause by hoisting a pair of fingers in the V-salute first made popular by Churchill, and by lesser men since.

"Even though the Senator doesn't know his rosy pink from a foot fault," Barney said, "he's welcome here. Right, Hackers? We let anyone in. Now on to the big meat. On one side of the net we have a lady who has won the hearts of all American women and the rods of all American men. I give you Shelly Blaine!"

There was appreciative laughter from the worldly crowd as Barney stuck the microphone in Shelly's face. She smiled and did a little wave of her hand that reminded me of that distinctive circular gesture the female members of British royalty make from the balcony of Buckingham Palace. I had no doubt that Shelly had picked up the gesture from the Queen when she interviewed her. Shelly Blaine was tall—5 feet 8 or 9 inches—and a thoroughbred. In the brief tennis dress she wore I could see her slim hips which thrust out, her lean flanks and her breasts which were considerably larger than you would imagine if you had seen her only fully clothed. She was a classic model of what the French call *fausse maigre*. Her face was all planes, extremely thin as if all excess of flesh had been pared away. Her complexion was soft, almost translucently white. There was a freshness about her. A freshness, and a carelessness—a splendid carelessness. Her mouth was on the large side, her lips always seemed slightly open. Her eyes were light blue, her hair pale red.

"Shelly," Barney was saying, "I have only one question. Is your game equal to your body?"

"I think I know what a girl is supposed to do with balls, if that's what you mean, Chester."

The crowd burst into laughter. "Let me know whenever you need a new can, will you, Shelly?" Barney said. The crowd laughed some more; they were having a good time. "But I do want to say just one thing in parting, Shelly." And he made a thing of looking down and around her. "You've got a mighty nice little ass there."

"It would certainly fit easily into your mouth, Chester."

Barney exploded his laugh. "And now, folks, on the other side of the net we have the man who has also won the hearts of American women albeit in a different way, and at whose very sight their fur stands on end. The American Heartthrob Spence Leland!"

He had been carved to order by whatever god is assigned to create Hollywood leading men in the old vogue. His shoulders were broad, his tummy flat, his legs sculpted. His face was made for the great profile shot, although a patina of wrinkles had just begun to appear, the first intimations of mortality. He wore shocking pink. One phenomenon of the tennis surge is that so many new players turn up in matching ensemble, always pastel.

"Too divine!" Barney said. "Are you wearing a pink jockstrap as well, Spence?"

"Would you like to take a peek and see, dear?" Leland said in his famous deep voice.

The quick line pleased the audience.

"We may ask you to autograph that garment later for a consolation prize," Barney continued. "Well, I know there must be something under there. I don't know about his tennis, but Spence assured me personally that he has the greatest strokes off the court of any swordsman in Hollywood."

"Barney for President!" the little girl yelped.

"Will someone shut that fat kid up?" Barney said. "Now that we've got through the hackers, let us move on to the authentic players. Ladies and Gentlemen, I give you the Big Cat and the Kitten!"

I remembered Catlo's summary: "If there's one thing in this world I loathe it's a Celebrity Pro-Am. Patting balls to jerks and fags who happen to have some fucking name so they can think they're big jocks." None of this was in evidence now. Catlo's living depended on the status of his club, and a good Pro-Am adds status. As Catlo and Billy stepped for-

ward, a different kind of applause came from the crowd. It
was genuine warmth: Catlo and Billy were liked around here,
though I think Catlo was feared as well.

"Even I," Barney said, "would not presume to instruct this
audience—or any tennis audience—about Robert Catlo. Or
a Palm Beach audience about his son, Billy. I will say one
thing, however. Now listen carefully."

Chester waited until a silence came over the crowd, until
there was not a sound except the blue Atlantic washing in
beyond the courts.

"A little sea gull has told me," he said, "—and the best
sea gulls bring all their secrets to Chester Barney—that a
couple weeks from now Billy Catlo may be going to Forest
Hills. So once more the game will be graced by one of its
greatest names. It so happens that the reigning champion of
that event, as well as Wimbledon, and the Number One
ranked tennis player in the world, will be arriving here tomorrow. Across this very net"—Barney reached over and
touched it, as if it were about to become an object of ven-
eration—"Tilly and Billy"—it was the introduction of that
phrase to tennis—"will meet *for the first time*. Those of you
who are fortunate enough to be present—it will cost you another hundred bucks and is worth twice that—will witness
an event that may go down in tennis history. In fact I, Chester
Barney, personally predict it."

Granted Barney had built up the event. Nevertheless he
had some material to work with: it *could* be a memorable
meeting, the king and the promising youngster with the great
name.

Barney's voice moved into its honking frequency. "On with
the Patty-Cake Championships! Playing with Shelly—tennis,
I mean—we have the Copper Angel! Playing with Spence,
the one, the only, Big Cat. It's *stroking* time!"

The Billy-Shelly versus Catlo-Leland match, with the Senator alternating with Shelly and Barney with Leland, was the

usual thing you see at Celebrity matches on the tube. It was corn but it was supposed to be.

"Those majestic crosscourts and down-the-lines!" Barney neighed as the Celebrities loped and reeled around the court and balls crept into the net, flew into the fence or sailed into the stands. "Those impeccable chips, dinks, drop-volleys! The acrobatic footwork! The exciting fusillades!" When the Senator flailed at a ball with his metal racket and almost caught Billy's head instead: "He's going to bludgeon Billy to death with that thing before the kid ever gets to Forest Hills." When the Hollywood Heartthrob continued sending lethargic lobs high into the air: "The Sky-king himself! One of those is going to kill a sea gull."

There was a lot of clowning around. Catlo was surprisingly good at it, but it was sad to see him playing the buffoon, cowering in mock fear at the Senator's serve, winding up as if to aim his own big serve at Shelly, then lollipopping it over the net to the delighted squeals of the crowd. I wondered what was going on inside Catlo during these antics, and whether he was thinking, how could it come to this? Occasionally he and Billy went with the big serve or the booming ground-stroke when hitting to each other. The crowd would applaud with genuine appreciation.

Of the Celebrities, Shelly Blaine was unquestionably the best player. It was typical that once she took up tennis, she would become good at it. For Shelly Blaine did nothing badly. Between shots she seemed to be having a problem keeping her eyes off her partner's body. On the odd-game changeover at net, she stood unnecessarily close to Billy, who made no great effort to move away. Once I glanced at Lindy sitting in the second row. She had a thoughtful expression.

Toward the end when the Senator replaced her, I was surprised that Shelly Blaine came over and sat down next to me.

"Well, well," she said. "It's been four years."

"I'm flattered you remember me," I said.

"I never forget anyone I've screwed."

Shelly Blaine had always been frank. But there was a joy in her frankness, so that while I didn't like the trait on most women, it was okay on her.

"How do you keep your sanity associating with these pricks?" she asked. "I mean Leland and Chester. Jesus H! They should call it the 'Pricks Pro-Am.' "

"Chester's not so bad," I said.

From down below Barney's voice interrupted us. The Celebrity match was over and the Senator and Leland were sashaying to chairs at the side. Barney trailed his mike back to mid-net.

"Folks, I have a surprise treat for you now. A special dividend that wasn't on the program."

Chester paused and everyone gave him full attention.

"Robert Catlo and Billy Catlo are now going to play a proset exhibition. All r*iiiii*ght!"

A murmur of pleasure coursed through the crowd. Barney raised his hand.

"As you know, in a pro set the first man to get eight games wins it. Today the winner receives a thousand dollars, the loser five hundred. That's just to make certain it's for real."

A rare treat indeed. Both opened up, the more so, perhaps, from having to repress their real tennis throughout the Celebrity-match farces. Catlo did not give his son anything—or vice versa. It was hard-fought, exuberant tennis. The man and the boy moved over the court with authority and presence, and with immense grace, the boy a long step faster than the man. Catlo partly made up for his gone youth with cunning and precision, finding the lines with his shots, but he was giving away more than twenty years. You could feel the crowd's gratitude for getting something so good and so unexpected.

It was Billy's finally at 8-5. Man and boy were walking off and I heard the father speak quietly to the son.

"That was pretty good, Billy," he said. "Do you know

something? I wouldn't like to have to face you at Forest Hills."

Billy had still hit some wild shots but fewer than usual. He was using more topspin and more shots were falling in.

The Catlo-Catlo set was a nice way to end the day—until I got this jolt from Shelly Blaine. Jolts could come from Shelly Blaine at almost any moment.

"He's absolutely beautiful," she said.

"Who?"

"That *boy*, for god's sake." She was watching Billy pick up his extra rackets.

"Yes," I said. "He's pretty good-looking for a kid."

"Good looking? He's gorgeous. I think I'm going to have him, Brinkley." She looked at Billy. "He's a young matador."

"But are you?"

She turned and looked at me. "I actually believe you're jealous. You always were," she added. She turned away to watch Billy. In a moment she said, "Do you think he might like to exchange lessons? He'd teach me tennis."

"Why don't you yell down and ask him?"

"Instead of that, why don't you tell him to meet me in Room Five-twenty-two of the jolly Jolly Roger?"

I knew she wouldn't do it that way—there was no scrap of coarseness in her—but I didn't like it anyway. I was very aware of her next to me, in that brief tennis dress, her bare legs. Those lanky thighs, soft-white.

"Tell him yourself," I said. "I've given up pimping."

Room 522 she had said.

"All you hackers!" Down on the court the voice of Chester Barney cut through the air. He was winding down the day. "Don't forget to get your tickets for Jack Tillotston versus Billy Catlo. Shelly and Spence will be here tomorrow too whether they get any tonight or not."

"Jesus H.," Shelly said.

How did all this nonsense get started? I wondered. But even I was looking forward to seeing Tillotston and Billy across a net for the first time. I looked up at the sky. Dark cumulonimbus was drifting across it. I hoped the rain held off. Beyond the courts, long, smooth swells were moving in from the Atlantic.

"Give you a lift?" Shelly said. "I've got a car and man waiting."

"No, thanks," I said stiffly. "I've got my Plymouth." I knew I was handling it in the worst possible way.

4

TILLY

COMING INTO A TENNIS STADIUM YOU WOULD KNOW IF ONE
of the players was Jack Tillotston by the sound of the ball
coming off the racket. He hit the hardest groundstrokes in
tennis. One thing above all made Tillotston a great champion.
In a tennis age of increasing safe playing, of laying back at
the baseline and waiting for your opponent to make the error,
he went for the winner. He hit out. He had nothing but contempt for the safe player.

"That's not tennis," he said. "That's a game we used to
play as boys in Virginia and its name is 'auntie over.' I don't
care to win on my opponent's errors. The only way I want to
win is on my winners."

There was a charm about Jack Tillotston, and something
wonderfully malevolent. He was a handsome man. He had
wavy blond hair and a strong curved line to his nose. He had
iron-grey eyes, active eyes, analyzing all the time, whether a
person, a remark or a situation. His face had a mocking cast.
His derisive laugh was directed toward the world, or life in
general, as if everything about it was faintly ludicrous. There
was a certain swagger to him, but it sat well when he did not
deliberately parody himself on the court to annoy an opponent. He was cool in manner, and could be frigid.

Most top tennis players have slender bodies. Tillotston
looked more like a football running back. His 6 feet 4 inches
and 210 pounds arranged themselves in long, strong thighs,

rugged shoulders and a hard tight stomach. He was the purest athlete the game had, beautifully coordinated, and remarkably quick. I have never seen anyone in sport as big as Tilly who also had his moves. When Tillotston lost a point, it was seldom because he couldn't get to it. He had huge hands. The 4⅞-inch racket grip he used was the largest in tennis, the 15-ounce weight the heaviest, its 80-pound tension the tightest. Tillotston's rackets broke strings so often that he brought a full half dozen to matches. It was always a sight to see that big man stride onto the court carrying that much firepower.

He didn't buddy around with other players—at tournaments he didn't even dress in the locker room but at his hotel. I think he felt above them. In honest truth, he was.

Like many big men Tilly rarely became angry. When he did, he could be fearsome, and he had the strength to back it up. Once after a match in which his opponent had made some personally obscene remarks about Tillotston's tactics, Tilly waited until the man finished his shower ("I didn't want to get my hands dirty"), picked him up and threw him against the tile wall.

Tilly was the leader of the new wave in tennis, of the revolution which was changing the game. A Tillotston match was as much a piece of theater as a sports contest. He made psyching a major resource: his gestures at linesmen, his discussions with umpires, his dialogues with spectators, his demands for the removal of officials. Tillotston had even insisted on the removal of a ball boy for allegedly "thumping" across the court in pursuit of a ball. He loved to tantalize, to bait, to mock. He could imitate an opponent to perfection— his manner, his language, his gestures, his way of walking. The mimicry often evoked laughter from the stands and no one played the crowds as well as Jack Tillotston. He often toyed with opponents. Once I saw him give a first set at 1-6 to a young Yugoslav named Kravlovic, keeping the crowd in stitches by copying him—his stern expression, his soldier-straight method of walking—and letting balls go by him completely, swinging ludicrously at the air. It was a comical performance—if your name was not Kravlovic. Then Tillotston turned it on and ran out the next three sets at 6-2, 6-1, 6-0.

Then there was the litany of his pre-serve specialty: his infuriating manner of walking slowly to the baseline, bouncing the ball interminably, blowing on his hands, adjusting his shirt by the shoulders, knocking imagined dirt off his shoes with his racket, forever stalling. Nothing forbids these rituals, so anarchistic are the rules of tennis, having been written for an age of manners. They could shatter an opponent's nerves and destroy his timing and concentration. Few of his opponents seemed to have the mental weaponry to combat it. As for Tillotston's own psyche, I had yet to see him rattled.

It was always a show when Jack Tillotston played. He drew the largest crowds in tennis. The funny thing was, he was so good that he seldom needed to do these things to win. He did them anyhow.

I got to know him pretty well last winter when the magazine sent me to follow the tennis circuit on its round-the-world tour.

"Why do you use all those tactics?" I asked him over some mastika at a bar in the Grande Bretagne in Athens.

"What do you mean, 'tactics'?"

"Come off it, Tilly. That ball-bouncing before serving. Blowing on your hand. Mimicking your opponent. Talking with people in the stands. Straightening your shirt. In a word, 'stalling.' "

Tilly grinned. "I don't know what you're talking about. Can I help it if I'm prissy and like my shirt to be nice and unwrinkled?"

"Catlo never did it."

"Well, screw Catlo. He's the old breed. I'm the new." He leaned across the bar table and was serious. "While we're about it, why should tennis be so prissy that it can't take what every other sport takes? Why do tennis players have to be such mama's boys that they fall apart if someone sneezes in the stands? What is this, a game or a religious service? If that's what they need, let them go off by themselves and hit balls against a backboard. That's a contest out there, not a high mass."

"Thanks for educating me."

"Somebody should educate tennis people. Every athlete has two things going for him, and he's entitled to use both to the hilt. His body, which is his basic skill at whatever it is he does. And his mind, which is his ability to reduce that skill in his opponent by anything short of going over and sticking the racket, handle first, up his ass, which wouldn't be a bad idea with most of these crybabies."

He sipped his mastika, then held the glass up and looked at it thoughtfully. "Brinkley, I can't understand how a place as great as Greece could manage to come up with a drink this bad. What kind of man would make a drink out of something I use so my racket won't slip? *Resin*."

"I think it was a Spartan who originated it," I said.

"It figures," Tillotston said.

Tillotston needed enemies the way other people need friends. He had a gift of penetrating to the specific thing that would most insult or infuriate a given individual. He fed on enmities and I am certain it helped his game, giving it that hard, fine edge.

"I have never looked upon a tennis court as a place to make friends," Tilly said. "Don't expect me to be nice to the man across the net. My idea is not just to beat him but to break him. He is standing in my way, and for doing that I am going to humiliate him if I can. Fair play and sportsmanship are overrated. Charity is the worst trait an athlete can have."

Like everything else, sex took its assigned place in Tillotston's geometry of life. It was one of those items to be taken care of without a lot of fuss. Above all it was not to interfere with what he did, which was winning in tennis. He was a dandy in many ways. When we were in London for the tennis stop at the Albert Hall, I spent a full morning making the rounds with him while just about every part of his body was measured for something: at Kilgour, French and Stanbury, for suits; at Peal's, for shoes; at Locke's, hats; at Beale & Inman, underwear, shirts and pajamas. He was always perfectly groomed. He spent one morning a week in New York in a hairstylist's salon having his blond hair done exactly so, styled back with that row of waves. The nails on the big hands that held the racket and tossed up the service ball were manicured. There was a polish to him, or a slickness—I guess the adjective you chose would depend on whether or not you liked him.

Jackson Claudius Tillotston was a Virginian. His family had a place about twenty-five miles from Charlottesville, where they had lived since the eighteenth century. They were decent people, I'm sure, though perhaps not quite as "genteel" as Tillotston's allusions sometimes suggested. They were sufficiently so to hold membership in the Farmington Country Club, which spreads over some lovely rolling country outside Charlottesville with the Blue Ridge hanging in the distance. The club provided a tennis court where, like all players who go to the top or anywhere near it in tennis, he became good very early. As a boy he started winning tournaments in his ascending age group and accumulating rows of little silver cups, which also got bigger. He did go a year to Washington and Lee, then left because his father ran out of money to keep him there. Not knowing what to do with himself, he wrote a letter to Gus Licata, who had been the tennis coach at W and L and had left to run the lush tennis program at the Acapulco Duchess. Licata told him to come on down. He went for a week and stayed for a year.

Licata was the first to recognize Tillotston's potential and for that year worked with him on his game. It must have been a pretty good life, playing tennis and filling in at undemanding hotel jobs. Licata may have been the best tennis coach this country has produced (and the best anywhere next to

Hopman). Licata taught him to "dance" on his toes on the court like a boxer, always ready to move in any direction. Licata helped him create the "fadeaway" shot, taught him that tantalizing, maddening soft drop shot that just plops over the net and dies.

To hone the "dancing," Licata made his tennis pupils endlessly skip rope. He also made them work on one shot for a week at a time. "What happened," Tilly said, "was that you came to hate that stroke so much that you mastered it, just so Gus would let you stop doing it. If you didn't he'd make you do it a second week. He was a great coach. The greatest, without a question. Look what he did with me. He was as queer as a seven-dollar bill of course."

"I didn't know." We were in a bar in Bangkok, at the Erawan, drinking rice wine.

"He never did it with his pupils. He had these little Mexican boys. I used to think they were the main reason he took the job at the Duchess, there were so many of them available and they had these nice smooth brown bodies. Actually I think the Duchess knew it and was glad. Their pro wasn't going to be off screwing the rich young girls who took lessons from him."

"He left that to you."

"How did you guess." Tillotston laughed fondly. "Old Gus. He'd be seventy now—and I'm sure flipping fifteen-year-old Mexican boys over and doing them on both sides."

"And he never made a pass at you?"

"Not once. I don't think he ever made one at any of the boys he coached. Point of honor with him, I think, not to mix coaching with cocksucking. He was a true Virginia gentleman."

Tillotston was a student of sport, interested in how far the frontiers could be pushed, how much more the body in a given sport could finally do—and, most of all, what would make it do it. He told me another time that he had considered making boxing a career until Licata talked him out of it.

"For one thing," he said, "I thought it was time boxing had a champion with a mind as well as a body." Tillotston never had to carry around the burden of modesty. "It's the stupidest of the sports of course—in more ways than one, but I'm talking here of how mentally stupid so many great boxing champions have been. Aside from Tunney and Ali and Sugar Ray, I can't think of one with an IQ much above seventy. That's *before* they got beat up so much. I went out for it at W and L and made the boxing team. I loved it—knocking the daylights out of people. If it hadn't been for Gus, you'd probably be talking with the heavyweight champion of the world instead of the tennis champion. He convinced me it was insane to get your brains bashed out, especially with the things that were happening to tennis, the big money and all. That came along just right for me, the timing couldn't have been better. I mean, just a year before I went on the tour, they were playing for money that wouldn't have kept me in handkerchiefs. Then suddenly the bread was all over the place. Incidentally, I do feel sorry for the old Cat. He just missed, and I came along to pick it up. But that's life."

He gently rocked his stengah glass—we were in Singapore —and watched the liquid swirl. I looked at the right arm lying across the table with its light covering of blond hair. It was like some great, perfectly tuned weapon in its musculature, so much larger than his left arm.

One of the most debated questions in tennis was what would have happened if Tillotston had met Catlo in the Big Cat's prime. Tilly was very honest in anything involving tennis and I think he came closest to the answer himself when I asked him. We were having gin pahits at the Peninsula in Hong Kong.

"Well, to tell the truth, I think if we had played a hundred matches, one of us would have won fifty-one times and the other forty-nine." He shrugged. "Too bad we'll never know." Then he laughed a little. "I'm glad we won't, of course."

And when later I asked Catlo, he said more or less the same

thing. It was the only thing I knew that they ever agreed on.

"I had a bigger serve and volley and bigger overhead smash," he said. "But I don't think anyone ever hit the ball harder off the ground than Tillotston." He shrugged. "At that level it's all character anyway."

This year Tillotston was going for something no man had ever achieved, winning the Big Four in one year.

"If I make it, I'm going to do something different," Tillotston told me in Tokyo at a bar in the Okura the night before we grabbed the 747 for the long flight home over the Pacific. We were sipping sake. "I'm going to retire undefeated at the age of thirty. But I want to retire having won everything the year I do—the Masters, WCT, Wimbledon, Forest Hills. If I miss one of them, I'll stick around till I do it. When I make them all, that's it. No one is going to take my racket. I'll just put it down."

He had a little sake. "Do you know I've got a million bucks in Governments stashed away? That's all I ever wanted. I'm not greedy. But I want to work. If I retire undefeated I'll go to CBS or NBC and show Barney how that job should be done. I'm at least as smart as Barney and his own mother would say better looking. CBS is talking about a ten-year contract at two hundred and fifty thousand per. I'd start as a voice but I'd expect to end up as their director of sports."

"You've talked with them?"

"Yep. It's on, all except for the fine print."

It sounded like a good plan and I told him so. I wasn't too happy for Barney, but as Tillotston said, that was life.

It was very late. I had long since lost count of the number of sakes. We finished this round and stood up. Tillotston looked at his Rolex.

"No point in sleeping now," he said. "It's only three hours till plane time. We can sleep all the way across the Pacific. I've got a bottle of Wild Turkey in my room. Now that we're headed back home, shall we clean the other tastes out?"

Since then Tilly had won the Masters, WCT and Wimbledon. Three down and one to go.

The day lay under immense floating clouds that kept colliding with each other. The air had that odd, total stillness that comes before big weather. The net on Court 1 had been removed to provide a landing pad for the arrival of Jack Tillotston from the Palm Beach airport. At noon an MBC point man stationed at the airport phoned to say that Tillotston had landed and even now was lifting off in the helicopter. At 12:10 the chopper could be seen approaching above the palm trees, the scudding clouds seeming to push it on its way. It was not Tilly's idea that he arrive in this fashion. The helicopter ride would save only twenty minutes over the land route. The idea came from Chester Barney, who felt that Tillotston's dramatic entrance would make an elegant opening shot for the Chester Barney Hour television show.

"I think this may be the first recorded landing of a whirlybird on a tennis court," Barney said, as if that were a pioneering event in the category of landing on the moon. "Personally I think it's a particularly classy idea with a *Celebrity* tournament where the time of all these freaks is so valuable. The copter will convey that idea."

A mild demurral had been entered by the *patrón* of the courts, Robert Catlo.

"Chester," he said, "you know that clay is fragile. It takes a long time to get it just right. I'm not sure what a chopper is going to do to it."

"Now don't worry about a thing, Cat," Barney had reassured him. "The network is just like strip miners. When we come in and tear a place up, we fix it when we leave so it's better looking than before we arrived."

"I don't want it looking any *better*, Chester. I like it the way it is. But I'll remember what you said."

The Green Tongue was standing on Court 2 ready to tape

the arrival to show to the nation at 5 P.M. when the Celebrity Pro-Am would be on the air. In its approach the chopper fluttered a little as a gust of wind caught it. The wind blew the craft slightly off course to a point over Court 2, where Chester and his mike courageously stood their professional ground, even when it appeared briefly that one of the blades might behead the Tongue, which would have been a real pioneering incident for television. Then the chopper corrected course and dug in safely on Court 1 in swirls of red clay. Jack Tillotston stepped out and was greeted by Barney and the committee. It made a considerable entrance, with Barney leading the champion and the welcoming delegation to mid-net on Court 7 where the opening ceremonies would take place.

Tillotston was flawlessly turned out in his Tillotston brand shirt and shorts, Tillotston shoes, Tillotston socks, the discreet lettering "Tilly" on all. There was not a single item on his body which he was not paid to wear. When he stood around he would often be holding a Dr. Pepper, which also brought in a considerable sum—his contract didn't even require him to be seen drinking it. For a moment he and Catlo stood face to face. To my knowledge they had not seen each other since that day in Wimbledon eight years ago. They shook hands. Catlo after all was the host.

"Okay, Hackers!" Barney addressed the crowd. Today his reverse-crocodile Lacoste T-shirt was in fuchsia. "Here we are again, all of us tennis topers. None of this is on the air yet so we can be as catty, chatty and dirty as we please. I'll let you know when we *are* on the air so you can take your hand off your neighbor's wife's ass. Now just to put everybody at ease, there's a hurricane floating around out there somewhere." Barney shaded his eyes and looked out at the Atlantic Ocean washing gently in beyond the courts. "But we have a Chester Barney Hour to do today and it wouldn't dare interfere. So welcome to tennis."

Like a drill sergeant about to take morning muster, Barney looked over his row of Celebrities. "All right, troops. On your marks." Today Shelly Blaine wore a tennis dress of pale green. She looked stunning. Barney checked his watch, then looked over at his television crew.

"And now, people, we're about to go out to the nation, Anchorage to Key West, Honolulu to the New York Island. Try not to watch the camera too much."

There were some brief rituals having to do with the great medium, all done with a brisk professionalism. Then Chester was speaking to his vast TV following. He told them where he was—"in beautiful, chic Palm Beach, where nobody ever goes in the ocean. There's too much happening ashore. Like right here today." He identified stars and players. Then:

"And now shall we create a little instant history? Are you people out there aware that these two, the reigning king of tennis Jack Tillotston and the brat with the great name who may challenge him—maybe right soon, at Forest Hills—have never even met? I mean not only not met across the net but not met at all. Billy Catlo, step up here."

Slowly, his face tight with reserve, Billy got up from his chair by the umpire's stand and walked forward. He looked so thoroughly a boy. And that is how they met, right there on the Chester Barney Hour as Chester was never to let anybody forget.

"Hello, kid," Tillotston said.

"Hello, Mr. Tillotston," Billy said.

"That's enough!" Barney ejaculated. "It's *stroking* time. Today, Hackers, we have one of the all-time great doubles matches. Tilly and Spence Leland going against Billy and Shelly Blaine. All riiiiiight! We'll be right back with it. Right after these words from Sniff. 'If it can make a jock smell sweet, it can make *you* smell sweet.' "

They spun a racket for serve and took places. Jack Tillotston raised his racket and as gently as a butterfly fluttering its wings hit a yellow tennis ball in the direction of Shelly Blaine on the other side of the net . . . and so the match was on. It was more of the same clowning and horseplay of yesterday, but I was not watching or listening to it. I was watching Billy on his side of the net and Tilly on his, the first time their game had been visible on the same court. No flaw would be visible here, and no excellence either. But one could at least observe them and seek comparisons. I saw Robert Catlo watching too, not seeming to look at Tillotston. But I knew he was registering everything. A mild breeze fluttered up. Beyond the courts I could see whitecaps on the dark blue.

I don't know whose idea it was to have Lindy be a ball girl, but as the set went on she got quite a bit of attention. From her kneeling position at the net post during a point, she would dart on the court for a ball, skirt flying. Then instead of tossing it to the server in the approved one-bounce fashion, she reared back and hurled it at him, baseball fashion. With her small body it made a delightful picture, and her throw was accurate and hard. After a while the crowd began to want her to go after the ball and to throw it as hard as she could, that funny and charming southpaw windup she had, the leg kicking up and across. She got some nice rounds of applause. Nothing was subtracted from this tableau by the fact that today she was wearing bright red panties.

I began to review my earlier opinion that when she wore her *bal pockette*, she was not aware of the thoughtful attention she attracted. I must have been stupid to think that. Of course every woman knows when a man is looking at her panties, for god's sake. Every woman knows when a man is *thinking* about her panties. Then, in a further series of lightning insights, I understood what was happening. Lindy had observed Billy and Shelly Blaine "messing around" with each other—I was convinced that was the precise phrase she would use to describe it—and she was employing an ancient sports tactic that began in Sparta when Pausanias decreed, "Fight fire with fire." Then I decided on still another slight modification: she was "showing" Billy where he got off. Her word, too, I felt sure.

I started to watch Billy and Tillotston.

On those times when they hit a ball to each other, it was as if they were playing their second game. Noticeable particularly when they served. Of course serving to Spence and Shelly, they would apply just enough force to get the ball over the net, enabling their foes occasionally to look fairly good. So here was Shelly Blaine hitting a winner off the serve of the Number One player in the world. And here was Spence Leland scoring off the serve of one of the bright new crop of challengers and son of the tennis immortal Robert Catlo. Which is what Blaine and Leland came for.

But even when serving to each other, neither Billy nor Tillotston used his first serve. The same on the groundstrokes. Nothing truly big, not one of those screaming returns of service that were Billy's best shot, not one of those shots that seemed to erupt from Tillotston's racket. Neither player intended to show the other his game, not the power, or the finesse, or any of his repertoire. Perhaps one thing more: each had too much respect both for himself and for tennis to put his true game on display in the ludicrous setting of a Celebrity Pro-Am.

After making this astute analysis I went back to watching Lindy. My god, I thought, what was happening to me. Yes, I found myself watching, not Tilly's shots, not Billy's, and not the sometimes pathetic, sometimes barely acceptable shots of those two household names paired with them. I found myself looking forward to the time when someone would make an error that would send the ball into the net so that Lindy could dart onto the court, pick it up and rear back with that windup of hers, skirt flying, and make visible those sweet thighs crowned by the gallant red bunting, the view now assisted by the slight wind off the sea. I found myself waiting for this moment like some fifteen-year-old schoolboy.

Not only me. In following Lindy I had begun to notice Leland. I became aware that when he was serving, he was deliberately hitting a few balls into the net for the express purpose of seeing Lindy's little act as she tossed the ball to him. After one completion of her throw to him, with its accompanying whirl of skirt, the actor spoke to the crowd:

"Isn't it nice they don't carry the all-white rule too far in Palm Beach?"

I had the impression it was two things with him: to see her and to get back on center stage, which Lindy seemed to have appropriated. The crowd laughed and the game continued. Then, a bit later, Leland netted a ball intentionally after he had served. Lindy did her throw to him, there was a moment of red and he spoke to her—and to his audience.

"Any time you want to ball girl with that in Hollywood, sweetie pie."

During the next two games it happened twice more, again with different lines. Pedestrian as they were, they amused the crowd. There was nothing to suggest that Lindy was in any way offended. Rather I had the feeling she was mildly flattered.

It was on the odd-game changeover at the net with only minutes left in the network TV segment. Billy's serve was due next. They were right there in front of me—Tillotston, Shelly, Lindy standing next to Leland, who had plopped into a chair by the net post, and Billy standing a little behind them both. Billy had picked up a towel to wipe his racket handle preparatory to serving and had just tossed the towel on a chair. They were all so close together at the net that I may have been the only one to see it. Leland simply moved his hand sideways and brought it under Lindy's skirt. I saw a flash of red panties again before the skirt dropped, the hand still under it. Lindy's head did not even turn. With considerable presence of mind and class, I thought, she simply walked away—and handed three balls to Billy.

"Your service," she said.

Before he went back on the court, Billy picked up the yellow bucket of balls that had been used in the rally warmups. The crowd's eyes were constantly on the "stars" and I doubt if anyone even noticed Billy carrying a bucket of balls to the baseline. Billy Catlo stood to serve to Spence Leland.

"Now, not too much, champ," Leland sang out across the net. "Remember us senior citizens."

The crowd laughed. I suppose I knew an instant beforehand that Billy was going with his big one. It was his mannerism. He would lean forward a little with his weight, pause the fraction of a second and with his ball-hand pat the face of the racket. In the workouts I had found it only interesting and a bit boyish, as if he were saying to the racket, "Do it for me." He made the gesture now so I knew that Spence Leland would not see the lollipop serve he expected. The ball went up in the toss, the racket fell back. Then, in one explosion of movement, the body crashed forward with all the strength of its youth. So Billy, too, had seen Leland's hand under Lindy's skirt.

I don't know how often you have stood behind a service box ready to receive and had a tennis ball come toward you at 125 miles per hour. I once had Robert Catlo do this to me so that I, the sincere and dedicated sportswriter, could at least know what it looked and felt like. What it looked like I never learned. What it felt like I never forgot. As the projectile hurtled toward me, my concern became that of a man with but one thought, to save himself. I had Catlo repeat the service a few times just so that I could concentrate on trying to touch the ball with my racket. Even when I managed to stay still long enough to swing at it, swinging at air about the time the ball crashed into the fence behind me, the fear never left me. Once I was able to get my racket on the ball. The racket was torn out of my hand. All this occurred under conditions where I was prepared and knew that a serve of that magnitude would be coming at me. The difference here was that Spence Leland didn't know. The result was interesting.

The ball took off from Billy's racket and hit the clay in front of Leland—I couldn't tell from where I sat whether it was in or out—and he spun around. Literally spun around like a top and came back to rest in position. I don't think he even knew what he had done. Almost instantly another ball was leaving Billy's racket and detonating on the court in front of Leland. Again he spun around. The crowd thought this was part of the show, a routine that Billy with his big serve and Leland the great actor had cooked up between them to add to the crowd's pleasure. Now the balls were flying off Billy's racket in a deadly bombardment.

A surprise ending made me raise my estimate of Spence Leland as an actor. As Billy reached toward the bottom of his bucket, Leland, as each serve hit the clay in front of him, mimicked his own fear, pirouetting like a ballet dancer, spinning now by design exactly as he had spun reflexively before. It was a marvelous imitation of himself, an acting performance so good that his pretended fear seemed more real than the real thing.

Billy's bucket was empty. Applause and shouts of "Bravo!" swept down from the stands over Spence Leland, who took a wide-sweeping Barrymore bow. Then he did a truly nice thing. He flung out his arm, the one holding his racket, toward Billy, as a stage actor will graciously do on the curtain to a fellow-actor.

Chester Barney jumped down from his umpire's chair and brought his microphone to the middle of the court.

"All riiiiiiight! Too much! Folks, even I didn't know that was on the agenda. Fool you never! If word gets around that Celebrities can expect serves like that, it'll be the finish of Celebrity Pro-Am. Billy Catlo, come here! Spence Leland, come here! I want to thank you two for giving us the finest moment of the tournament. Also for one of the greatest acting performances I have ever witnessed, which believe me is saying a lot. That's it, Hackers. Until next time on the Chester Barney Hour—where everything that is anything in tennis happens— this is the Green Tongue saying good-bye for Sniff. Sniff. 'If it can make a jock smell sweet . . .' "

I was standing just behind Leland and Billy when the actor leaned over and spoke in a low voice.

"Christ Almighty, kid, you could have taken my head off," he said. "Or what is worse, my balls. How was I to know she was your girl?"

But I was thinking about something more important than Leland's manhood. The first serves that Billy had had such trouble getting in when I watched him practice . . . well, I had kept track of the last dozen balls today. All of them landed in the service box. Maybe all he needed for accuracy was to get really mad about something. I looked over at Catlo and saw something bright in his eyes.

Just one other thing happened that day before the great Celebrity Pro-Am came to an end. They had resumed play and all were patting soft balls again. Billy was standing nonchalantly at the net when with no warning a groundstroke came off Tillotston's racket and boomed across the net straight at him. Unprepared, Billy stuck his racket up in a reflex movement, more to protect himself than to play the ball. It went past him without touching the racket, stirred the line behind him and curved away from the court. It was as if Tillotston wanted to remind Billy who he was.

"Scare you, kid?" Tilly said, and laughed.

I gave Shelly Blaine a lift back to the Jolly Roger. On the beach road the Atlantic had chopped up. Whitecaps stood on the dark sea to the horizon and a freshening southeast wind was ramming high waves ashore, where they hit with a hard, gathering rhythm. Above, great black clouds rolled across the sky and I knew there was rain in them.

"It's going to be a wet night," I said.

"I imagine."

"I suppose you're going to tell me you and he were together last night?"

"That's right," Shelly said. "You've got it ever so right."

"Well, did you do it?"

"I never do it the first night."

"Only the second," I said.

"That's right. It's a rule I set for myself a long time ago."

"We didn't go to bed till the sixth night," I said.

I could feel her looking over at me. "You remember the exact night," she said in wonderment. "Well, I was younger then," the crispness back.

"Yes you were. So tonight is the second night," I said stupidly. I knew I was losing this conversation.

"How well you add."

"But tonight's the party, sweetness. It's going to be a probblem slipping off. You're such a great star."

"Don't you know by now—sweetness—that I know how to manage things if it's something I really want? And tonight I happen to want that boy."

"To suck or to fuck?" I was trying what I knew was impossible, to shock her.

"You're incredibly gross. But since you ask, I would imagine both. And if I may use one of your sports terms, you've got the probable order of finish."

I didn't know, or wouldn't admit, why I should feel so miserable. The rain began as we reached the hotel marquee.

5

THE TENNIS BALL

I USED TO THINK THAT EVERYTHING OF IMPORTANCE THAT
happened in Washington and New York happened at parties,
though very different things. In Washington the party was
where the deals were struck that determined the tally of a vote
in Congress or a few sentences were exchanged that determined who would fill a Cabinet post. In New York the party
was where a divorce got started, or a baby, or a love affair (or
all three at once). In Washington the party was where things
were resolved; in New York it was where they began. But in
both cities it seemed to me that the party was where things
happened. After the night of Tish's party I began to think this
might be true of Palm Beach, too.

Surely the rain had much to do with what took place there.
It drew people more closely together, enhancing, magnifying
the emotions between them, making them more vulnerable.
The rain had stopped for a while, then resumed about the time
the last guest arrived. After that it never stopped. In fact it was
to go on without letup for four days. Rain makes a special
sound on Spanish hollow tiles. It has been compared to the
percussion section of an orchestra, or to a pipe organ, but I
hear the ringing of bells, tiny, medium or heavy bells, depending on how hard the rain is coming down. As the party continued into the night, the rain's sound on those hundreds of
roof tiles grew insidiously louder, bringing the partygoers ever

more closely up against each other's inner selves, inner desires.

Afterward people referred to it as the hurricane party. I don't know what Catlo or Tillotston or Billy called it, but to me it was always the Shelly party.

Shelly: America's highest aristocracy may be that handful of people who are identifiable by their first names alone. It is the ultimate accolade, our knighthood: Jackie, the Duke, Walter, Johnny, Liz, Frankie, Judy, Chester, Shelly.

Shelly: Her daily network talk show mainly covered Washington and the city's doings as the capital of the world. Her special field was the interviewing of very large names, whether they operated in Washington or visited there on affairs of state. These days no one turned down a request from Shelly Blaine. There was almost no one left she could interview whose name was as big as hers. Perhaps for this reason she ranged afield, to Moscow, London and Rome, to Cuba and New Delhi, Tokyo and Peking, to Cairo and Tel Aviv. Her questions bore in as sharply as a diamond drill. She didn't let anyone off the hook until either he had answered the question or it was clear to 40 million viewers that he was ducking it. Most of those interviewed chose the first alternative so that many Blaine shows ended up making news themselves.

Shelly's success was surely at the root of the rumors about her, since so many of them originated in the Washington press corps. Washington reporters are paid as little as $225 a week. Shelly was paid $350,000 a year. Certainly there were grounds for envy. But what really got them, I always felt, was her ability. She was a hell of a lot better reporter than most of them, and an incomparably better interviewer. The rumor circulated most often by these gentlemen, naturally, was that to get her interviews she employed a weapon they didn't possess. For the story to be true it would have meant that Shelly had slept with Leonid Brezhnev, Fidel Castro and Pope Paul VI among others. Her male colleagues in the press liked to say that she did it only with individuals of at least Cabinet rank.

They got back at her for her talent and the money she made by calling her stupid and cruel things, like "Miss Accordion Thighs." Though the Washington press corps told a lot of stories about her alleged bedroom habits, I doubt it boasted one male member who would not have broken all existing District of Columbia speed records had Shelly phoned and said, "Honey, I'm in my apartment and I have a great idea. Why don't you come over and screw me?" I know whenever I used to receive such a call, I was over there fagairtrans, as we said in the Navy.

Off-camera she certainly played on her sex. Personally, I was thankful that Shelly crossed her legs a good deal. She never wore pants, which she considered an abomination for a woman. "Why should a woman conceal one of her nicest resources," she said once in an interview in *Vogue*. Her dresses tended to be clinging or cut on the low side (show the best of both worlds, as she said in the same interview). Which meant, in sum, that she had the good sense to punctuate her two chief assets—legs and bosoms, both. She had a magical body. I never saw it clothed in a dress that lacked either taste or invitation.

For such a well-organized person, Shelly had the messiest apartment I ever saw. Books, records, slips, bras—everything was strewn everywhere. And the bathroom! The apartment reminded me of those cartoons of George Price in *The New Yorker*. Still, for a while there was no place in the world I would rather have been, and no place to this day where I was the recipient of so much pure, giving pleasure. In those days she worked from 11 A.M. to 7 P.M. and I from 2 to 10 P.M., but even with this difference in hours, I began to spend nights there. It seemed silly, as Shelly said, and I agreed with alacrity, to get out of bed at midnight, especially in February in Washington. She had so many "boyfriends"—she still referred to them by that archaic term—that she devised a telephone code system for her favorites. If Jack called he was to ring once, hang up and ring back; Jim was to ring twice, hang up and ring back. In this manner she would know who was calling and decide if she wanted to see him that night, or talk with him or do something else. It was flattering, since none of the men knew that the others had their own mantras. She told each only that the code was for him so she could answer immediately. I didn't find out about the system's other subscribers until, having been assigned three rings, I stayed afterward one night and the phone began to beep. Two rings and a hangup, two rings and a hangup, on and on. She did not answer, either because Number Two had fallen from grace or because I was there. Thus I ended up being pleased rather than furious at the discovery that I was not the only "boyfriend" with a code.

The thing that used to make me the angriest about Shelly was that however good we were together, she was ready for anyone else who attracted her. She couldn't understand why I couldn't understand this. She was not promiscuous, she was extremely selective. But if she wanted it with someone else, she would simply say, "How does that take away from us?"

"I don't think anyone should own anyone else's body," she said. "Heart yes. Maybe soul, even. I think you can share your heart with just one person, share your soul. But to limit your body to one person—no, that's wrong. It's unnatural."

Since we parted four years ago I have had a few women but not one like Shelly. I merely had to think about her to get excited. I think we would have got married. But then she got the big job in television and pretty soon she was authentically famous. I didn't want to be Mr. Shelly Blaine. I took the job in New York and Shelly left my life. Except that from time to time I could not help, when that hour of the day came, turning on a television set just to see her. Until the silly Celebrity tournament that was the only place I had seen her in four years. Sometimes as I looked at that screen, along with several million other viewers, I even thought she did things on it, little secret things known only to us, as a signal to me alone. Surely a very grand illusion.

Tish Milam was what is called in her part of the country "big rich." I know of no definition of the specific sum of money required to qualify for this category but those who do can buy a place like buying a bauble. Tish Milam had quite a place. A Mediterranean villa all blue and white and clay-red, capped by those hollow red Spanish tiles. It stood on ten acres of high ground in the northern part of Palm Beach along a row of ocean estates that included the homes of the Kennedys, Otto Kahn, Atwater Kent and the owner of the Kentucky Fried Chicken enterprises. It stretched from ocean to intracoastal waterway. You reached it after a winding drive through a dark tropical forest so luxuriant that you had to use your lights until you emerged to see that astonishing villa perched in the sunlight on the sea. Tish told me that the first time she drove out of that forest and saw the house, she decided on the instant to buy it, even before she set foot inside.

From that high land one could see across the blue Atlantic as far as one could anywhere in Florida. The house had long galleries, spaced with Moroccan columns, from which opened luscious rooms with the highest ceilings this side of Rome, and possibly the largest bathrooms anywhere. The sea winds moved and murmured languidly through the great free spaces of the house. Pillows were everywhere, great Turkish pillows covered in paisley prints. One felt that harem girls in baggy Arab pants had recently reclined on them and were still around if one went looking.

The crown jewel was the two-story ballroom. Across its Carrara marble and parquet floors and over a half century of time every dance from waltz to Charleston to tango to rock had been danced beneath its trinity of cut-glass chandeliers. Rustling taffeta had swept across that floor and floating silken gowns, and challis miniskirts. It had been filled with the names of the Republic, including four Presidents of the United States. For the Tennis Ball, five hundred people had been invited. Four hundred of these—the ball's quota for the Charity—had paid $250 each for their invitations. For the remaining hundred the price of admission was what they personally brought to the ball as decoration.

Tonight tennis motifs were everywhere. Crossed rackets of assorted flowers—camellias, cornflowers, yellow daisies—adorned the walls. Hundreds of plastic yellow tennis balls dangled from the ceiling between the chandeliers. Miniature nets separated the bushels of stone crab, buckets of calico scallops, acres of salads and mountains of fruit which rested on long buffet tables. Drinks were served by teenage "circulating ball girls," outfitted in ingeniously scanty tennis costumes. The Everglades Club band wore tennis blazers and long white flannels. But the most original and charming touch was the life-sized effigies of tennis history's giants. Created in the Madame Tussaud wax-figure style but in papier mâché, they were the work of the notorious Mexican art-deco designer Jesus Sanchez. The gallery of tennis titans stood in a great circle around the dance floor, looking on like observer-consuls from some tennis pantheon: Suzanne Lenglen and Bill Tilden, Jack Crawford and May Sutton Bundy, Gottfried von Cramm and Margaret Osborne duPont, Norman E. Brookes and Hazel Hotchkiss Wightman and—installed near the bandstand like a quartet of featured vocalists—the French Four Musketeers, René Lacoste, Henri Cochet, Jean Borotra, and Jacques Brugnon. The effigies, done in blazes of color, were eerily real. The charming thing about them was their expressions, which had been cleverly varied by Jesus Sanchez to show a sly, knowing grin (Tilden), a Gallic leer of delight (Lacoste), a devilish play-face (Suzanne Lenglen). Famous in papier mâché, they watched the Tennis Ball.

I stopped at the bar and instructed the attendant to prepare me a double Tanqueray Gibson in a Scotch glass. I wandered over to the buffet and stood at an enormous tub of shrimp, my favorite food. I had never seen so many shrimp at one time, large and firm and white-pink. I speared one after another, placing the toothpicks in a neat crosshatch. I took care of about a dozen while listening to the rain fall on the hollow tiles and give out its bell-bell sound. It was a deeply sensual feeling, close to euphoria and even beatitude. Seeing that so many shrimp remained and that no other predators were in the immediate vicinity, I decided I could take a break.

I went into the ballroom and danced with one of those saucy-looking circulating ball girls. Holding her, with so few garments between her and me, I began to feel familiar arousals. Someone cut in and I had the bartender fix me another Gibson. The beatitude grew. Maybe the combination of shrimp, Gibson and circulating ball girls would get Shelly out of my mind. I looked around but could not find her. I danced with Tish.

She was wearing a pale yellow chiffon evening gown, surely an original from one of the great Paris houses, cut to display both her rounded shoulders with their stunning Palm Beach tan and her full white breasts. An emerald of considerable size hung from her neck.

"You throw some party."

"I like to see people have fun. Almost as much as I like having it myself."

A scent of Femme came from her. She was comfortable to hold, all rounded. As I danced, I looked into an ardent earth-face, with large discerning eyes that seemed always to be laughing at something. Holding her gave me a sense of peace and reassurance, a vision of long, bawdy lovemaking in a heaven of white flesh.

She was a beautiful dancer. "I like the effigies best," I said. "Next to the circulating ball girls, of course."

"An alive body is always best, isn't it?"

She had a bland, innocent way of saying things that seemed

to reach right inside me and pull out all my secret thoughts. I looked into her eyes. Yes, the eyes were laughing, ever so gently, at me.

"Did I say something wrong?" she said. I guess I was really looking at her.

"No, my dear. I don't think you could. It is better with something really alive, isn't it?"

I danced her around within the pantheon of tennis immortals she had decreed. "Is Billy going to Forest Hills?" I asked.

"Do you think he should?"

"I don't know."

"How is it up there?" Tish asked.

"Very rough. I remember Booth Nelson the first time he played in the Stadium. He managed to spin for serve but then he couldn't pick up his racket. His hand was shaking too much. Every time he tried to grip the racket it just fell out of his hand. It wasn't very funny. There were fourteen thousand people watching."

"You're saying it could happen to Billy?"

"It's possible," I said. "There's a lot going on inside Billy, isn't there?"

She waited a moment. "A lot goes on inside Billy that I don't think any of us knows too much about. But isn't that always true of the best people? So couldn't it be good?"

"Maybe so. Provided Billy can hold on to his racket."

We swept past Louise Brough, Maureen Connolly, Fred Perry and "Little Bill" Johnston.

"Jack Tillotston is a very impressive man," she said. "I don't imagine Billy would get much mercy there, would he?"

"Don't look to Tillotston for mercy. Is it important to Catlo for Billy to go?"

"My goodness no. I think Catlo would rather he'd never taken up the game."

I did not believe her. She would simply lie automatically if doing so would help Catlo. I believed Billy's going to Forest Hills might be the most important thing in the world right now to Robert Catlo. A speculation occurred to me: she would be glad to support Catlo in all the elegance money could buy, taking him away from those lessons at the bath and tennis club and from all other drudgery. He could never accept this. So her wealth was the one thing that stood between them.

"Why don't we consult Bill Tilden about whether Billy should go?" I said. I danced her to the papier mâché figure. But Tilden wouldn't tell us much. The sound of bells playing over the roof grew louder. "You like Catlo very much, don't you?"

Her face became bright, delighted, as if touched by some quiet, secret joy.

"Like Catlo?" she said, as if that were such an insufficient word. "Oh, my yes. I like Catlo."

I waited a moment, and then I said something. I don't know why.

"Let me tell you this," I said. "I can't really discuss why, but this may be Jack Tillotston's last year."

She looked up at me, alert. "Oh? That seems odd. But I don't know much about tennis."

She knew plenty. Certainly enough to register precisely the implication of what I had told her.

"You mean if the Catlos want Tillotston, it will have to be this year?"

"Very possibly," I said.

If that was what Robert Catlo wanted, it would be what she wanted. And if it was what he wanted, she would do everything in her power to get it for him. She would be a cool, astute ally. I had the feeling she could be very rough, maybe ruthless, if she had to be.

We danced past Alice Marble. I felt a strong hand on my shoulder and turned. He looked great in navy jacket and white flannels.

"Brinkley, I'm cutting in," Robert Catlo said.

I went over to the windows. They were wide and tall and ascended to Moorish arches to form a frame, so that one seemed to be looking at a Winslow Homer painting. I could hear the big sound the sea was beginning to make as it assaulted the shore on the incoming tide. The rain was coming down hard. Chester Barney joined me. Tonight his wrong-way-crocodile T-shirt was off-apricot, which more or less went with his light green jacket.

"Brinkley, step in here with me," he said. "I've got something serious to tell you."

He steered me into the library, closed the big double doors, looked at his watch—chronometer, I should say, an immense thing which had everything but radar on it—and switched on the television set. A voice said, "We now take you to the National Hurricane Center." A nice-looking man appeared on the screen. He wore a short-sleeved white shirt. Behind him was a wall-sized Mercator projection of Florida and the Caribbean.

"This is Vernon Page at the National Hurricane Center in Miami," he said. "Here is the latest advisory on Hurricane Agatha."

He began to read in a calm voice from a piece of paper he held, at intervals poking a pointer at the map.

"Agatha has now become a very dangerous hurricane. She is a vast storm system 400 miles in diameter. At ten this evening Hurricane Agatha was located at 22′ 10″ North Latitude and 75′ 6″ West Longitude, or 425 miles south southeast of Miami. Maximum winds near the center of the hurricane are approximately ninety miles per hour and as she moves across open water, Agatha is gathering strength. At present Hurricane Agatha has a forward speed of eight miles per hour. A hurricane watch is in effect for the area extending from Jacksonville to Key West. Small craft in this area are advised not to venture from harbor. High tides three to four feet above normal may be expected . . ."

The station announcer came on. "Residents along the coast should be prepared to board up their houses, to remove all loose objects such as garbage cans and playpens from yards, fill bathtubs with drinking water, and lay in canned food and flashlight batteries. All interests should stay tuned for further advisories. The next advisory will be issued by the National Hurricane Center at seven A.M., with intermediate bulletins."

Barney switched off the set. "I don't like the looks of it, Brinkley," he said. "I can't afford to get stuck here. I have major commitments. You were in the Navy, weren't you?"

"Yes. Well, it's still a couple of miles out there, Chester," I said.

"Listen," he said, "anytime they start talking about laying in canned food and filling bathtubs with drinking water, you may be sure it's serious." I realized Chester had had a few. "I absolutely can't get stuck here, Brinkley. There's Forest Hills coming up, and next weekend there's the Chester Barney Hour."

"They'd probably postpone Forest Hills if you didn't make it, Chester."

"Would you mind not being so sarcastic about this? Why do you think I brought you in here? We may be the only two normal people at this party."

"Well, there's plenty of time," I said. "Anyhow these hurricanes are unpredictable. Maybe it'll change course and go to Texas and wipe out Galveston."

"I hope so," Chester said. "But we can't count on that, can we? Jesus Christ, if they're talking about filling bathtubs with *drinking* water. I definitely can't afford to get socked in here."

"Listen, Chester, I just had another idea," I said. "MBC could always have the Pentagon fly you out in a jet fighter. They can fly in anything. Rainstorms, windstorms, hailstorms, even hurricanes."

"I'll keep the Air Force in mind," Chester said. "You wouldn't dream the clout MBC has in all sorts of oddball places. Besides, I've got friends personally at the Air Force. Greenie told me he never misses an edition of the Chester Barney Hour."

"Greenie?" I said.

"Four-star General Armstrong Green, United States Air Force. He's a tennis nut. He's also Chairman of the Joint Chiefs."

"Maybe you could get him for a Celebrity Pro-Am," I said. "Especially if you could find a four-star admiral who also plays the game. It would be kind of like the Army-Navy football game, only tennis."

Chester's face lit up for a moment. "Say! That's not a bad idea." The smile faded. "What the hell does that have to do with my problem?"

"Just a thought," I said. "I'm trying to stay with the big picture, which is your show."

"That's true. The Chester Barney Hour is what's important. Not me but the Hour. Hell, I know that. But how could there be a Chester Barney Hour unless Chester Barney is on it?"

"That's a good point," I said.

"It's the only point," he said.

We stood at the big windows looking out to the sea. Water was everywhere. The wind was whipping the palm branches, which were making snapping noises. Beyond them the sea smashed against the seawall.

"Look at that sea," Barney said. "Have you ever seen a sea like that?"

"You'll get out all right, Chester," I said. "MBC wouldn't let you get stuck down here. You have my word on that."

"You're probably right." He settled into a big leather chair. "Well, I feel a little better. I tell you what. I'll keep the hurricane checked out and keep you informed, right? Stay available."

"Don't hesitate to count on me, Chester," I said. "I could be of considerable technical help to you if the hurricane strikes. Remember I was in the Navy."

I waited a moment. "Now that I've got us battened down for the hurricane, let me ask you something. Does Billy Catlo stand a chance against Jack Tillotston? I've got my own ideas but I want a second opinion."

"Providing Tillotston gets tennis elbow. Or breaks a leg."

"That bad?" I said.

"I think Billy should wait," Barney said. "For his sake. Of course, I'll be delighted if he goes ahead. It's good copy, the son going against the man who finished off his old man. But he really ought to wait a year."

"Tillotston might be gone."

"Gone? He's got five good years."

"Not necessarily . . ." I caught myself. Chester Barney knew nothing of Tillotston's plans.

"Maybe," Chester said, "if all the stars were just right in their various constellations, the sun didn't get in his eyes, and he didn't throw up from the tension, maybe, just maybe, Billy could pull it off, providing he was hungry enough. I've seen hunger do some strange things on the court. Is he hungry?"

"I don't know."

Barney paused for a moment. "Brinkley, I offer you a friendly piece of advice. It's not healthy for a reporter to take sides. We should be blind like Justice while keeping our balls tucked in. Journalistic ethics, you know."

"Of course, Chester. I rejoice in your ethics."

I started away, then stopped. I liked Chester. I thought I owed him this much.

"The Chester Barney Hour may be in a touch of trouble," I said.

"Trouble? Impossible. We have no competition."

"You may have," I said.

Suddenly Chester Barney was at Condition One alert. "Brinkley, as you know we're old friends. I hope we can continue to be. So let's knock off the cuteness, shall we? What is it?"

"I'm not sure I should say anything more. There may be a question of journalistic ethics here."

"Fuck that! Anything that concerns the Chester Barney Hour, that's where all rules are down the drain, out the window and up Idi Amin's ass. Let's have it."

"Very well. If Tillotston wins at Forest Hills, he plans to retire and go on the tube. To do tennis. In which case there'll be a Jack Tillotston Hour. But only if he wins—wraps up the Big Four for this year. Something just occurred to me. That gives you a stake in his losing, doesn't it?"

I'll say this for Barney. Despite the momentous news, he remained very cool. But something came into those sharp green eyes. It crossed my mind that Chester Barney, off the streets of Boston, might be a very dangerous enemy. And it was not until I had told him of Jack Tillotston's plans that I realized I had taken at least one step on the road from observer to participant.

"Well, well, well," he said. "The son of a bitch, the asshole, the motherfucker. 'The Jack Tillotston Hour' indeed." He spat out the phrase. "If there's anything I detest it is jocks trying to muscle in on our profession. Well, well. I'm deeply obliged to you, Brinkley, and Chester Barney never forgets a friend or a foe. There's an old saying from Bunker Hill we use in Boston. When you see the whites of their eyes, stick it up their ass. We reporters have to stick together against the jocks."

The double doors burst open. A noise in the upper reaches of the soprano register split my ears.

"Here he is!"

Into the room flooded a platoon of circulating ball girls, all clothed in those minimal tennis costumes. They swooped on Chester Barney and formed a ring around him, holding hands and jumping up and down in that peculiar jack-in-the-box mannerism indigenous to ecstatic young females.

"Chester!" they squealed. "All *riiiight*! Chester Barney!"

Then their leader announced their mission. "We've been looking everywhere for you, Chester Barney. It's *stroking* time!"

Another chorus of frenzied shrieks went up. The spokeschild continued, "Every one of us wants a dance with you. And we're going to have it or smother you to pieces!"

One of them reached down and began playing with the hair

above Chester Barney's fire-hydrant ears. Another threw her arms around his neck and actually cradled that ridiculously ugly head against her tiny bosoms like Salome with John the B. It was a preposterous scene, like seeing Benjamin Franklin fondled by underdressed pubescents.

Barney, swathed in teenage flesh, gave a shrug of helpless modesty.

"My fans, Brinkley. Isn't this terrible?"

Then these agitated nymphets in their flagrant dress that showed three-fourths of what titties they had and four-fifths of their little asses extracted Barney from his chair, a full half dozen of them pulling and tugging on various parts of him. I detected no signs of resistance.

"My fans, Brinkley," Barney repeated. "I'm absolutely at their mercy."

I went back to the party. The noise level seemed to be growing: the band, the roaring niagara of talk, and always the rain on the hollow tiles, up a few more decibels now. Some man had picked up Althea Gibson and was dancing her around the floor. Somebody asked me if I was Lew Hoad. I looked around for Shelly, moving in and out of the mass of dancers and drinkers. She was nowhere. But I did see Billy, which comforted me. The rain seemed to pull the party together. Everybody was having a good time.

I found myself looking straight at Suzanne Lenglen, the "Maid Marvel" of France, the greatest woman tennis player ever. She wed ballet to tennis. She danced away the nights at brilliant parties and sucked brandy-soaked sugar cubes on the odd-game changeover. I wished we had her today. She was dressed now as then. In her famous bandeau, she wore a low-cut, one-piece dress that stopped at her pretty mid-calves, clothed in white stockings rolled to just below the knee. This daring costume had shocked and delighted Wimbledon in an age when women played in corsets, layers of petticoats, long-sleeved blouses and ankle-length skirts. No one in tennis has ever so provoked the adoration of the crowds. I fancied she winked at me. Maybe I would take her home to bed with me. A nice French girl with rolled stockings would be just the ticket on a night like this.

Suddenly I thought of what Billy would be doing with Shelly this night. I didn't want to think about that so I wandered around the party looking at the girls. I danced with a couple more of them. It didn't mean anything. I could not stop thinking of Shelly. I kept looking for her over shoulders. Then I saw Lindy and cut in.

She was light in my arms. She wore a white linen skirt with a halter top. Her legs were bare. There was some wonderful scent to her.

Out of nowhere she said brightly, "I think Shelly Blaine is a nice person. I was talking with her today and you'd never know she was such a big name. A girl can tell whether another girl is really nice."

"I'm sure of it," I said. "Girls are very perceptive anyhow."

She looked at me and giggled a little. "You're funny."

We whirled by Francis X. Shields. A thunder solo went off right over the rooftop, so close that everyone looked up at the ceiling. The three cut-glass chandeliers did a brief chorus of tinkles. It startled her a little closer into my arms.

She giggled again and smiled up at me. "Wow, I really jumped. That's a heavy storm."

I thought how much I liked them. I thought of all the wonderful girls with their wows, their you-knows, their far-outs, their fantastics and their heavys and I loved them all.

"Anytime," I said.

"You're not flirting with me, are you?"

I danced her past Don Budge, Jack Kramer and Sarah Palfrey Fabyan Cooke Danzig.

"It's almost that time for you to go back to school, isn't it?" I was talking to get my mind off certain things. One of them was the sudden intensity of wanting to put my hand farther down on her. "Maybe you should take Billy back with you."

"I wish I could," Lindy said. "I'd like for him to do both,

the college and the tennis. He says he can't do both."

"Well, he's right about that. Not the way tennis is today. They don't pay that kind of money for part-time work."

"No, I guess not," she said. "And it's not my right. No one has the right to take anyone away from two hundred and fifty thousand dollars a year. As if I could."

I was surprised at her precise remembrance of the figure I had given her that day at the bath and tennis club. She said it almost as if it were the minimum guaranteed annual wage.

"Well, he's a couple steps away from having it in the bank," I said. "So I suppose you have the right to try if that's your pleasure."

"But he really has the chance for that money?"

It seemed quite crass. She was always surprising me.

"The money's there," I said. "Of course a lot of other young men want it too."

"It's a gamble then?"

"Isn't everything?"

"You mean like making love?" she said suddenly.

She had such fine hair, white-blonde with the lights on it. I could feel the marvelous scents of youth from her.

"Making love is the biggest gamble of all."

Suddenly she said, "May I say something? He wants to go to bed with me. There, I've said *that*."

Reporters are like priests, there is something about them— that is, away from their work—that makes people tell all to them.

"Well," I said, "that's hardly the news item of the year. It would be odd if he didn't."

She cocked her head in that way she had, rather funny and charming, when she was intent on something. "I have the feeling that if I go back to school, that'll be the finish of Billy and me. Should I let him? It's terribly important to him. Maybe it would be to me. He could remember that, remember me." She laughed a little.

"What's stopping you?" I said.

"I think I know Billy. You probably think I'm old-fashioned."

"I did. I'm beginning to reassess that thought." We slid by Pancho Gonzalez.

She looked up at me and smiled comically. "Anyhow, he's really old-fashioned. What I think is this. I don't think he'd ever marry anyone he'd slept with before. Or that *anyone* had slept with."

"I'm beginning to see the battle lines."

She cocked her head, looking at me. "Oh, yes, that's exactly what they are."

Somebody cut in on us. Some oaf. I realized I didn't know the first thing about her.

Over there Chester Barney was interviewing Bill Tilden. He was mobbed in people, none of them men.

"All you hackers out there," Chester was saying. "It's *stroking* time."

"Fool you never!" a girl squealed.

"Bringing you Bill Tilden live!" Barney reached up and threw an arm around the towering papier mâché. "Big Bill, say a few words for Chester Barney."

The pubescent shrieks went off.

Tish walked up and Barney interrupted his Tilden interview. "What do you do here during a hurricane?"

"We board up and get drunk and screw."

Barney looked over at the great windows and at the rain pounding them. "It must take a lumberyard."

"Actually you could screw on one plank," Tish said blandly.

"Listen, baby," Barney said. "Tell me just one thing. Could a man get stuck here?"

"You can always outrun a hurricane," Tish said. "They only go nine or ten miles an hour. Any car can outrun one. You simply drive north."

"Drive! My time's too valuable to drive." Chester went back to interviewing Tilden.

I went up and introduced myself to Helen Wills Moody and
looked her up and down with careful appraisal. I decided I
preferred Suzanne Lenglen. Someone had started to conga
chain and I got into that, snaking around the room, holding
hips, in and out of the effigies, under the trinity of chandeliers
and the ceiling covered with those hundreds of yellow tennis
balls. The conga chain kept getting mixed up and suddenly I
found myself holding hips I knew.

I pulled her out of the line. She was wearing a black silk
jersey dress scooped to her breasts.

"Oh, Miss Blaine? Are you the famous Miss Blaine?" I took
her in my arms and danced her in the direction of the Winslow
Homer windows.

"And who might you be? Are you one of the famous tennis
players?"

"Permit me to introduce myself. My name is Bjorn Borg.
The B in the first name is silent. You pronounce it in the
second."

"Well I should hope so."

"Yes. I wear Tuborg on my headband, SAS on my sleeve
and 'Drink Aquavit' across my chest. Altogether this brings
in two hundred thousand dollars a year. That's not counting
the tennis."

"My god, you're a walking billboard. Have you thought
about renting out the seat of your pants?"

I could see the tops of her breasts, all white, all silken and
smooth and the black lace bra holding them. I danced her
along the battery of windows with the rain flailing them.

"Listen to that rain and wind," she said. "Is a hurricane
really on its way?"

The tide was reaching its highest. We could see the sea
slamming in violently now against the shore.

"Shelly," I said. "Shelly."

"Yes," she said. She thrust hard against me.

"It's been forever."

I could feel her pressing up into me.

"God, how I've missed it," I said. "Missed you."

"Yes, me too. Me too. You were so stupid."

"I wish you hadn't taken that fucking job."

"What difference does a job make?"

"It just does," I said. "I don't like the rules either but that's one of them."

"*Your* rules. How can anyone be so jejune. You must work at it."

I could feel her so. "My god, Shelly."

"All right, come down to Washington some time."

"I can't wait for Washington."

"Say it."

I held her very close against me, only the thin black silk in the way, and said it because she liked that.

"That does excite me. Ever so much. Tell me one more thing."

I did. She put her face against my chest.

"Say some more."

I said the words into her ear. She pressed her face hard against my chest and her fingers reached into my shirt and bit into my ribs. "I wish you were in me this instant." She waited, then her head went back. "But I couldn't. Tonight I'm spoken for."

She was the only woman I ever knew who could be totally passionate and totally ruthless at almost the same moment. Maybe that was why she was so good at her work. It was certainly part of why she was so difficult to love, and yet impossible not to desire, to have to have.

"Billy," I said. I was cold and angry.

She smiled up at me. "Thanks for helping get me so very ready for him."

And started off.

I was very angry and could not stop. "I didn't know you slept with anyone as lowly as Billy Catlo," I said after her.

The moment I said it I would have given anything in the world to have the words back. She paused, turned and looked at me.

"You, too, Brinkley?" And she was gone.

I have never despised myself so much as at that moment. How can people hurt people so? Especially with words.

6

CANADIAN DOUBLES

STANDING BY THE SEA WINDOWS, THE RAIN WASHING DOWN a foot beyond them, Jack Tillotston and Barney were surrounded. Spence Leland and Shelly were near the front. She didn't look at me. I could see Billy on the far rim of the group. A very bad thought went through me that if I saw him leave and saw Shelly leave, I would ask Lindy to go for a drive in the rain and just see. It was in me tonight. If he didn't leave, I would stay away from Lindy. I have a rule never to sleep with the wives or the girlfriends of my friends, but this seemed to permit an exception. Chester Barney was holding forth.

"I'm not a mouthpiece, mouthing what someone else has written." Chester had a pretty good load on by now. His slight figure swayed, as though the wind were inside the house. "Anyone who thinks that is what my job consists of doesn't know his ass from a foot fault. I write my own—nay, I compose it as I go along. Could you ever do that, Tilly? Or would you freeze? It's a born gift. I doubt seriously that you—just to take the nearest example—have it. Being a great player and being great on the tube call for separate genes entirely." Chester belched.

"I don't know what tennis would do without you, Chester," Tillotston said. From his smile he clearly thought there was an alternative.

Chester did not miss the smile. "You're right. No one can replace me." He was certainly trying to demolish the Tillotston Hour before it could get started. A burst of thunder broke massively over the roof.

"By god, they're getting close," Barney said.

Now Tillotston was being asked questions by the tennis nuts. In spite of all he had had to drink, he looked superb— male and muscular, urbane and commanding. A beautifully-tailored white linen suit showed his body to perfection. A grey paisley tie picked up his eyes, those active iron-grey eyes. Every wavy blond hair was in place, the nails on those big hands manicured. A bit lofty, cool, holding court as the reigning King. The questions came from all over, from fans with names and fans without names.

"Would you rather win Wimbledon or Forest Hills?"

"I wasn't aware it was necessary to choose." Appreciative laughter.

This was his public-figure role. Tilly enjoyed the idolization but had just a shade of contempt for the people who indulged in it. A tinge of condescension crept out. But he could play this game as well as he could play the game of tennis.

"Do you know what the betting odds are on Forest Hills?"

"I never bet, honey. My daddy taught me that gambling is a sin and the work of the devil."

A quartet of low rumbles moved about above us. I knew Tilly knew what the early-line was. I also knew he would have down a large bet on himself.

"Does it bother you that some players complain about your methods?"

"Methods?" Tillotston said with that faintly derisive air of his. "My method is to win. That's the only method I have. I imagine tennis will always have its mama's boys, don't you? When they can't win on the court, they complain and they whine off of it. Tell them for me that if any of them can ever start beating me the only place it matters, the tennis court, I'll listen to their talk about methods."

A soaring procession of thunders commenced. Not just one burst but a series of rolling, approaching claps, like big artillery sounding off across the sky, seeking the range. I could see the tracer shafts of lightning through the big windows. Then finally one zeroed in and detonated right over the house as if attacking it, and silencing all talk.

It came right after that.

"Tilly, old sot, tell me this," Barney said. "What did you think of Billy's game?"

"He moves well. And I never saw him close his eyes. Otherwise I didn't see enough of it to say," Tillotston said. "Is he coming to Forest Hills, Roberto?"

"Why ask me?" Catlo said. "It's up to him. I'm not sure he should—yet."

"You're probably right," Tillotston said. "Be a shame if someone with the Catlo name was embarrassed. It's been a great name."

"I don't think he'd be embarrassed," Catlo said. His voice had that fierce cold politeness. "But thank you for being concerned."

"Any time, Roberto." Tillotston smiled a little. "Of course if you'd like, I'll take you both on in Canadian doubles."

This is the game where two play against one. Therefore an insult, no matter how lightly it was said. Catlo's face became icy, but before he could answer, another voice spoke up.

"That Canadian doubles match won't be necessary."

It was a young voice, from the fringes of the crowd. Everyone looked over in the direction of it.

"No Canadian doubles," Billy Catlo repeated. His voice was stronger the second time. "Just one of us will be enough."

All I could think at that moment was: how admirable, how almost touching in a way—and what sheer bravado. I looked at Catlo, standing just beyond me. He was doing something he didn't often do. He was grinning. Like some big fat owl. I suddenly thought: the crafty, wily, cunning son of a bitch has got just what he wanted, and got it the way he wanted it. Billy speaking for himself. I wondered if Tish had told him my news that this year might be Tillotston's last at Forest Hills. Suddenly I suspected that Catlo had wanted Tilly down here on the hunch that this would happen—that Billy would see Tillotston's cockiness and something would go off in him.

Everyone looked up, startled. The lights had gone out and from the great ceiling of the ballroom, from their nests among the cut-glass chandeliers, hundreds of plastic yellow tennis balls were tumbling down on upraised faces, and on hands upraised to catch them. It was midnight. The balls were fluorescent and they descended glowing like legions of giant fireflies. The rain sledge-hammered the roof in a sound that was wild and deafening in the darkness. Then the lights were back on.

I looked around and Shelly was gone.

The plastic yellow balls had all fallen. The partygoers had started throwing them at each other across the great ballroom, yelling and laughing with that shrill, hyped-up idiot laughter of the inebriated at big parties. There was a fearful din. I felt absolutely empty. I looked around for Suzanne Lenglen. She wasn't in her proper place. Finally I found her propped in her countryman Borotra's arms. I took her in my own arms and went to find Tish.

"May I borrow Suzanne Lenglen?" I asked. A yellow plastic ball flew toward me but hit Suzanne instead.

"Borrow her?" Tish said. "Keep her. Is that the best you can do tonight?" Her voice was friendly, concerned, her eyes laughing a little.

I put Suzanne over my shoulder and started to leave. Lindy and Billy stood alone in the entry hall.

"Billy, what *was* that?" Lindy was saying. "I don't understand what that was about you and Jack Tillotston."

"Just a minute," Billy said to me. "I've got something for you." He turned back to Lindy. "I said I'm going to Forest Hills."

"That's what I thought you said. Are you sure?"

That seemed to make him angry. "Would I say it just to hear my voice? I want you to go with me."

They were talking as if I were not there.

"I don't have any money," Lindy said.

"Who does? We'll drive up in the MG."

"I don't know. There's school."

"Do you have any more excuses? Lindy, I'm asking you. I need you." I thought how difficult it must be for him to say that. "Are you going? Yes or no."

He appeared tense, urgent. She must have known that he would not ask her again. Everything was going too fast for her. She knew only that large things in her life were being settled this moment and there was no time to think about them.

"Of course I'm going!" she said. She was still very young, but I thought then what a marvelous woman she would become.

Billy reached in his pocket and handed me something. "Would you see that this gets back to the owner?"

I took it, cupping it in the hand that was not holding Suzanne's pretty little papier mâché rump. Lindy could not see it. It was a key, with a pirate relief superimposed. On it were the numerals 522.

Billy and I looked straight into each other's eyes. I admired him quite a bit at that moment.

"I'll see that it's properly returned," I said. "Where are you two going?"

"Going?" Lindy said, as if that were the most inane question she had ever heard. Her face was radiant, as if everything of any real importance in life had now been decided. "Why, we're going for a walk in the hurricane. Aren't we, Billy?"

Billy stood there a moment. There was a certain fierceness to him, a bit comical in its youth. Still, I would not have wanted to be on the other end of it.

"Canadian doubles," he said to no one except himself. He

made the two words sound like the worst kind of obscenity. "The son of a bitch."

Why, they've made Billy mad, I thought.

He took Lindy firmly by the arm. "Let's take that walk," he said.

And they were gone.

I put the key in my pocket, covered Suzanne Lenglen with my Burberry and went out into the rain. The wind hit me and held me in place. I had not realized it was that big. Force 7 or 8, I judged. The rain beat into my face. I could hear the roar of the sea as it fell against the shore. I gripped Suzanne tighter and pushed against the wind to reach the Avis. I propped her on the front seat, using both hands and my weight to get the door shut. I felt my way around the car. I drove slowly through the forest, where the sound was momentarily muted. As I emerged the storm was on me again, beating savagely at the car. I got onto A1A and drove along the ocean. The car rocked in the wind, the rain lashing the windshield. Through it I could make out the sea, raging in against the shore, and hear its wild rhythm as the great waves hit home. From the beach the water rushed over the highway and the car went through it like a boat. I got to the hotel and parked and ran for it. I left Suzanne below in the car. She would be nice and dry there. Surely I wouldn't need her now.

No more dank and dismal place exists in America than Florida under rain. No place is so leaden and grey. But for now I could not have been more glad to have the rain, for the exception that proves the rule had come to Florida: there was more to do indoors than out. Shelly phoned Washington to say that the rain had given her a sore throat so that she would be no good for her talk show. I was in the room running my hand lightly through her light red hair while she made the call. Her voice was a ghastly croak.

"I'm in bed with the virus," she said, rolling her eyes.

The network wanted to fly in a doctor but Shelly assured them that while primitive in some ways, Florida did have doctors.

"In fact one is in the room right now," she said, putting her hand over on me while I moved one up her thigh. "He's going to examine me."

She hung up and we made love.

They were gallant days, those three, with the rain falling on the roof, never stopping. We ate in, drank in, and made love in and listened to the bulletins on Hurricane Agatha: she had stalled, was simply standing still two hundred miles off the coast, as if making up her mind what to do next. At the end of those three days I was as close to being happy and in love —can one ever really be the first without being the second?— as I have ever been.

"I wonder if it would ever work," I said one day, making it as offhand as I could. "I don't suppose so."

"I don't suppose so," she said. She was as soft as a summer cloud, no hard edges to her now, soft and vulnerable and somehow innocent. I knew the shield that she kept around herself. I knew why, too, because of the world she moved in. It is still very much a man's world, do not let any one kid you. The one terrifying aspect of the woman's movement— and they should hate men for this above all other reasons— is that in seeking simple equality, so many of its practitioners have had to pay the penalty of losing those qualities that make them women. With the armament dropped, I found a gentle and loving human being. We were better together even than before, better than the earlier years when we were younger and new.

"Well, I guess there's an outside chance," I said casually. "Possibly as good as one in ten. For one thing, to be objective, we're pretty nice this way."

"We'll do," she said. "Why don't you move back to Washington and we'll do it every night. Twice on Mondays." Monday had been our day off on the paper.

"I work for a magazine now, remember? In New York. They like me there. But not enough to move the whole operation to Washington."

"You could get your job back on the *Post.*"

"I've gone on to better things. Magazines are bigger than newspapers, don't you remember?"

"That may be the greatest fallacy in journalism," she said.

"I'm beginning to think so."

"Maybe the network would move me to New York."

"But the whole idea of you is Washington."

"We could commute," she said. "I'd come up to New York one weekend and you'd come down to Washington the next. We'd just lock the door and screw and screw and screw. When we got tired of that we'd fuck."

"That sounds very pleasant. The only thing is—weekends are a sportswriter's main working time."

"Let's not talk about it now," she said. "Not about anything bad."

"Something good then," I said. "Why don't you come up for Forest Hills. At least the weekends. There are two of them. I'll have to cover some stories."

"I'll come with you."

Even having a name like Shelly Blaine with me could create problems while I went about my reporting. I didn't say so. I didn't want to spoil anything now, especially since the same kind of thinking had once destroyed our love. My hand moved on her.

"Good," I said. "I like it when we come at the same time."

"You're so vulgar." She threw a pillow at me, then threw herself over me.

I pulled her down and kissed her on the nose. "I think I love you, Miss Blaine."

"And I think. I don't *know.* Anyhow I feel different. So maybe it's love."

I kissed her again.

"Yes I do," she said with sudden urgency, turning in to me.

"I love you, love you, I love you so. Let's do it right now. Shall I spread my pretty white thighs for you? Shall you fuck me this very instant?"

The rain beat on the gravel roof of the Jolly Roger. Not the music of bells on the Spanish hollow tiles of Tish Milam's great house, but as sweet a sound as I have ever heard. To both of us, I think.

"No, I don't suppose we could make it," she said later. "Maybe someday."

I did not press her again, from that time until the morning of the third day when I took my Burberry off Suzanne Lenglen and put it over Shelly and drove her to the airport. The planes landing and taking off kicked up long trailing ropes of water. We stood in the rain and looked at each other. She was bareheaded and drops of rain glistened in her hair, cradled there. A crystal raindrop sat on the end of her nose. I touched it away with my finger.

"Well, all things considered, I suppose I'm glad you came instead of Billy." She traced a finger across my chest. "You've probably got much more hair here. All the same he is a very beautiful boy."

"Probably not as virile."

"I hope not. By the way, why didn't he show? Imagine being stood up by a child."

"He probably got a better offer." They were calling the flight. "See you in Forest Hills," I said.

"I think I will come up," she said thoughtfully.

All at once it came over me. "You mean Billy would be there? Yes, he would. He just decided the night of the party."

"How does that take away from . . . "

We both broke into laughter. Nothing had changed. Billy was still on her list and I would have to take her that way or not at all. Strangely, I was no longer angry. I would take what she had to offer me, and others too . . . well, as she said, that had nothing to do with us, subtracted nothing from us.

And if it did . . . well, I accepted it. There are advantages
to being older. I didn't have to like it.

So this time I grinned. "You mean how does it take away
from us? It doesn't. Nothing at all."

She looked at me quizzically. I had the feeling she was not
all that pleased with my new equanimity.

"What is it?" I said.

"You don't have to look as if you just swallowed the canary.
You know, Brinkley, in so many ways you are such a really
terrible son of a bitch." The look on her face made it one of
the nicest compliments I ever got.

She turned quickly and walked through the rain to the 727.
I watched her until she had gone up the ladder. She turned for
a second at the top of the stairs and stood there in the rain
and waved at me, then ducked inside. I watched until the
plane had taxied out and was pounding up the runway in a
gale of water and into the sky, banked, then was swallowed
by the grey-blue overcast. I didn't know until I turned away
that I was soaked.

I drove around in the rain for a while. Then the thought
came to me that I had better do some work on the cover story
or New York would very presently stop liking me even there,
let alone in Washington.

Of all the dank and dismal places in Florida under rain
none is worse than a bath and tennis club. It was like coming
into lake country. The nets had long since been taken in.
The water was creeping up the net posts as on the depth
markers on a ship of the line. I was about to drive away when
I saw a light in the pro shack—it was ten minutes to noon. I
parked the car and ran through the rain.

Robert Catlo was there, and Billy and Tish and Lindy.
They stood by the window looking at the flooded courts with
the rain still coming steadily down. It was a scene of gloom.
I felt sorry for Billy. The rain was taking away precious, indispensable practice hours for Forest Hills.

"Where the hell have you been?" Catlo said.

"In bed."

He must have grown used to my being around. He threw up his hands and addressed the universe. "Does anyone know of an indoor court anywhere around?" It was a rhetorical question. Florida doesn't believe in indoors.

"I know one." They all looked at me. "On Jekyll Island."

"Where?"

"Georgia. Three hundred fifty miles north of here. It's quite a court. It ought to be. J. P. Morgan built it."

Catlo looked at the body of water that the South Palm Beach Bath and Tennis Club had become.

"All right, all right," he said brusquely. "Let's hear about it."

So I told them.

Robert Catlo had always been decisive. "We'll leave in one hour. That last bulletin said Agatha has started to move. Headed straight for Palm Beach."

There was a big noise at the door and we all turned. Standing there framed in the doorway, the rain coming down like a waterfall behind him, and wearing the frontline drill longcoat, the safari-yellow rainhat and the big rubber boots that could only have come from the Royal Poinciana branch of Abercrombie and Fitch, was the Green Tongue.

"Surprise! Surprise!" he said. "Here I am, all ready to take on Hurricane Agatha. I fool you never."

He moved into the room, his presence immediately filling it. "Chester Barney heard that last and he's coming with you. Unzip your ears! I've decided to do a Chester Barney Special just on Billy—the first time ever any upstart tennis player has been honored with a full Chester Barney Hour Special. Two days on the phone but cleared with the network and committed. You heard that right! On Billy and his daddy with the immortal name and the big push up the golden ladder for Forest Hills."

"Good god," Catlo said.

"Besides, someone here told me the way you beat a hurricane is to drive north. Didn't you, Tish baby?"

Catlo looked at Tish as if she had arranged the whole trip and was personally responsible for Barney's inclusion. "Yes I did, Chester baby," she said.

"I'll tell you something else," Chester said. "You need me a lot worse than I need you. I'm very familiar with the great Morgan court. I've *played* it. You probably wouldn't get within a mile of J. Pierpont's old court without me. After all, Brinkley's only a print journalist. He doesn't have the clout. But nobody—I said nobody, doctor!—says no to Chester Barney. Isn't that right, Brinkley?"

"That's right," I said. "And thanks for putting it just the way you did, Chester."

"My pleasure!" Chester Barney sang out. "The fresh picaresqueness of the trip is going to make this Chester Barney Hour Special. Well, what are we waiting for? Let's get off our rosy pinks. Tish and I will ride in the back seat. All riiiiiiight! Let's go. It's *stroking* time!"

PART II

JEKYLL
ISLAND

7

THE J. PIERPONT MORGAN COURT

I COULD SEE THEM PLAYING THERE, MONEYED GHOSTS MOV-ing over the russet clay. William Rockefeller, Cyrus McCor-mick, F. H. Goodyear, George F. Baker, James J. Hill, Vincent Astor, Edwin Gould. The Pulitzers and the Pullmans, the Drexels and the Biddles, the Vanderbilts and the Marshall Fields. What an entry list for a tournament—perhaps the greatest Celebrity Tennis of them all. The Robber Baron Classic at Jekyll Island, the most exclusive of all social clubs. So exclusive that the boast was made: "For sixty years no unwanted foot ever walked on Jekyll soil." During its heyday as a retreat, one-sixth of all the world's wealth was said to be represented here. Here the barons took their leisure while they took the rest of the country.

But what a lovely artifact they left us in J. Pierpont Mor-gan's indoor court. Pillars of sunlight pouring through the huge vaulted ceiling with its hundreds of individual panes spilled over a man and a boy moving across it with a grace that sent a tingle up the spine. And never, surely, had the sound of tennis balls being hit rung out in this remarkable room with such a decibel count. In my wicker chair I closed my eyes and listened. A boom of sound reverberating in the enclosed space, a fractional interlude, another boom. I opened my eyes and watched.

They were hitting from the baseline, and both were hitting

out. On one side Catlo, cascading his deep shots with ease and elegance. On the other, Billy, crashing them back. He wore shorts and no shirt. Converses and white gym socks. A white handkerchief was tied around his neck. In the heat of August and under the TV lights his copper body gleamed in sweat. One two-man camera crew at one end of the court, one at the other. In the umpire's green highchair, Chester Barney with his mike. Kneeling at net, Lindy. She wore raspberry shorts and a white T-shirt. Keds and no socks. Her white-blonde hair was held back by a yellow ribbon. In the wicker chair next to me, Tish in a light summer frock. Nobody else. Not a sound save the cyclic crashing of tennis balls like waves hitting a shore. Oh, yes, one more body was present. Sylvia, Barney's "script girl," who had flown in from New York. She was stacked and pert and redheaded. Large, lovely, liquid eyes. When they looked at you they kept saying perhaps. She wore hot pants and one of Barney's T-shirts. It looked a lot better on her than it did on Barney. She apparently didn't own a bra. She stood always at Barney's side, her blank clipboard on the ready.

Arrayed on one side of the court over against the teakwood wall were the tools and implements of Billy's quest. Six Wilson rackets. The rackets were wood. No one could convince Robert Catlo that any other substance—aluminum, graphite, fiberglass, tungsten, boron—could replace the "feel" of wood. These were regular Wilson rackets, each picked with great care by Catlo out of the shipments he received for his pro shack in Palm Beach. On each he had stripped off the leather grip. With a wood file he had filed down the sharp edges of the handle to produce the rounded grip that Billy preferred, then re-gripped the handle. At the top of the bow he had affixed two strips of leaded tape to make the rackets slightly heavier in the head, as Billy also preferred. The grip on each racket was four and three-quarters inches in circumference, fitting Billy's long fingers. Each was strung with light 16-

gauge Victor Imperial gut to a tension of 66 pounds. Each had been strung by Catlo himself.

Alongside the stack of rackets were four large boxes, each containing twenty-four cans of Wilson tennis balls, the kind used at Forest Hills. One day of workout would run through three dozen tennis balls, the way Catlo and Billy hit them and destroyed them. Catlo had insisted that Chester's network pay for everything—all living expenses and all tennis balls. Also stowed there were six boxes of adhesive tape. Catlo was a fanatic about a tennis player's hitting hand. He had always taped the first joint of each finger before a match to prevent blisters. He did the same for Billy. Also: three boxes of plain wood sawdust, the kind used on the floors of butcher shops. Catlo said nothing equaled it for combating hand-sweat. He and Billy played with sawdust in the right pockets of their shorts. Also: a duffel bag containing a dozen large white handkerchiefs—Billy always played with one tied around his neck to trap sweat; extra wristbands; a bottle of tincture of benzoin—an expectorant that Catlo had discovered was the best treatment for hand blisters; a repair kit for broken racket strings; extra packages of gut; a bottle of salt tablets. Also: three large thermoses of fresh orange juice.

At 11:30 in the morning we were already five and a half hours into the working day. The day had begun with Billy doing a five-mile run on the beach, including fifteen minutes of sprints. Barney and a camera crew followed in a beach buggy, shooting from it. Catlo believed that nothing prepared tennis legs like running in sand—and legs are all in tennis. Many a big match between equal players has been decided in the fifth set not by who had the best forehand but by who had the best legs. Then breakfast. Then three hours of workout on the Morgan court. Then the hour of playing points. An hour and a half break for lunch. At 1:30 the man and the boy would be back on the court. They would not leave it until the last usable light died.

"No, no, *no.*" Catlo was walking to the net, talking as he came. Billy was walking more slowly in from his side. He stopped at the service line and steadily watched his father across the net.

"You know the big difference between one top player and the one just above him?" Catlo said. "It's not that the one above has a better forehand, backhand or serve. They both have the best or they wouldn't be there. The big difference between Number One and Number Two is that Number One hits the ball farther in front of him, takes it higher on the rise. Don't wait for the ball to come to you. Move into it. *Attack* the ball. You got that?"

"I got it," Billy said. His face was tight.

They went back. Catlo put a ball into play, Billy returned it. Catlo cross-courted it, forcing Billy into the alley, took his return and rammed it down the opposite line. But Billy, in an explosion of speed, was there. He feinted, then, as his father was crossing, crashed it back down the line. The ball skidded an inch inside the chalk, barely came off the clay, and flew like a bullet into the far teakwood. It was a breathtaking shot, a tremendously dominating shot. Catlo, caught ten feet from the ball, just stood there with his hands on his hips.

"Is that what you had in mind?" Billy said.

"That's a little better," his father said. "Let's go again."

I was beginning to see a new Billy. In this short time on the island he was becoming more his own man. He was beginning to buck his father, talking back more to him. Putting up resistance against Catlo's efforts to control him. A tension beginning to build between them. Billy's game seemed.to be improving in direct ratio.

They played off six more points. Billy took four of them, losing the last.

"You should have had the sixth," Catlo said. "You . . ."

"Cat," the unique voice of Chester Barney came down in a honking rasp from the umpire's highchair. Barney climbed down. He was wearing Jamaica shorts, Greek sandals, an

Aussie hat and his reverse-crocodile Lacoste T-shirt, in puce.
"I need a scene of you and Billy at the net talking."

"At the net talking!" Catlo said. "That's what we've been
doing all morning."

Catlo had been on a short fuse, trying to cram everything
into Billy in the little time left. Barney's recurrent demands
for the television necessities had shortened the fuse even further. None of this bothered Chester or in any way stemmed
his demands.

"Big Cat, I'm aware of that," Chester said. "I'm aware
you've been talking all morning but I'm not getting enough
face there. I want to move the camera up close, by the net
post here. I've got to have more face."

"More face!" Catlo said. "How about more ass, Chester?
All right, all right. Move your god-damn camera."

One of the cameras was brought up to the net post. Barney
squinted through the viewfinder.

"All right now, Cat. Say something to Billy."

Catlo waited a moment as if counting, if not to ten, at least
to three or four. Possibly in Spanish, his anger language. Then
he began to talk to Billy.

"Cut," Barney said. "All right now, let's run through that
one more time. Just to make sure it's natural and spontaneous."

"Natural and spontaneous!" Catlo exploded. "Jesus Christ,
Chester, I don't feel natural *or* spontaneous. All right, but
this is the last one. You've got two minutes."

"Roll tape," Chester sang out, as the father-and-son col-
loquy ran through again. Then: "Cut."

Chester straightened up. "Will you put your arm around
Billy in a fatherly fashion, Cat."

"Absolutely not," Catlo said. "I will not put my arm
around Billy." He looked at his watch. His voice now came
low and menacing. "You've got thirty seconds, Chester."

"Roll tape," Chester brayed. Finally: "Good, good. Got it.
Break for lunch."

Catlo glared at Barney then shrugged his shoulders.

Tish had offered to see to all lunches during the five days we had on the island. She planned them for different places to take advantage of the scenery. The Croesuses had chosen well for their hideaway. The island spanned from a wide beach where long-leaf pine came down to the sand's edge to deep forested recesses where little sparkling streams flowed amid a sweetness of trees, holly and magnolia, bayonet palmetto and live oak, white cypress and wild orange, and meadows of wisteria, trumpet creeper and Cherokee rose. This was the home of deer and duck, quail and wild turkey and wild boar, the last a gift from King Humbert of Italy to Morgan the Elder. The island air was filled with the perfumes of the flowers and the songs and sounds of the mockingbird and the flicker, of the pine warbler and the American widgeon and the great blue heron.

"The different settings will provide a relaxation for Billy from the tennis," Tish said brightly.

"Well, I don't want him to relax too much from the tennis," Catlo said. "But okay. And ninety minutes at the outside. Portal to portal."

Lunch that day was on the beach. Tables a few inches high were covered in checked tablecloths. Different kinds of crustless sandwiches were arrayed, and fruit, and white wine for people who wanted it, like me, and milk for people who needed it, like Billy. Billy had added fifteen minutes in the water to the schedule. We older folk sat in the sand. I sipped my wine, a fine 1971 Bernkasteler Doktor, and watched Lindy and Billy disport in the sea. We had had rain most of our time here, but today the sky was bright and blue, the sea all glass with the sun playing across it. The same sea, but how different from the raging water we had left behind. We talked a moment about Agatha. Tish said she had called about her house and Agatha, after moving a hundred miles north, had stopped again and was standing off Florida, undecided. The rains she left behind her were flooding Palm

Beach. I watched Billy duck Lindy's head under and saw her
come up and go after him. Mating rites, I thought.

Catlo seemed resigned to Lindy being along, since there
was nothing he could do about it. Before leaving Florida she
had put in a call to her parents in North Carolina. Only
after Tish, with her coping ways and her reassuring manner,
had got on the phone with Lindy's mother was permission
given for her to make the trip. It was clearly established
chaperonage would be furnished by Tish. Some chaperone.
I was sure Tish felt that the best possible thing, for tennis or
anything else, was to hop gaily into bed, if that is what they
wanted. I watched Lindy and Billy plunge under and disappear. Then two bodies, one English-girl white and one
Aztec-copper, rose through the surface like porpoises playing.
What a fine body each had. I thought about the other condition entered by Lindy's parents: the moment the tournament was over she would fly directly from Forest Hills to her
Carolina school in time for semester-beginning. I sipped my
wine and thought about them.

"Does it bother you having Barney and his TV troops
around?" I asked Catlo. "One surely is conscious of their
presence."

"I'm happy to have them aboard. It puts on the pressure
and tension."

"Oh, is that what you want?"

"Yes, that's what I want. What do you think Forest Hills
is, anyway? All it is is pressure and tension. Twelve days
of it."

I knew there was another element. Barney would never do
this television special on the Catlos because he thought Billy
was going to win at Forest Hills. He was doing it because of
the Catlo legend. So Catlo's own pride was on the line. If
Billy failed after the buildup of a Chester Barney Hour
Special, Catlo failed. His own pride and his hopes for Billy
and the big money and getting Tillotston: all of it was on the
line. So what Barney was doing was a plus, putting added

pressure on everybody. Catlo was a natural champion. The more there was at stake, the more he rose to meet it.

After lunch it was back to the Morgan court.

As a coach, Catlo was a hammer. A great deal of the time he stood at the net—in part because from there he could talk to Billy, in part because he could blister hard balls at him with his volley, the part of Catlo's game to show the least diminution with age. Volleying is much easier on aging legs than chasing. He kept two yellow baskets of balls by him. Lindy scampered about like an overworked cottontail, keeping them full and not getting in the way. If Billy hit a ball down the line or crosscourt, Catlo let it go by unless he could reach it without moving. He just reached down for another ball from the bucket and drove it at Billy. There was no letup and it was wicked and rough and hard out there. And hot! The court had never been meant for summer play. It was withering heat, devastating. For a half hour Catlo would hit balls to Billy's backhand where his son stood on the baseline. "Attack the ball, *attack* it," he kept saying. The word carried the whole freight, the essence, of Catlo's concept of tennis. "Don't wait for it. Attack the ball. Move into it. Rip its cover off. And get *down*. Tennis is a low-level game." Then a half hour on the forehands. "Smooth. *Stroke* the ball. Don't club it to death." And: "Go for the lines. Don't play it safe. *Go for the lines.*"

Then Catlo moved back to mid-court, putting Billy between the service line and the baseline for a half hour of overhead smashes. Catlo lofted the ball high toward the vaulted ceiling with its myriad of panes, and Billy moved to it. It was my favorite picture of him. Backpedaling to the ball, then waiting in all stillness, his side turned to the net, his eyes following the ball like a hunter, stalking it, as it floated down from the glass panes, his shirtless wettened body bronzed and cocked, tense to where the ribcage showed, the sunshafts through the skylight rippling across it, now the racket going up high, dropping back. Then, in an explosion of young strength, his arm whipped across the ball with a sound that crashed through the enclosure. The ghosts of the long-ago tennis balls must have murmured to one another that J. P. and Vincent A. had never treated them in such fashion.

Then Billy back to the baseline while for another half hour Catlo fed drop shots just over the net. "Short steps. Short steps. You're not a kangaroo. For every step you're taking, take two. Keep your body together," Catlo yelled as Billy raced for the net with his racket full out. "Keep the racket under all the way. You've only got a second or two. The ball's not going to rise up and wait for you." Indeed the ball didn't. With Catlo's underspin it fell just over the net, ascended a few inches, then died. It is the most maddening shot in tennis when executed properly. No one executed it better than Jack Tillotston. I had seen him destroy opponents virtually with that shot alone. Billy's thighs pumped and his feet dug the clay. It was the hardest of the half-hour segments in terms of what it took out of the body. At the end of it Billy stood at the net breathing hard, his body wrapped in sweat. Even his shorts were soaked. I had never seen him pant before. Panting and glaring across at his tormentor.

"I guess they never heard of air conditioning," Billy said.

"No, they hadn't," Catlo said brusquely. "The Stadium at Forest Hills has never heard of it either. All right, I'll give you a rest with something easy. You can receive my serve."

As much tennis as I see, so that even I need a rest from it now and then, to watch Robert Catlo serve for a half hour was a high pleasure, very satisfying. The service sublime in its execution: the toss, the knee motion, the cock of the arm, all flawless, then out of these lovely rhythms, to see a tennis ball explode with such speed. Catlo sent the yellow balls one after the other at Billy, the serves booming through the room, the balls screaming over the net. The wonder of Catlo's serve had always been his accuracy at that speed. He must have served over a hundred balls in those thirty minutes, 90 percent of them in the service box. I kept count of Billy's returns. Well over half came screaming right back to Catlo's feet. It was Billy's best shot. Once, without warning, Catlo did something else. Cunning, tricky, he went with a fairly soft serve that caught Billy so unprepared it actually went in for an ace. Catlo walked to the net, talking as he came.

"Whatever happens to your body, don't let your mind get tired. Your opponent is not required under the rules of tennis to announce to you the velocity of his next serve. Be ready to come in. Be ready for anything. Got that?"

"Got it," Billy said tightly. "You want to play some points off the serve?"

"I'll let you know when you're ready to play points," Catlo said.

When the time for point play did arrive—Catlo always ended a practice session with point playing—Billy, exhausted as he must have been, played with anger, with ferocity. I was certain that this emotional condition was precisely what Catlo was after in his son. He wanted Billy to hate him on the tennis court. If Billy could learn to hate him, he could learn to hate anybody across the net. To Catlo that was an ingredient absolutely indispensable to a champion. They played 100 points —it was always 100 points. Billy played as if life depended on it. Catlo's body had been spent much less—all that time just standing at the net. Even so Billy won 64 of the 100. I checked my notes. His best in Florida had been 58.

It was so dark by now that even yellow tennis balls could barely be seen. Catlo looked up at the skylight.

"I guess that's it for today," he said. "Let's make it an hour earlier in the morning. Five o'clock instead of six. You can't hit tennis balls in the dark but there's no reason in the world you can't run on the beach in the dark. You can get that five-mile run out of the way before daylight. We'll use the extra light for tennis."

"Get it out of the way!" Billy screamed in outrage. I had never heard him scream.

"Wake me when you come back," Catlo said.

8

BRAHMACHARYA EVERYWHERE

WHEN I WAS A BOY, GROWING UP INLAND, WHEN I BEGAN to spend all of my free time thinking how to get it, the overwhelming problem was *where* to get it. Since then, having known many beaches of the world, if I could choose a place to be a boy, I would choose somewhere near a beach. It may have been what drew me to the sea and the Navy. I thought what a temptation it must be for Billy and Lindy, with everything so accessible, and on a very lovely island, and summertime. Of course I had no way of knowing that they hadn't. Yes I had. You can look at two people and tell if they've slept together. Then Lindy herself told me, one evening when we took a walk around the deserted old cottages before dinner.

The night before they had been for a walk on the beach, barefoot and in their bikinis. The moon was near to full, the beach windless on a soundless sea. They wandered over to the darkened tennis court and went in. In an eerie quiet, the moonlight fell shimmering through the immense glass skylight and spilled over the court. Perhaps because the astonishing court was such a relic of another and grander age, the place seemed spectral under the moon. They walked up to the net and she climbed into the umpire's green highchair. I could imagine her up there, gently enthroned, and the moonlight softly illumining her sweet thighs in the bikini. And Billy standing just below her in his bikini trunks. There was a lot of splendid body showing there.

"It's spooky," she said.

"Yes."

"I think Mr. Morgan and Mr. Vanderbilt and all those people are wondering what we're doing here. Whether we belong."

"Yes." Even for Billy, he seemed preoccupied, away somewhere.

"Well, you belonged today," she said. "You hit lovely."

He turned away and walked all around the court, barefoot, no sound even of footsteps marking his route on the clay, stopping at various places to look at it. As if he were taking the measure of this, his arena, to see if he had what it took to conquer it. He was moving up toward a rarefied level of the game, where the number of men in all the world who could say yes to that question could be counted on the fingers of two hands. Moving up to that terrible plateau where even the shots scarcely count since there they all have the shots, where the final difference, the only thing that matters, is character.

She could see his figure in the moonlight and the shadows, moving from one part of the court to another, looking almost naked, Greek. He came back and stood below the umpire's chair and looked up at her. He grinned.

"How does it look from up there?" he said.

She thought she knew what he was thinking. "You mean do you want to spend your life on this?"

"Yes, something like that." He waited a moment. "Is it big enough?" He laughed a little, to take off any over-seriousness.

"It depends."

"It depends on a lot," he said. "To start with, only if you can be the best."

The moonlight touched down over them. They were two dark shadows on that space.

"Oh, yes," she said. "Only if you can be the best. You have to want to be the best. Do you?"

"I don't know."

"Let's say you could, just for instance."

"Well, you can be the best in any sport only for a few years," he said. "There has to be something else. Then what?"

"Yes, then what?"

"Live off the money."

"That isn't good enough," she said. "What do tennis players do when they're not up there any more?"

"Most of them start tennis camps or go with clubs and teach other people how to hit tennis balls."

"Like your father?"

"Yes. Like him."

"Do you want that?" she asked.

"No. I couldn't stand it." Then he said, "I'm not sure I want to be the best. Not sure that's such a great thing as people say it is."

"You're saying ambition isn't a good thing?" she said. "What else is there?"

"Maybe this. I don't know. Maybe quietness."

She waited. "It's not enough to know what you don't want. You better decide what you *do* want, Billy Catlo." I could see her, speaking in that way she had when she was firm and intent on something, her head cocked a little. "You're not a baby anymore. You're almost a man."

"Almost?" He shrugged. "All that other's probably just an excuse. The truth is I'm scared."

"I know."

"I'm scared of being scared."

"I know."

He looked up at her, the moonlight touching her thighs. He reached up and rested the tips of his fingers gently on one.

"Can I come to your room tonight? I know I want that, *you.*"

"No. I don't want it that way."

"That way? What way is that?"

"Not in a motel room. Especially not in a motel room with your father on one side and Tish on the other and everybody else *around*."

"What way *do* you want it?"

Now she said his phrase. "I don't know. I just know how I don't want it to be." She laughed shortly. "That's like you about things, isn't it? Knowing what you don't want but not what you do. Maybe that's the big difference in life."

"Well, there's the beach. Nobody around there for miles. Do you want it that way?"

"No."

He nodded across the court. "There are rooms over there. The massage room would be perfect. It's got . . ."

"I certainly don't want it in a *massage* room."

"You require more space?" She could feel an anger rising in him. "How about right here?" He looked around him. "Plenty of room here."

She could feel his fingers moving on the inside of her thighs, just brushing them.

"No, Billy. No . . ."

"You mean not in the umpire's chair?"

The fingers stopped. "You want it. Why don't you say you want it?"

"Have I said I didn't?" She could feel the beating inside her, feel the heat.

"Let me get this straight." She could hear the anger again. "I don't want to misunderstand you in any way. Are you saying you won't sleep with me unless we're married?"

"I haven't made up my mind. A girl has a right to have time to make up her mind."

"But how much time? I'll tell you what. If I win in New York, why don't we get married?" She didn't know whether he was bantering.

"What kind of proposal is that?"

"Then why don't we say if I lose we'll get married."

"Listen." She was firm and intent again. "Whether we get

married or don't get married, it is certainly not going to depend on a game of *tennis*."

"I was just trying to pin you down to something. I'm just trying to find something you'll say yes to."

"Don't con me, Billy Catlo."

He leaned forward, close and serious, insistent, urgent. It must have been hard for Billy to plead. "Lindy, go to bed with me."

She felt his fingers moving up her thigh. She could feel things hammering in her, a physical excitement or hunger of a kind she had never known until then. Then for one moment he touched.

She got up immediately and started down the steps of the chair and his hand fell away.

"Let's go look for turtles on the beach," she said.

Every August a mighty thing happens on the Atlantic beaches from the Carolinas through Georgia through Florida. The thousand-mile beach becomes a massive maternity ward. The great mother turtles swim here from thousands of miles away to give birth where their ancestors gave birth before. They come to the very same beach. The oldest living things, some of them living when Thomas Jefferson did, they ascend out of the sea, come ashore with their weight up to a ton, stay on the beach ninety minutes, their bodies land-chained, immensely vulnerable. With their hind flippers they dig a huge hole in the sand, then deposit 150 or so eggs, maternally covering them with layers of sand, to hatch forty days later. Then they lumber back to the sea, leaving a track a yard wide, and disappear in the dark waters, until another season for birth. See you next year, Georgia.

"All right, let's see the turtles," Billy said. "At least they know what they want and where they want it."

"It's not so much different from what I want."

"You mean have babies?"

"What's wrong with having babies?"

They went down to the beach. They found two turtles that

night and watched them give birth to approximately 300 babies.

"Those eggs look like tennis balls," Billy said.

They went back to their separate rooms.

I spent a lot of time at night with Chester. Sylvia the script girl was always present. She was nice to have, nice decoration.

"That's quite a script girl you have there, Chester," I said once to him.

"Isn't she? The best in the business I think. Everyone at MBC tries to get her. She's very loyal to me."

"She looks like a loyal person. What does she do, Chester? I mean besides looking terrific and carrying around a clipboard with blank paper."

"Can't you recognize a script girl in full uniform?"

"But she isn't writing anything."

"That's because the script is all in my head."

What Sylvia did mostly was just watch us talk, looking from one to the other as each spoke, like watching a tennis match. I have never been so watched by such large and liquid eyes. It was very flattering. We talked in a booth over dinner or in Barney's room in the old Clubhouse over fifths of The Glenlivet. Chester had had two cases sent down.

"Brinkley, " Chester said to me one night, "I can't understand why anyone in journalism would waste his time being in the print part of it. The action is all in television. That's where the kings and the princes are."

"I know, Chester," I said. "But you can't have kings and princes without serfs."

"Serfs is right. How much do you make, Brinkley?"

"Not enough, Chester."

"Whatever it is, I'll double it for openers if you want to come with me. My operation is getting so big I need a chief of staff."

"There are too many chiefs and too few Indians."

"I will never understand the false snobbery of the print

people," Chester said. "After all, it is television which chooses our heroes, elects our Presidents and in general makes the world go round. Isn't that right, Sylvia?"

"Just like you say, Chester." Chester gave her a Buddha smile.

We were in a booth after dinner. We had driven over the causeway to Brunswick. We could see out the window the fishing boats which brought the fish straight to the restaurant, berthed three alongside. The rain had come again, along with a freshening wind, and a fine drizzle was spraying the decks. The proprietor owned both the restaurant and the boats. It was great fish we ate there. We had had stone crabs and red snapper. We had preceded these with a few Glenlivets and were digesting them with a few more.

"Take one example close at hand," Chester said. "Today Billy Catlo is absolutely a nobody. After my show airs, he will be a household word to the forty million people in this country who play tennis. But here's what's important. The perception these forty million have of Billy will be the perception *I* give them. The way I *present* Billy will determine pretty much what they *think* of Billy. By god, if that isn't about as near to being God as you can get on this earth! Wouldn't you like to be in a medium with that kind of influence and power?"

"No."

"I don't believe you, Brinkley. Everybody in our racket wants to have influence. Otherwise why be in the racket?"

"I don't think a man should try to be God. It sounds too dangerous and I'm too chicken. Sylvia, may I have a little more of that Glenlivet influence."

Her youthful hand, hardly out of baby fat, sweetened us all from the bottle on the table. I felt her sandaled toe touch mine under the table. An accident perhaps.

I had some fine conversations with Chester. He really knew tennis like no one else and for all his Green Tongue nonsense he loved the game, as I did.

"Chester, tell me," I said late one night in his room. I gave a minor belch. "How do you perceive tennis players as different from our gladiators in other sports?"

"The chief way is that they fall apart far more easily. If Johnny Bench gets a ball called a strike, he doesn't fall down on the ground, burst out bawling, beat the sod with his fists, and refuse to play for three minutes. He's just as likely to hit the next pitch out of the park. But among tennis players: well, you and I know, Brinkley, that it's quite normal for a tennis player to be winning and then get what he thinks is a bad call. Immediately—after having a tantrum, of course—he starts losing. Or simply throws the match. For one silly little call."

"Yes, that's true," I said. "That happens only in tennis."

"No sport has so many unprofessional professionals. They tank matches. They fake injuries. They give the finger to linesmen. They show their asses to umpires. They walk over and call a spectator a motherfucker or an asshole. They pout and they sulk. They spit on their own playing surface. In short they befoul their own nests. All the while making a mint of money out of the game. As a class they are without grace. They are spoiled and pampered. They are vulgar and insolent. They are the worst batch of crybabies professional sport has ever known."

Chester spun the ice cubes in his drink. "I love this game—it's the greatest game we have if you want to get into that —and I'd love to personally saw the balls off every one of them who fucks up the game. If pro football players behaved on the field like tennis players do on the court, the fans would storm out of the stands and massacre them."

"What I've never understood is how tennis players get away with it."

"I think it's just because tennis itself has always been such a *nice* game. When all this sudden bread lured a lot of unmannered brats into the game, tennis people didn't know how to handle them. There's such a simple way. The moment they start it, throw the young punks off the court. I think we'd all be edified by how quickly they'd learn some manners."

"You're speaking of the men, of course," I said. "The girls are nice."

"Girls are always nice, aren't they, Sylvia?" Barney said. They smiled at each other.

I sipped the Glenlivet and looked down into the glass. The fathom line was getting dangerously low. "The pro tennis player starts his career so much earlier than other professional athletes. Maybe it's a matter of education. Do you know something? Billy can't decide whether to get an education or to be a great tennis king."

"He'd better see if he has that choice first."

"You don't think he will have?"

"I watched him today," Barney said, "and I think he may have the tennis. To go all the way. Oh, some flaws here and there, but he's young. He's a baby. He very possibly has the gift. I don't know if he has the will."

"I think he may find it."

"Where? When? Time's getting on. Also I don't think he has the slightest idea what he's getting into. The tennis part is almost the easiest part. The Stadium's a different world."

"Sylvia, pour me a little more of that Glenlivet, will you," I said.

"It's called *The* Glenlivet," Barney said.

"Sylvia, pour me a little more of that The Glenlivet, will you?"

She did and then went back to the big double bed. Chester and I had the two chairs. Seeing her installed on that bed in her T-shirt, which made her look more topless than topless, and her hot pants, with her lavish, teasing thighs, was one of the best parts of the conversations. I could hear the rain coming down on the Clubhouse roof.

Chester looked at me and said suddenly, "Tell me, Brinkley. Do you get the feeling he depends on that girl? Lindy."

"For what?"

"Well, I don't mean just for fur. To give him what he needs to make it."

I thought a moment. "It's possible. But no, I don't think so. I don't think he could depend on anybody that much. Even on his old man. He's not the kind."

I looked into my glass. "This The Glenlivet is a fine drink, isn't it? Do you know about Catlo's thing on sex?"

"I can't say that I do. Is it different from mine, which is, 'Get all you can as often as you can while you can'?" Chester looked fondly at Sylvia.

Sylvia giggled. "You're so witty, Chester."

Chester smiled at her.

"Catlo thinks for a tennis player to do it before a big tournament is like defaulting or tanking the match."

"Nonsense."

"Catlo may have a point." I gave a delicate belch. "Gandhi, for one, believed that going without sex made you better in anything else."

"Gandhi? Was he that tennis player from Bombay?"

"Why, I've never heard of anything so silly," Sylvia said. "Sex helps you all over. Especially oral sex. Especially two-way. Don't you agree, Chester? I get positively irritable if I don't have it. Sex is what everything else comes from. Isn't that what you think, Chester?"

It was her longest speech. Clearly it was a subject on which she held deep feelings.

"Well, not quite," Chester said. "But I wouldn't want to interfere with your beliefs in any way, Sylvia."

"To the Hindus of India," I said in somber tones, "deprivation in this realm is a first principle. The Hindus call it brahmacharya. They feel it makes you a lot better in your work."

"Nonsense," Chester said. "I have it almost every night. And in my work I'm not only Number One. There is no Number Two, Three, Four, or Five."

I looked into my drink. We were in the shoals.

"Well, I must go," I said. "I've got a hard day tomorrow watching Billy work out. Can I escort you to your room, Sylvia? There are a lot of wild boar running around out there. They're Italian and you know how the Italians are about pretty girls."

Sylvia giggled. "You're cute." She looked at Chester. "Why if . . ."

"That's very good of you, Brinkley," Chester said. "You're most thoughtful, as always. But I have a few technical problems on tomorrow's shooting schedule to go over with Sylvia. You wouldn't understand them. I'll escort Sylvia safely to her room and past those Italian boars when we've worked through these technical problems."

Nothing distorts like jealousy. Next to anger it is the most dangerous of the emotions. Mainly because so often we don't recognize it for what it is.

I had to make a decision. We were leaving the island day after tomorrow. I found I didn't know if I even wanted Shelly to come to Forest Hills. But I phoned her that night. I was lonely for her on that island. It was too beautiful. Nothing makes me more lonely than to be alone in the presence of beauty.

Unless it's rain. The rain was never going to stop. The rain came from the whim-like behavior of Agatha. She had finally turned in toward Florida, sideswiped Cocoa Beach, then continued up Highway 1, in the process being weakened by the movement over land. Then, with her winds down to sixty miles per hour, she had decided to go to sea again to renourish herself. Now she was moving steadily north, getting stronger, and sending the rain ahead of her. I could hear it coming down hard on the roof of the old Clubhouse, now a "guest cottage." The rain was there when I went to sleep and when I woke up. The rain was going to go on forever, falling on the just and the unjust. But not on the Morgan court. The

Catlos could thank God and J. Pierpont for that indoor court.
I phoned her at 8. I knew her habits. She would be in bed,
reading fiction. For thirty minutes and at 8:30 she would turn
out the light. She did that every night five nights a week. The
only exception was if she screwed. The last thing before sleep
every night it was one or the other. I knew her habits all right.
I hoped she had found a good long novel tonight.

"Are you screwing or reading?" I said.

"I haven't screwed since Florida."

"I feel better already."

"Don't let it go to your head."

Before long she said, "How's Billy?"

"Billy?" I said as if I didn't know which Billy.

"Yes, Billy. Isn't he why you're where you are?"

"I assume you mean his tennis game. I think he's moving
into the zone. Also," I added, "I think he and Lindy are falling more in love by the day. Isn't that nice? I always like to
see the young in love."

"Oh? I thought I was speaking with a sportswriter. Is this
Abigail Van Buren?"

"You can forget all that about Billy. Anyhow Catlo is a
disciple of brahmacharya." I was getting this thing myself
about brahmacharya.

"Disciple of what?"

"It's a Hindu idea. The Hindus believe going without it
makes you better in anything. Your tennis game is better if
you don't do it right before a big tournament."

"I didn't realize the Hindus went in for tennis."

"The Hindus are very big on tennis. The biggest Hindu
player was Gopal Ramachandran. He had great staying power
—at least on the court. He played Davis Cup for India twelve
years running—1949 through 1960 if you want to write it
down. He was an Indian national hero. He reached the semifinals at Wimbledon. Then the night before the semifinals
Ramachandran—"

"That name. I love it. It sounds like a Kipling story."

"The night before, Ramachandran saw a girl in a miniskirt somewhere in Soho. One thing led to another and the upshot was, he went out in the semifinals at Wimbledon the next day. In straight sets. Two-six, one-six, love-six."

She burst out laughing. "Brinkley, the reason I like you is that you make me laugh. Poor Ramachandran. Anyhow, I don't think that proves anything. She may not have been talented."

"Well, it's all academic anyway. I don't think Billy will violate brahmacharya, but if he does, it'll be Lindy he violates it with. Not someone a lot older."

"Speaking of older, are you sleeping alone these nights?"

"I did last night. Chester's got a script girl here. She's absolutely stunning. She has to turn sideways to get her tickets through the door. She's eighteen. I imagine she wants to sleep with me."

"Then why doesn't she?"

"Well, you know Chester. He doesn't like sharing unless it's yours. Et vous-même?"

"I'm practicing brah—what is that word?"

"Brahmacharya. Just say it slowly."

"Anyhow that's what I'm practicing. When you have to get up at five in the morning, you have no idea how it cools all that down."

"You used to like it in the afternoon."

"Maybe that's for the very young. I find if I do it in the afternoon, well, you know how I always fall asleep immediately afterwards."

"Yes, I know all of your habits," I said.

"Isn't that nice? Knowing each other's habits, and yet still exciting the hell out of each other. If you've got both, maybe you've got a lot. Is that possible?"

"It's a thought," I said. "I wish to think about it before committing myself."

"Please do. Anyhow if I fall asleep in the afternoon, I find I can't get to sleep later to get up at five. I refer to five next morning."

"It looks like a choice between the flesh and your career."

"That's truer than you know. I'm thinking of buying myself a vibrator. How I still hate getting up at five in the morning. I'll never get used to it."

That fucking job, I thought, that motherfucking job. "You could quit. Marry me. I never get up before eleven. No sporting events are played in the morning. The sportswriters wouldn't stand for it."

"I'm scared of marriage. It sounds too much like prison."

"So am I. But how will we ever know? After all we've got those two things."

"What two things?"

"You just said them. Knowing each other's habits and still exciting each other. In fact I'm pretty excited right now."

"So am I. And I'm in bed. If you were here I'd permit you to fuck me this very moment. For just as long as you pleased. Brinkley, am I really very good at my job?"

"You're the best. That's the truth."

"You really think so?" she said seriously. "You're not just being polite?"

"Have I ever? You're the best in the business."

"What if I've got used to this job and everything that goes with it? It's an awful lot of money. Maybe I've got used to it and the other things." She spoke lightly: "Do you know that if I call Hamilton Jordan I'm put straight through?"

"I don't see how you can give that up."

"Is it right that I have to give up something I'm the best at to get something else I really want?" she said. "Is that fair?"

"No it isn't."

"If we got married, could I do it with someone else who came along? Just now and then?" She sounded almost like a little girl speaking of her cookie jar someone was trying to take away from her. I could hear the rain coming down.

"Like Billy?" I asked.

"All right. Like Billy."

"I wouldn't like that."

"You're very old-fashioned."

"Yes."

"What are you supposed to give up?" she asked.

"We'll have to think of something. Reading in bed. No. I've got it. Tanqueray martinis. I could switch to Gordon's."

"So I'm to give those other things up and cling to you only. And give up my job I'm the best at. Isn't that asking quite a bit?"

"Yes it is. It's asking too much."

"Oh, Christ," she said.

"Yes."

"God I like doing it with you. I like you kissing me everywhere. Getting me ever so wet. Like I am right this very moment. And then coming in and staying ever so long. And holding me afterward while I go to sleep. That's best of all."

She could excite me so. Just with words. Just over a telephone line.

"I even like having you around when we're not doing it. Maybe that's it. If you like doing it with someone very very much and like having them around when you're not doing it —maybe that's everything. Maybe if you've got that you've got it all."

A roll of thunder moved overhead. The connection was broken for a couple of seconds.

"What was that?" she said.

"Thunder. I'm here."

"I'm glad. Do you know I'm very glad you're here, Brinkley? When do you come up?"

"Day after tomorrow. Listen." And I said it. I knew I would ask her, Billy or no. "Before you pick out a vibrator, why don't you come to New York for Forest Hills. I know the best vibrator on the market and I'd like to show it to you."

"Oh?"

"But there's just one left and I think it'll go. To somebody. You'd better come up if you want it. Well, are you coming?"

"Don't be so brusque. I've already booked the flight. I arrive at La Guardia at twelve-oh-five noon Saturday. Eastern. Flight two one nine."

And I thought I had been deciding it.

"The planes fly right over the Stadium coming in," I said. "When I see yours I'll break away and meet you. You don't have to get up at five Sunday, do you?"

"Not Sunday. I can fall asleep right after Saturday night. Right after we try out that vibrator. God you've got me all raunchy. I wish you'd walk through the door this instant. Brinkley?"

"Yes?"

"Are you familiar with that phrase, the one about reassessing priorities? It's a big phrase in Washington, everyone is always talking about reassessing priorities. Not that they ever do. Well, maybe getting fucked properly on a continuing basis is a more important priority than getting put through to Hamilton Jordan. Not to mention having someone around that you like to have around. Brinkley?"

"Yes?"

"Why do you want Billy to win so much? What's it to you?"

"I think youth should have its chance."

"What's the real reason?"

"I honestly don't know. But you're right. I'd like to see him win." I waited. Then suddenly, I knew. "There's something about him. In Tennessee the blacks had this thing about any new boy baby. They'd look at him and ask, 'Are you the one?' I feel a little like that about Billy. Is he the one?"

She was silent a moment then said slowly, "Yes, I see what you mean. Brinkley?"

"Yes?"

"Will you promise to stay away from that script girl?"

"Who's being old-fashioned now?"

"Brinkley?"

"Yes?"

"You wear well."

The phone clicked.

I had difficulty sleeping. I didn't know how it affected your tennis, but as far as I was concerned, brahmacharya was for the Hindus.

Catlo had told me he wanted to get Billy to New York a few days before the tournament opened. "Not so he can visit the Statue of Liberty," he said. "So he can start getting used to people. There'll be a lot of people on top of him at Forest Hills. He's never been around anything like that. He's got to start getting accustomed to the mobs. Otherwise the tennis means nothing."

To this end he had traded Barney the extra time he wanted for TV shooting for Barney's getting the MBC company plane to fly down and pick us up. We were meeting the plane tomorrow in Jacksonville. It was our last day.

I saw them when I took a walk down the beach. I think Catlo had begun to fear he might be "over-tennising" Billy and he had decreed this day off. Or so I thought.

The wind was freshening. It must have been twelve knots that morning as I walked south into it, with gusts of twice that. The wind brought sea spray into my face. The tide was running big and foaming up the sand. Immense clouds moved across the sky like black tall ships. I had been looking for seashells and wishing Shelly was there with me. I must have been thinking of Shelly more than of seashells. I did not see the man and the boy until I was quite close.

They were standing on the beach. Both were wearing jeans and tennis shirts. I saw yellow objects rise into the air and as I came nearer I could make out two ball-buckets. Catlo would reach down and pick up four balls—with one hand—and feed them one by one to Billy. Billy would then serve each ball exactly as if he were on a tennis court. The only difference was that the balls were falling into the Atlantic Ocean instead of a service box. They went on as if I were not there. Billy serving, Catlo talking to him about the toss, the position of the feet and the angle of the racket coming over the ball. A third yellow bucket bobbed on the waves and Billy aimed at it. Toward the end he was serving with considerable accuracy, coming closer to the yellow bucket and even hitting it now and then. Not until the last bucket had been emptied did Catlo take notice of me. He stood holding one last yellow ball.

"You have to learn how to use the wind," Catlo said. "Just in case there is wind. Here's the last one, Billy. Keep the toss low. Don't let your racket fall back so deep."

Billy took the ball, made a toss much shorter than usual, whipped over the ball more quickly with his racket. The ball sailed toward the sea and hit the bucket with a sharp click.

"Bull's-eye," Catlo said quietly.

He touched Billy's shoulder for a moment, his hand resting there lightly. I thought suddenly, *this is his son.* The touch seemed almost to be saying to Billy that whatever happened, that was so. And saying something else: that that was what was important and it would not change. Whatever happened that would never change.

The hand came away and Catlo looked up at the darkening clouds coasting before the wind, then out to sea.

"Well, let's hit the road," he said. "Leave the buckets, Billy. We won't need them anymore. Maybe some Georgia fisherman can use them and that'll bring us luck."

Catlo's voice was uncharacteristically soft, as if he were saying that they had done everything that could be done. Now it was up to Billy. I looked at the boy. Standing there, on that lonely beach, with the wind from the whitecapped sea blowing at him, he seemed too frail, too young, to have this weight thrust on him.

We walked off the beach and came to a little rise where the long-leaf pine began. We stopped and looked back at the sea. The dozens of yellow tennis balls rose and fell on the ever-rising waves. The bucket had disappeared.

9

THE WHITE SEA

I HEARD THE SOUND FIRST. I HAD HEARD IT TWICE BEFORE
in my life, once aboard ship, once ashore. No other sound of
the sea is like it. It is the deepest of roars, as if it came from
the very bottom of the ocean. It never changes and, if you
have ears for it, you can hear it explicitly beneath, above and
around any sound of the wind. The sound of the wind varies
and moves over a wide melodic scale. That sound of the sea
never varies, the deep note that says this is a hurricane.

I went to the window and looked out. The sea was white
to the horizon. White literally, no greys or blues or blacks but
solid white as far as one could see. The white seemed to stand
up above the land as it came on. This was not an illusion,
for the waves were riding in on walls of twelve or fifteen feet.
That meant they were marching on a long fetch, perhaps as
long as a third of the ocean. A great wave of it came majesti-
cally on, riding ashore, hit in a wild rhythm and spent itself
in a white flood on the land. The sea's great orgasm, the hurricane wave of white, mightiest of ejaculations. Standing
there, watching the waves come in, I heard the pounding on
doors in the old Clubhouse. I pulled on trousers over my
shorts and went barefoot to the door. A Georgia trooper was
standing there. A yellow foul-weather slicker wrapped him
beneath his campaign hat. Water dripped off him. The hall
light flickered, then came back on. The trooper looked up at
the bulb, then at me.

"That light," he said, "is why we have to move pretty quick."

I understood at once, but he went ahead and finished it. "Light goes, no electricity to operate the drawbridge to the mainland. So in thirty minutes they'll put the bridge up for good so the boats can get to harbor. No way off then."

"I know," I said.

"How many others in this place?"

"Two here. The others are in the Annex."

"How many?"

"Nine."

"Cars?"

"Three."

"What are they?"

"Eldorado. Ford van. MG convertible."

"Might be a problem with the MG. Let's go."

We went down the old staircase and knocked on Chester's door. Beyond the walls I could hear the sea's deep roar and the long whining, almost keening sound of the wind. Chester had always told me he slept soundly—"possibly the foremost of my various professional assets." The trooper's big fist pounded and finally Barney was there. He looked like a new species of anthropoid. I had never seen him this way and didn't realize he had hair all over, completely furry. Maybe that was what the girls liked. Then I saw why he was sleeping even more soundly than usual.

"Chester, what is it?" Sylvia said from the bed. She sounded slightly cross. "It's not even light."

One less door to knock on anyhow. "Folks," the trooper said, "we've got to get off the island before we get cut off. The hurricane's moving in."

Chester shifted instantly from sleepiness to action. "Sylvia," he said, "get your ass dressed."

Sylvia needed two items to do that. Hot pants and one of Barney's T-shirts. We got our things together fast and followed the trooper down the staircase. The ceiling light downstairs flickered off, longer this time, then went back on. We went out into it. The wind drove us against each other and sand blowing in from the beach stung our faces.

"Look at that sea," Sylvia said. "That sea is *white*."

The sea was advancing in wide tall waves, mounting, cresting hurricane water that could overwhelm anything it could reach. The sea looked capable of devouring the whole island. The rain slanted at us as we walked down the covered passageway to the Annex. Barney went to the second floor to rout out the camera crew. We went to the four doors downstairs and knocked.

"Everybody in the lobby in five minutes," the trooper said. "Pack whatever you can. You'll have to leave the rest. Let's have the car keys please."

He took the keys. "Caddy first, then the MG, then the van, then me," he said.

The trooper, Barney and I went back out and pushed through the wind to the cars. We lined them up that way and popped back inside. The others were waiting. The cameramen looked bleary and hung over. Tish seemed completely alert. Catlo stood easily and watched the trooper with those eyes, assessing, as if to make sure he was in the hands of a pro. Billy and Lindy looked kid-sleepy. The trooper spoke to everybody.

"Now there's no problem if we beat the bridge. We better move a little."

Stepping outside woke everyone up. The hard roar of the sea came at us and the wind-lashed rain, sweeping down in long sheets now, found us even under the portico. The trooper began making the assignments. He had to talk loudly.

"All right, Mr. Catlo, you go first in the Caddy. Then the MG. Next the van. You'll keep some of the wind off it. I'll follow. Ass-end Charlie. Excuse me, ma'am," he said to Tish. "Everybody with lights on dim—you'll see better than with brights. Okay, let's hit it."

Catlo got one door of the Eldorado into his arms and held it hard while Tish got in and I did the same for Sylvia, then

Barney. The trooper went with Billy and Lindy for the MG, then with the cameramen for the van. He came back to Catlo at the Caddy wheel and leaned in.

"Keep it at a steady thirty," he said. He had to yell over the wind. "Speed'll hurt more than help. Watch for downed trees. Animals too. Let's go!"

First light was just coming on as we moved out. The sea surged in behind us. The wind tore through the forests, the branches snapping and sighing. I knew birds and game were seeking cover in there. The birds would head below the cracking branches, down among the roots where the hurricane could not reach them. A mockingbird or a blue jay could thus survive the worst of hurricanes. I saw a flight of gulls sweep across the sky, the wind flinging them slantwise, then come in for a landing and disappear beneath the trees.

I was in the trooper's car. We drove past the Morgan court. I rolled down the window and looked at it through the rain. I could hear faint tinklings. I realized the wind and the hard rain were taking out the skypanes. The trooper suddenly braked, throwing me forward. Through the sheets of rain slapping the windshield I saw two deer loom up like terrified ghosts and hurl themselves in great bounds across the road directly between the van and us.

"Close," the trooper said. "They looked about two. That would make it their first hurricane. Their mamas saw the one in seventy-three."

We listened to the hurricane reports coming over the police band. "How high is it?" I said over the wind and the radio.

"About eighty-five last report. They think it'll go to a hundred ten. Maybe a hundred twenty."

"How about Jacksonville?" I asked.

"Jax will get it before we do. The center's just south, near St. Augustine."

I told him about the plane picking us up at Jacksonville.

"It won't get through," he said. "I surely doubt. Unless it's already there. What about Savannah? Just eighty miles north. That should be a winner. Better chance than Jax anyhow."

"Would you see if you can get word to the plane?"

"I'll try."

I gave him the information. "Tell the pilot to try for Savannah. Sign it Barney."

He picked up his mike from the dashboard cradle and gave the instructions.

"They'll try," he said.

The fast wipers were leaving just fractional moments of visibility. Between swishes we could see the drawbridge up ahead. Water was breaking over it in high, hard waves. We drove across slowly. All the cars stopped on the other side. The drawbridge man, completely wet, was standing at the trooper's car window. He was black. He had to shout.

"That everybody?"

"Everybody, Jim. Put her up. Then get out yourself. And thanks. We all surely thank you."

The trooper swung his car around the other three and took the lead for the long causeway. The caravan started to move again. I looked through the rear window and saw the two halves of the drawbridge rise slowly until they formed a V. The island was locked off, sealed, left to the waters and the hurricane.

Water was over the causeway and we went slowly through it, feeling our way to stay out of the marshes, the trooper huddled over the steering wheel for what visibility he could muster through the sheets of rain whipping down on us. I looked back and saw the dim glow of headlights, the El-dorado following in the wake we were making. We came through it and stopped and got out.

We pushed against the wind and went back to the other cars. Catlo and Barney got out. We stood there on the road, huddling against the Eldorado. Far away we could just see the white sea, moving in great sheets against the island. We

could no longer hear the sea and stood there watching, free
at last of its terrible sound. But the wind was rising. The
trooper had to speak up.

"I've got to leave you," he said.

"We're very grateful, Trooper," Catlo said.

"Well, that's what they pay me for."

"We surely are," Barney said and everybody murmured the
same thing. "Trooper, if you're ever in New York," Barney
said. "I mean that. Anything."

"Sounds like a winner. I've never been fortunate enough
to get there but if I do I'll take you up. I've always wanted
to see New York."

I suddenly realized how young he was. Maybe twenty-four.

"Sounds like a winner," Barney said.

The trooper grinned. "Yes, sir. It surely does. You go
straight ahead to Highway Seventeen. I suggest you go north
and drive out of this. The hurricane should be moving into
Jacksonville about now. She's pushing along at about twelve
miles per. You can outrun her."

I told Barney we were trying to get word to the plane about
Savannah.

We drove to Highway 17, Catlo leading now. We got out
again at the intersection. We had to turn left and south to
Jacksonville or right and north to Savannah. The wind was
driving at us out of the south.

"How about trying it south?" Barney said. "Case the pilot
didn't get the word. If we go to Savannah first, we'll never
get back."

"Let's try it," Catlo said. "Billy, you go first. We'll see."

Billy and Lindy pulled out and went ahead and turned left
onto Highway 17. Catlo followed and the van came behind.
We went about three miles. Then the MG stopped. Just
stopped. Billy got out and came back, the wind hurtling him
toward us. Catlo rolled down his window and the rain came
in.

"Won't go anywhere," Billy said. He had to yell a little. "Had the pedal down flat and it just stops."

The wind had literally brought the little MG to a halt.

"Let's go to Savannah," Catlo said. "We'll follow you."

Billy made a U-turn and the Eldorado and the van turned around and followed north. The cars flew over the road now, the tail wind pushing and flinging them on. When we got into Savannah, the traffic was heavy with cars moving north ahead of the hurricane. A cop in black raingear stood in the middle of an intersection directing traffic. Catlo got directions to the airport while the cop held on to his hat. The plane was there. We locked the cars in the parking lot and went on out to it in the wind and rain. Lindy and I helped Billy carry his rackets.

We got in the Gulfstream and flew north to New York and Forest Hills. As soon as we were aboard, Catlo made us dry off the rackets.

PART III

THE NEW YORK
ISLAND

10

NIGHT DEPOSITORY

THE HOOKERS HAD STAKED OUT THE SUMMIT. THAT PROVED they didn't know tennis players. Hookers ordinarily know more about the city's conventions than does the New York Convention and Visitors Bureau. But tennis players rarely use hookers. With their young good looks they don't have to. But the main thing the hookers didn't know was that tennis players like things free, or at least cheap. That is why, incidentally, they pay officials $5.25 a day at Forest Hills.

The lobby was a mess, but a very handsome mess. Good-looking Swedes, good-looking Spaniards, Italians, Frenchmen, Englishmen, Czechoslovakians, Rumanians, Russians, Indians, South Africans, Japanese, Australians and possibly two each of Argentinian, Bolivian, Colombian, Japanese, Peruvian and Pole were all trying to check in. Good-looking bodies and tanned skins and sun-streaked hair. They were all there, the men and the girls, standing in long lines at the check-in desk. Everyone holding three or more rackets, waiting and talking to the players behind and ahead of them.

The lobby was strictly from function, a motel kind of lobby. It was not large at all—another dozen people and they'd have to extend the lines through the revolving doors and onto the sidewalk. No frills, just plain vinyl couches and chairs on which more tennis players sat waiting, all speaking English since that is what they learn on the circuit, especially "Fuck you" for use in discussions with linesmen. The lobby didn't even have the virtue of being dirty and frayed, hence picturesque. You could almost smell the Clorox. The Summit was picked as the tennis hotel because it was two blocks from the Forest Hills subway and gave the players rooms for half price. The players liked that part.

They were all here for the big dream. Most of them actually expected to win the tournament and go home burdened with dollars and fame. I didn't believe that for a long time, but it's true. They all felt that somehow this time everything would fall into place. Half their opponents would have off-days and the other half would get leg cramps and there they would be. There was some substance to it, at least in men's tennis. Most of them in that lobby could beat any of the top ten of the world, on a given day as they say—if they were very hot and their opponent was really off. The only thing is, none of them could do it twelve days running. That was what made Forest Hills—and Wimbledon—the toughest of all sports tests. Save only for the Olympic decathlon, no ordeal in sport is like Forest Hills, no place is an athlete tested, punished, so hard for so long.

I worked my way past the bodies to a house phone, rang Catlo's room and waited for him in front of the elevator. In a few minutes he stepped out wearing slacks, a beige jacket and a pale yellow shirt open at the throat against the copper Aztec skin. A handsome, striking man. A good many players looked at him as we went through the lobby. Three or four of the older ones spoke and Catlo answered with a reserved dignity. We pushed through the revolving doors to the sidewalk and into the warm August evening. The sky was still light above the tall buildings.

"Let's walk," he said. "Tish won't be ready anyway."

We went west on Fifty-second and turned up Park.

"This is some city," he said. "You like it here?"

I think it was the first question he had ever asked me, the first practically I had heard him ask anybody. He considered questions a form of weakness.

"I wouldn't live anywhere else," I said.

It was true. I never returned to New York without having that feeling. A feeling of anticipation, of excitement, that just around the corner of the next tall building something wonderful will happen to your life. More than anything else, that feeling makes New York what it is.

"I'd like Billy to see it sometime when he's not playing. Of course he's going to see some of it now. But not too much before it's over. Not if I can help it."

"It's hard to go to bed," I said. "I remember my first time in New York."

"Well, I'm not doing bed-checks, but there's one way that'll help. He has to be running in Central Park at eight every morning. Five miles. Then an hour on the courts. Maybe that'll keep him from staying up all night."

"It should help," I said.

"I'll be glad when they make the draw," he said.

He was tenser than I had ever seen him. We waited for the traffic before crossing Fifty-third Street.

"You feel good about Billy and Forest Hills?" I asked, deliberately.

"I never feel good about Forest Hills. I hate the son of a bitch. How could anyone feel good about it?"

I think he felt it more for Billy than when he had been there himself.

"Resigned is more like it," he said. "It's up to Billy now."

"He's going to be all right," I said, but of course I didn't know.

"We've done everything we can about the *tennis* part of it," Catlo said. We walked in silence. Then he said almost angrily, "Wouldn't it be lovely if after all that, the other thing fucked it up."

"She's a pretty girl. Smart, too."

"What does that have to do with it? That makes it worse. Do you remember what falling in love, I mean really falling in love, can do to you? I do." His voice had become soft.

"I remember when I fell in love with Billy's mother. It had never happened before with me. I remember all right." He laughed briefly. "Hell, I couldn't even get the ball in."

Walking there alongside him, I felt the pang, though I never knew her. I remembered photographs of that beautiful, lovely girl, remembered what that plane crash had done to Robert Catlo. Then his old voice was back, stern, demanding.

"Any fool can see that Billy is falling in love. It's the last thing he should be doing right now. You can't do anything in a pressure pit like Forest Hills if your mind is on something else."

We turned off Park at Fifty-fifth. I wondered how it felt to be no older than Catlo and to know that all the great moments were in the past. That must be the worst part of being a jock. Knowing that all the mountaintops were gone, knowing that for the rest of your life there would never be another one, that from here on you lived off the clippings. Unless, of course, you had a talented son.

We picked up Tish at the St. Regis. She had taken one look at the Summit and announced that she preferred something civilized. Tonight she said she wanted some good Italian food, so I took them to Il Valetto on Sixty-second. We had honeydew and proscuitto, linguine, veal limone, a green salad, some bel paese and three bottles of Barolo. Everyone felt soothed, mellow, all that good feeding and the Barolo lacing through the system.

"In my experience it works the other way," Tish said. "You're more relaxed. Your food, even your bourbon tastes better. You're in balance. Did you ever hear of anyone jumping up and going out to hurt somebody after a good screw?"

"I'll say amen to that," I said.

"But hurting someone," Catlo said, "is exactly what you're trying to do. Do you know what they do with fighting bulls in Spain? When those bulls are raised they never get near a cow. Not once. The bull goes into the bullring a virgin. Obviously it has something to do with why they have so much fire and bravery."

"Poor cows," Tish said.

"Poor bulls," I said.

We drank our espressos.

"Well, there may be something there," I said. "Baudelaire wrote a little bit on this subject. Not concerning tennis—I don't think Baudelaire was ever seeded—but concerning writing. He speculated whether the same energy that went into the act of sex went into the act of writing. He thought there might be just so much of that particular energy and that you put it into one or the other. He also imagined the possibility that just the opposite could be true: that having sex actually increased what you had to give to writing."

"Which did he finally decide?" Tish asked.

"So far as I know he died without ever finding out," I said.

"Well, I *know* what I'm talking about," Catlo said. "After Forest Hills Billy can do what he likes."

"Robert, I really don't think you have to worry," Tish said. "It still takes two, and I think I know Lindy."

"I hope so," Catlo said grimly. "I hope so."

I took Billy and Lindy to an early dinner at A La Fourchette and then to see *A Chorus Line*, with scalper's tickets. The magazine is very liberal about expense accounts and I've always been a liberal myself.

Lindy wore a black linen dress with an interesting V that set off her white skin and short blonde hair. Billy wore a tie and a white jacket, also linen, which set off his copper skin and black-black hair. I felt a silly pride just to have them with me. After the theater we walked over to Times Square. They stopped on the sidewalk and took in its sights and sounds. They were seeing and doing all these things for the first time and I was glad to be with them. They looked at the lights, at the people, at the stall-sized stores. Billy bought a big panda bear for Lindy.

Billy had been staying out late. With the tournament so near Catlo was under increasing pressure to control him. But more and more Billy didn't want to be controlled. Catlo was committed to the tournament. I think Billy was determined about it too, but tennis was not his whole world. He had the city he had never seen and he had the biggest distraction of all, to be with Lindy every moment possible. He and Lindy were stuffing themselves on the city. I think Lindy was beginning to feel responsible for him. More now, she would get him back to the Summit reasonably early. Billy was now a nominal member of the grownup world. We would see if he really was when he stepped onto the courts at Forest Hills.

We went up Seventh Avenue turning east on Forty-ninth Street, making our way through a file of hookers, both girl and boy, and over to Fifth Avenue. We walked up Fifth looking into windows. Then we strolled the three long blocks to Lexington, but when we got to the Summit we kept on walking east, unwilling to leave the night. Just before Third Avenue, a hawker wearing a wing collar and a stovepipe hat stood under a gaudy marquee that said "The Peeled Onion."

"Come see the girls!" the hawker shouted. "They're young. They're beautiful. They're wearing nothing."

Lindy stopped on the sidewalk. "What's that?" she said.

"You don't want to go in there," I said.

"Why don't I?"

The hawker spoke directly to us. "Don't miss these girls. Wearing ab-so-lute-ly nothing! Watch these young, beautiful girls do things to excite you."

"No thanks," Billy said.

"Maybe I can learn something," Lindy said.

Before I could say anything she walked past the hawker, who opened the door. We followed her. It was dark in the entry. A young man in a red vest guided us to a place where overhead cone lights shone on a horseshoe-shaped counter. Men sat on stools looking up at four girls, two on each side, dancing on the counter. The room was very narrow. The young man in the red vest put us at a small table near the counter. Billy propped the panda in the fourth chair. A waitress in the high black net stockings that have become the

national uniform for cocktail waitresses took our order. We
watched the two girls nearest us. They were very near.

"The man told the truth," Lindy said. "They're very
pretty."

They were. They seemed like real dancers, too, not just
naked girls moving their bodies around. The young man in
the red vest came by and I asked him where they got the
girls.

"They're all modern dance students," he said.

"How much do they get?" I asked.

"Sixty-six dollars a night," he said. "Plus what they earn
that way."

Each girl had a section of counter to herself, each section
with six bar stools. The girls were around twenty. Their breasts
stuck straight out, nipples alert. I thought how nice it was
that breasts came in so many different configurations and
nipples in so many different shades. What good bodies they
had. That was the big change of course, and we were in-
debted to the sex revolution for this gift. There had been
shows like this around for quite a spell. But in the past all
the girls up there would have been cows, with mushy pumpkin
breasts, elephant thighs and Dorian Gray faces. There were
no cows up there tonight. Only marvelous-looking girls,
proper, intelligent-looking, girls you'd like to take out.

Each of the four girls would pick out a man on one of the
stools and do her dance in front of him. If the man placed
a bill on the counter, she would slowly gyrate down with her
body until her mound was directly in front of the man's face,
just inches away, and keep rotating. Then she would pick
up the bill, fold it expertly until it made a neat little wad,
then tuck it deftly away there. Then move on to the next man.

"My goodness," Lindy said. "They're very nifty at that."
She was watching totally absorbed. Billy looked straight
ahead at the girls.

The customers were well-behaved. They were mostly men
in their thirties, some in their twenties. There were no whistles,

no vulgar comments. They sipped their drinks and watched a girl quietly, as if they wanted to show their respect for her having this marvelous device. We had one more round of drinks and left.

"*Muy simpatica,*" Billy said, holding his panda bear. "They were *muy simpatica,* I'd say."

"*Muy,*" Lindy said.

I felt excited and I could imagine Billy. They say it builds up to about age nineteen for a man. After that it's downhill all the way. A sobering thought. Billy *was* nineteen. We went back to the Summit. Tennis players were standing around the lobby talking, men and girl tennis players. I heard one say to another, "The topspin lob is what gets him. If you can get him to the net you can pass him half the time and topspin-lob him the other half." Tennis players are generous about giving tips to each other on possible opponents. It is one of their nicest traits. We got our keys at the desk and went to the elevator. I had taken a room at the Summit with the magazine's money to be near the action. Because of our early start next morning I would try out the Summit bed. Billy punched the buttons for the seventh, ninth and sixteenth floors. At the seventh floor he looked at Lindy, their eyes met.

"G-r-r-r!" he said and pounced, shoving the big panda bear into her arms. She giggled and grasped it. He was gone. The elevator went on up to the ninth and rocked to a stop.

"It was a nice evening," Lindy said, hugging her panda. "I thank you."

"My pleasure."

"That man was wrong about one thing. When he said they weren't wearing anything. They wore shoes." The elevator door opened. "Safe place to keep your money too."

The door shut. I went on up to the sixteenth floor and to bed. I thought, all Billy had to do was walk up two flights.

I met them in the coffee shop at 7:30 A.M. I had some black coffee and they had Danish rolls with strawberry jam and tall glasses of milk. People glanced admiringly at Billy and Lindy in their shorts and T-shirts. When we had finished Lindy had the waiter fill her thermos with milk and we went outside to a cab, Lindy carrying the thermos and two bath towels inscribed "Summit Hotel" and in need of retirement. It was a pretty morning, a slight haze hanging over the city, but it would be hot later.

"Central Park at Sixth Avenue," I told the cabdriver and we got into the back-seat cage. They held hands, something they hadn't done much in front of anybody, and looked out the windows at people going to work in the midtown buildings. At the Bernardo O'Higgins statue we got out and entered the Park and rented two bikes at the concession.

Lindy put the thermos and towels in her bike basket and Billy took off his shirt and put it on top of them. She took a man's handkerchief from her purse and knotted it around his neck. In just his shorts and that knotted handkerchief and that copper body and blackest hair and that Aztec-coin face, I think he was the best-looking boy I had ever seen.

He started trotting and she pedaled alongside and I came behind them. He ran down a little incline past a place where two old men bent over a chessboard painted on a concrete table and on past the sheepless Sheep Meadow. He circled around the lake where a small boy and a young woman were sailing a model of a tall ship. The boy was on his knees and he looked up at Billy running. The woman didn't look up at all. Then she did and watched the boy in white shorts running through the trees. Billy had a wonderfully easy stride and rhythm to his body. There was no effort to it. His body gleamed in the early morning sun, his hair bouncing as he ran. We left the lake behind and he led us up a rise over a little bridge and past the old Dakota with its peaked roofs. For a while the path was too narrow to ride alongside him and Lindy followed him on her bike. He passed under an arch and almost bumped into a horse and rider crossing the bridle path where it intersected the trail. The big reservoir came into sight, a low mist hanging over it like the mouth's breath on a cool morning, and a long clear stretch opened up. He sprinted for about two hundred yards, she accelerating alongside him now. Then, back to pace, he went around the water and they crossed the East Drive just ahead of a taxi which whipped around a curve and sped past them to contribute its first halo of black exhaust to the New York day. He ran past the back of the Metropolitan Museum. They went down a little slope and entered a deeper forest and ran and pedaled on single-file between the trees. Here a sweet haze hung down through the draw, forest-fragrant in the early morning, and he ran through it. The woods opened up and gave way to a straight stretch where he sprinted for another two hundred yards. He went back to pace and ran past a playground where mothers were beginning to push their small children in swings and past William Shakespeare in stone and came over an incline. Above the trees we could see the black-and-white slab of the Gulf and Western Building at Columbus Circle. We went down a little valley and up another rise and from on top of it saw the Carousel ahead of us. "Race you," Billy said and poured on a hard sprint for the remaining three hundred yards, she pedaling hard beside him. He stopped at the Carousel, the end of the five-mile route his father had staked out for him.

Billy grasped a pole on the Carousel, put his arms around it and stood panting, bent over a little, winded and sweating. Lindy got off her bike and held it by the handlebars and looked at him. He straightened up and she leaned the bike against the Carousel and got a towel out of the bike basket and mopped his face and then his chest. She looked dedicated and determined rubbing down his chest. Then she stood on her toes and kissed him very lightly on the lips like a reward for all that running. She poured milk for him into the thermos cup and he swallowed it. She unknotted the wet handkerchief and got a fresh one from her purse and tied it around his neck.

"There," she said. Pride and ownership hung in that single word. Billy didn't seem to mind.

We stood and looked at the tall buildings caught in the haze. Real haze, the smog would come later. We rested five minutes and walked the bikes back to the concession. Catlo was waiting there, dressed in tennis gear and carrying four rackets and a bucket of balls. We got in a cab and rode to the Central Park tennis courts.

"You in the tournament?" the cabdriver asked. "Forest Hills?"

"Yes," Billy said. "Forest Hills."

The courts were crowded. Two middle-aged men were on the one Catlo had reserved. Catlo and Billy waited for them to leave. When they did not, Catlo looked at his watch and spoke to the man about to serve. "Finish this game," he said, "then it's ours. You're five minutes over." The man did not look at him. They played six more points, including some suspicious deuces, before they finally left the court. One of the men looked curiously at Catlo.

"Aren't you Robert Catlo?" he asked.

"That's right," Catlo said.

"I didn't realize. Do you mind if we watch?" he asked politely.

"They're public courts," Catlo said.

Billy went to the other side and Catlo started feeding balls to him. From the sound of the balls coming off the rackets it became clear down the line of courts that these were not two hackers hitting on a summer morning. Soon people from the adjoining courts stopped their games and went behind the fences to watch. More people arrived and joined them. "It's Robert Catlo," one said. "It's the Big Cat." Catlo divided their hour: ten minutes to loosen up, ten minutes for the forehand, ten for the backhand, ten for the overhead and volley, ten for receive-serve, ten for Billy's serve.

Critical analyses, all favorable, came from behind the fences, oohs, ahs and gasps now and then and various running commentary, some of it quite loud. The audience participated right along. After all these were New Yorkers. At the end of it the man and boy stood a moment at the net. Both were wrapped in the sweat induced by the already humid, hot August day; the lovely haze of the glens and dells had all faded away. Catlo said nothing to Billy about his game, gave no words of advice. It was too late for that. They picked up their rackets and their bucket of balls and started back through the gates. The people surrounded them and several held up tennis balls or pieces of paper for Catlo to autograph. They carried their rackets and the bucket of balls to Central Park West and hailed a cab.

"You in Forest Hills?" the cabdriver asked Catlo through the grill.

"Forest Hills is for young men," Catlo said. "He is."

The best way to enforce a jock curfew is not to run a bedcheck but to require your jock to be doing something at eight o'clock the next morning. Billy still stayed out but not as late as he would have liked. Lindy wouldn't stay late with him. She was the real enforcer of the curfew. Billy did his run for five mornings and then the workouts with Catlo.

Catlo had it figured right. After the first day there were stories in the *Times, News* and *Post* about the workouts. Starting with the second day the crowds were bigger—and then much bigger. Middle-aged people at first. They came to see the Big Cat of their earlier years. Then younger people came as stories about Billy got in the papers. The papers were beginning to hype the Billy-Tilly thing. There was no fence room if you didn't arrive early. Play on the two adjoining courts had to be stopped to accommodate the crowds. Volunteers acted as ball boys. The third day a couple of policemen were there to keep some kind of order. This was not Palm Beach or Jekyll Island. Billy was certainly getting exposed to the crowds, which was Catlo's purpose more than the court workout. Catlo had his crowds. Each morning more people were there to observe and to make their running commentaries. The crowd was filled with volunteer tennis critics, all highly articulate.

"Notice that topspin."

"That wasn't a topspin. It was hit flat."

"I say it was topspin."

I watched Billy's tennis closely to see if what Catlo said about Lindy affecting his game was true. I looked especially for mental lapses. I didn't see any. So far at least I was prepared to say that falling in love did not lead to serious deterioration of one's tennis game.

11

THE HARVARD CLUB BET

I WALKED OUT OF MY PATCHIN PLACE APARTMENT ONTO Tenth Street and over to Sixth Avenue and took the subway up to Fiftieth. At my office I found a note stuck in my typewriter saying that Cy Bannon wanted to see me.

Almost all good magazines in this country reflect one man to a degree almost entirely unappreciated by outsiders. At my place that man was Cyrus Bannon. Every week he read every word and selected every picture that went into the magazine. I walked down the corridor to his office. It was a very large room, not because Bannon wanted a big office but because all that space was required to spread layouts and for the several editors, researchers and art people who were always in the room when this activity was in progress. In my years at the magazine I have not once seen the door of that office closed. Nor is there any receptionist. If anyone wanted to, he could come up off the street, walk right into that room and drop a typewriter on Cy Bannon's head. I've thought of doing it myself on certain unhappy occasions. He was seated at a desk-height shelf that ran the length of the room, looking through a magnifying glass at 36-frame contact sheets of 35-millimeter pictures. He wore a white shirt with the sleeves rolled and no tie. When I walked in he turned to look at me for a moment, then put down the magnifying glass and contact sheet.

"Well, now," he said. "Georgia. I hear there was a little hurricane."

"Not much. The troopers got us out."

His shoulders shrugged. "Evidently."

Cy Bannon does not talk a great deal. What words he does use come out in a hoarse whisper so that you have to pay attention to hear them. People meeting him for the first time think he has laryngitis. He swiveled in his chair to look at a wall on which hung cover mockups. These were cover candidates for the magazine's next issue, exactly as they would appear, if they made it. There were four candidates. Along with Bannon I studied them and said nothing. One was of the football running back Pump Pilchok, who was being promoted as next year's probable Heisman trophy winner. It showed him in uniform running off a field past a cheerleader with some really terrific legs. I knew at once that Buzz Gilroy, the photographer, had set up the cheerleader and positioned himself in that exact spot to get Pilchok, with his great pumping legs clothed in padded football pants, running past those other legs padded in nothing. There would be fifty shots of this moment, almost exactly identical, as Gilroy made Pilchok and the cheerleader do it over and over again to be sure he had a good cover. It was a strong candidate. Two of the other candidates were pretty enough, both showing nice water: a beautiful scene of a fly fisherman casting in the Restigouche; and, sea this time, a sailboat running before the wind.

The fourth was the shot of Catlo and Billy taken by Dusendorf. Billy and Catlo simply stood in their tennis clothes looking into the camera, both in whites, Billy with the handkerchief knotted around his neck. Obviously father and son. It was their faces that made the picture. Dusendorf, a man who probably had never seen a tennis match, had captured the essence of the Catlos, their dignity and their beauty, something sad in their eyes yet defiant, smoldering. Technically anyone could have taken the photograph. But

Dusendorf had captured what the two men were. That was why he could ask for and get double our normal cover rate. The cover slug said, "The Catlos at Forest Hills. Like father, like son?" Bannon would have been the author of that.

"I think it's Pilchok, don't you?" he said in that hoarse whisper.

This was his way of provoking disagreement and dismay. I was duly dismayed.

"Well, that's a nice picture," I said. "But it's August. Too early for college football."

"It's never too early for football. Everybody's going to do Pilchok soon. The longer we wait, the more Pilchok covers there are going to be. Besides, it's quite a picture."

"So is Dusie's."

Bannon looked at it. "Yes, but no action."

"Well, about the Catlos," I said. I spent two minutes sound-tracking the Catlos. I wanted the cover. I went through the Tillotston thing, the father-and-son thing. I made a pretty heavy pitch. Then I described the forthcoming Chester Barney Special. That got to him. Cy likes to be ahead of television, or at least even.

"What if the kid bombs out in the second round?"

"Well, it would be better for the cover if he won a couple, of course," I said. "Better yet if he went some distance. But even if he loses right off, I think the cover holds up. Catlo's return to tennis through his son—that's a pretty big tennis story all by itself." And I said two things he already knew: "Catlo is one of the four biggest names in the history of the game. And he's stayed out of sight pretty much for eight years until now, not *allowed* a story on him. Some people probably think he's dead. The cover will correct that impression. We put this all together and I'm saying it's a hell of a tennis story. Anyhow tennis is big now. We've probably got more readers who *play* it than play anything else. I think we've been neglecting tennis lately," I said piously.

"Oh, do you?" Bannon gave me a sardonic look. "How far do you think the kid will get? First round, second round? Quarters? Semis?"

So I had come to it. "Finals and semis," I said, "are very outside. Quarters: a chance." I swallowed and said it. "Depending on who he draws, a pretty fair chance to reach the quarters." So I was risking something on the Catlos too.

"We could just use Catlo alone," Bannon said. "The original plan before you got excited about the kid."

"We could. But if Billy does much, it'll look like we left out three-fourths of the story."

Cy Bannon said something. I don't know why I hadn't at least thought of it. Maybe that was why he was the editor.

"What about putting Tillotston on the cover with the Catlos. That way we have the whole feud. Pretty certain he'll get to the quarterfinals?"

"Oh, yes. Jack Tillotston will get to the quarters all right," I said.

"I don't like three on a cover any more than in a bed."

"It wasn't my idea."

Bannon sighed. Even his sigh was hoarse. "I know. Nobody around here has any ideas. Anyhow, that way we'd know someone on that cover would be playing tennis when we come out."

"Catlo would never do it."

"Is it permissible to ask him?" he whispered.

"It's permissible."

It was time to go.

"Incidentally."

"Incidentally" is Bannon's warning word. Especially "Oh, incidentally."

"Oh, incidentally," he said. "We're pretty liberal around here on just about anything. But I have a note from the accounting department that you seem to purchase a complete tennis outfit, including a racket and a jockstrap, every story you do. Naturally we want you to have whatever you need to cover the story properly. I don't suppose it's occurred to you to carry at least a racket with you."

"Well, it might mean a charge for excess baggage on the plane."

"I think we can afford that," Bannon said evenly. "Incidentally. How many tennis rackets do you—or should I say the magazine—own?"

"Fourteen."

"Bring me one. We own so many, I'm taking up the game."

Cy Bannon is the most unathletic person I know. Now I knew tennis was truly catching on.

"About the cover," I said. "Pilchok might break a leg."

He gave me that look. "The Catlo kid might break an arm. How much have you written?"

"I've got the lead and maybe four pages. It'll go very fast from here."

"Let me see the story and we'll decide."

He picked up his magnifying glass and bent back to the contact sheets.

I have never considered myself a true Harvard man—much as I admire them—as one hardly could who has spent a total of perhaps fifty days in residence. Not that I was the first Nieman Fellow to set such a precedent. Others have carried this absentia much further than I ever did. A friend of mine named Stanley Korbut, who got his Fellowship working out of the Washington *Post*, spent a total of six days of his "year" from September to June anywhere near the famous Yard. Most of the rest of it he spent in Key West. Stanley liked the sun. By comparison with Stanley, I was a tall tree in the groves of academe.

The Nieman consists of a year at Harvard, including not only all tuition and fees but also whatever salary the Fellow might have been receiving from his regular employer. It is given annually to deserving reporters who want to broaden, or deepen—I forget which word is used—their knowledge in something or other. Like Stanley I got my Fellowship off the Washington *Post* where I had been covering the Hill for four years. Sometime between then and the end of my Harvard year, I decided I had had it with politics. I can't explain why. Maybe I got fed up with politicians and decided I would rather spend my professional life with athletes, as a relatively less devious group. It may have been nothing so grand. Most of my Nieman year was spent in New York and it may have been simply the crass desire to live there instead of Washington, a city which required my presence on my former beat. But for whatever reason I crossed over.

That Harvard year meant a lot to me. It enabled me to play squash forever afterward in New York. I have an emotional need for exercise. If I do not get it, I growl at people, cannot eat, write or screw and in general become unfit for decent human society. Tennis is difficult and expensive in New York and squash provides an acceptable substitute. Without the Harvard squash courts I do not believe I could stay in the city.

The squash courts are the only part of the Club I ever see. Except that day I invited Jack Tillotston to lunch there. I think it was a mock way of impressing him, which it didn't.

Jack Tillotston is one of the great athletes of our time and certainly its greatest tennis player. Since I have been covering sports, I have become fascinated by the riddle of what distinguishes the great athlete from those on the level just below him. I haven't found out and I am not sure anyone ever will, despite the considerable scientific research in the field, conducted mostly by attaching various electronic devices to various parts of an athlete's body. Certainly the difference is a matter of fractions, especially in tennis. The hit tennis balls of the great player touch the lines, the hit tennis balls of those just a step below him are out by an inch. But I don't think it's that. Nor do I think it is coordination, reflexes, strength. These are necessities, not differences. Everybody near the top has them in very high degree, so much higher than you or I. Whatever makes for the razor-thin crucial difference lies in some inner quality. I wish I could define it. The most I can do is spot just the *possibility* that someone coming up possesses that quality, that faint glimmer that signals he just might be the one to reach those heights where so few ever dwell—being the one best in the world, in anything. To me the chief fascination of sportswriting is trying to spot such a person, and seeing how far ahead you can do it. *Is he the one?* And so, Billy.

Jack Tillotston of course had been there for a long time. There must have been someone who once spotted it in him, probably gay old Gus Licata at the Duchess in Acapulco. The only question was, had his ascent reached its apogee sometime in the past year or two and had he just barely, almost imperceptibly, started down, to run into someone in the same way that Robert Catlo ran into him. As they all do, sooner or later. I could not tell. It is so subtle when it starts. Certainly the raw physical power of Jack Tillotston's game had been greater five years ago than now. But he had long since made up for that with accuracy and shrewdness. By such things as his ability to anticipate so precisely where a tennis ball was going to land. This may be the greatest asset a tennis player can possess, and the rarest. It was as if radar had been installed in Tillotston. I think the Tilly of today, even with less pure tennis power, would have beaten the Tilly of five years ago. But this is only a guess.

I knew something else, though. He could never have looked more magnificent than now. It is a word I do not like to use in sports—save it for the Sistine, for the Beethoven Concerto in D—but it fit. I had picked him up at the St. Regis—no Summit Hotel for Jack Tillotston—and we walked from Fifty-fifth to Forty-fourth. On the streets of New York one looks at the pretty girls passing, and if they are pretty enough, when they have passed, one turns one's head to contemplate the complementary perspective. People did that with Tilly. Girls, and men, and now and then a child, stared at him as he strode along, then turned to look. He was beautifully dressed, as always, but that did not explain it. He moved with unthinking grace, but it was not that either. It was his bearing, a presence that dominated whatever space he was in, even a few yards of sidewalk during the moments he traversed them. A confident, put-together air, with a certain cockiness, an overlay of arrogance. He was tall and that helped. He was always highly tanned beneath the blond wavy hair. But it was presence really. Few of the turning heads could have identified him by name or sport. But I think many would have guessed, first, that he was an athlete, and second, that he was a great one.

"Brinkley," he said after the first sip of the first martini, "did you enjoy a good screw last night?"

It was an odd question from Jack Tillotston, even in rhetorical jest. One nice thing about Tilly, in fact, was that he seldom talked about sex. No talk bores me so much, none is so tiresome, as another man talking to me about sex. Sex is a performing, not an oratorical, art.

"When I think of New York, I think of screwing," he said now. "They should call it Fur City, not Fun City. Here's another advantage of tennis. Tennis players move in a far higher social stratum than any other sport and so get silkier fur. No upper East Side people I know of play football, basketball or baseball, but they nearly all play tennis. Naturally they want to meet and frolic with the players. They are Tiffany lays. Most big jocks in other sports get their fur from hookers as they travel around. They may be the very best but they're still hookers. That's not necessary in tennis. That reminds me."

This was a lot of talk on this subject coming from Tillotston. "I must be out of here by two. She's just eighteen and she feels like the French about what you always do first. Do you find that as you get a little older, you like them a little younger each year? It seems to be almost an actuarial law. Well, fill me in. But first, is another of these permitted?"

I ordered the second round of martinis. "You know I'm doing a story on the Catlos," I said. "I'm trying to talk my editor into putting father and son on the cover."

Typically, Tilly was immediately aware of the implications. "Do you think you should do that?"

"Do you think we shouldn't?"

"Well, now," he said. "It won't look so good if the kid isn't even around when the magazine shows up on the newsstands. If they have to ask who's that on the cover."

"The magazine would survive, I suppose. I can only hope I would," I said with an attempt at lightness. "Naturally it'd look a lot better if he lasted a few rounds."

"Don't do it. The feeding and care of sportswriters is not normally one of my charities, but why be embarrassed?"

"You don't think he has a chance?" I asked.

"Sure. Fawcett-Majors has a chance. Do you realize that, depending on the draw, he could meet me or Shnayerson or Foote or Graves in the first round? You don't think any of us is going to let a kid like that beat us in the first round, do you?"

"Well, maybe the kid will get lucky," I said. "Maybe he'll not have to meet you for a couple of rounds—when, naturally, you'll put him out at love and love."

Tilly grinned. "Oh, I might let him hang in for a game or two. Like I did his old man. Even if I don't get him, he'll have one or two players to get through who don't have reputations for rolling over just because someone named Catlo is on the other side of the net. Don't put him on any magazine cover. You'll regret it."

"My editor suggested you with the Catlos on the cover. It was a good idea. I wish I'd thought of it."

"Well?"

"I asked Catlo. He just said the only place any Catlo would see you would be across a net."

Tillotston burst out laughing. It was honest laughter but I noticed something in his eyes.

"So Catlo won't be seen on the same magazine cover with me."

"He didn't make a lot of fuss. He just said no and that was it. You know Catlo."

"Oh yes, I know Catlo," he said. "I'll have another of these."

I had the waiter bring another round. "What do you really think of Billy's chances?"

Tilly sipped his martini and thought some more. "Well, I think this," he said. "I saw the kid in Palm Beach, of course. He's good. He may get a lot better. I think I know why Catlo's pushing him. One, getting me. Two, the bread. But his judgment is bad. He's rushing things. It'll take a year or two before we'll know *what* the kid is, one way or the other. But you know what I think mostly?"

He took a swallow, not a sip, of his martini. He set the glass down and looked at it, holding it lightly. I looked at that right hand of his. It was an eloquent hand, long and strong and beautiful, a devastating weapon with a racket in it.

"This is a guess judgment," he said. "But what I think mostly is that he can't take the heat. I don't know why but I have this feeling that the kid just won't be able to take it in the Stadium. I've seen it too often before. He has the signs. Forgetting about what strokes he does or doesn't have, I think it'll take him apart. I don't think I'll have to do it. I think the Center Court will."

He waited a moment, looking at his glass. And then he said something I never forgot—and never, for one second, doubted was the purest Tillotston truth.

"I hope that doesn't happen," he said. "I'd rather beat him myself than have the crowds and the pressure do it for me."

I looked at him, watched his eyes. They were good, right then, Tillotston at his best.

"We'll see," I said. "Let's order."

"Let's have another of these to go with it."

After lunch when we were drinking coffee and stingers, Tilly said, "Well, look who's here." I looked up and saw Robert Catlo.

"Brinkley, I need to talk to you. Your office told me I'd find you here." He was ignoring my guest.

"Well, Roberto," Tilly said. "Well, now."

With a glance Catlo finally acknowledged him. "We were just talking about you and your place in tennis history," Tilly said. "I know you've reached the age where you've been inducted into the great Tennis Hall of Fame at Newport, which we really couldn't live without. It was a sure thing, of course. I'd get up in honor of it but I'm not sure I'd ever get back down again. Instead, let's have another stinger. Will you join us, Roberto?"

"Why not?" Catlo said.

I ordered three stingers. It was not tense, actually. At least not at first. We just talked idly for a few minutes about the tournament. Then, inevitably, the subject got to betting, to odds. It always did.

Before the big prize monies, a player *had* to bet on himself—and win, both ways, more often than lose—if he was to stay on the circuit at all. In his high days I don't think Robert Catlo ever played a match without betting on himself, though there came a time when it got harder and harder to find takers—and Catlo responded by devising some interesting spreads, such as how many points he would allow an opponent in a match. Tilly, I knew, always bet on himself. Not because he had to but because he was a bettor. The circumstances were attractive to a great, dominating player. In a tournament like Forest Hills, with seven rounds for one player to get through in a field of 128 players, long odds are standard even on the best of players, even on a Tillotston. Tillotston bet plenty on himself.

"I have a little down," he said, as we talked of betting and the odds. "Just for fun, of course."

"Of course," I said.

In one sense it was for fun. But it was much more. There are people who bet—there are millions of these. Then there are bettors. They will bet on anything and they are enormously shrewd at it or they would not still be bettors. All the true bettors I have ever known are unemotional about it. Ruthless. Jack Tillotston was a bettor. It was part of his life. He was an exceptional bridge player, for instance, but he would not have dreamed of playing without stakes. When I went around the world with him and the circuit, we played gin every day. Until I ran out—in Bangkok, only halfway around—even of expense-account money. Catlo over a period of years had had to bet as his chief source of income. But unlike Tillotston, he was never a bettor.

"Roberto, I was just thinking," Tillotston said. "Just for fun of course."

That phrase should have told me something. "Just for fun," Tilly repeated, "shouldn't you and I have a little something down? Of course we are all realistic people here. We all know the odds are against Billy and me meeting. Too bad, because I would sincerely like to play the kid. But if we should meet. Shouldn't you and I have a little something down for fun— and of course for old times' sake?"

"Well, my betting days are pretty much over." Catlo smiled. "Like the rest of my tennis." He gave a shrug, palms up. "I don't have it to bet," he said, without a shred of embarrassment.

"I understand," Tilly said. "All the same I think we ought to have *something* down. Makes it more interesting. Of course I'd prefer to make it even *more* interesting. Oh. I just thought of something."

Then he said it. He had a gift for that. I honestly think Jack Tillotston couldn't help saying those things. Not that it was ever anything but intentional. He had a meanness in him, no doubt of it. When some true hostility existed, he was outwardly even more polite. He was like Catlo that way. But he could not help saying something, something one would not forget. In Florida it had been the Canadian doubles remark. Now he said:

"I just thought of something, Roberto. You could always have Tish underwrite it."

Something caught in me. Catlo just smiled. "You know something, Jack?" he said quietly. "That's the kind of remark I expect from you. You know something else? I simply consider the source and it doesn't bother me." He looked straight at Tillotston. "Some people just naturally piss when they open their mouths." Then: "You know my club in Palm Beach?"

"Know it?" Tilly said. "Who else was the star attraction at the great Celebrity Pro-Am?"

And suddenly it was like something of long ago—eight years ago, to be exact. We were back at Wimbledon. It was like a match between them. But this time not across a net. This was across a table at the Harvard Club. Catlo was no longer interested in playing random shots, in *rallying*. He wanted something and he went straight to it. It was the only way he knew. It was like the Catlo of old, going for it, with no concern other than to destroy an opponent.

"I have a fourth interest in that club." He spoke totally without emotion. "If you and Billy meet, I'll bet that fourth on Billy. Naturally if you don't meet, there's no bet."

"Do you mean that?"

"There's an easy way to find out. You can just decide if you think I mean it. Then we can get on with it and I can get out of here instead of having to sit here and listen to you run off at the mouth."

Yes, it was like a match between them, as it had been once on the tennis court. And it was as if Catlo had called a bluff. Tilly knew it.

"You've got it," Tilly said. "All we need to do is decide against how much."

"Good. That fourth interest was valued at twenty-five thousand when we started," Catlo went straight in, as if he wanted to get it done with as quickly as possible. "Sixteen years ago.

It's worth a hundred now. You can look at the books. My quarter interest against a hundred thousand cash."

I caught my breath. Tilly smiled. "Well, now. That *does* make it interesting. I'd rather like owning a piece of a club in Palm Beach. It'd be a nice plaything. But the hundred, Roberto. I don't think just your share alone is worth that. Your deal down there must have included your being the pro."

"Of course," Catlo said.

"No, I don't think your share is worth a hundred." Then Tilly twisted it in. "Unless you mean to go on giving lessons to the ladies—in the event I win, I mean. I'll take the bet if you'll agree to stay on as the pro, oh, let's say for a minimum of three years." Tilly grinned. "I'd keep you on at the same salary—whatever that is."

"Done," Catlo said.

He stood up. And then he twisted his own. "Brinkley, you're the witness. Would you ring me before four about the other thing. I'll be at the hotel."

And he was walking away between the tables. I watched that tall figure go, as erect, as graceful as always. I saw a member, slightly greying, turn to look at him, startled, as if he knew who *that* was all right, that it couldn't be anyone else. I sat shocked and appalled. I turned on Jack Tillotston.

"Jesus Christ, Tilly!" I felt responsible. "That club may be just a toy to you. To Catlo it's all he's got."

Tilly shrugged. "Then he shouldn't have bet."

"It's a terrible bet." I was very angry. "You at even money against Billy!"

"No one held a gun to his head. He could have asked for odds—I'd have given them. What am I supposed to do? Make it easier for him?"

"So you just have to rub his nose in it." I sat back and spoke more quietly. "That's it, isn't it? You already drove him into retirement at Wimbledon. You already beat him. Isn't that enough?"

"Yes. But I only beat him *once*." A look came over Jack Tillotston's face. Behind all that loquacity, yes, that charm, was a hard-core ferocity that was chilling to see. I remembered that merciless performance at Wimbledon when Tillotston didn't just defeat Catlo but exterminated him. Tilly must have seen my reaction. He shook his head in annoyance.

"Sportswriters!" he said. "You'll never understand. You think it's all a question of winning matches and making money and being famous. Being on top, being the best. Well, all that is very nice. I love it. But you know what it really is? Catlo knows. It's being the best *man*. There's only one way to do that. You can't just beat the other man. You have to destroy him. You have to kill him. The survivor is the best man. That's what the Center Court is all about."

As soon as Tilly and I separated I phoned Catlo.

"What did you want to see me about?"

"Oh, I didn't want to see you. I wanted to see Tillotston."

"Why, for god's sake?"

"I wanted to see what he was doing these days."

"Did you find out?"

"I did. Having lunch with martinis for the first course and stingers for dessert. And Tish tells me she sees him around that hotel with luscious young things."

"He's also making big bets."

"He's made bigger ones."

"Yes, but have you? Couldn't you at least have asked for odds?"

There was a pause at the other end of the line. "Brinkley," he said, "there are things you'll never understand. Don't tell Billy." He hung up.

12

EXOTIC FRUIT

WHEN CHESTER BARNEY INVITED ME TO LUNCH, I KNEW IT was for a reason. I am quite fond of Chester, but I don't believe his own mother would accuse Chester of asking any male to lunch because he was enchanted with his company. I was sure when he named the place, "21". I never go there. I am never very happy where the customers address the man who takes their food order as "Captain." Chester waited until after the drinks and some really first-rate scallops and a green salad. Only when coffee was served did he sit back, light up a thin long "21" cigar which he had selected from a cedar box brought by the "Captain," blow out a gust of smoke and come, by a circuitous route I knew was intentional, to the point.

"The reason I like this place is that it's all quality," he said. He held the cigar sideways and examined its rich-brown six or seven inches. "I can never understand why anyone would choose to go second-class in the one-time-around journey when it's just as easy to go first. Here the scallops are always bay scallops, the Bibb is right out of a Jersey garden, and the cigars are vintage leaf. I don't think there's a second-class thing on the premises." He maneuvered the cigar expertly, deftly, now sucking on it and actually blowing out a perfect circle.

"Wait'll you see my Special. They'll have to think up some new Emmys. I've dug up the old footage of Catlo and Tillotston at Wimbledon."

I thought that was a good idea and I said so. "The whole thing is like a symphony," Chester went on, rotating the cigar over his lips, "orchestrated in allegro, larghetto and rondo movements. Guess who's the maestro. It's not even primarily a tennis show, if I'm right about this thing I think I've got. It's really a study of a young boy going up against the adult world for the first time, all that pressure and the biggie question—what will happen? Is he going to make it? Same theme as *The Red Badge of Courage*. Personally I feel the show has a depth far beyond tennis. When you get that in a sports show, you get what I call Art. Brinkley, I've had my eye on you for quite some time."

"I'm glad to hear that, Chester," I said. "I've always had my eye on you. I hardly ever take it off."

"Always the cynic, aren't you, Brinkley? Well, a touch of cynicism might not be such a bad thing in the world as we know it. It helps give a balance to someone like myself, the original eternal optimist, always looking on the best side of people, provided they have one. Why, we might make a team. Brinkley, I'm considering opening a door for you. The golden door."

There was nothing for me to say. Chester waited, rotating the cigar.

"I said *the* golden door."

"Come off it, Chester. We're grown boys. Spit it out."

"The thing I like about you, Brinkley, is that you don't play along. You leave the bullshit to others. Nothing would give me more pleasure than to tell you myself. But I promised Fred. Fred wants to look you over personally. You should be very flattered."

"I would be, Chester, if I only knew what there is to be flattered about."

I had heard of Fred. I had never had an audience with him. Barney went into a little soliloquy. "Fred, of course, is one of the most powerful men in America, never mind that most Americans have never heard of him. Fred tells the Cotton Bowl that they are going to have their game on the morning of New Year's Day, not in the afternoon like they thought. He tells the World Series they won't have theirs on any *day* at all. He tells them they'll play at night. He is sometimes referred to, not in jest, as Pope Fred the First. You can't imagine how powerful Fred is."

"I have a large imagination, Chester. I probably could imagine it if I knew what this is all about."

"Fred insisted on doing this in person. You should be extremely flattered. It should tell you what level we're operating on. Let's saunter over and drop in on Fred."

"Do I have to kiss his ring?"

"Not the first time. Captain! The check."

Chester signed and we went out, Chester pressing green bills on various bowing attendants on our progress to the doorway amid a litany of "Thank you, Mr. Barney." It was like checking out of a hotel in Naples.

"I like this place," Chester said as we mounted the steps to the Fifty-second Street sidewalk. "They can tell the wheat from the chaff. As a matter of fact the chaff never gets beyond Raymond."

"Raymond?" I said. "Who's he?"

"Don't you know anybody? Raymond is the maitre d'. One of the most powerful men in New York. He decides where you sit. Let's take a little saunter over to The Magic Mountain."

At least I knew what that was. The Magic Mountain was the MBC headquarters in the Fifties on Sixth Avenue, the great bronze skyscraper whose emanations determined how 30 million Americans would spend three hours of every night of their lives. That's power. I guess.

An executive elevator took us to the sixty-first floor as smoothly as a successful NASA launch and about as rapidly. I followed Chester out of the elevator and down deep-pile-carpeted corridors where heads looked up from desks and murmured, "Good afternoon, Mr. Barney." Chester dispensed his benediction along the way by unfailingly calling everyone by his—usually her—first name. We landed at a considerable desk where a sharp-looking young lady in horn-rims like picture windows said it again.

"Good afternoon, Nancy," Chester said. "You're looking even more beautiful than this morning."

"I always get better as the day goes on, Mr. Barney," the young lady said in a bright manner. "By night I'm pretty terrific."

"I'd like to check that out sometime, Nancy," Barney said. "Is His Holiness engaged?"

"Not for you, Mr. Barney. Go right in."

We went through a leather-padded door into a large room with two walls done entirely in the same lovely, rich-looking glove leather. The remaining walls consisted of massive pieces of plate glass. They presented a vast panorama of downtown clear to the Battery and of great ships at dockside on the Hudson. It was like being on an island in the sky over Manhattan. On a tripod by the window sat a telescope of a quality I had last seen on a heavy cruiser.

A man of under middle age sat behind a rosewood partners desk with a leather top, wearing an open-necked, long-sleeved, coal-black silk sports shirt. As he stood, he revealed Cambridge-grey doeskin slacks held up by a gold double-G Gucci belt. From his neck hung a large gold medallion. He was short, frail, slightly bent at the shoulders. He had a cherubic face with rosy cheeks, no wrinkles and long wavy greyish-white hair descending in well-tended curls to his ears and neck. He looked like an overage choirboy.

Three 25-inch television sets were going quietly against one leather wall. He pressed a button on his desk which shut off the sound on all three but left the pictures on. He came out from behind his desk and extended his hand. He was looking up at both of us.

"I've already shaken hands with Chester today," he said, "and I have a rule against shaking hands with the same person twice in one day. Chester, I see you've brought the prize himself."

No one had ever called me a prize before. "I never miss your tennis stuff," he said. "Did Chester tell you I'm one of his new hackers? Is anybody *not* taking up tennis? I've reached the point where I know which end of the racket to hit with and which to stick up your opponent's ass when his back is turned. I'm a real fan of your stuff. Would you talk a little?"

"About what?" I said.

"About anything. Chester tells me you know the game better than any of the print people. But of course I knew that."

"Well, for a print person," I said, "I try."

He looked at me intently, then turned to Chester. "I think it may be there, Chester."

"Didn't I tell you, Fred? You'd never know he's from Tennessee, would you?"

They spoke as if I were absent.

"Well, we shouldn't knock-knock Tennessee, should we, Chester?" Fred said in a smiling, baiting voice. "Andrew Jackson came from Tennessee. More important, Tennessee is one of those states we practically own. Way up there in our demographics. I've never understood why. And doesn't Roscoe Tanner come from Lookout Mountain?"

I was impressed by that arcane bit of knowledge.

"Yes he does," I said. "But he made up for it by going to Stanford."

Fred burst out laughing and looked keenly at Chester. "Oh, oh, oh, touché! Touché and once more touché. Don't I know when someone's feeling up my hairy leg and squeezing my pinky rocks? He has the wit on top of everything else, Chester."

"Didn't I tell you, Fred?"

I looked out the plate glass. That was the *Elizabeth II* down there, just backing out into the stream.

"You have a hell of a view," I said. I turned back. Everything in the room that could be in leather seemed to be. "Nice walls, too."

"I'm a leather freak," he said. "But if there's any buggering to be done I do it. Pitch but never catch, that's one of the two secrets of life. Now that we've done the obligatory admiring of the wardroom and the view, shall we do a little talking?"

He went back behind his desk—bridge, I almost said—and we took two leather armchairs across from him. I wondered what the other secret of life was.

"Chester tells me you're not too keen on TV," he said. "I like that. If I liked the way things were on TV, I wouldn't be here myself. Do you know why I'm here, Mr. Brinkley?"

"No," I said.

"I'm here to shake up the assholes," he said. "I'm here to show the assholes are wrong three times out of five. You're seated right next to someone who's a perfect example of what I'm talking about. It's hard to believe now when Chester is Number One, Two, Three, Four and Five in tennis telecasting. But every asshole I know in the TV business—and believe me, that's covering a wealth of people—opposed taking Chester on. I had to fight even to get Chester a flier. Of course today everybody claims to be the discoverer of Chester. What was it Jack said? 'Victory has a thousand fathers, defeat, nobody's to be found who stuck it in.' Well, every TV hit has a hundred assholes saying they were the father. I had to fight them all to give Chester a chance."

I glanced at Chester. I had never known Fred's role in Chester's ascendancy. Chester's face was a mask now. I'm not sure he had known either.

"Do you know what I was fighting for? I was fighting for *one transcendent principle*. Do you know what that principle was?"

"I don't believe so," I said.

"TV was at a crossroads in deciding the kind of people to put on the air. I'm talking about sports shows and news programs. Was it going to be regiments of Terry Splendids all looking and sounding alike, like windup toys, and still trying to find out what their little peckers are supposed to be used for. Or was it going to be knowing what the shit you were talking about. One of my greatest prides is that MBC Sports and News have the ugliest on-camera men in the business. I go for knowledge. I've always gone for knowledge. That's why you're sitting where you are, Mr. Brinkley."

"Who won at the crossroads?" I said.

"It's too early in the ballgame to tell. We're barely into the first quarter and every play is third and eight. But I'm in there fighting every down. I am proud to be one of the quarterbacks on the knowledge team. I've read your tennis stuff. I like the stuff. I want another booth man for Forest Hills to help Chester out. It would involve the weekend of the finals plus some taping early in the week. But I'm thinking beyond Forest Hills. You know where I'm thinking?"

"Not really."

"Way beyond the big F. H. If things at Forest Hills go, I'm thinking of a *lot* of tournaments. Do you realize we doubled the number of tournaments we covered this year over last? And we're thinking of doubling that."

"I know," I said. "I sometimes think tennis is going to get overexposed."

"I like this guy," Fred said to Chester. "He's my kind of guy. Chester, tell this guy how I hate yes-men."

"That's the gospel foursquare," Chester said. "Fred can't abide a yes-man."

Fred sat back and looked keenly at me across the leather-topped rosewood.

"You wouldn't believe how difficult it is to find someone who knows tennis and doesn't fart when he opens his mouth," he said. "The most uncrowded field in the business. What I'm thinking of is phasing you in. Chester is going to be doing more and more Specials, and while we all know Chester wears a pair of iron balls, he's going to need help. It's phase-in time."

He looked over at the three silent TV sets, at the pictures galloping along like ghosts.

"Look at all that crap," he said. "If manure is the world's greatest fertilizer, roses should bloom in there. I'm trying to plant a few roses."

He turned and looked right at me. "For the Forest Hills washup, I have this figure in my mind." He leaned forward, picked up a pencil and made four noiseless taps on the leather desk.

"Rat-a-tat-tat," he supplied the sound track. "Ten big ones for Forest Hills."

"Ten thousand dollars?" came out of me. Just out the huge windows I saw a helicopter float by. I saw the face of the pilot. He was smoking a cigar.

"That's quite an offer," I said carefully. "I'd like to think it over."

"Just the answer I wanted. I would have been disappointed if you had grabbed it. Always be just a little hard to get. That's the other great secret of life and I learned it at my mom-mom's knee. I want a man who thinks things over and doesn't grab both tits the moment the clothes come off. Chester, let's talk about the Special scheduling."

The subject of me was over, just that abruptly. Fred opened a leather looseleaf book on his desk.

"We're penciled in for Tuesday. Night before the opening," he said. "You wrote me a note about that."

"That's the time for it, Fred. Our opening gun for Forest Hills."

"Now let's have a little think-think about that. Point one. The tournament hasn't even started. Low interest. Point two. Nobody's ever heard of this Billy Catlo. Low interest. Point three. He hasn't even won a match. Low interest. Low interest, Chester, means low ratings. Maybe we should hold it for a few days. Let the kid win a few."

There was a hard silence. Something had changed in the atmosphere. Games were over and it was hard lines now. And then I saw another Chester. He was all cold business.

"Wrong, Fred, all wrong. On your point one, just before the tournament is a *good* time for the hackers, who're ninety-nine percent of our audience. They know the early matches aren't important, but they're all primed for Forest Hills, ready to punch on their sets for something on tennis that *is* important. We have it. Your point two, it isn't just Billy Catlo. It's the *Catlos*, father and son. Everybody has heard about the Big Cat and now he's back. Your point three, Billy hasn't won a match. But he might never win one. He could get knocked out in the first round and that knocks out the Special too, everything we've done."

Barney leaned forward, hammering in his case. "Now my point four. There've been newspaper stories on the Catlos up in Central Park. Brinkley's magazine has a cover story coming. The other networks could do a quickie. What do you want to be, Fred? Last man in town to discover the Catlo story? When we were on it first? My point five. I've got a terrific show. My point six, seven, eight, nine and ten. If you've got it, run it. I learned that in the newspaper business so I didn't have to learn it in the television business. Go with what you have. Do you know something else, Fred?"

Fred sat silent as a piece of granite, and as expressionless, his eyes never leaving Barney. I imagined it could be unnerving if you were on the other end of it. Especially with the touch of sadism that I felt was present here. Chester's voice dropped a little and came on in tones of conviction.

"This show is the best thing I've ever done. In a way, it's not even about tennis. It's about a boy going up against the adult world for the first time, and all the pressure on him, and how is it all going to turn out? It's like *The Red Badge of Courage*." I realized Chester had been rehearsing on me. "Something people will talk about for as long as they talk about sport shows. Or at least beyond next week. I'd hate like hell to see it dumped in the Gowanus Canal because we waited to see if Billy won a couple and he didn't. Letting the fact of a fucking tennis match, won or lost, decide whether a show this good even runs, for Christ's sake."

The piece of granite stirred. The case for the prosecution was over. I had confronted another of Chester Barney's gifts: a rich power of advocacy if he really believed in something.

"Just off the top-top, Brinkley. Do you agree or disagree with Chester?"

"Go with it," I said.

Fred sat looking a long time at me now, or at least it seemed a long time. Abruptly he stood up.

"All right. I buy. We'll go with it."

If you could convince Pope Fred . . . We were standing now, too.

"I hope I can say welcome to television, Mr. Brinkley. Say welcome to MBC. We don't run a bad shop here. I'm biased, but personally I think our asshole quotient is the lowest of The Blessed Trinity."

"I'll let you know," I said. I glanced out the plate glass. "May I look through that telescope?"

"Help yourself."

I went over to it, a shining thing in black and bronze. I tipped it down toward the river and looked through. The *Elizabeth II* was starting down the river, a white goddess in the afternoon sun, off to faraway places. I wished I were aboard. I straightened up. Fred walked us to the door and opened it.

"I hear you know Shelly Blaine," he said.

"Yes, I know Shelly."

"We're going to steal Shelly away from those other people. You watch. Maybe you can help. Shall we say Tuesday?"

"Fine," I said. "I'll have an answer to you then."

We waited a moment. "I wonder," Fred said casually, "if there's anything to this rumor that Jack Tillotston is quitting tennis if he wins at Forest Hills. Going behind the mike."

"I've heard the rumor," I said.

"Well, the woodwork is always full of rumors. Isn't that true, Chester?"

"Yes, indeed, Fred. And they all seem to be crawling things."

Fred smiled and we walked out. Going back down the deep carpets I had the wildest feeling that this had all somehow, for some reason, started with Shelly. Or at least had something to do with her.

"Thanks for voting with me," Chester said as we waited at the elevator. "About the timing."

"Thanks for asking for me on the show."

Neither of us was given to going on in this vein, but we had heard each other. We got in the elevator and started down.

"What did you think of Fred?"

"I like him. I think he honestly wants to plant a few roses in it."

"Brinkley, I'm not sure I want you on the show. There's room for only one of us."

The elevator glided to a stop and we went across the lobby and out into the afternoon sun. I knew I would take it and I knew what I would do with the ten.

"It's a pretty day," I said, "but I have a story to write. Walk me back to my shop-shop."

I had assigned myself a day off with Lindy. I could scarcely have chosen a better one. Sunlight flooded even the crosstown streets, reaching down to cleanse the dark canyons. She wore a light summer dress of blue and carried the sweater, a tan cashmere, I had suggested she bring in case coolness came in early evening. She looked what she was, a girl off a southern campus, alive in the fabled city. I was aware of the lightness, the coltishness, of her body beneath the dress, the scents of girlhood. At Madison and Fiftieth we got on the Fort Tryon Park bus. She walked all the way to the back.

"We'll sit here," she said firmly. "That way we can look

back if we miss anything. Tell me places as we go by."

So I told her as we passed the St. Laurent boutique, the Whitney Museum, the Mount Sinai Hospital. At 110th Street the bus turned left and moved across the north edge of the park.

"Central Park," I said. "To your left."

"I know *that*. I may be new here but I'm not a dummy."

What a happy thing it was just to be with her, how it brought life alive. Never mind what you were doing. Anything would do. If the word "comfortable" is the most important in the language as defining what makes things right between two people, well, it was that. But it was something more. A feeling of joy, very close to exhilaration. With this girl all things remarkable might come to pass. How fortunate some man was going to be. I half-turned to the rear window.

"Quick!" I said. "You mustn't miss this."

She turned quickly and looked back with me.

"Central Park," I said. "What you see back there is Central Park."

"You're *awful*," she said and looked at me. Her face was bright, her eyes dazzling.

The bus rumbled crosstown, then swung wide onto Riverside Drive. Clear now of the annoying in-and-out traps of the congested streets, the harassing Chevvies, Fords and Volkswagens snapping at its heels, it growled and gathered steam for the clean shot uptown, then lurched forward up the Drive. Over the clouds of black exhaust we viewed the river, shining in the sun. Two far-apart bursts of pure-white cumulus stood against the blue. Between them, like some walkway of the sky, hung the George Washington Bridge. The bus swung up a long hill and stopped at the Cloisters.

"We get off here," I said.

We went through the Fuentidueña Chapel, the Romanesque Hall, the Cuxa Cloister, the Nine Heroes Tapestry Room, the Early Gothic Hall, the Glass Gallery and lingered in the Hall of the Unicorn Tapestries, looking up at the fabulous animal.

"You really do want to catch the unicorn, don't you?" I said.

"Only if it wants to be caught."

We went back out and got a Checker. The front and back seats were separated by a steel grill like a patrol car bringing in rapists and murderers. I told the driver to go to the Forty-third Street pier.

"Well, that surprise was nice," she said. "I'm grateful to you for taking me to that. What's the reason for the grill?"

"It's so we won't attack the driver."

"Oh."

At the pier she read the sign, "Circle Line, Three Hours Around the Island of Manhattan."

"I figured this was the one way you could say you had seen all of Manhattan," I said. "We get the one that does the first two hours in daylight and the last part coming back down the river with the lights in the big buildings beginning to come on up ahead of you. The city lighting up for the wicked night."

We boarded and went forward. The boat backed out into the stream and began to move down the river, opening up the city before us. Great ships stood at their piers in midtown —the *Rotterdam* sat there, white and gleaming. Then, as the boat moved into the water off the Village, the freighters. We went back and took seats in the stern. We were off Tenth Street.

"Right up that street is where I live."

"I'd like to see your place sometime. I've wondered what New York apartments look like."

It was not mock innocence. It was certainly not the come-on talk of seduction. I wished it were. I think I would have taken her there and done whatever she would let me do. You learned not to put more meaning in her words than were there. No, that wasn't right. Sometimes there was a lot more meaning than appeared. She baffled as well as allured me. Is that what the really best girls do? Up ahead we could see the Statue.

The boat proceeded into the bay past the Lady and began to make her turn. She came full about and suddenly there it was, broadside on. The greatest of all views, from land, sea, or air, of the New York Island. It was about like the Messiah. We stood up.

The great bouquet of skyscrapers stood just above us. From the low freeboard of the boat, they seemed twice as tall as they were, immense, dazzling slabs reaching to the clouds. I wondered why I had never done this before. We spread our legs and planted our feet and strained our necks to the limit, looking way way up. Then it was gone, too soon. We rounded the island, moved under the Brooklyn Bridge and stood looking up at its belly.

The boat chugged slowly up the East River. Ahead were the midtown skyscrapers.

"Madam, may I have your attention," I said.

"You have it, sir."

"May I direct that attention to the port side. Just off our port bow you see approaching the famous New York East Side. Notice over there the United Nations, the Franklin Roosevelt Drive, the Empire State, Chrysler and Seagram's buildings, the Queensboro and Triboro bridges, Sutton Place, New York Hospital, the River Club, P. J. Clarke's. Just off the bow now! Look alive. Gracie Mansion there. Home of the mayor of this city."

"Why is it called Gracie Mansion?"

"Madam, please don't ask impertinent questions the captain can't answer. Starboard side! The big round thing. The famous Yankee Stadium. So called because it is the home of the famous New York Yankees." We moved on. "Steady as you go! We're coming about."

"Coming about what?"

"About to the end of the blooming island."

I realized I was *performing* for her. It was something I

seldom did for any girl, for anybody. "The famous New York subway yards, madam. And now we enter Spuyten Duyvil. A Dutchman, one stormy night, vowed he'd swim it in spite of the devil. He's below us."

"Poor Dutchman."

The boat crossed through the canal, chugged under Henry Hudson Bridge. Suddenly we stood at the Manhattan mouth of the Hudson.

Far away and wide the river stretched, going to the sea, the blood rays of the evening sun spilling across the water and sending up immense bursts of gleaming white light. In the distance, lining her bank, stood the great city, spectral, unreal, the end of all visions that ever were. We stood and watched, the boat pitching just slightly under our feet.

"You picked the right trip," she said.

A breeze was coming up. She put her sweater around her. I went down the ladder to the lower deck and brought up paper cups of coffee. We sat and watched the city approach. We watched night come to the city, the lights turning on in the tall buildings like hosts of nearby stars.

"Up there," I said, pointing to the Cloisters, "is where we were."

"It looks better from here. When I was there I didn't think it was too happy there. From here it belongs. It belongs on that bluff."

The earth-tan medieval haven did seem serene on its Manhattan rock, as if it had reigned there from the twelfth century. The breeze caught her dress and fluttered it for a moment. I was aware of her body. I had to remind myself that she was Billy's girl.

"How's Billy?" I said.

The air off the river had turned cool and crisp. Her boyish, blonde hair moved in the breeze. She sipped her coffee, both hands holding around the paper cup for warmth.

"This is good. It feels even better. I think he's having fun in New York."

"Is that all?"

She knew what I meant. "Well, he's pretty tense I'd say."

"I'd say that was natural."

"I guess so. But he *is* tense. Uptight. Speaking of Billy. I have something to say." She waited a moment, thoughtful, as if gathering herself. "I had an idea of what's going on in Mr. Catlo's mind. This morning I got Tish to tell me."

Her head was cocked in that funny, somewhat angry way she had when intent on something. "I'm beginning to feel if I sleep with Billy and he loses, Mr. Catlo will blame me. If I don't and he loses, Billy will blame me. I have a message for both of them. I'll deliver it personally to Billy. Will you deliver it to Mr. Catlo?"

"Yes ma'am."

"I want Billy to win as much as anybody does. But I'm infuriated at being placed in this position and I'm more infuriated at it being discussed *at all*. Who do they think they are? You will tell him exactly that."

"I will. And may I say that I think you're right? You're quite right."

"Tell him if I hear one more word about this, I'm going to tell them both to . . . to buzz off. You got that?"

"I got it."

"Who do they think they are, discussing what *I* should or should not do. He makes me sound like some sort of groupie, some, some . . . *camp follower*."

She turned away and waited a bit, watching the apartment buildings of New York go by across the water. We must have passed four or five blocks of them when she turned back to me. The other was out of her now. She spoke now in a shy, tentative voice.

"Should I sleep with him? Mr. Catlo knows everything about tennis," she said. "I'm not sure he knows everything about Billy."

I was surprised to find myself so impatient. "Do you think

anyone can answer that question for anyone else? Anyway you shouldn't talk about it. It'll hurt it if you do."

And then I really said it. "Also I don't want to hear any more about it."

She looked up at me. She was really very small. I was aware of a pool of night around her face, but I could see her eyes and they looked all through me, with a knowledge I didn't want. I was aware of her holding the coffee with both hands, between us.

"Why, you're jealous," she said.

"Don't be ridiculous."

She bent down and placed the Dixie cup on the deck. The breeze was beginning to agitate the river. Then the boat pitched. I was vaguely aware of the cup flying off somewhere toward the darkening water. She stood a little on her toes. She looked up at me and she kissed me on the lips. Not a great amount of kiss, just barely damp, but fresh and sweet as some exotic fruit. It was over before I really knew it had happened. I remembered only thinking that I wished I had never met Billy. I wished that I had only met her. It was over and she was turning to the city.

The city was all lit up, every last light. The whites and the blues and the yellows and the reds, the streets and the high buildings, all ablaze. All on, waiting for whatever you chose to find in it. If you didn't find it, it was not the city's fault.

"Was there ever anything so beautiful as that?" she said.

I never knew how we got from the Nineties to the Forties, but there we were, home. The boat heeled to port and came in, stuttering and clanking, to the Forty-third Street pier.

They bring the silver winners' trophies down from Cartier's to pull the names out of, the men's names in one big sterling silver loving cup, the women's in the other. For the men, there are 128 entries, including sixteen seeds—the top sixteen players in the world, picked by computer ranking according to tournament performance over the past year. The Number 1 seed has slot Number 1, the Number 2 seed has slot 128. If everyone played according to the seeding, the Number 1 seed would meet either Number 3 or Number 4, depending on the draw, in the semifinals, and Number 2 would meet the other; the finals would be Number 1 against Number 2. That seldom happens in men's tennis where there are plenty of hot and hungry unknowns. As I write this, I note that Arthur Ashe, a Wimbledon champion and one of the half dozen best tennis players alive, has just been eliminated in the first round of an Australian tournament by the world's 157th ranking player. This is unheard of in women's tennis, where there are only four top tennis players, who all reach the semifinals with tiresome consistency. If you have a little girl who can do a good backhand with her rattle, you might want to start training her to make $661,395 a year by the time she's nineteen—which is what one of those four made last year.

It's quite a ceremony, the draw for the U. S. Open Championships. It's held in the grand ballroom of the Roosevelt Hotel, which should give you an idea. Like any good shootout it starts at high noon. Few of the players whose fates are being decided ever show up—maybe it's because the tension would be unbearable—but everyone else connected with tennis does. I went over with Catlo to see it and get some of the free champagne passed around by the USTA. Chester Barney was there with Sylvia, his script girl. I'd never seen her out of hot pants, but the ultrasuede she was wearing, which clung to her like magnetized polishing cloth, did very well. Her breastworks were as undefended as ever. While she chatted with several members of the male sex who were buzzing around her, I whispered to Barney, "Chester, I think this is the first time I've seen you with the same one twice. Does it mean we can expect the publishing of banns?"

"Jesus Christ," Chester said, alarmed, "keep your voice down. She's got ears too." His face suddenly held a far-off expression. "I'll say one thing. If they were seeding for the

U. S. Oral Championships today, it would be Sylvia in straight sets all the way."

The tournament referee, wearing soft-grey slacks and a blue blazer with the U. S. Open emblem, read off the seeds in solemn tones. Jack Tillotston, of course, was Number 1. The sixteen seeds were written on the master sheet on a big easel board set up by the speaker. All the rest of the 128 players are treated as equals. Their names and hometowns (if American) or home countries (if foreign) had been put on pressure-sensitive labels, about 1 inch by 3 inches. Now these were placed in the loving cup and stirred. Then they started plucking out the names. As each name was drawn the label was stuck on the master sheet.

Pretty soon there was a nice folksy little ritual. Carrying the men's loving cup, high like the chalice for the Eucharist, the tournament referee, Pat Hargraves, went around the ballroom inviting people to draw one name out of the trophy.

When it was over we went out and walked to Pearl's where we were meeting Tish for Chinese food. Billy had drawn Art Leachman for the first round.

"Oh, sure, we all know Art," Catlo said as we idled up Madison. "Hell, I've played old Art myself."

Art Leachman had been around the circuit for years but had never done anything much. Five years back he was a semi-finalist in the Italian Open and that had been his career high-water mark. He was thirty-seven now and he was never going to better that victory beneath the Roman pines in Il Foro Italico. But he was not to be taken lightly. Once in a while, on some given day, he would come on dangerous and give a seed a scare, or even knock him out. Especially a seed. And he was still winning first, second and third rounds. I liked Leachman. He had a kind of fiendish glee about the game and his mission in it.

"I just love knocking out one of those big motherfuckers who thinks his fucking balls are made of brass and his prick of galvanized iron and thinks he's going all the fucking way,"

Art once told me, hardly for publication. "I really love sticking it up the bloody fucker's royal fucking ass."

He broke into a cackling laugh that sounded like the devil receiving a fresh shipment of sinners. Leachman was an Aussie. From his language I always assumed that he had served a hitch in Her Majesty's Royal Navy, where, as we all know, the famous word is indispensable to communication.

"Well, I could have asked for a better first draw for Billy," Catlo said. "But he could have done a lot worse." Catlo chuckled. "Old Art. We used to call him Fart Leachman on account of what came out of his mouth. I don't believe I've ever heard Art speak a sentence that didn't contain The Word. I'm satisfied."

Billy and Tillotston had landed in the same half of the draw but in different quarters. This meant that if they met, it would not be in the early rounds. They could only meet in the semifinals. It reduced their chance of meeting at all. Billy would have to get past five other players even to see Jack Tillotston across a net. It meant that Billy and thirty-one other players, including four seeds, would be fighting viciously among themselves for the rare privilege and high honor of meeting Jack Tillotston in the semis.

"If you want to see Leachman play," Catlo said, "show up at Central Park tomorrow."

"Oh? Will Leachman be there?"

"You're looking at him," Catlo said.

Robert Catlo had decreed no tennis for the final two days before the tournament. "When that tournament opens," Catlo said, "I want Billy to have *missed* tennis, to be hungry to play." So it was the last morning of the workouts on the Central Park courts. A considerable crowd was on hand, watching through the fences and from the adjoining courts. Today was all point-play, Catlo playing Art Leachman's game. Leachman's game was mostly serve and volley but of a special kind.

He had a wicked twist serve, with a combination of sidespin and overspin, which cleared the net by several feet then came down like a dive bomber into the service box near the doubles alley and "kicked," pulling the receiver off court. Leachman followed this serve to net, hoping for a pop-up return to be put away crosscourt. When it was working, Leachman's serve could drive you up the wall, putting you into some embarrassing acrobatics as you dived into the next county to get it. Billy had trouble with it at first. Then Catlo positioned him closer in and closer to the alley, to pick the shot off the clay more quickly and blast it back down the line.

Catlo and Billy were just finishing when a small commotion started in the crowd behind the fence. Heads turned away from the court to see the source.

"It's Jack Tillotston!" I heard someone say.

Tilly was making his way through the crowd toward the courts. He was followed by several men carrying cameras, including one from my magazine, and by several sports reporters I knew. I realized at once they would have suggested this idea to Tilly. Bringing together Robert Catlo and the man who had toppled him from his tennis throne would provide nice copy and pictures. Tilly would have gone along as a lark.

The retinue of sportswriters and photographers convoyed the champion through the crowd, which opened and closed behind them. The crowd wanted to see now more than ever. Out on the court, Catlo and Billy had finished hitting. Catlo opened the gate and they walked through together. Billy was toweling his face. I don't think they even saw Tilly until they were surrounded.

"Roberto, the boys wanted some pictures and I didn't see why not," Tillotston said, looking at Catlo and ignoring Billy. "I've always found it's a good idea to do what the boys want, haven't you?"

He smiled lightly. Everyone knew that while Tilly cooperated with the press to their mutual benefit, Robert Catlo had at best tolerated the press and more often avoided it.

"Anyhow we might as well be charitable and do our bit to help the gate, hadn't we, Roberto?"

"It's always nice to see the gate helped," Catlo said in that even way he had, of handling something completely on the outside, not letting it get inside him at all.

The photographers started taking pictures and issuing various commands. I noticed with approval that our man, Harry Bender, had blocked out a good position and was holding it.

Catlo and Billy were sweaty in their white shorts and polo shirts. Billy's black hair was damp and mussed from the toweling. They obviously would have preferred to be on their way. Tillotston's tan and his blond hair were set off by pale blue slacks and a dark blue Jack Tillotston signature sports shirt, with the word "Tilly" in small white script at the edge of the left sleeve. He was entirely at ease, the champion holding court.

"Hey, how about you two standing closer together," a photographer said. "And the kid too."

The Catlos didn't move but Tilly obligingly stepped closer. Billy was between them, just behind his father's shoulder. It was a nice grouping for a picture. The reporters gathered around.

"Do you remember the last time you two met on a tennis court?" one asked.

"Yes," Catlo said evenly. "It was a couple of weeks ago in Palm Beach."

Tilly laughed in admiration. "I don't think that's what he meant, Roberto."

"No, I mean at Wimbledon," the reporter explained.

"Wimbledon?" Catlo said in the same even tone. "I played Wimbledon a lot, but that was a long time ago."

Tilly laughed again, appreciating the performance. One of the reporters brought us back to the present.

"Billy, are you hoping to meet Tilly at Forest Hills?"

Billy started undoing the handkerchief around his neck. It was very wet.

"Hoping?" he said. "Sure, I'm hoping."

"Are you *expecting* to meet him?" the reporter said. "You'd have to get to the semifinals."

"Expecting?" Billy said. "Well, I'm always expecting something. We'll have to see."

He wanted to go but they were holding him.

"What he means," Tillotston said with a grin, "is that he doesn't answer hypothetical questions." The reporters laughed. I thought how lordly he was, how sure of himself, but how easy. That was what gave him his charm.

"Is it that hypothetical?" a reporter said.

"How do you like New York?" a reporter asked.

"I like New York," Billy said, answering an inanity with an inanity. It's a good practice. "Great city."

"Do you get to bed early?"

"Not early enough," Billy said. The reporters laughed a little.

"Are you going on the circuit after Forest Hills?"

"Well, right now, I'm just thinking of Forest Hills," Billy said.

The young boy was catching on. Of course he had the master model. He was learning, as his father had, the ritual to be followed in handling these matters. You had to learn the ritual if you were going to leave yourself free to handle the tennis.

"You mean it depends on how you do at Forest Hills?" a reporter asked.

"Depends?" Even that mindless trick of echoing the operable word of the question. "Something like that."

"Tilly," a reporter said, "are you hoping you and Billy meet?"

"I just try to play whoever's on the other side of the net.

I just play the best I can," Tillotston said with mock humility, "and hope for the best."

"What's this about a grudge match between you and Billy?"

"Grudge match?" Tilly said. "What grudge match?"

"Well, the story goes," the reporter said with some sarcasm, "that Billy wants you because you beat his father eight years ago at Wimbledon. Something like that."

"Let's grow up, boys," Tilly said. "Shall we just grow up? Anyhow, to have a grudge match, there has to be a match. If you carry a grudge, you have to be good enough to get to where you can *have* a grudge match. Boys, I'm afraid I'm being too cryptic."

"Oh, no," a reporter said. "A few of us went to college. It isn't cryptic at all."

"I'm delighted," Tilly said.

"What's your training program these days?"

"Spartan as usual."

"I hear it's been a little less Spartan and a little more Babylonian lately," a reporter said.

"I understand Billy does a five-mile run every morning at eight," a reporter added. "Do you think you should be getting in some roadwork?"

"A five-mile run in New York?" Tilly said, appalled. "At eight in the morning? I thought we were playing tennis at Forest Hills. I didn't realize it was the marathon."

"It could be," a reporter said.

"Too bad we can't get you and the Big Cat on the court hitting a few," a photographer said.

"Well, I wouldn't mind playing a friendly social set," Tilly said. "Between old friends. How about it, Roberto? Shall I go in and change? I'll spot you thirty."

"My playing days are over," Catlo said, outside himself. I never knew a man who wasted less emotion.

"How about you, Billy?" Tillotston said. "Just a little friendly social set. I'll spot *you* fifteen."

"My playing days begin at Forest Hills," Billy said. He had called, now he raised. "You want to give me fifteen at Forest Hills, Mr. Tillotston?"

The reporters looked alert. There was something suddenly in the air that had not been there a moment ago.

"Are you asking for fifteen?" Tilly said.

"I'm not asking for anything. It was your figure."

Tilly smiled. "I don't give points at Forest Hills. I take them."

"So it's just talk," Billy said. "Talk doesn't count." He smiled—just like his father, the smile of ritual. And he walked off.

"Where have you been?" Cy Bannon said in that whisper-voice. "I'm going with the cover."

I didn't want to overreact. "It's a great Dusie portrait," I said.

"Yeah. I'll use that inside as the lead picture. But the cover is Bender's."

He gave me the magnifying eyepiece and indicated a single color transparency on his light table. I bent over. The three of them: Tilly smiling arrogantly in profile, Catlo staring back in deadly calm, Billy's face just over Catlo's shoulder, the young tense face looking straight at Tilly. The picture was so sharp that you could read the white lettering on Tilly's shirt-sleeve.

"Pretty good," I said. "The background's a little busy."

"We'll knock it back in the engraving," Bannon said. "Better get to your typewriter."

I decided this was the perfect time to request my television leave.

"I don't see why not," he said. "As long as you get your copy in. How much they giving you?"

"Ten thousand." I felt a little ashamed of it.

"Well. Nice piece of change for a week's work. I assume

this isn't for keeps. Not that I'd blame you."

"They said something about afterward if it worked out. It wouldn't work out for me. Anyhow I'll probably choke. I just happen to have a use for that money."

"Wouldn't anybody."

I closed my story. It ran much longer than it was supposed to, and while Bannon grumbled about the length, he must have liked it because he fiddled with the mockup, threw out a story that had already closed and gave me two-and-a-half additional pages, muttering about long-winded writers.

When he went in, it was not to pray for victory. He would have considered that obscene. These days there's quite a bit of asking God to give you victory. Even in locker rooms, before games. God must laugh at that. If I were God I'd make sure of one thing. I'd have a rule that anyone who asked me to let him win, well, I'd make sure that son of a bitch lost, and big.

Billy didn't go in to pray for anything like that. But it's a good place to go at night. I do it now and then myself and I'm not even Catholic. Every so often when I'm passing St. Pat's I stop and walk up the steps. I don't know why. I just go inside and stand there for a minute or two.

I like the way it sits down between the tall buildings. From high up in the building where my magazine is located, I can see it doing that. It is far below the buildings on either side of it, yet it seems higher than they, the way the spires reach up toward the sky. The most expensive real estate in the world, Fifth Avenue and Fiftieth, and it's only one-story, two if you count the choir loft.

It would all begin tomorrow. Billy would play his first match. Billy, Lindy and I had had dinner. We walked out of the night and up the steps and inside. As the Catholic of the three, Billy crossed himself, touching his lips with a kiss as the fifth point, as his people do, and dipped his knee toward the altar.

Aware of him beside me, I found myself feeling a strange thing, wishing that he was not there, not entered in the tournament at all. He seemed too much a boy to be carrying the burden that would be his starting tomorrow. He should be somewhere having fun, going to college, chasing girls. We stood and looked at the altar in the distance and saw the heads of the people praying, bent on their prie-dieux.

We stood there in St. Pat's, Billy and Lindy holding hands. Lindy had taken one of Billy's handkerchiefs out of her purse to cover her head—she carried a supply of them now so he would always have one on the court to tie around his neck. I wanted to light a candle—I often do when I go in there— but I was afraid they would think it meant praying for Billy. I certainly didn't want them to think that, or God either, for that matter, in case He invoked the new sports rule I had recommended to Him. We stood awhile looking at the altar far away, at the crucified Christ, lit by the glow of the altar candles.

We walked back to the Summit. The lobby was all fluorescence, harsher than ever after the candle-glow of the cathedral. Some players were sitting around talking. "If you play him at night, hit into the lights," I heard one of them, perched on a couch-arm, say to another sitting on the couch. "He can't handle the lights." The bar was just to our right. Through the open door we could hear the sounds of conversation. Just inside stood two cocktail waitresses in uniform, high black net stockings, red short pants, black-girdle tops.

"You like a nightcap?" I said.

Billy waited a moment, looking at the cocktail waitresses but not really seeing them I don't think. I don't know what he was seeing.

"No thanks," he said. "I'm playing tennis tomorrow."

PART IV

FOREST
HILLS

13

ONE TENNIS PLACE

FOR THE FIRST FIFTEEN SECONDS THERE WAS NO PICTURE at all. Only the sound of a tennis ball being hit back and forth. But differently. Any tennis player would have known that this tennis ball was being hit exceptionally hard. Then a picture came on and as the metronomic sound of the hit ball continued, the camera moved slowly around an enclosure, showing a cathedral roof of hundreds of small window panes, a grouping of white wicker chairs, walls of gleaming teak-wood, and then an exquisite rust-clay tennis court in the sun-light through the panes. The camera came to rest on the source of the sound the viewer had been hearing, a man and a boy hitting out from the baseline.

Now the camera on each side of the net showed the ball coming directly at the viewer with bullet speed, as if it were going to burst through the screen. It was superlative camera work. Still not a word spoken. Now the camera came in close to show the beauty of body-movement. First the man, with a copper face and legs, tall and handsome and wearing tennis whites, hitting with command and grace. Then a matching closeup of the beautiful young boy in tennis shorts but no shirt, his hitting style virtually identical. Now the screen filled with the man's face, his very black hair, the greying at the temples. Then back across the net to the face of the boy, the same black-black hair, longer than the man's and with none of the grey. The faces were so much alike that the boy had to be the son of the man. Two lines came on the screen: "The Tennis Kid, a Chester Barney Hour Special." Then for the first time a voice was heard.

"Ladies and Gentlemen," said the voice in the raspy twang known across the Republic, "you are watching Robert Catlo, one of the four greatest tennis players of all time, and his son, Billy, who is about to restore a magic name to tennis. This is Chester Barney. What you are seeing, for the first time anywhere on camera, is the most remarkable indoor tennis court ever built, created by the top-seeded indoor bandit of them all, J. Pierpont Morgan. We are coming to you from the legendary Jekyll Island, Georgia. We'll be right back, right after this word from Sniff, 'the fragrance of the jocks.' "

We sat in comfortable black leather easy chairs, each with a small side table for drinks and ashtrays. In the windowless MBC screening room sixty-one stories in the sky over Manhattan, we were watching Chester's special on the Catlos, along with, it was hoped, 40 million other Americans.

We were Chester, Fred-Fred and a half dozen MBC executives of assorted rank. Then the commercial was over and we were back on the tennis court.

"Billy Catlo," the familiar voice twanged again. "Remember that name. Tomorrow Billy Catlo goes for the dream at Forest Hills. He is out to beat one hundred and twenty-seven other players, and especially one player you all know, Jack Tillotston. He goes for the dream of being the best tennis player in the United States. How did he get here and how far can he go? How does any boy get *here* in the immensely rich lottery that tennis has become? We are going to show you . . ."

When it was over we pulled ourselves out of the big chairs and went to a room next door. As if to make up for the submarine-like windowlessness of the screening room, this room had a thrilling view. Two massive pieces of plate glass rounded a corner to present a spectacular picture of downtown and the West Side, of New York in its night glory, of the great black buildings rearing themselves into the sky in a vast nest of twinkling lights, of the Hudson and the lights of the berthed ships reflected in the quiescent water. The walls were wallpapered in leather. I had been here by day but never by night. It was Fred-Fred's office.

"A little toast," he said. He wore an open-throat chocolate silk shirt and fawn slacks held up by a huge silver belt buckle, and around his neck a matching silver medallion on a chain.

"I believe," he said, "we have just seen a milestone in sports telecasting. It had that extra thing. Let's uppercase that: That Extra Thing. Even I don't know how to produce it in a television show, if you promise not to tell anyone. But if it's there it's there. Chester, this one was there. I think we showed the assholes something tonight."

He raised his glass higher.

"But one thing I do know about That Extra Thing. You never even have a chance to get it unless you've got someone in charge, like our Chester, who *knows* his subject. What we've just seen is another vindication of MBC's policy of going with people who know what they're talking about. Chester, I think we planted a rose tonight. In the shit-shit."

As we hoisted our glasses, Chester responded with admirable brevity. "There was only one thing missing," he said. "I think Stephen Crane should have been given a credit line."

"Stephen Crane?" Fred said. "Oh, was he the second camera?"

I don't know if he was putting us on. That's the thing about people like Fred-Fred in high places. You never know when they really don't know or when they're putting you on. But he was right about Chester's special: it was there. It really captured, as they love to say, that quality of the young boy about to make his first run at it. It was Red Badge all right.

I was picking Billy up after breakfast to teach him about the subway. At Forest Hills a player is defaulted, no excuses accepted, if he is fifteen minutes late for a match, so he had best take the right one. Today Billy was going out early to get his locker assignment and get the feel of the place. Catlo had gone ahead to arrange a warmup court. I phoned Billy's room and Lindy's room from the lobby. They came down on the same elevator. Both were wearing jeans. Lindy had a yellow ribbon in her hair. Billy was carrying three wood rackets and a blue duffel bag. We walked out onto the street and Billy looked up instinctively at the sky. Not a scrap of cloud. I looked at my watch to time the route for him: 8:37 A.M. We walked the two blocks to the subway and went down the first flight of steps. I gave the woman in the cage five dollars and she slipped the ten tokens through the slot, two at a time. We went down the long escalator and stood under a sign that said "Third Avenue-Lexington."

"Take any train that stops here. Either E or F," I told them. I found myself speaking more to her than him. "On this side of the track. Got it?"

"Got it," Lindy said. "E or F. This side of the track."

One came along in a couple of minutes and we were swept in. Billy guided Lindy into the one empty seat and we stood over her. I think she would have liked for him to take the seat but didn't dare suggest it. She did, without asking, take the duffel bag from him. She placed it on the floor and put her feet on it. She took his three rackets and stowed them in her lap. It would be Lindy's first subway ride, and Billy's too, unless his mother took him on the subway to see his father play that time when he was two. The subway hurtled and swayed down the track. I leaned down a little toward Lindy so both could hear me and showed them how to look for the signs at the subway stops. "Forest Hills is the fourth stop," I sounded off above the train's roar. "There'll be a sign there." Then it was coming up and Billy took the rackets and the duffel bag and we got off. I showed them the best route to the surface. "Go up one flight and cross over and go clear to the end," I said. "Then up again. It'll save you having to cross a street above." We climbed out of the shadows into the sunny day. My watch showed nine o'clock.

"Twenty-three minutes," I said. "Plus five minutes' walk to the club. I would allow an hour. Train schedules can vary depending on the time of day. So can waiting time."

"Allow one hour," Lindy said. "Got it."

From here all you had to do was follow the crowds. They were all moving one way to one place. We passed the block of stores, went under the viaduct of the Long Island Railroad, then turned right and walked the one block and then across the dead-end street that ended at the club and the address "One Tennis Place." We showed Billy's player's pass, my press pass and the clubhouse pass I had got for Lindy. We went past the guards and up the steps into the clubhouse. We moved slowly through the crowds and then out onto the terrace.

"So this is it," Lindy said.

"Those are the field courts, those Har-Trus. Those grass courts—Billy, you'll have to practice on them sometime for Wimbledon. And way down there is the Stadium."

Holding his three rackets and duffel bag, Billy looked off across the grass courts to the Stadium and the Center Court about three hundred yards away. The concrete shell stood tall and fort-like in the bright morning sun, its horseshoe shape open toward us. High on its rim, spaced clear around its circle, hung the eleven flags, representing the nations which had players playing today. The shell would hold 14,000—12,644 paid, the rest us freeloaders—and it was beginning to fill up for the opening. Billy stood and looked at it in silence.

"I better get changed," he said.

I found Lindy a chair on the terrace and Billy parked his rackets with her. He kept his duffel bag and I took him past the pink-coated Burns Security girl at the foot of the outside winding staircase and up it to the players' lounge. Furnished with eroded formica card tables and decayed vinyl couches, it looked like the waiting room in a West Side dentist's office. Players were standing around talking or sitting on chairs and couches blankly watching the elevated TV set. Two were playing backgammon at a card table. Billy and I went through and past the players' bar to the locker room. It was crowded with players sitting on benches changing. A man gave Billy his locker assignment, number 237, an upper locker with an open wire grid to let the gear air. From the two casement windows immediately beside it you could see the Stadium in the distance. Billy did not look out.

He took off his shirt and hung it in the locker. He took off the rest of his clothes and placed them neatly in the locker and stood naked, that almost perfectly sculpted body, a copper David. He opened the duffel bag and dressed out, pulling on jock, tan shorts and a matching shirt. He sat down and put on socks and his Converses. He took two wristbands out of the bag and put them on. He put the duffel bag in the locker and we went back out and down the winding staircase.

Catlo was waiting at one of the three practice courts by the clubhouse. He had the free can of Wilsons they had given him for practice and he opened another can he had brought. Billy went to the far side and they started rallying. Word moves mysteriously through Forest Hills. Soon people were coming up to look through the fence. I looked up and saw players gathering on the sun deck above to watch. It had been nine years since Robert Catlo, once ruler of all tennis, had stepped onto a Forest Hills court, even to rally. They wanted to see Catlo and, mainly because of Barney's TV Special, Billy. The man and boy hit for thirty minutes, a little of everything, loosening up. Then Catlo nodded to Billy and they talked a few moments at the net, then walked through the fence gate and started through the crowd. The autograph cultists went into action, wanting both of them now. Catlo and Billy gravely signed objects thrust up at them, pieces of paper, albums, tennis balls, racket covers, then Catlo said, "No more now" and they went through them. Billy left his rackets with Lindy and they went up the winding staircase. Catlo believed you were better if you took a shower between practicing and playing. Lindy and I waited for them on the terrace.

"I'm extremely nervous," she said. "Does it show?"

"No."

"Good. It does on you."

They were down in twenty minutes in fresh clothes, Catlo wearing slacks and carrying Billy's duffel bag. The fingers on Billy's right hitting hand were taped individually now, as his father had always done his to prevent blisters. Catlo would have wrapped them for him in the locker room. Just beyond us crowds of people, club members and others with enough drag to get a clubhouse pass, were massing against the terrace bar to receive their initial Bloody Marys of the day.

Lindy took a white handkerchief out of her purse and put it around Billy's neck and knotted it. Catlo looked at his watch.

"It's time," he said. "You've got Court Number Four. The boondocks. That's good."

Billy took his three rackets from Lindy and came down off the terrace and started down the walkway toward the court. In the distance he could see the Stadium, now nearly full, the mass of people visible in the open horseshoe. There, at the same time Billy began, Jack Tillotston, as the reigning champion, would be opening the tournament against the Number 1 player of the University of Michigan.

Billy opened the fence gate and stepped onto Field Court 4. He and Catlo exchanged a last quick glance. None of us spoke.

It was a pretty good match. The 300 bleacher seats were filled only because of the Barney show on Billy. As he played, Billy could hear the occasional roar from the 14,000 in the

Stadium. The opening of the horseshoe served as a funnel which poured the sounds over the field courts. Billy was shaky at first and dropped the first set to Leachman at two. The Australian's twist serve was kicking in fairly well. Then Billy settled in and began attacking the serve. With his speed he flew at the balls angling off court and started sending them down the line, passing Leachman. When Leachman tried to compensate by coming to the net closer to the sideline, Billy cross-courted him. Billy looked good to me, although I reminded myself that he was playing someone twice his age. He had the match at 2-6, 6-4, 6-3. Leachman went to the net to shake his hand and walked off with his arm lightly around Billy's shoulder, the net between them, to the bleachers where Catlo, Lindy and I were sitting. We got up.

"Big Cat," Leachman said softly. He was red-haired, freckle-faced and thirty-seven. He grinned that big Aussie grin of his.

"Hello, Art," Catlo said. "It's been a long time."

"I never could handle you, Cat," Leachman said. "But then neither could anybody fucking else. Do you have to bring the fucking kid along now to do it to me?"

Billy went off to change.

"He's all right," Leachman said. "He plays Kerby next. I was hoping to play the motherfucker myself. I know just how to handle him. Tell the kid to give him a lot of short balls. He can't handle the fucking short ball."

"Thanks very much, Art," Catlo said. "I'll tell him."

"I hope he goes a long fucking way," Leachman said. "It's good to have a Catlo back in the game." And walked off, carrying his rackets.

"Not bad for openers," Catlo said. "Art Leachman is nobody's patsy."

"He's nice," Lindy said. "He's fucking nice."

Catlo turned and stared at her, startled. She looked entirely bland.

In a little while someone came by and told us that Tilly had taken the University of Michigan 6-1, 6-0.

I was watching Jack Tillotston attend to Karl Dessauer, the young and promising West German, in the second round in the Grandstand when I became aware of friendly aircraft overhead. Every few minutes a big jet would amble across the sky and start floating down to La Guardia. One of them presently would be carrying Shelly. I was the recipient of major news. She had mysteriously got two extra days. I felt a quickening enlargement down there just thinking of her getting so near and looked furtively at the girl sportswriter sitting next to me. She was watching Tilly destroy Dessauer.

Tillotston had the first set at 6-1 and was leading 4-love in the second. Here in the Grandstand, with the bleachers coming right down to the court's edge, you could see the true ferocity of Tillotston's game. Here the big shots boomed in the ear, the ball streaking over the net with all the brute force of that strong, big body behind them. They seemed almost to be driving Dessauer from the court, to refuge. He seemed like a spectator at his own match. Not a single game had gone to deuce. Tillotston was in the killer mood. Of course he had that mood as a permanent part of his tennis weaponry, but I had often seen Jack Tillotston fool about in the early rounds, toying with his opponents, letting points, games or even a set go away with a carefree air before he decided it was time to annihilate somebody.

There was no carefree air here. He seemed, even this early, to want to wrap it up, as if he were already tasting his Big Four sweep and wanted to get it over with—and retire. Retire. The word seemed ludicrous watching him take Dessauer apart now. It seemed he should be years away from it. But of course retire was a euphemism. He wanted to retire into the money and power of television. Watching him now, I remembered something Jack Tillotston had once said to me.

"I have no intention of waiting until I am driven out of the game by the young pricks coming up. Like Catlo. I'm going to wipe out everybody in sight and leave with the trumpets sounding. Nobody is going to take my racket."

It was time to go. I got a cab to La Guardia, fifteen minutes away. I found the gate number and went on up the concourse to wait. Beyond the gate I could see the DC-9 taxiing in and pretty soon there she was, coming through the covered bridge toward me. How stunning she looked, how expensive, with that air of splendid carelessness. People turned to stare at her. She wore a summer dress of mauve paisley and a Panama. The dress seemed to nestle and insinuate around her body, clinging gently, with just hints of the treasures inside it. Then I felt them against me.

"My god," she said. "You can't be that way here. I am too. I don't suppose we could go somewhere right now."

"I know a man in the baggage room."

"No, I don't think so. Why don't we just let it build during the day?"

"Build?"

"I also came to see the tennis."

"Of course. The tennis."

The taxi driver actually got out and held the door. An absolute first.

"Good morning, Miss Blaine," he said.

For some reason I felt I had to give a big tip when I was squiring Shelly Blaine. We made our way through the clubhouse—more turning heads—and joined the crowds moving past the field courts. Fourteen thousand people would be on these rather tiny and cramped grounds, and most of them seemed to be constantly in motion, as if determined not to miss a single one of the twelve matches going on simultaneously. People would be watching a match on one court, then hear a roar go up from another and dash to that court to see what they were missing. Start watching that match, hear a roar from still another court and dash there. Except for the Stadium and the Grandstand, the courts have very few seats. Some short bleachers seating a few hundred at the most. There are a few priceless vantage points if you know them and can stake them out. For instance, you can stand at the top of the bleachers on Court 15 and simultaneously watch matches being played on Courts 15, 17, 18 and in the Grandstand. All at once and by the top players in the world. It's as if you could watch at one time the Dolphins playing the Cowboys, the Steelers playing the Vikings, the Rams playing the Patriots, and the Colts playing the Raiders. We worked our way through the thick crowds moving back and forth between the courts. It was tough going.

Whenever we stopped to get a glimpse of a match, other people would stop to stare at her. Then lay siege. The autograph freaks went into action. I was elbowed aside, pushed and body-blocked or body-spiked, usually on the blind side, in a manner that would have brought unsportsmanlike conduct penalties in another sport. I got pretty irritated. I couldn't decide whether she liked it or not. Whichever, she smiled, she had to smile, be nice. Once when she was signing, a fully grown man waiting his turn asked me, "Are you Mr. Blaine?" "Yes, sir," I said. I leaned close to his ear. "I'm the one who screws her." He looked at me peculiarly and moved off. One less to sign for, anyway. But I walked alongside wondering if I could ever be Mr. Shelly Blaine.

At four o'clock we went over to watch Billy take on Kerby on Court 6—a little closer to the Stadium this time. The 300 seats soon filled up. Again it went to three sets. Again Billy dropped the first set. It came out at 2-6, 6-3, 6-2. Billy's pattern was beginning to trouble me. He had dropped first sets in both rounds. He seemed to have a problem getting going once he stepped onto the court. At the end I heard Catlo say to him, "What were you *thinking* in that first set? I know what you weren't thinking about. *Tennis.*"

"I won, didn't I?" Billy said.

More and more, I had noticed, Billy was talking back. More and more he was being his own man.

Shelly and I were back in a taxi, crossing the Queensboro Bridge with Manhattan lighting up, when she told me.

"Brinkley, I've a surprise," she said. "I've arranged to do the show in New York all next week."

"You mean we have a whole week?" I leaned forward and told the driver, "Will you please scrub the Carlyle. Make it Patchin Place."

"Patchin Place?" he said. "What's that?"

"It's right across from where the Women's Jail used to be."

"Do you really want that?" Shelly asked me. "Remember, starting Monday I have to get up at five. I could stay at the Carlyle and we could see each other every night—early."

"Out of the question," I said. I lowered my voice so the driver couldn't hear. "When you're in my town, we screw at my apartment."

"What a filthy mouth you have."

"And I know where I'm going to use it."

"Don't be too smug. If you're smug or take me for granted, you'll only get to screw."

14

CROSSROADS

THAT WAS A NICE NIGHT. I GUESS RAVENOUS WOULD BE THE
operable word. I could not get enough of her, of her or of
her body. I could not look at it enough, touch it enough,
taste it enough, enter it enough. Lying there, that body so
splendid, so magical, with such a freshness about it, with its
clean lines, lanky, lithe, with no excess of flesh anywhere.
That heartbreakingly smooth flesh, its secret scents now in
blossom and making my body pound in desire. Flesh of soft
white, almost translucent, radiant, the hard breasts coming
alive in nipples of pink, echoing that pale red sparse crescent
below which guarded the moist entrance, that wild nectar
which came so sweetly flowing at the touch, of fingers, of lips.
That face, all lovely planes, transfigured in the act of love
into a face she would never see, only I.

We slept in until ten and were at it again.

"I call this rutting," she said.

I traced fingers lightly over her. Here, there. Her body
began to move softly.

"Just to be able to sleep until ten," she said. "And then
this. Oh, yes. Yes. Do that. Keep doing that. *Oh*. God, I like
doing things with you. Anything. Everything."

We had coffee and went on out to the tournament. One of
her perks was a chauffeured Rolls-Royce. "The network feels
it should furnish me with a proper saloon," Shelly said.
Theodore Dreiser, John Masefield, Djuna Barnes, e.e. cum-

mings, Eugene O'Neill all lived at one time or another in Patchin Place. But I don't believe any of them ever had a Silver Cloud waiting outside. After all, none had been the hostess of the Morning Show.

I felt silly sitting in the back seat of the Rolls saloon with her, immersed in the rich aroma of Connolly Brothers leather and surrounded by Circassian walnut panels that shone like glass and mirrored each other, my heels resting on the deep pile carpeting and my toes on the footrest, with a uniformed chauffeur dead ahead. This one was about sixty, with a tall, lean body of erect bearing, encased in a hauteur that said he knew exactly who he was and would be dislodged by no possible circumstance into being anything else. His gunmetal-grey uniform was immaculate, his white shirt speckless and starched, his chauffeur's cap square on his head, the black visor polished to the same sparkling gleam as his black shoes. His driving gloves spotless, his greying-white hair and steel-grey mustache trimmed to the millimeter, his accent cultivated, all of him proper, unbending, all of him *British*. I had never been sirred with such unservile assurance. I was not too surprised, one day while I was chatting with him and waiting for Shelly, to learn he had done nothing his whole adult life except drive a Rolls. He was rather like a Rolls-Royce himself and actually had been turned out by the Rolls Works at Crewe by the chauffeur-mechanic division. His name was Edwards.

Edwards at the helm of a Rolls Silver Cloud made for a remarkable driving experience through the streets of Manhattan and Queens. He had that touch of the pure driver, not the jerk-and-stutter of the average hackie, but a caress of the wheel and a synch with the machine itself. We glided through the streets. Or sailed. It was not like being in a car at all. Rather like a boat which never rolled and never pitched but slid soundlessly over a glass sea. At the clubhouse Shelly and I had some toast with apricot jam and more black coffee and watched each other as we ate and once touched crumbs off each other's lips. We were silly, we were surely in love.

That day I watched more Shelly than I did tennis. How I liked her for the way she saw and enjoyed little things. Like the ball boys and ball girls in their yellow shorts and blue shirts kneeling at net, leaning forward, fingers on the ground like a track runner in the starting blocks, while a point was played, then scurrying onto court, bobbed hair bouncing, snatching a ball and scurrying back and kneeling again, all in one rapid balletic movement. It was a charming act but not everyone would have seen it. Shelly did and was amused by it, got pleasure from it and so gave pleasure to me. How I liked being with her. Not being with her beginning to seem like dullness itself.

She was fascinated by the deportment of a number of the players. A casual tour of the courts produced a typical menu. Obscene gestures were popular today. The Finger was given on four occasions, two to the crowd, one to an official, one to an opponent. Two players walked over to specific spectators in the stands, one to say "Shut up," the other to say "Fuck off." A third went over to address the spectators as a group: "Assholes." Temper tantrums were in vogue. A player spat at a linesman. A player evinced his displeasure at a line call by walking to his chair and sitting down and pouting while the umpire pleaded with him, like a cowed father, please to come back and play. A player slapped a ball at a linesman. A player hit a ball at a cameraman. A player hit a ball at a spectator. A player went over and sat in the lap of a linesman. A player called an umpire "Dummy." A player swung a racket at an umpire. A player stuck out his ass at a linesman whose call he disliked. Called for a foot fault, a player furiously kicked off his shoe toward the guilty official. A match was delayed eight minutes in a dispute over a point while both players played not tennis but acute melodrama.

"Why, it's like *The Lord of the Flies*," Shelly said in fascination. "It's children-time and there are no rules."

"It's brat-time all right."

"I thought tennis was such a *proper* game," she said.

"That's all gone. It's evidently hard to tell a twenty-year-old making four hundred thousand a year how to behave. Somebody better start finding ways to tell them or they're going to tear the game apart."

We had lunch in the place below the stands where you can see the legs of the players through the screens, along with their asses, but not their heads. We drank rum collinses to deaden the taste of the food. We had shifted to iced coffee when Chester Barney hove into sight. He was wearing expensive multicolored patchwork jeans of half-foot squares of cloth. He wore his reverse-crocodile Lacoste and thonged sandals. The hair that flowered up above his fire-hydrant ears seemed to be in a somewhat new style. He greeted Shelly with a rush of the Barney effusion.

"The lovely Shelly Blaine. all r*iiii*ght!" he said, pulling up a chair. "Forest Hills is honored. Shelly, I'm free for funsies tonight between six and eight."

"What have you done to your hair, Chester?" Shelly said.

"Isn't it a pretty thing?" Chester said, trailing fingers back through his frizzies, now more pubic than ever. "It was my hairstylist's idea. Gives my image a touch of the radical-chic, Jules said. Jules says that's pretty important. Speaking of Jules, I must bring him here. Look at all those legs through there and those buns! This table would be heaven itself for sodomites. Well, Shelly doll, what do you think of our friend here moving into our terrain? My territorial imperative already feels threatened."

"What are you talking about, Chester?" Shelly said, but looking at me.

"I was going to tell you," I said and explained to her my new job on the Great Medium during the semis and finals.

"Well, well," Shelly said. "So the great superior print man has succumbed."

"Yes," I said. "I decided the time had come to sell out. Sooner or later they were bound to meet my terms."

"What might those be?" she said.

"Speaking of money," Chester said. "Shelly love, there's a big one going the rounds in the New York chitchat circles that you're about to abandon ship and sign aboard with us. They even say that's why you're in New York all this week."

"Do they?" she said.

"Fred admires you very much," Barney said.

"That's nice," Shelly said.

I had never known her so monosyllabic, as if she were watching herself very closely. As if this were much too important a subject for any horsing around with Chester Barney.

"Well, the bread I hear Fred's ready to shell out," Chester said. "I thought for a moment they were referring to the defense budget . . ."

I felt it was coming too close for comfort. "Chester," I said, "I don't think I've ever seen Tilly in such a hurry to get it over with. Have you?"

"I see," Chester said. "End of subject. And Billy's slow-starting, isn't he? He seems to get stronger the longer the match goes on. He likes to use that body of his. And isn't it a lovely body, Shelly?"

"Lovely," she said.

"He is playing it a little close to the bone," Chester said. "Those first sets. And of course he hasn't played in the Stadium yet."

"No, he hasn't," I said.

Chester looked thoughtfully through the screen at the disembodied legs flying back and forth.

"Somebody came up with the figure that this championship is worth about one million to the winner when you count everything. Any wonder they do naughty things now and then?"

He stood up abruptly. "Got to run, troops. I'm granting an interview to the tennis reporter of the Cedar Falls *Gazette*. Doubtless the football, baseball, basketball and skateboard reporter as well. He wants to know my secret."

"What is your secret, Chester?" Shelly said.

"Keep the bastards off balance," Chester said. "See you on court."

And he was gone.

"Let's get out of here," Shelly said. She stood up. "Let's go see some tennis."

I was looking up at her. "Does Fred have a prayer?"

"Oh, yes. Fred's the master genius at dreaming up an offer you can't refuse, then making it."

I decided to be direct. "Has he made it?"

She stood there a moment looking down at me. "Have you heard about the crossroads of life, Brinkley? Well, I'm there. Let's get out of here. I'm tired of looking at legs. And asses."

That night at Patchin Place she asked me, "What time is it?"

I looked at my watch. "Eight o'clock."

"I've got to go to bed."

"At your service," I said.

"No, I've got to go to sleep."

"Go to sleep! It isn't even dark."

"It will be when I get up at five o'clock tomorrow morning."

I must have seemed huffy. "It isn't my fault," she said. "I don't do it deliberately."

"Yes, I know that," I said.

"I'm not trying to hurt you by having to get up at five."

"I know you aren't." She seemed hurt herself, like a little girl. I must have been very forbidding. I was being unreasonable and I couldn't help it.

"Isn't it worth it?" she asked.

"Worth it?" I knew what she meant. "Of course it's worth it. I'd get up at two o'clock if it meant I could have you. It's just that—"

"Do you want me to go to the hotel?" she said.

"Don't be ridiculous."

When the alarm jangled at 5:00, I reached over and shut

it off. I turned toward her. She was all warm and she slept in nothing. The best is when you wake up with somebody, sleepy and full of desire. But she was quite awake. I guess she had learned to be.

"You know," she said, "I like what I know you are just about to do. But I've got to get up in five minutes."

"Five minutes is enough."

"Not if I'm not concentrating."

I had learned that, that a woman needs to concentrate. A man can do it half thinking but not a woman.

"So concentrate," I said.

"How can I concentrate if I have to remember that in five minutes I have to get ready for the studio."

I was getting too awake now myself. I could hear my own annoyed voice. The talk was killing it.

"Do you want to come or don't you?"

"Of course I want to come. But I also have to go."

More than once in that week we went at the subject again, just touching it. She was gentle, trying, coming more than halfway. In the end I felt compassion for her. I felt it for us.

And yet, beginning with the moment I saw her walking down that concourse ramp and straight into my arms, sometime between then and now I had made a decision. When had I made it? When I sat beside her in the Stadium and saw her joy at watching the scampering ball boys and ball girls? When I lay beside her and touched her nakedness? When she didn't go with me to Forest Hills but stayed in the city on some television business and I felt lost and lonely all day, some part of me missing, until I could get back to her? In truth the decision must not have been made. It must have just happened. The decision to do everything in my power to see to it that I spent every possible moment of my life with her. Nothing in life is so important as making sure, should you be lucky enough to find someone to love, that you get her for as many moments as possible. With Shelly's life and mine, I didn't know how much was possible.

15

PRIDE AND PREJUDICE

I HAVE SOMETIMES FELT THAT TENNIS IS ALMOST SECOND IN the skills required for victory at Forest Hills. If you cannot handle the other part, all the tennis skill in the world will get you nowhere.

The other part. The thing that happens when the body of an athlete is invaded by tension. We call it pressure and it is made up of many things, some unseen and unheard, some quite visible and audible. One of the audible ingredients is that Forest Hills lies on the approach lanes of La Guardia and on the main tracks of the Long Island Railroad. Above the courts the big jets roar in to land. Helicopters eggbeat the clouds. And of course there is the ubiquitous Goodyear blimp, without which no major American sport event could be held. The trains rattle by not a hundred yards beyond the Grandstand. Tennis players are notoriously sensitive to noise. In the Stadium it is common for a player about to serve to stop, catch the uptossed ball and complain angrily to the umpire of a phone ringing in the Marquee, or of people walking around in the seats above him. The only reason he does not complain about the other sounds bearing far higher decibel-counts is that he cannot complain to a train or a helicopter. Nonetheless I have seen the world's Number 2 player stop between his two serves, having netted the first, and scream to the umpire: "Tell the fucking blimp to go away!"

The other part. Even the mere act of getting to the courts

to play. The clubhouse sits at one end of the grounds and the Stadium at the other. Most of the field courts lie nested near the Stadium. The player cannot pass directly from locker room to playing surface, as in all other sports. Here the player—uptight, testy, on edge—must pass through 200 to 300 yards of fans. No player of any note can get from the locker room to a court of play without several or more assaults by the autograph fiends, grabbing him, thrusting paper, racket covers and tennis balls into his face for him to immortalize. There is no place to hide, to be alone, to think. No refuge anywhere. Even the players' lounge is crammed with commercial representatives, players' lawyers and advisers, and hangers-on who somehow got a pass.

And there is one thing more. The Center Court itself. The decision as to who plays in the Stadium is simple. A well-known, ranking player plays there. Unknowns never face each other in the Stadium. In the first or second round, a newcomer has a remote chance of playing there—but only so that a big seed can take him apart. By the fourth round the seeds are normally playing each other there. If an unseeded player survives, he will likely play his first Stadium match in the later rounds, under the absolute maximum of pressure: meeting a world-rank player, and one carrying a hot streak in this very tournament, before a full house. It will probably be the first time he has ever played before an audience of more than a few hundred.

The Stadium. I have seen players there in seizures of tension, some vomiting into their towels on the odd-game change. I have seen players of much skill at the game of tennis entirely come apart. For until a young player takes the long walk from the clubhouse, past the courts of grass, past the field courts, through all the people and on through the striped Marquee and under the Kipling quote about how you're supposed to treat victory and defeat, and steps at last onto its surface and looks up to see the thousands waiting to observe his every move and shot and hears the umpire say "Play," he can never be sure what will happen when he faces his most merciless, unforgiving enemy of all, the Center Court.

Nobody had solved the harassment problem like Jack Tillotston. He never even set foot in the locker room. He simply did not choose to fraternize with the other players. Tillotston changed at the St. Regis Hotel in midtown Manhattan and got into a rented Carey limousine. It was timed to arrive shortly before his match. The limousine would enter the Forest Hills reserved parking lot and drive to the very end, next to the Grandstand. Tillotston would get out, carrying six rackets, and proceed to his court, whose number he had obtained by phone before leaving the hotel. The prestige courts are all situated near the Grandstand and Stadium and hence near the parking lot. Jack Tillotston was scheduled only on prestige courts. There he would go about the business of demolishing his opponent. Having completed his work-load for the day, usually in an hour or so, he would gather up his rackets and go straight back to the parking lot where the limousine would be waiting. He would then be conveyed back to the St. Regis.

One thing this daily pattern meant. Tilly was not even taking practice hits before playing. And this could only mean one of two things, as far apart as could be imagined. Either he felt so sure, had such an edge that he did not want to leave it on a practice court. Or he felt he had to save all his reserves. Which of the two it was could say everything.

Two brief conversations.

Tish was an anchor for Robert Catlo. Someone to count on. Like the men who had come to Jekyll Island she had great wealth. Behind that air of luscious appetites, of using that wealth to gratify them wherever wealth would help her do so, I felt she could have dealt and connived with Jekyll's champions in shrewdness—with a Morgan, with a Vanderbilt. In fact I had the impression she was using her time in New

York, aside from shopping at Bergdorf's, to do something not far from that—there had been passing references to conferences at United States Trust Company at 45 Wall, with her attorneys in the General Motors Building three blocks from the St. Regis. But like all of us who try going it alone, who come back to empty living spaces, whether a New York apartment or a Palm Beach palace by the sea, I knew she knew she was missing the one thing that makes life worthwhile or even bearable. Someone to share it with, someone to *be* with once the door is closed, whether it be the hollow-core door of the apartment or the vast solid teak double doors of the palace. She said as much to me one day in the King Cole Bar while we waited for Catlo to join us. Then we were picking up Shelly at her studio for dinner. Tish had been to Forest Hills once. "I don't mind tennis," she said, "but sitting eight hours in an oven is not my idea of how to spend your time in New York." The real reason, I think, was that she felt Catlo was better off without any outside distractions. But she was making her own contribution to reducing the joint Forest Hills pressure effort. Catlo was less and less at the Summit and more and more at the St. Regis.

"Isn't it ridiculous," she said as we stroked our drink glasses, "that the money is what keeps me from having Catlo. I don't know anything sillier than male pride. Pride! What does it matter who has the money. The important thing is to *have* the money."

"It makes that much difference?"

"Oh, yes," she said. "Money is the real difference in life."

"I'm not so sure," I said. "I haven't known that many rich people—I mean *rich*—but I've known a few. I'm not ready to say that it's bought them all happiness."

She looked into her drink. "I think you'd agree with me that more unhappiness comes from not having money than from having it. But you're right. It's not that it will buy you happiness. It's more that money will buy you out of the grey times. But . . . well, the bright times are not all that bright and shiny blue if you have to have them alone. Catlo!" she said in exasperation.

Suddenly, with something of the same exasperation, she turned on me.

"What about you and Shelly?"

"What about us?"

In the enormous twin mirrors across the room we could see reflected Maxfield Parrish's mural of King Cole.

"You'd be as stupid as Catlo to let that get away from you."

Into the mirror came Robert Catlo.

"What are you two talking about?" he said.

"Stupidity," she said.

Two days later. Same place. Talking and now and then looking at King Cole in the great mirrors. Waiting for Tish to come down for drinks.

"By god, I'm glad Tish is here," Catlo said. "I couldn't do it without her."

Quite an admission coming from him.

"No, you couldn't," I said. "What's more, I have a notion that when a man finds someone like Tish, he'd better tie her down—with knots."

Catlo shook his head. "It doesn't work if the lady has the big stuff. It's that simple. Not with me. Hell, you're the same way. You couldn't be Mr. Shelly Blaine any more than I could be Mr. Tish Milam."

How much better we see others than we see ourselves. Even in the biggest mirror in New York. In it Tish was standing there. We stood up.

"What are you two talking about?" she said.

"Knots," I said.

It was the fourth round. In the third, Billy had received a pure gift. That morning the tournament referee's phone rang to tell him that Adriano Barzini, Billy's opponent for the third round, was down with severe stomach cramps, due to undigested cherrystones. The young Roman lay moaning and immobile in his hotel room, cursing all clams in a language beautiful for such expression. Grateful to the unseeded shellfish that had removed Barzini from play, Billy and Catlo had spent the free time of the forfeited match in the stands, studying Jack Tillotston as he sent Zeijko Jausovec, the fine Yugoslav player, back to Belgrade with a 6-1, 6-3 tourist-class ticket. Now Tillotston and Billy each had to subdue two more opponents if they were to meet across a net.

Both were playing at 11:30. Tillotston and Curry Arlen, who had reached the quarterfinals last year, were in the Stadium. Billy and Ron Whitcomb, seed 16, were in the Grandstand. Whitcomb was thirty-four years old, once ranked ninth on the world list and was now better known as a doubles player. In doubles he and Rowan, the Australian, were ranked third. Doubles is as different a game from singles as is the married life from the single one, and for some of the same reasons. Like any good doubles player Whitcomb was a tactician more than a shotmaker. He had a round, even somewhat tubby body. He based his game on making his opponent run as much as possible. To achieve this, Whitcomb employed a fine repertory of spins and lobs, touch shots and placements. A relatively soft game but a dangerous player, even in singles. He had the baldest head in tournament tennis.

I wanted to see both matches and had seats for the only way you could do it. I bought two icy Coors and guided Shelly to the sun side of the Stadium. We climbed to the highest row at the very end of the concrete. From there we could watch Tillotston playing in the Stadium before a full house of 14,000. By turning our heads, we could see Billy playing in the Grandstand below to a full house of 1,500, his largest crowd so far.

It was the worst kind of New York day, wet, sticky. On our side of the Stadium it was like sitting in the mouth of a blast furnace. People covered their heads with newspapers or their eyes with the Mr. Peanut visor sunshields given free to spectators. The flags of the player nations hung limp against the poles. We sipped our beers, sweated and watched. We would suffer cricks in our necks before the matches were over but it was a sight to see, the big man straight ahead, then with a turn of the head the boy below us. It was eerie: as they played, Tillotston and Billy could hear very clearly the roars that went up from some point played by the other.

Tillotston finished quickly. Nothing bothered him. Neither his opponent nor the heat. No fooling around, no coasting, no fun, no mercy. Six-1, 6-1, and the points themselves going quickly as Tillotston brutally closed them off. In fifty-two minutes by my watch he was on his way back to the St. Regis in his limousine.

In the Grandstand, Billy was having as different a match as could be imagined. Not only were he and Whitcomb playing even in games. Most of them also went to deuce. When Tillotston left, Billy had just dropped the first set at 6-7 on a tie breaker.

"Let's go down there," I said.

We made our way down the long flights of seats and out and across and climbed through the ropes into the press section of the Grandstand. Beneath the far windscreen I could see people lying flat on their stomachs looking under it. Above them some boys were perched in an oak tree. Across the court in the stands I saw Catlo and Lindy just behind him. A long makeup of the Long Island Railroad went by with a shattering roar just beyond the Grandstand.

The press box in the Grandstand is so close to the players that you can almost reach out and touch the one receiving serve in the ad court. Billy would have known that the Tillotston match was over because the roars had stopped. And he would have known by the quickness of it that Tillotston had won. Nevertheless as he was walking back from a volley at the net he looked over at me.

"How did he do?" he said.

"One and one," I said.

Billy turned to receive serve, crouched, body swaying. I heard him talking to himself, in Spanish.

The second set seemed to go on forever. The two players were dead even, locked in an embrace from which neither could free himself, the games themselves going repeatedly to deuce before one or the other took it. The crowd had become exceptionally quiet, watching strong tennis. Watching the boy down one, down to a set he had to win, fight to stay alive in this tournament. He was going for it, not playing conservatively but hitting out, staking everything on his big shots, blazing away at the ball, *slugging* the ball. His opponent, giving up fifteen years, summoned all the sly artistry of those years to drive the boy out with spins, with lobs, with placements. It went right into another tie breaker, which Billy took with three points to spare. Sets were 1-all. Six-7, 7-6.

"Ay, Catlo," someone in the stands sang out.

Two sets had gone as far as sets could, twenty-six games— long games at that. Two men testing each other to the limits. The midday heat testing both. The heat was demonic, draining, an airless, wet, malevolent calm, a heatstroke day. One seemed to gasp for breath. The players, drenched in sweat, continually wiped the handles of their rackets with towels between points. On one point Whitcomb's racket flew out of his hand and slid across the court. When he was receiving serve close to me, I could see his cranium sunburned a fiery red. On it stood large globules of sweat. His fair hair was plastered wet against his temples.

Then it was the third set and it began to happen. At the odd-game crossovers Billy would be out on the court, ready to go, and Whitcomb would still be sitting in his folding chair by the net post. "Mr. Whitcomb," the net judge would say, "it's time. It's time, Mr. Whitcomb."

The legs were gone, the body was gone. And Billy still strong. I thought of that big dune in Florida, of Billy pushing himself up it in the August heat. I heard Catlo driving his son, *"only eighteen more,"* and I saw Billy's body wrapped in sweat, heard him panting as he struggled up it. Toward the end I felt pity for Whitcomb.

But it was the way Billy went through the third set. He never let up. Having seen his opponent near exhaustion, he went at him with ferocity, his cocked body erupting against the ball, scorching shots low and hard down the line and as far away from Whitcomb as possible, cross-courting to one side and then the other, delicately slicing underspin drop shots just over the net to make him run. As a doubles player Whitcomb was used to having help on the court. He had no help now. Twice Billy put away overheads so fiercely that the ball bounced high over Whitcomb's head and over the fence. After each that strange chilling cry came from somewhere in the stands, "Ay, Catlo." I had to remind myself that it was not for that other Catlo who had once ruled all of tennis. Now it was for Billy. The cry seemed to send fresh strength and resolve through Billy's body. Going for every point, not letting one point get away from him if anything in him could prevent it. Going at Whitcomb ruthlessly, with all he had, all his youth. Billy had it at 6-3 and the match.

It was a Billy I had never seen. I knew what had been born within Billy Catlo in that third set. Killer instinct. He had seen Whitcomb's exhaustion, had smelled blood, and had gone for him.

I walked across the court to where he was standing next to his father. Catlo was looking at him as one looks at a stranger.

We stood on the scuffed and battered court, knowing that Billy had reached the quarterfinals. The win had given him a new confidence. Standing there, the three rackets tucked under his arm, he had a certain air. I had the feeling of something being repeated, something from the past, elusive and tantalizing.

"Now for Wilkins," Billy said.

Lonnie Wilkins was the great moonballer. Seed Number 4.

We took the Rolls back to Patchin Place, Shelly and I. I was watching the back of Edwards' head, still trying to remember.

"Some win," I said. "Billy did it to him, didn't he?"

"I'm not sure I liked it. Something about him . . . it scared me a little. I think I liked him better the other way."

Then I remembered. The way Billy had gone after Whitcomb, the savagery of it, going at him without any mercy at all when he saw his weakness, going for the kill: I had seen it before. At Wimbledon. Eight years ago when Jack Tillotston did it to Billy's own father.

She told me about it after dinner at Mistral. "Brinkley, I have something to say," she said.

We were over coffee and I looked at my watch. "But it's bedtime," I said. "It's eight-thirty."

"Well, screw eight-thirty," Shelly said. "I'm planning to get very sick tonight—I feel faint already—and you're going to phone and tell them. The offer from MBC is this." She went right to it. "First off they will give me a lot of money. So much money I don't even like to say it."

"That's a lot of money."

"Second, they will give me my own show. Sunday night at seven. Called 'Shelly Blaine Interviews.' It's a terrible title but we can change that. I'll be able to concentrate on one show a week and the one thing I think I do best, which is interviews. Instead of that carnival midway of two hours every day trying to do everything. And oh yes. I'll never have to get up at five A.M. again. I can date like other girls."

We waited while I tried to digest all this. "Well," I said. "Well. Old Fred-Fred. You were right. He knows how to make the unrefusable offer. When do you start?"

"I haven't accepted."

"Haven't accepted? What do you want. A third of the network?"

"I'm still thinking about it," she said. "I'm to let them know Monday."

It would be the day after the finals at Forest Hills. Altogether it promised to be quite a weekend for crossroads.

"What do you need to think about?"

"I don't know." I had never seen her so indecisive. She had always known exactly what she wanted, where she was headed and how to get there. "I just want to think it over."

She waited a moment and looked at me.

"I almost forgot," she said. "There's another item in the switch if I make it. I'd be doing the show from New York."

"New York?" I said. "That's where I live."

"Will you go make that phone call now and come back?"

I stood up. "What is it you're down with?" I said.

She looked up at me. "Well, I'm really down with you, aren't I? But I don't think they'd understand that. You'll think of something."

16

A PROPER SALOON

MEASURE BY MEASURE LINDY HAD TAKEN OVER. SHE CARRIED
the subway tokens. She carried the handkerchiefs to tie around
Billy's neck. One day she asked Catlo how to tape fingers.
After hesitating and looking at her suspiciously, he showed
her, using his own hand, and she took over doing that for
Billy too. When Billy got a trace of a blister she applied the
tincture of benzoin from the small bottle she started carrying
in her purse. Every night she packed his duffel bag with the
shirts, shorts, shoes, socks, wristbands he would require the
next day. By the fourth round even Catlo grudgingly admitted
to me that she was not just a camp follower. "She's earning
her keep," he managed to say.

When Billy ran low on some of the battle dress of tennis,
she went shopping for him. She asked me to guide her to the
best store. We went out the afternoon of the night Billy was
to play Lonnie Wilkins. His first match against a moonballer
and his first night match. And something else new. Starting
with the quarterfinals, the sets would be three out of five.
Stamina would become a more important factor.

We left the hotel about 4 P.M. and I took her to Bloomingdale's.

"Four jockstraps and two dozen wristbands," she told the
sporting goods clerk in a crisp, businesslike manner.

"What?" the clerk said. "How many?"

"Four jockstraps," she said. "And two dozen wristbands."

After making these purchases we walked down Lexington where she halted at a drugstore and bought four bottles of rubbing alcohol.

"That's a lot of alcohol," I said as we went out. "Do you drink it?"

"No, I don't drink it," she said tartly. "I use it to give Billy his rubdowns."

"I see," I said.

"A tennis player uses a lot of muscles," she said, as if educating me in the nuances of the game. "Also Billy gets pretty tense and a rubdown at the end of the day helps him relax."

"I imagine it does. His room or yours?"

"You needn't be so smart about it. *All* I do is give him a rubdown."

"Did I say anything different?"

"No. But I know what you're thinking."

The match with Wilkins was scheduled for 7:30 P.M. Billy, Catlo and Lindy were leaving the Summit at 6:00 to take the subway to Forest Hills. Shelly was meeting me at the hotel at 6:30 and we would go out in our usual stylish fashion, in the Rolls. Due to surface traffic, a subway was the fastest way to get to Forest Hills but I willingly gave up speed for grandeur. At the hotel I waited for Lindy in the lobby and she came down in fifteen minutes, carrying Billy's duffel bag. I handed her the Bloomingdale's package of jockstraps and wristbands. Catlo appeared a few minutes later.

"Where's Billy?" he said. Catlo still talked rather briskly to her.

"What do you mean?" she said, brisk herself. "In his room, I guess."

"No, he isn't. I thought he was with you."

"Well, he isn't. As you can see."

Catlo looked at his watch. It was six o'clock. We waited fifteen minutes. No Billy.

"God damn," Catlo said. "Where is he?"

He kept looking at his watch. He got a key from the desk

clerk and went upstairs to get Billy's rackets. He came back and another quarter hour went by. Promptly at 6:30 P.M. the Silver Cloud made port in front of the marquee, Edwards alighting and holding the door. I leaned past his tall, at-attention body in its impeccable uniform and told Shelly the situation. She got out and we joined the others in the lobby. By 6:45 Catlo was really worried. And angry.

"For god's sake, where *is* he?" he said. "That match starts in forty-five minutes."

With perfect subway connections they could leave right now and be at Forest Hills in thirty minutes. Perfect connections, a subway just sitting there waiting. Subways didn't often do that in my experience. But if they were very lucky, that would give Billy a quarter hour to change and he could make it in a squeeze. The only trouble with this marvelous plan was that he wasn't there. Catlo looked at his watch again.

"Six-fifty. Mother of God."

"What happens if he isn't there at seven-thirty?" Lindy asked.

"What happens," Catlo said sharply, "is that they give him fifteen minutes and then, if he's not there and ready to play, default him. On the dot. At Forest Hills they would default Jesus Christ if He was sixteen minutes late for the Second Coming."

It was seven o'clock. Catlo kept pacing the lobby. At 7:05 Billy came through the revolving door. Catlo sprang at him.

"Where have you *been*?" he said. He was shouting. People turned to look.

"I went to Brinkley's place," Billy said quite calmly. "I couldn't find Lindy so I went to Brinkley's place."

"*My* place?" I shouted too. The whole lobby was looking at us.

"*His* place?" Lindy shouted, angrily. "What would I be doing at *his* place."

"You tell me," he said. "What would you be doing at his place?"

"I was *shopping* for you," Lindy said. She was furious. "You said you needed some jockstraps. Well, here they are." And she rammed the package into his hands. "*Four* jockstraps."

"Knock this off!" Catlo said coldly. "I don't know what this is all about and I don't care. All I care about is how we get Billy to Forest Hills."

He looked at his watch. "It's seven-ten. *If* the subway is there waiting for us we might make it. *If* it doesn't get stuck somewhere underground."

Actually there had been more than one case of a Forest Hills default due exactly to that: a player failing to arrive because of a subway delay.

Catlo thought for a second. "No, we can't risk it. We've got one chance. A taxi."

"How about the Rolls?" Shelly said. "I think it'll be faster. Billy can change in the car. And I've got a good driver."

It was exactly what I would have expected of her in a crisis. Cool, decisive, cutting through to the best available solution.

"Right," Catlo said immediately.

We started through the revolving doors. The Silver Cloud stood in front of the parked cabs, dignified, majestic, the famous slender stainless steel panels of her radiator brilliantly reflecting the early evening light. Behind her a barrel-shouldered hackie was leaning out of his window and giving Edwards what for.

"Will you *move* that motherfucker?" the hackie said. "Those spaces are for taxicabs, limey."

"Watch your language, my good man," Edwards said with his Rolls hauteur. "Don't you know that public obscenity is a punishable offense?"

"Edwards," Shelly interrupted, "do you think you can get us to Forest Hills in"—she looked at her watch—"twenty-seven minutes?"

"Twenty-seven minutes, madam?" Edwards looked at the Rolls saloon as if he were seeing in a new light the vehicle he had spent his life driving. An expression of anticipation touched those austere features. "Would that be a serious matter?"

"Very serious," Shelly said.

"With pleasure, madam," Edwards said. "I've always wondered what she could do."

And he opened the rear door.

Lindy, Billy and Catlo piled into the back seat. Shelly and I hurried around and got in the front. Edwards swung the Rolls into the Lexington Avenue traffic. The saloon hummed to Fiftieth, the engine purring richly as if wanting to be given rein, picked up a green light and turned left on Fiftieth to Third Avenue, caught another green light onto Third with its six lanes of one-way traffic. Accelerating, Edwards weaved the vehicle expertly in and out of lanes as a space opened, making for the far right lane as Fifty-ninth Street approached. He took the Bloomingdale's corner in a glide, whipped crosstown to Second Avenue, crossed Second and angled the saloon left into the chute for the upper level of the Queensboro Bridge.

The five-lane bridge across the East River came quickly into sight. I could see two lanes green light going to Long Island and three lanes red light coming into Manhattan. As traffic piled up ahead of the fast-rushing Silver Cloud, Edwards hopped into the nearest red-light lane and whipped down it. Then, its top coming up from a rise in the bridge like a ship's mast over the horizon, I saw a big semitrailer roaring down on us. I closed my eyes and then opened them at a continuous blast of truck horn to see the face of the truck driver, screaming something I could not hear. The Rolls spun to the right and slid down the aluminum length of the huge trailer with inches of freeboard, swinging back into the green-light lane.

"For Christ's sake, Edwards!" Shelly said.

"You said it was serious, madam." Edwards' proper British voice had a note of donnish reproof.

The saloon leaping to his foot, Edwards aimed it on the bias toward the far right lane and took the curve off the bridge into Queens Boulevard. He squeezed into the one lane under a subway which roared overhead. Almost immediately a stoplight on red gleamed ahead of us. Edwards, cool eyes glancing at the cross-traffic from either direction, sped through it to face still another red light no more than fifty yards on. On the left I saw the elevated subway on an arched cement structure that looked like an ancient Roman aqueduct. The Rolls and the subway were neck and neck on their parallel roadways. Edwards went through the second red light, skillfully aiming his way between two cross-traffic cars, the second expressing its outrage in a blast of car horn and a screech of rubber.

"Way to go!" I heard Lindy say from the back seat. She looked exhilarated. Between her and Catlo, Billy was beginning to change. Lindy was ready for him, the duffel bag open on her lap. Catlo ignored the drive. He was talking to Billy as calmly as though they were conversing across a net. He was giving him reminder advice on how to play Wilkins.

"He's all topspin. Remember, you like to play those big-topspin characters. The ball comes up and sits right there like a piece of cake. You're going to smash it down his throat. How's the time?" he asked me.

"Seven twenty-three."

"Remember," Catlo said, "he's got something more than a moonball. He's got a great passing shot."

Across the glistening hood of the Rolls the Boulevard was broadening into five lanes with the lane on the far right for parking. A McDonald's whipped past and a whir of cheap-looking one-story shops and bars. Edwards seemed transformed. I was certain he had never driven a Rolls in this manner, but he was doing it eagerly, as if this was his chance of a lifetime, one he never dreamed of having. We were approaching a huge Mobil gas station at an intersection with a traffic light showing red and a considerable line of cars waiting for it to change. Edwards swerved the Rolls and screamed

into the station. I saw an attendant leisurely filling a Volks-
wagen with gas while chatting with the driver. The attendant
looked up to see the Rolls racing toward him, abandoned
the gas nozzle and jumped to the raised gas-tank platform.
The Rolls swung left and through the station and out of it
toward the green light from the cross direction. Edwards
gave her hard right helm and she went through the light and
back onto the Boulevard.

"Jesus," Shelly said.

"Beautiful!" I heard Lindy say. "Just beautiful." She looked
out. "We're beating the subway!"

In the back seat Billy had removed his shirt and jeans.
Lindy, looking the other way, had opened the package and
was feeding him one of the brand-new jocks.

The scene ahead was changing. The subway, now bested,
curved away to the left as if quitting the field in ignominy and
the Boulevard became grander and wider, the view more
open.

"Ah-h-h," Edwards said in the tones of a prospector finding the mother lode. "Look at those islands. Aren't they just
lovely?"

Over the Spirit of Ecstasy sitting like a ship's figurehead
atop the radiator, three lanes appeared in the center for the
main road and three lanes on the outside as a service road
feeding into it. Separating the two, a series of islands, between
which traffic could leave or enter. The islands were no more
than six inches higher than the roadway and were adorned
with thin lampposts and small trees.

Edwards immediately began using the islands. When traffic
jammed up ahead of him he swerved between two islands,
hummed down the service road until he saw free space opening up on the main road, then swung between two more
islands and back onto it. He kept cutting smoothly in and
out of the two roads between the islands. The maneuverability
of the car was a wonder, the steering brilliantly responsive,
the handling astonishingly light. But I also knew we had a

passionately skilled driver handling her. It was less speed that was moving us onward than it was masterly driving, picking and diving into the holes as they appeared, weaving us in and out of the maze of traffic. Suddenly as the Rolls started between two islands, a car entered. Edwards instantly veered left and took the saloon over the island itself between a lamppost and some trees. We all rose abruptly in our seats before settling back.

I looked into the back seat. Billy had his shorts on and was taking his shirt from Lindy and pulling it over his head. She helped him straighten it in back.

"Remember, the greatest danger in playing a moonballer is impatience," Catlo was saying. "Along about the eighty-fourth ball to come over a net on one point, you get so furious that you charge the net without setting up for it and he passes you. Take the net, but only after you set up with the right approach shot. Get your approach shot right and you can take away his passing game. What's the time?" he asked me.

"Seven twenty-nine."

Sixteen minutes to make it. We were throttling straight down the Boulevard now. I did not choose to look at the speedometer. Ahead on our right I saw a sign "3rd Calvary Cemetery of St. Sebastian" over a stone pillar entrance. Beyond the eight-foot walls I got a glimpse of acres of tombstones. My god, I thought, there must be enough people in there to populate the entire city of Syracuse. Still they'd have room for six more of us. Six blocks of tombstones and a couple hundred thousand stiffs rushing past us and giving way to long rows of the living in drab two-story buildings, motels, gas stations, used-car lots.

We came onto traffic and Edwards took the Silver Cloud between two islands and shot down the service road, whipping around some vehicles in the near lane. He was cutting back onto the main road ahead of the traffic when a car in that lane bore down on him. Instantly Edwards swung the wheel hard right and straight toward a Mercedes Benz Service and Repair lot where two superb German shepherds stood at attention behind a wire fence. As the Rolls headed for them, they charged the fence and started barking violently at it. They probably like only Mercedes, I thought stupidly. Edwards swung the saloon and slid along the curb, cut across the service road, plunged between two islands and went sailing back up the main road.

"Did you see him accelerate that way!" Edwards exclaimed. "No consideration at all. When it comes to driving, the motherfuckers don't know their arse from the Queen's bonnet. Begging your pardon, madam."

"Not at all, Edwards," Shelly said.

A shopping center appeared ahead. The vehicular density thickened greatly and Edwards cut between islands to the service road and hummed down it. Cars were parked heavily in the far right lane. Suddenly the Rolls was blocked entirely by a retinue of double-parked cars.

"Look at that!" Edwards said in outrage. "Double parked! Absolutely illegal!"

He rolled around the parked cars and jumped the Rolls onto the wide sidewalk. Moving rather slowly now to give the foot traffic time to disperse and for the first time using the Rolls horn, held continuously, he scooted down the sidewalk. We cruised past Seaman's Fine Furniture and the Queens Delicatessen Restaurant and Coffee-Shop, where people looked out windows with forks or cups raised and studious expressions. At the end of the block was a "Learn to Drive" office. Here a subway entrance blocked the sidewalk, forcing Edwards back onto the more customary passageway for vehicles. The saloon departed the sidewalk between parked cars and came back onto the service road.

We could see the main road funneling into an underpass, the service road remaining at street level. Edwards dived between two islands onto it and shot through the underpass. I looked back and saw Lindy put a handkerchief around Billy's neck and knot it.

"He'll try to play you all night," Catlo was saying, "and make every point last an hour and take you to five sets and collapse you. He'll try to make it an endurance contest, not tennis. He'll try to slow-ball you to death. Hit at him so hard he can't do it. Make him think it's a rocket coming back at him." Catlo looked at me.

"Seven minutes," I said. Billy was putting on his shoes.

"It'll be close. Hit at him the way *you* hit. Hard, deep, low, clean. Put the ball in the corners. Put the ball on the baseline. Billy?"

"Yes, sir."

I had not heard that "sir" in a while. When Catlo spoke his voice was quiet, soft, but it had steel in it.

"I know he's favored. He shouldn't be. You can take him. If we can get there, you can do it. You can have him for supper. Give him a tennis lesson."

We came out of the tunnel onto a plain of four- and five-story apartment buildings separated by blocks of neighborhood stores and shops. "Forest Hills Bakery—Everything Fresh Daily," a sign read. Then another sign showed "Yellowstone Boulevard," and a curving exit road. When Edwards took the curve, a tire blew—the curb-hopping, no doubt. The Silver Cloud stumbled a moment, then bounced onto the sidewalk and into the red canopy of the Tung Shing House and settled there in a shroud of canvas. A furious elderly Chinese came out shouting in shrill Mandarin, followed by a retinue of waiters and cooks. Billy was tying on his shoes.

"What have we got?" Catlo said, getting out.

"Four minutes," I said. "It's four blocks."

"Leave the rackets. Take off, Billy," Catlo said.

"Edwards and I will see to this," Shelly said, already fending off the Chinese hordes.

"No problem," Edwards said.

We all grabbed rackets. Catlo, Lindy and I started running down Yellowstone, Billy widening the lead. Somewhere behind us I could hear a police siren. Above, September's new moon was starting up the sky. We ran left on Burns Street past some Tudor houses. Suddenly there it was, all aglow, rising above the trees. Up ahead in the dusk I could see the white shadow of Billy running hard toward the great concrete Stadium.

17

FORGETTING TENNIS

THE 14,000 IN THE LIGHTED STADIUM HAD BEEN WHISTLING —the polite tennis version of the Bronx cheer—to show their displeasure at being kept waiting. They were startled to see a young man wearing tennis clothes burst from the Marquee in full flight, sprint across the court, black hair flying, and come to a sliding stop in front of two men standing at the foot of the umpire's chair. One of the men was Lonnie Wilkins, also in tennis clothes. It was said of Wilkins that he was the shortest player and hit the highest balls on the circuit. The other man, wearing a navy-blue blazer and grey slacks, was the referee Pat Hargraves, a tall, unflappable man from Bath, Maine. He had spent a lifetime officiating at tennis matches and dealing with tennis temperaments. He was looking at his watch.

"Seven forty-three and thirty-nine seconds," Hargraves said as Billy almost plowed into him. "I wouldn't want to see you cut it much closer. Are you ready to play?"

"Yes, sir!" Billy said. He was breathing so heavily from his long sprint that he could barely get out the words. But relief flooded his face. He was in. Then he looked up and for the first time became aware of the thousands of faces looking down at him. They were more than he had ever seen at any tennis match, much less a match that he himself was going to play in.

Hargraves held the watch for Wilkins to see. "Well, he made

it, Lonnie," he said. "Isn't that nice? Bad business having a default as late as the quarterfinals."

Lonnie Wilkins was born querulous and tennis had made him more so. He found it possible to get through life without the grace of humor. With those high, lofting balls of his, a game in which the idea was not to go for a winner but to keep the ball in play until your opponent made an error, he had kept many other men waiting, and exasperated, across the net. But he had not liked to be kept waiting now, and he liked even less missing a free ticket into the semifinals by a minute and twenty-one seconds.

"Doesn't the rule say he has to be ready to play?" Wilkins said. "Where are his rackets?"

Billy looked across the court where his father was standing at the edge of the Marquee.

"My father has them."

"Your father? I didn't realize that was the Catlo I was playing."

"All right, boys," Hargraves said.

"Just because his name is Catlo," Wilkins said, "I don't see why he has to be given special consideration."

Wilkins had gone too far. No one questioned Pat Hargraves' impartiality, his absolute integrity. "No special consideration is being given," he said with a warning note in his voice. "The rule states that a player has fifteen minutes before being defaulted. Billy Catlo had to be there at seven forty-five. He was here at seven forty-three and thirty-nine seconds, in his tennis clothes, ready to play. He is going to play. That question has been decided. The question now is, are *you* going to play? I wouldn't want to consider the possibility of a second default in the same match."

Wilkins waited a moment, glaring. "I'll play," he said. "Under protest."

"Your privilege." No protest against a Hargraves ruling had ever been upheld. He looked up at the umpire and said, "Charley, I think you can announce the match."

The incident may have been a blessing. Billy had been too preoccupied with just getting there to incur any very bad case of Stadium terrors. But he couldn't get going in the first set and Wilkins took it easily at one. Then Billy, back to full strength, went at Wilkins with those deep, hard-hit balls. It turned into a tightly-played match with two tie breakers. Wilkins could not crack Billy either physically or mentally by imposing his slow moonball game on him. In the fourth set Billy's attacking game finally broke the spirit of the Human Metronome. It was nearly eleven when Billy closed it out at 1-6, 7-6, 7-6, 6-2. He was in the semifinals against Jack Tillotston.

Catlo had called Tish to tell her what had happened. When the match was over there she was, waiting for us with a Carey limousine. Going back to Manhattan Billy sat tired and quiet in a corner of the car listening to us plan the coming day. I wondered why he wasn't excited over beating Wilkins and having Tillotston finally on a court. Maybe now that he was there, he suddenly realized what he had to face.

Catlo wanted Billy just to relax during that day of grace between the moonballer and the match with Tillotston. See a musical, see Wall Street. Anything but tennis.

"Don't even tell me where you're going," his father said to him. "Just take off. Forget tennis. I don't want to see you until tomorrow morning. Only one thing. You're to be back here at ten. Sharp. In bed by ten-thirty."

Catlo had the same prescription for himself—away from tennis. Shelly had the long weekend off from her show. She also wanted away. Crossroads day was Monday. She had to decide whether to stay in Washington, which had always been her beat, or take the new offer, new show, new network in New York. Tish had come up with the best plan, something that suited everybody's purpose.

"Let's get out of this city. Let's drive into the country. It's going to be too windy to do anything in the city."

"That's fine with me," Shelly said. "There's a house at Red Hook I want to look at, if that's all right with everyone else. Edwards can drive us."

"Red Hook?" I said.

"It's up on the Hudson."

"Oh." It was pretty far from Washington, D.C.

I was meeting Catlo at noon at the Summit. Shelly would collect us in the Silver Cloud with Edwards. Silver Cloud II, actually, since Silver Cloud I was in repose for radiator-grill and front-fender attention. Oddly, Shelly told us, the Spirit of Ecstasy figurehead on the radiator had escaped pristine, not a scratch from the dive into the Tung Shing emporium. Edwards had the first ticket of his life—for "careless driving," of all things.

"Did it depress him?" I asked.

"On the contrary," Shelly said. "He said he'd have it framed as the only time a graduate of the Rolls-Royce chauffeur-mechanic school had been charged with that."

Rule Britannia.

It was gusty and sunny. I too looked forward to spending it away from tennis. I wanted to forget that I was making my national television debut tomorrow. Chester Barney had coached me extensively. He had taken me over with the director and crew for some run-throughs in the green booth overlooking the Stadium court. I had been pretty calm until Chester started talking to me about not being nervous.

"The biggest thing of all," Chester had counseled, "is to be your natural, humble self. That's why Fred went for you. You talk naturally."

"Doesn't everybody?" I said.

"Hardly anybody," Chester said. "Most people talk in high voices when they get nervous or excited. Keep your voice in the same 'weight.' *Never* get excited. If Tillotston takes that big prick of his out and pisses on a linesman, don't raise your voice."

"Do you think he might?"

"Don't let talking to forty million people throw you. Your hands might shake a little at first. Keep them under the table until you stop. We only shoot from the waist up so you can play with yourself if that will steady your hands. I used to when I was new on the tube. It doesn't work for everybody. People are different."

He told me about the statistician always available if, for instance, you wanted to know who beat whom and by what score and what the color of his hair was in the fourth round in 1933. We went through it all.

"When in doubt," Chester said, "there's one thing I daresay will always save you. Do as I do."

"Of course," I said. "My natural, humble self."

"I wish you dry palms," Chester said. "Let's don't have two cases of Stadium terrors tomorrow. I don't care about the forty million so much. What's important is that Fred is always watching. I fool you never."

After this calming counsel, I was looking forward to the country drive. To forgetting about volleys and half-volleys, backhands and forehands, slices and smashes, lets and lobs. Topspins and backspins and drop shots and netcords and double faults and foot faults and Fred-Freds. Forgetting about young, greedy, misbehaving princes of tennis and Forest Hills—and everything that had anything to do with tennis.

It didn't start out that way.

I was sitting in the lobby waiting for Catlo to come down. I flipped to the sports section of the *Times* and scanned an interview with Jack Tillotston, granted just after he reached the semifinals yesterday afternoon by destroying Scot Linder in straight sets. "Tillotston was asked whether he was concerned about Billy Catlo's impressive performance so far. 'Concerned?' he said. 'No, I wouldn't choose that word.' What was his game plan for Billy if they met? 'Game plan?' he said. 'My game plan is to win. That's the only game plan I ever have.' "

I looked up to see Billy coming toward me, dressed in jeans

and tennis shirt. I got up, something I don't often do for
nineteen-year-olds. But after all he had come all the way to
the semis. Considering the exhilarating events of the previous
night, I thought he looked a bit intent. *Quite* intent. Perhaps
he was hung over from playing a moonballer. Or perhaps it
was Jack Tillotston in the Stadium tomorrow.

"Why did you let him do it?" he said.

It hadn't been that long since breakfast. "Him? Do what?"

"Why did you let Dad make that bet?"

Oh, my god, I thought. No. Something felt very still inside
me. "How did you find out?"

"Why wasn't I consulted?"

Consulted. He was growing up all right.

"Why did you let him do it?"

"Now listen, Billy. I don't know where you got your information. But I haven't heard of anybody *letting* your father do
anything. Or keeping him from doing anything either."

"You could have stopped him."

"You don't really believe that."

"*Betting his tennis club.* It's all he's *got.*"

"Does he know you know?" I said.

"He knows all right. I chewed him out."

We were silent, held by that chilling knowledge of an irre-
versible deed. Then Billy said, "To let that son of a bitch trap
him into making a bet like that. Having to prove what a great
big macho he is by calling his bluff."

No one needed to identify the son of a bitch. If three people
know a secret, it isn't a secret. Had Tillotston told him deliberately or had it come out accidentally? But of course Jack
Tillotston never did anything accidentally. Son of a bitch all
right.

"Billy, let's sit down."

The Summit lobby was empty and antiseptic now. All the
losers had gone home, to Bakersfield and Bombay, to Chatta-
nooga and Moscow and Bucharest and Goose Creek, Texas.
Only winners remained. Four of them. And one of these was

there before me on the stained vinyl couch in this thrown-together lobby. He had been hit with something devastating.

"Billy, listen to me," I said. "I wish your father hadn't made the bet. But he had a damn good reason not to tell you. He was thinking of you. He didn't want to add to the pressure."

"What do you think it does now?" he said coldly.

"I know, Billy. I know."

"What is he supposed to do if I lose tomorrow. Start over? At his age?"

"I don't think your father's all that old."

"He's old for tennis," he said brutally. "For tennis he's an old man."

"Your father could always get a job in tennis."

"A job?" Billy said. "He has a job." His voice was bitter. "That son of a bitch told me Dad promised to stay on at the club. Working for him."

He waited a moment. "He's never worked for anybody. I don't think he could. He can work for himself. And he's worked damn hard at that club ever since I was about three years old. You know something?"

He had not raised his voice. That was not his way, any more than it was his father's. But I could hear the anger and pain. And something else, too. I knew suddenly just how much he loved him.

"The first memory I have of my father was that he was always on that tennis court. When I was about six, I thought he didn't work like other kids' fathers. He just played tennis. Then when I was around ten I began to realize he was the hardest working man around. He works twelve hours a day, giving those fucking lessons. But at least it's *his,* that club. He's supposed to lose that now?"

That news would be shattering, overwhelming, to a young boy. I understood that. Knowing that his father had bet his living on a stupid tennis match, *his* match. It was too much to ask of a young boy, that he carry a burden like that into tomorrow's match. What a stupid thing that bet had been. I felt horribly depressed myself, that any of this could happen. That it could happen now, of all times. I looked across the lobby and saw a charman begin to swab the floor. I could smell the Clorox.

Billy stood up. I got up with him.

"I'm scared," he said. "I was scared before. Now I'm *scared*."

"I know, Billy."

"No you don't."

"You're right. I don't."

"What do they think I'm made of."

I wondered later why I said it. But I really always knew I said it deliberately.

"I guess we'll find out tomorrow."

For one moment I thought he might swing. I saw the first real anger I had ever seen on that handsome young face. Then Lindy was walking up, bright, face aglow at the prospect of the adventure ahead. She was wearing jeans and a white sleeveless Fred Perry. A yellow ribbon tied her hair. She always looked so clean and fresh.

"A whole day to do nothing in New York," she said. "A whole day to do everything." She gave a mock sigh. "And a whole day to forget tennis. Let's not waste a minute of it. Let's go!"

He took her abruptly by the arm. I watched them walk across the lobby and disappear through the revolving door.

I felt awful. I remembered seeing Tillotston at last night's match. That was an odd thing in itself. He never went to matches. He only played in them. To me it had meant only one thing. He had begun to take Billy seriously. He had decided he better have a look at his game in case he was his next opponent. Sometime after that match, in the locker room, somewhere, he must have told him.

I did not know what that news might do to Billy. I did know this: at the last possible moment Jack Tillotston had come up with his *coup de main*. He had played it as cunningly as he played the game of tennis.

Soon after Robert Catlo joined me, Edwards and Shelly and Tish arrived with the Rolls. We drove off into the country to forget tennis.

18

THE MAN ACROSS THE NET

THE STADIUM AT FOREST HILLS IS A THEATER IN THE ROUND, the concrete horseshoe with its wooden plank seats surrounding the court on three sides. On the fourth, broadside to the court, is the Marquee, rows of chairs covered by a long blue-and-yellow-striped canvas shelter, where sit the press and people said to be important. In front of the Marquee, on the playing surface itself, is a single row of folding chairs, separated from the court only by green tin window boxes planted in red geraniums. The geraniums are plastic.

Our green television booth sat like a treehouse amid some oaks between the Marquee and the stands, at one end of the court. Directly below us, on one of the folding chairs behind the fake geraniums, sat Robert Catlo. He wore slacks of soft yellow and a white tennis shirt. He sat tall and straight, dignified, impassive, looking straight ahead. Across the court from our booth was one of the "V.I.P." boxes, also sitting directly on the Har-Tru. In it, in the first row, sat Lindy. Somewhere in the Marquee, under the canvas shelter, not visible at all but attended, I knew, by at least three lord high executives of television, sat Shelly.

It was cloudy with a forecast of rain. More important right now was the wind. High around the rim of the Stadium the flags of the nations were flapping steadily. Occasionally a gust of wind unfurled them so that they stood straight out. Below the flags, every seat taken, the 14,000 waited.

A ragged cheer went up as the man and the boy stepped down from the Marquee and onto the Center Court. The boy looked up at the crowd for a moment. The man, who had been here many times before, ignored the crowd as incidental, a necessary nuisance to the job he had come to perform. The man knew that he performed that job better than anyone in the world. They walked along opposite sides of the net, across the court toward the umpire's green highchair on the far side.

I was seeing them for the first time from the perspective of a television booth. The man looked more like a football running back than a tennis player. Muscular, handsome and fair-haired, he carried himself with an easy, almost arrogant air. He wore all white and carried his six rackets under his arm with the casualness of a hunter carrying weapons he knows and uses with absolute mastery. In his other hand was a canvas duffel bag with the frettings of his profession, the wristbands and the sticks of resin, the spare shirts. The boy looked almost slight alongside the man. Lean, lithe, the kind of boy to whom you might apply the word beautiful, with the copper skin and the hair they have that is as black as any black on earth, with the erect posture of his blood, the face grave, reserved. His shirt and his shorts were light tan. He wore a white handkerchief knotted around his neck. He came with three rackets and a duffel.

They went to their folding chairs separated by a yellow "ball conditioner" filled with tennis balls. This refrigerator kept the balls at 68 degrees and thus preserved their truest bounce. They stacked their spare rackets next to their chairs. They spun for serve. They moved to opposite ends of the court. They rallied, offering each other easy but firm forehand and backhand shots. Then each hit a dozen or so volleys, a dozen overheads, a dozen serves. After five minutes of this they returned to their chairs.

"Ladies and Gentlemen," the umpire said into his microphone, "this semifinal-round match will be the best of five sets. In the event the games in any set reach six-all, the twelve-point tie breaker will be in effect. The first player to win seven points with a margin of at least two points wins the tie breaker and the set. Tillotston has won the toss and has elected to receive. Catlo will serve. Linesmen ready? Play."

It was an unusual gambit on Tillotston's part. Usually the winner of the racket spin elects to serve, especially if he possesses a serve as big as Tillotston's. Tillotston was trying to demoralize Billy from the start by breaking his serve in the very first game, when Billy would be most on edge, uncertain.

In the afternoon grey the tennis ball rose high off Billy's left hand, his racket dropped back, and as it whipped up and over, he leaned in with all his strength. The yellow bullet streaked over the net and hit the clay deep in the service box and inches inside the sideline. Standing a step behind the baseline, Jack Tillotston took the ball on the forehand and blazed it down the line. Low over the net, the ball skidded deep and just inside. Heavy with sidespin, it curved away from the court. Billy lunged for it, dipped low and with a ferocious backhand drive sent the ball flying crosscourt at an acute angle. Tillotston, reading the shot perfectly, was there waiting for it. The court was opened up. He stepped into the ball and blew it viciously down the opposite line. Billy was half a court away. Love-15.

Billy set up in the ad court and looked at the champion across the net. Tillotston bounced on his toes like a boxer then crouched, waited. Billy boomed his big flat serve directly into the champion's body. Fault. A foot long. Tillotston moved slightly inside the baseline for the second serve. Billy delivered it with spin, a yard inside the service line. Tillotston pounced on it, taking the ball on the rise, and sent a violent backhand down the line. The ball hit the very corner of baseline and sideline. Billy dived for it, just managed to get his racket on it and the ball came floating up, high and weak to Tillotston, parked at the net. Nonchalantly he tapped it crosscourt. Love-30.

Billy, the wind abetting his big serve, sent the ball crashing down the middle. It netted. Tillotston moved in two steps. Billy went for his big one on second serve. Once more a foot long. Love-40.

Billy crashed a big serve in and they exchanged forehand drives. Billy got an approach shot, hit deep and followed it to net. Tillotston threw up a lob. The ball appeared headed for the stands. Billy looked up, hesitated, then, his black hair flying, raced back. The topspin and the wind together brought it down. He saw the ball fall on the baseline and head toward the Stadium barrier. First game to Tillotston, at love.

"Well, that vindicates Tilly's choice on the racket spin," Chester Barney said into his microphone. "Billy broken in the very first game."

The two players walked to their chairs beneath the umpire's stand. Tillotston sat barely thirty seconds before he got up and headed to the opposite end of the court. A light cheer followed him. The way he carried himself, his straight shoulders, gave the appearance of a strut. Billy sat for the full time, then got up and walked to his end. The same light cheers. Tillotston stood in to serve. Billy, a step behind the baseline, crouched, swayed. The big man rocked forward, rocked back, the ball rose, the racket came over. The serve caught the corner of the service and center lines, unplayable. Service ace. Billy walked the few feet to the ad court, crouched, swayed. Tillotston delivered. Billy moved into the ball and sent it screaming back to Tillotston's feet. Tillotston blistered it up the middle. The two traded crosscourts. Then Billy caught a shorter Tillotston shot, sent it deep to the baseline, and moved quickly across no man's land, between baseline and service box, toward the net. Tillotston sent up a lob. The ball soared and Billy raced back for it. The ball dived onto the clay behind him. With its topspin and blown by the wind, the ball was traveling so fast that no quickness could run it down. Tillotston had shown he could lob successfully both with and against the wind. He was trying to teach Billy that the net belonged to him. Thirty-love.

Billy took the serve on the forehand and sent his big return of serve flying crosscourt. Tillotston seemed to have an eerie ability to anticipate where the ball would land. He was waiting there and blew it down the line. Billy, racing, took it and sent it crosscourt. Again Tillotston was there and hit crosscourt and short. For Billy it was a good chance for a deep approach shot to be followed to net. But, stung twice by lobs, he hung back and they exchanged forehand drives from the baseline. Tilly, disguising beautifully, coming under the ball at the last moment, suddenly undercut. The drop shot floated toward the net, the ball spinning backward. Billy, far back, raced flat-out, black hair flying, racket extended. The ball fell just over the net, rose not a foot and spun back. Billy slid on the clay into it. His racket head dug and scooped the ball up and over the net.

"Not up!" the net judge called.

There are thirteen officials arranged around a playing surface measuring only 27 by 78 feet. In no other sport is there anything remotely like this ratio of officials to players. Nothing could testify more to the fineness of the game. Tennis is not a game of inches, it is a game of millimeters. Twenty-six eyes are needed to distinguish the in-millimeter from the out-millimeter in a tournament match. This call meant that Billy got the ball on second bounce. Forty-love, Tillotston.

The champion tossed up the ball and for the first time sent his serve sharply to Billy's backhand. Billy was pulled out of court and simply blasted away, slugging. The ball sailed high over the net, over the court, over the baseline. A good five feet out. A wild, wild shot. Billy could not find the lines. Games were 2-love Tillotston.

Again Tillotston broke Billy's serve after giving up a couple of points. Three-love.

"Does Tilly have an important date at the St. Regis at two?" Barney inquired into his mike.

"I don't know about the date at the St. Regis," I said. "He does seem to have a date with the finals."

As they crossed over, I looked down at Robert Catlo. He was seated no more than thirty feet from our booth. There was nothing between him and the court but a few yards of Har-Tru. He reached down to the green window box and snapped off one of the plastic geraniums.

Again Tilly was up first. He gave the impression of a man who wanted to get the business over with. The light cheers followed the champion to the baseline. Billy took his full rest before starting for the other end. The cheers that trailed him were louder, not out of partisanship but because the fans wanted to see a tennis match. They had not come to watch a tennis lesson. "Come on, Billy" a lone voice came down from the upper stands. It sounded a bit forlorn.

In the fourth game Billy was digging for everything. He stretched, he chased. He got shots few players could. Little it helped him. Tillotston yanked him from one corner to the other as if he were tied to a string. The crowd was dead quiet, watching not so much a tennis match as one player displaying the game at its best. The champion was in complete command of the court. Finally he had the short one he wanted. He sent back an approach shot to the corner and moved in. Billy blazed the ball down the line. Tillotston was at the net.

He had fantastic reach. It seemed as if, standing at the midpoint of the net, his arm could reach clear to the lines on backhand or forehand. With his reach, with his big body, he stood there as though owning it, daring you to get by him. Now as the hard-hit ball raced down the line, the big body lunged, the arm went out full length and the racket full length beyond that. The racket caught the ball and cracked it cross-court at a sharp angle.

"Tillotston!" Barney said into his mike.

A dazzling get. The ball hit the sideline. Billy was nowhere near it. The first loud cheer went up from the stands. Fifteen-love.

"What gives with Billy, expert commentator?" Chester fed me a line.

"He's not playing his natural game," I said into the mike. "Only responding to the other man's shots. His natural game is aggression, boldness. But of course he's never seen this big a game coming at him."

The two players in motion presented a classic antithesis of the athlete's body. Tillotston with his big frame, immensely strong, but with lightning reflexes and astonishing speed for his size. His strong thighs pumped him over the court surface. His racket forearm, more than a foot in circumference, pounded at the ball. A great, fair-skinned, all-American body, relentless, controlled. Turn this knob and the body would lash out at the ball. Turn that knob and the body in sweet calm floated a drop shot just over the net. Billy's body with its thin frame, a supple, effortless body. His moves, however desperate, seemed natural, unplanned. He had a limitless, thoughtless energy, a liquid strength. Even when he was being blown off the court, chasing unreturnable shots, there was a wild beauty about him.

In the ad court Tillotston powered in his big serve. Billy hit crosscourt. Over the sideline. Serve into the deuce court. Billy slugged it. Eight feet over the baseline. Serve. Billy slugged it. Into the net. Games were 4-love.

"Do you think Billy realizes the object of the game is to get the ball inside those white lines?" Barney said.

Billy toed the line. Across the net the champion bounced on his toes, crouched. Billy lifted the ball, the wind behind him. The ball boomed over the net and hit the center line dead on and deep.

"Catlo!" Barney said, delighted to be able at last to say that word. "Service ace!"

The shot was unplayable. Tillotston made no attempt to get to it. He smiled and bowed toward his opponent. A titter of laughter rewarded him from the stands.

"Uh-oh," Barney said. "I don't think Billy liked that gracious bow."

Billy pounded another raging serve into the ad court and charged the net. Tilly sent it singing down the line. Billy leaped, caught it on his racket and lashed a volley crosscourt far from his opponent. A burst of applause came from the stands. Thirty-love, Billy Catlo.

At 40-15 Billy delivered his big one and after trading shots again attacked the net. Tillotston threw up a lob. This time Billy did not wait to see what the wind would do with it. He sprinted back, picked it out of the sky. Blasted off. The ball slammed into the champion's court where it seemed to dig a hole in the clay. First game to the challenger.

"Ay, Catlo." And the first of those. "Ay, Billy."

Games were 4-1 Tillotston. They crossed over. They sat on opposite sides of the refrigerator. Each toweled off. Face, hands, arms, thighs, racket. They never once looked at each other. The only place they looked at each other was across the net. They went to their ends.

Tillotston served with the wind behind him. As if to make clear that the last game was only a momentary lapse, he ran off three points on serve and three jugular volleys. Billy passed him. Forty-15. Tillotston blew an ace past Billy. Games were 5-1.

Billy served into the wind. They played to the first deuce of the set.

Billy leaned in and lifted the ball. Across the sky the clouds were starting to darken and move before the gusting wind. The serve came in deep and Billy moved in. The champion drilled it up the middle, short and low to force Billy to volley up, and also moved in. Billy scooped up the ball on a half-volley. Each man now stood dead astride the service and center lines, facing each other. Each was looking straight into the mouth of the cannon. Tilly took it on the volley and slammed the ball back full force straight at Billy. Billy slugged it back at him. At point-blank range they exchanged savage volleys, slamming the ball at each other. In six shots the ball never touched the ground. Then Tillotston blew it through Billy.

The crowd was on its feet cheering wildly. It was a thrilling display, one of courage on the part of both players.

"Tillotston!" Barney said. "He loves to hit right through you. You'd better get out of the way or he'll hurt you with it. I mean *hurt*."

"At least Billy didn't get out of the way," I said. "At nineteen, he has the courage."

"Yes," Barney said. "But does he have the game? Set point."

Billy delivered both serves full out. The first hit a foot beyond the service box. The second, an inch.

"Game and first set to Tillotston," the umpire said.

Six-1. They crossed over.

"Somewhat wild, wouldn't you say?" Barney said into his mike. "Center Court jitters?"

"Some of that, I imagine," I said. "But mainly it's that he's playing Jack Tillotston."

I looked down at Robert Catlo. I counted four severed plastic geraniums on the clay in front of him. I wondered if he was thinking about the bet. I wondered if Billy was thinking about it. Surely it was one of the most important things down on that court. And yet I could not tell it. I felt a conflict between my journalistic loyalty to the people who were listening and my promise to Billy and Catlo, my word given.

But of course Catlo was losing much more than any bet. Jack Tillotston was doing to Billy something not unlike what he had done to Robert Catlo at Wimbledon. I looked down at that proud man and thought how much I respected him. Sitting there in the open, nothing between him and the court, he was as exposed as Billy.

He was looking straight across the court at Billy. Billy was holding a racket in each hand. He moved them up and down as if his hands were two scales. He did not look up. He looked only at the two rackets. He was in his own world. Slowly I realized that Robert Catlo was losing something else. He was losing control of his son.

"What do you imagine the Big Cat is thinking, Brinkley?"

"That he'd like to walk across that court and have some words with Billy. Tell him to settle down, to stop slamming that second serve. And a few other things."

"And of course any on-court coaching is forbidden. Brinkley, do you consider that a good rule?"

"It's an excellent rule. If a player can't win at this level on his own, he doesn't deserve to win. No one, not even a nineteen-year-old, should be in the Stadium at Forest Hills if he needs nursing."

Billy did one final hand-weighing of the two rackets, then laid one down. He had not looked at his father. It was as if he were saying, I will do it on my own. Make it or go down, it will be on my own.

He got up and started for the baseline. As he moved toward it he was walking directly toward Lindy. When he reached there he was no more than twenty-five feet from her, at eye level should he want to look at her. He had not done so throughout the match. Now he did. She gave him a little wave and a smile. His head made one short up-and-down movement. Then he turned to face Jack Tillotston.

In set 1, Jack Tillotston had shown the fans some tennis. In set 2, he decided to show them some theater. If Billy could not supply decent competition, the fans must not leave feeling cheated. He would give them their money's worth. They would now be treated to a dramatic performance.

In game 1, Tilly started bouncing the ball before each service. Three or four times at first. Then five or six. Finally as many as a dozen times. As the number escalated, Billy, crouching and swaying at the opposite baseline, stood up for a moment and turned his back, the equivalent of a baseball player stepping out of the batter's box. Later in the game a gust of wind blew a Tillotston lob out by a couple of inches. Tillotston turned to the crowd. He licked his finger, then held it up as though testing the wind. This was an instant hit. The crowd laughed and cheered. Tilly held serve. One-love.

In game 2 a baby's cry whined down over the court. About to receive serve, Tillotston turned around. He looked up in the direction of the mewling infant and said loudly, "It isn't mine—I hope." Laughter. Billy immediately aced him. The boy held serve. One-all.

Game 3, first point. Standing in serving position at the baseline, Tilly lifted his left foot. With his racket head he knocked off some Har-Tru, real or imaginary. This may have dislodged a shoelace for he bent down and retied it. He then tested the tension of his racket strings by pressing his fingers against them. He straightened his shirt at the shoulders. He cupped his hand and blew on it. He bounced the ball one, two, three . . . nine times. Finally he served. The ball hit on or near the service line. It was a very close call.

"Fault!" the service linesman cried.

Tilly walked around the net and entered Billy's domain. He approached the service line. He leaned down and gazed at a ball spot, real or imaginary. There must be *some* spot there. He circled it with his racket head.

"Mr. Tillotston," the umpire said. "The serve was out. May I remind you that 'play shall be continuous'?"

"I *am* sorry," Tilly said. "By all means let us continue." He turned to the service linesman. "Let us also *begin* to keep our eyes open." Laughter from the stands, though not from the linesman.

Tillotston walked back around the net to his baseline. Billy immediately blasted a winner down the line off the second serve. The game went to four deuces before Tilly held serve. Two-1, Tillotston.

Games 4 and 5 mercifully passed with only tennis being performed. Tillotston won both, but both were hard-fought, both went to deuce. Game 5 went to four deuces. Something had happened. Billy's game had begun to ascend. He was playing on a higher plateau of tennis. It was as if he had passed through some barrier. He was in better control of himself and of his game. Tilly's game was no less, but Billy's was more. Both men going for everything, going full out.

In game 6, the theater curtain went up again. At 30-all Billy served his big one. It crashed just over the net, caught the center line deep and raced past the champion. Billy walked to the ad court to serve the next point. Tillotston remained standing in the deuce court in the receive-serve position.

"Mr. Tillotston," the umpire said, "the score is forty-thirty. You are in the wrong court."

"Wrong court!" Tillotston shouted. "That ball was a let."

The net judge is a remarkable figure in tennis. He spends an entire match, up to three hours or more, seated at the net post, with his fingers resting on the net cord during serve. If the fingers catch the slightest tick of the ball against the cord, he sounds off "net" and raises his hand. This net judge was a very fat man named Arthur Constance. He weighed at least 250 pounds. He specialized in net-judging. He was said to have the most sensitive fingers in tennis.

Now Tillotston approached this Falstaff in a menacing manner. Arthur Constance did not budge or even look. Leaning forward, he looked down the length of the net. He obviously felt most secure in that position.

"Arthur?" the umpire said, looking directly down at him.

"The ball was clean," Arthur said. "I felt nothing."

"Maybe his fingers fell asleep," Tilly said.

"Mr. Tillotston," the umpire said. "I didn't hear anything."

"Well, I did."

"Jack, the ball cleared," the umpire said. "Arthur had his

fingers on the net and I was right above it. Arthur felt nothing, heard nothing. I saw nothing, heard nothing."

"Maybe you were both asleep," Tilly said.

The performance had now continued for a good three minutes.

Barney said into the mike, "I can't begin to count the number of players I've seen fall apart when Tilly used tactics like this on them."

Suddenly Billy left his service position. He walked past the rubberized mats where the photographers crouched, past Tillotston and on to a white container bearing the legend "Pepsi." He took out two cans. The umpire, leaning over from his highchair, watched in wonderment. Billy tore off the tabs. Carrying the two cans, he walked across the court, continued across the baseline toward the stands. Barney and I were following the pilgrimage in fascination. So was the camera. Billy reached the V.I.P. box. He handed one of the Pepsis to Lindy, sitting there in the front row.

"Folks, that lovely is Billy's girl," Barney informed our 40-million viewing audience. "Her name is Lindy."

Lindy received the offering as if she and Billy were hanging out on the beach on a hot summer day in Florida. Billy leaned comfortably against the box. He and Lindy began to chat. The still photographers popped off their mats, swarmed onto the court and began shooting close-ups of the handsome couple.

"Will the photographers return at once to their assigned positions!" the umpire said over his mike.

Naturally they kept on shooting.

Tillotston was still at the net, alternately glaring at the net judge and glancing over at Billy surrounded by photographers. Billy was nonchalantly sipping his Pepsi and shooting the breeze with Lindy. They appeared to be enjoying each other's company.

"Gentlemen," the umpire said. He was addressing the players. "Mr. Tillotston. Mr. Catlo. Isn't it time to cut out this nonsense, this . . . *spectacle*? Mr. Tillotston, can we play tennis please?"

"That's what I'm here for," Tillotston said. "But it takes two to tango." The crowd laughed.

Lindy was utilizing the break. She undid the sweaty handkerchief from Billy's neck, opened her purse and got out a fresh one. She carefully arranged it around his neck, then deftly knotted it. I fancy I heard her say, "There." It was as if she had said, "My knight." The crowd around her followed this charming ritual with delight.

"Mr. Catlo," the umpire's pleading voice came across the court.

Billy took another swallow of his soda. He turned toward the umpire. "Yes, sir. Just remember I didn't start this." The crowd applauded. Billy started walking toward his baseline. Tilly waited a moment, then started toward his. The crowd broke into laughter and cheering. They had had their show.

"Gentlemen," the umpire said with relief. "The score is forty-thirty. Catlo. Catlo is serving."

Billy leaned in, the ball went up into the grey-black sky. His racket came over it with savage force. The ball stormed over the net and hit near the corner of the center and service lines. Tillotston was ten feet from it. He did not move his racket.

"Games are four-two Tillotston," the umpire said.

Tillotston served. Billy hit two huge returns of serve. Love-30. He netted the next one. Fifteen-30. He slammed two more returns of serve past Tillotston. Four-3 Tillotston. For the first time Billy had broken the champion's serve. The crowd burst into cheers.

"This is very instructive, fans," Chester said into his mike. "There are two kinds of players when the squabbles start. One kind falls apart. The other gets fired up. That's the way Robert Catlo always was. The worst thing you could do if you were playing the Big Cat was to make him mad. Six out of the last seven points to Billy. Like father, like son."

But Jack Tillotston was that kind of player too. There was no more theater in the set. After three deuces he broke Billy's serve, then held his own. He had the set at 6-3. Sets were 2-love Tillotston.

They took their seats on either side of the yellow refrigerator. Tilly took his full rest. This time it was Billy who got up before that and started for his end.

The winds were swirling around the enclosure now. A photographer's empty film carton blew across the court. A ball boy retrieved it. At the baseline Billy came into the service position, toed the line. He paused and looked across the net at Jack Tillotston. He leaned in. The ball went up into the ever-darkening sky, up into the freshening wind.

"Here it is," Barney said to the 40 million. "Sets are two-love. Three sets win it, remember. Fans, it is truly stroking time. It is now or never for the Copper Angel. I fool you never."

The mouth of the Stadium horseshoe opens to the southeast, to the prevailing winds off the Atlantic Ocean ten miles away. This mouth was now taking in the wind, in gulps. The wind was not steady. Rather it came in sharp gusts. Usually the server could play around it. If he tossed up a ball and the wind veered it, he caught it, waited for the gust to blow through, then served. Generally a point would be finished before another gust arrived. The tennis was being played chiefly between gusts, around the wind.

But the gusts were coming through the horseshoe's mouth more frequently now and, it seemed, stronger. They came surely off some dark and whitecapped sea. In my mind's eye I could see it running against the beaches of Long Island. Above, the dark clouds coasted across the sky like fat supply ships. I have always loved this kind of sky at sea, a ship suspended between dark sky and dark sea, away and alone. So the elements seemed to embrace the two players in the arena below us. The dark clouds above, the 27 by 78 feet of clay-bounce, pulverized greenstone gypsum below, across which they were contesting for every point, locked in battle. The shots burned the damp air. They came off the rackets with a loudness which the elements seemed to magnify as the two figures raged across the court. The man more gifted than anyone who plays this game today. The boy knowing that he will have to summon from within himself a resource he does not even know if he possesses. Every shot seemed bigger now. Each looked for that vulnerable opening, that tiny crevice, to break through. One game only.

It all seemed to rest on that, on one service break. For Tillotston, the one game that would enable him, by holding serve only, to close it out in straight sets. For Billy Catlo, the one game that would enable him to take a set, and thus stay alive. It was hard and gallant tennis. The crowd sat hushed under the darkling clouds. Thousands leaning forward, many resting their chins in their hands, watching each point fought out in fury. Often the hush was broken by a burst of applause at some dazzling crosscourt, some impossible get, some put-away volley.

In tennis terms, what had happened to Billy's game was this: he had become accustomed to Tillotston's driving game, to the shots coming at him with such tremendous force. He had never really seen this game before from across a net. He was a different player now from the player he was in the first set, simply because he had played against it and learned he could handle it. This proved one thing beyond all doubt. Billy Catlo could play as an equal with the best, including Jack Tillotston. It did not prove that he could beat Tillotston. For it was no longer enough just to play as well as Tillotston. He must surpass him.

How those first four games were fought for! It was as if each player assumed, not just that any single game could decide it all, but that any single point could decide that game, and any shot the point. So all must be contested to the limit.

For Billy, time running out. For Tillotston, the time at hand to close it out.

Jack Tillotston had always been at his best in just this situation, smelling victory, going for the kill. He was at his most unmerciful, his game relentless. Today of all days he was not going to make an exception. He was on his way to being through forever with tournament tennis. To as glorious a leave-taking as a champion could wish. Winning the Big Four in a row. Bowing out undefeated. Entering into a world of television riches. The trumpets would sound him out. Was he thinking of any of this? I think not.

For Billy? What was going on in that nineteen-year-old mind as he fought on in that white-bounded rectangle below us? Thoughts of the importance of today to his father, thoughts of some ghostly revenge for what the man across the net had done to his father eight years back at Wimbledon? More hard, practical thoughts of what would happen to his father if he lost his tennis club? What would happen in that case to *him*? Dreams of The Glory and The Cash that victory today would lead to? None of this, I think.

I think none of these facts was in their minds. The crowd thought they were playing for them. They were not. The crowd did not exist. They did not even know it was there. They might have been all alone on some patched, scruffed, unattended tennis court in some distant small town. No crowd, no umpire, no linesmen, no ball boys, no one watching. Just the two of them. Each knowing that he had to beat the man across the net at all costs, just to beat him. Not for wrongs past, not for money, not even for glory. But for a deep animal reason: for Tillotston, to remain what he was; for Billy, to become something new. Nothing else.

And so between points they looked, now and then, stared at each other across the net. They were in a world from which the crowd, the officials, all of us, were shut out. It was their world, theirs alone.

Tillotston was serving thunderbolts. So big, so close to the lines that Billy was diving for them. Service shots that would be aces except for Billy's extreme quickness. Glorious tennis. Billy's quickness was his greatest weapon. It was enabling him to play even with the champion of the world. Games came to 2-all.

The Stadium mouth was taking in more gulps now, and bigger ones. Billy to serve game 5. Across the net the champion bounced on his toes. Crouched. Now quickly it became apparent that Tillotston was going for the break on this one. He attacked the serve, he charged the net. Billy answered with everything he had. A Tillotston stop volley with Billy far back seemed unreachable. Billy raced for it, racket full out, black hair flying, sliding almost into the ball. He flicked it over and crosscourt for a winner. The game went to deuce. The game rocked back and forth. Three deuces, four. Billy would not surrender the break. Five deuces, six. On the seventh deuce, Tillotston hit Billy's service crosscourt, wickedly angled. Billy flew at it, his racket miraculously made contact and flailed it down the line. The ball smashed into the net cord, its force almost pushing it over. It teetered there for a moment, uncertain whether to fall over or fall back. Then, as the crowd sighed in unison, the ball slid down the net into Billy's court.

"Breakpoint for Tillotston," Barney said into his mike.

Billy's service came in deep and he attacked the net behind it. Tilly sliced short and low to force the volley-up and moved in behind the shot. Once again they were only a few feet apart, at flash point. Exchanging volleys, they blazed away at each other. Each slamming missiles straight at the other. Brilliant, speed-of-light tennis. Then one of Billy's volleys caught the net cord, slid over and touched down near the sideline. Tillotston was on it and flicked a perfectly disguised, gentlest topspin lob, tricky and sly. An incredible shot to try from there, a shot so full of danger that it was likely to be hit back between his teeth. Caught by surprise, Billy looked at the yellow ball drifting up into the darkened sky. He raced back flat-out. If he could get there, it was an easy smash putaway with Tillotston at net. The ball outran him. Its topspin forced it down. It was very very close. All of us waited, hushed, to see if the linesman would speak the word "Out."

He said nothing.

"Game to Tillotston," the umpire said. "He leads three games to two."

As the players crossed over, a needle drizzle of rain began to fall.

"Well, Tillotston has his break," Barney said into his mike. "My, how he went for it. Killer tennis. Tillotston holds the copyright."

As the two walked to their baselines after the crossover, the crowd stood to applaud for the tennis they were being given. So high was the level of play, the crowd seemed without partisanship, equally grateful to them both. The hush fell as the champion leaned in to serve.

"All Tilly has to do now is hold serve," Barney said.

Game 6 went to one deuce before Tilly held for 4-2. Billy Catlo stood at the baseline to serve game 7.

All around was such a strange light. It was only 3:30 in the afternoon but it was as if night were closing in. Wrapped in clouds huge and deep grey, the sky hung low. The light drizzle continued, whipped by the wind. The wind was freshening, singing through the Stadium opening now. It wanted something, the wind did.

Billy leaned in. He hesitated for a moment longer than usual, looking at Tillotston across the net. I saw the boy's face and on it was a defiance that made my eyes glisten. He stood eight points from defeat. He would not go down easy. He would make those eight points a trial by fire. Every point would have to be taken from him. Like his father at Wimbledon those long years back, they would have to come after him. He would fight to the last point.

I thought: my god, what a champion he will make. For I

no longer had any doubt that is what he would be, some year.
How he would grace it. And, I thought also, how tennis
needed such a champion.

He threw up his first ball. A gust carried it so that he had
to catch the ball without swinging at it. The gusting was almost continuous now. Men spectators were holding onto their
Aussie hats. I saw skirts go up over some fetching thighs and
over one very fat pair—not a tennis player, obviously. Billy
waited for the gust to die. He wiped his hand, wiped the
drizzle moisture from his racket. He tried again. A stronger
gust caught the ball and carried it toward the Marquee, toward
Catlo and his box of fake flowers. There was quite a pile there
now of decapitated geraniums. A ball boy retrieved the ball.
Instead of bouncing it to Billy as they usually do, he brought
it over and placed it firmly in Billy's hand.

The fine drizzle went on. It was the kind that could be
either a momentary event or the harbinger of a real rain.

"Gentlemen," the umpire said through his microphone.
"Would you please step over here?"

It was instantly obvious what was going to happen.

"Uh-oh," Barney said. "It looks like they are going to delay
the match. That would be a real break for Billy Catlo."

Tillotston walked toward the umpire's chair. He was all
confidence. He did the wind-testing, finger-in-the-mouth bit
again. The crowd laughed.

At his baseline Billy stood for a moment, half ready to try
his serve again. Finally, his hair blowing, he started walking
toward the chair.

Below me Robert Catlo stood up, obviously relieved. He
clasped his hands in approval. If the match was postponed
until tomorrow or even delayed for a while today, it meant
another chance for Billy. Maybe in the interval they could
come up with something. At the very least it meant a break
in the fatal momentum of the match.

"Technically," Barney explained to his TV audience, "the

umpire has the right to call or delay the match, subject to confirmation by the referee. Either player can appeal to the referee, who has the ultimate authority. There's the referee Pat Hargraves coming out to joint the discussion."

Hargraves looked tall and Maine-like in the wind.

"Those are the rules," Barney went on. "What happens in actual practice is that if conditions are borderline, the referee consults the players. If the players want to go on, the match normally continues—that is, if *both* players want it. This is very unlikely to happen here for this reason. Billy Catlo is losing. He is down two sets and down two-four in this set. He might still be losing later today or tomorrow or next Christmas. But at least he could go over strategy with his father, try something new."

The wind whipped the drizzle over the conference at the umpire's chair.

"This match is temporarily delayed because of weather conditions," the umpire announced.

"Let's get to the Marquee," Hargraves said.

The players and the umpire followed him to shelter, walking close to where Robert Catlo was sitting. They stood there, just under cover. I saw Catlo get up and slide down the row of geraniums to join them.

They all stood watching the elements, waiting to see what they would do. The drizzle began to let up, but the wind did not. It was still gusting through the Marquee, slapping the canvas shelter.

Hargraves sent the groundsmen onto the court to spread ordinary bath towels over the Har-Tru. The drizzle had not lasted long enough to soak the surface, but Hargraves was taking the proper precautions. He turned to the players.

"Gentlemen," he said, "if there is no more rain, the surface is probably playable. A few soft spots, perhaps. We don't want any injuries. But if both of you want to continue the match and take your chances on court conditions, I would agree.

However, that is a tough wind. We can delay. Mr. Tillotston?"

Our courtside camera was getting everything. Jack Tillotston's face on our monitor said it all. He wore the winner's smile. Now he did a pure Tillotston thing. He turned to Robert Catlo, as though consulting his old rival.

"I think the conditions are pretty bad, don't you, Roberto?"

It was so unorthodox, bringing Robert Catlo into this. Tillotston was ignoring Billy as if he were a ball boy. The Tillotston tactics never stopped.

"Yes, they are," Catlo said curtly. He obviously hated to agree with Tillotston, but he knew where the odds lay. He had no choice. Delay was Billy's only faint hope.

Tilly took a moment to savor the concession. Then he turned to Hargraves. "The conditions are certainly poor," he said, "but I've played in worse. Why don't we let the Catlos decide? Either way is fine with me."

It was so grand, so outrageous, that I had to admire it. He was giving up nothing, of course. The match was going to be delayed whatever he said since the Catlos wanted it. But his apparent generosity, his sportsmanship, seemed magnificent.

"Then we will delay," Hargraves said, "and see what the weather does. All right, gentlemen?" For the first time he turned to Billy, almost as an afterthought. For the record he had to have Billy's approval. "I assume you are in accord, Mr. Catlo?"

On the monitor I saw Billy's face close up. On it was a wonderful fierce look.

"No," Billy said in a clear, firm voice. "I am not in accord. I'd like to play."

An array of startled looks: Tillotston, Hargraves, the umpire, and especially Robert Catlo. I saw Lindy standing there. She had made her way over to the group and now she stood just behind Billy, watching the faces.

"You want to continue?" the referee said. He just managed to keep the disbelief out of his voice.

"No, he would not," Robert Catlo said.

"Yes," Billy said. "Yes, I would." A strange grin was on his face. "Unless Mr. Tillotston objects."

Tilly's face registered it: what is this? He had already granted the decision to the Catlos, thinking there was no decision. He could not believe what he had just heard. "Of course it's the referee's final decision," he said. "But sure—I'm willing."

Robert Catlo spoke up. "You can't play good tennis in that wind on that court. When it's impossible to play good tennis, you delay or postpone."

"I can't argue with you, Roberto," Tillotston said. "If you want to quit, that's fine with me."

"But my father isn't playing," Billy said. "I am."

They all looked at him. In the booth I felt a sudden surge of emotion. Billy was his own man. Right or wrong, his own man.

Robert Catlo now turned directly to his son. "Call it off, Billy."

Suddenly Billy looked at Lindy. She had been standing there, saying nothing. He did not ask for her vote. But the look asked her.

I saw her glance at Catlo. She had that angry, lid-on look. She had never wanted his father to run Billy's life. And she had never wanted to run it either. She wanted Billy to run Billy's life. She glared around the circle of men, then turned back to Billy. She had his same fierce look.

"Billy," Lindy said. "Billy, I think you can whip his ass."

The MBC studio had to be in consternation. A three-letter word! And from a young lady! During family viewing time. What would Sniff say!

Hargraves looked up at the sky. The wind was still there, but the rain had stopped entirely. He looked over the court. The groundsmen were finishing the sponging of the fast-drying surface. Referees always want to continue a match if at all possible, and Hargraves had his pieces in place.

"Gentlemen," he said, "Mr. Tillotston has left it up to Mr. Catlo. Well, Mr. Catlo, do we play tennis?"

Billy grinned. He seemed positively cheerful. "You heard what the lady said."

It was as if the wind approved of the decision. During the talk it had seemed to abate slightly. Say, from Force 6 to Force 5, edging toward Force 4.

Billy was going for it. He would win or lose with the all-out game. He would not play percentage tennis. His serves attacked the lines. Behind them he attacked the net. He fired his volleys at acute angles crosscourt, the balls flying off the clay for the stands or the Marquee. He held serve at 15.

"Tillotston leads four games to three," the umpire sang his litany.

They crossed over, took every scrap of their time on their folding chairs, got up and marched to their baselines. The champion looked across the net and tossed up the ball for his first serve. Billy jumped on it for a crosscourt return and headed for the net. No one takes the net behind his return of a Tillotston first serve. Not unless he loves being slaughtered by a passing shot. But the return was so deep, so angled, that Tillotston had to scramble for it. He was behind the baseline as he hit the ball down the line. Billy did not have Tillotston's reach—but he had a body that could fly. He leaped, both feet actually leaving the ground. His racket caught the ball and cracked it crosscourt. Tillotston was nowhere near it. Love-15.

"Quickness!" Barney said into his mike. "We have not seen anyone as fast as Billy on the Center Court in years. Who could imagine he's been out here two hours?"

It was apparent that Billy had picked his game to go for the service break-back. This one. Tillotston's first serve came in. It is an enormous thing as it comes at you, a serve which has scared fine players everywhere. Billy sent it back in a shot which seemed to tie it in speed records. It is difficult to imagine tennis balls being hit harder, the shots seemed to echo off the Stadium walls. Tilly got his racket on it but his body was tilted out of position and his down-the-line missed. Love-30.

The champion seemed perplexed by the ferocity coming at him from across the net.

"That decision of his to play appears to have exhilarated our young challenger," I said into the mike. "He's on all ahead full."

"Tilly obviously expected to be on his way back to the St. Regis by now," Chester said. "Instead he's got this wild kid across the net. I'm not sure he knows what to make of it. Hurts his concentration I should think."

The concentration came back. Tilly ripped off his great down-the-line shot for one point. Won a baseline exchange of shimmering forehand drives when one of Billy's ticked out by inches. Thirty-all.

But then the ferocity came at him again. Big serve, big return of serve, deep to the baseline. Again Billy used the return as an approach shot and charged the net.

"And he's approaching on Tilly's first serve," Barney said. "I don't think I've ever seen a sane man do that. I didn't know it was possible."

Tilly was standing behind the baseline as he blazed the ball up the middle. The ball smashed the net cord, hesitated, tottered, and for once fell back. Thirty-40.

"Only fair," Barney said. "Tilly's been getting most of the net cords. Breakpoint for Billy."

In the ad court the boy crouched and swayed. He seemed eager for the serve. He leaped on it and smashed it crosscourt. The two played off deep forehand drives on each other until Billy got a shorter ball and headed for the net. Tillotston threw up a lob. Billy backpedaled. A swirling wind held the lob and as the ball started down Billy tracked it, stalked it, his body cocked and waiting, the racket on high. In a marvelously-timed convulsion he came over the ball for an enormous overhead smash. It was as if a cannon had been fired across the dark skies. The ball smashed into the opposite court for a winner and took off high over Tillotston's head in the general direction of the Long Island Railroad tracks. The crowd burst into cheers.

"Ay, Catlo . . . Ay, Billy . . ."

"Games are four-all," the umpire sang.

But Tillotston settled. He was not a man who could be panicked by one game. For the next four games they traded serve. Three of them went to deuce. It was tennis of fury, vicious, flat-out—glorious. Nothing held back, a full commitment by each player to each point. Tillotston to shut the door and lock it, in this set. Billy to keep the match going. Neither could penetrate the other's serve. Games came to 6-all. They were into the tie breaker.

They play the 12-point tie breaker at Forest Hills. First man to win seven points—but he must win by two.

"The pressure is squarely on Billy now," Barney said. "Now it's all down to guts. Now we'll really see what Billy's made of. Look at Tillotston."

Waiting to receive serve, the champion was bouncing on his toes.

"You can almost smell the kill fever in him, can't you?" Barney said. "He wants the set, the match, right now."

The champion crouched and waited. Billy's serve came in. One after another the points went to service, in the precise choreography prescribed for the tie breaker. At 3-3 they changed ends without stopping for rest—none is permitted in the tie breaker. They passed each other in mid-court like enemy destroyers at general quarters. It came to 6-5 Tillotston.

And suddenly it was there, the moment had arrived.

"Match point," Barney said. "Well, here it is, fans. We have been out here over two hours and it all comes down to this one point. Match point for the champion. If I know Jack

Tillotston he will pull out everything. He will go for it all."

The crowd was dead quiet. Only the wind could be heard singing through the Stadium opening. I looked down at Robert Catlo. He was sitting absolutely still. Erect, dignified, impassive, showing nothing.

Billy toed the baseline. The ball went up. His big one screamed over.

"Fault!" the service linesman cried. It was an inch long.

"This match is down to one tennis ball," Barney said into his mike. "It is the one Billy Catlo is holding."

Now, almost arrogantly, Tillotston moved a full step inside the baseline. He was going to jump all over that softer second serve. He was going to close out this match on it.

Billy turned the second ball in his hand, toed the line. He stood a moment as though undecided about something, looking at Tillotston standing there close. He saw him bounce on his toes, then crouch, watch. He knew Tillotston would go for the kill.

He took a deep breath. He patted the face of his racket. I had not seen him make that boyish gesture since Florida. It was as if he were saying to the racket, "Do it for me." I remembered, with a sinking feeling, what it meant. He was not going with the safe second serve. Jack Tillotston did not know the gesture. If he did he would step back. Billy was going, on match point, with his big first one on second serve. My god, why must he do that, I thought. Can't he be *slightly* cautious for once. I also remembered that I was a commentator.

"Billy is going to risk all," I predicted into the mike. "He is going with his biggest serve."

The ball rose high off the boy's hand, reached its zenith and seemed to hang for a moment, a round topaz against the black sky. The racket whipped over with all the strength of the young body behind it. It was an immense serve. It just cleared the net and streaked on. It was going to be deep. The service linesman was looking straight across the line, leaning out of his chair with his face not a foot from the clay, blocking in his eyes with his hands like a racehorse's blinkers for maximum focus. The ball hit and blew past Tillotston. He was standing much too far in to have any kind of stab at it.

"Was it out?" Barney seemed to inhale and hold his breath. And so, too, the fourteen thousand. Tennis is a game of millimeters.

The linesman's hand flashed the "safe" signal. It was a service ace. The crowd erupted in cheers. It wanted the match to go on.

"My god," Barney said in a rare television slip. He expelled the long breath. "This is too much, fans. Six-points-all."

Tillotston did not question the call. He simply started for the opposite end, as did Billy.

"You called that one, Brinkley," Chester said with a certain amount of respect. "Was that foolhardy and did he luck out?"

"I'm not so sure," I said slowly. And, on second thought, I was not. "With Tillotston standing in so close, he might easily have killed a normal second serve. Maybe the risk was the best choice."

"You mean the kid's got brains as well as that body?"

"Oh, yes," I said. "Brains were always one of the best shots in the Catlo repertoire."

They passed midway, continued to the opposite baselines. The ritual of the tie breaker proceeded. But not for long.

Billy held serve.

"Seven-six Catlo," the umpire said.

"Set point for Billy Catlo," Barney said into his mike.

The champion served. They exchanged forehand drives up the middle from the baseline. Then Tillotston, disguising, waiting until the last moment to commit himself, drilled a wickedly-angled crosscourt, sending Billy into the alley, took the crosscourt return and slammed it down the opposite line, seemingly unplayable. But Billy, on legs that were just as fast as in the first set, in a burst of speed was there. He feinted, then, as Tillotston moved crosscourt, crashed it back down the line. The ball skidded on the white, barely came off the clay and flew like a bullet toward the Stadium barrier. Tillotston was ten feet away from it. It was a breathtaking shot, a dominating shot. The crowd exploded to its feet in a tumult of applause.

"Game and third set to Catlo," the umpire sang. "Seven games to six. Tillotston leads two sets to one."

They crossed over. They sat and toweled off. I looked down at Jack Tillotston on his folding chair. He was sitting very straight, his feet flat on the clay. I remembered. I remembered Robert Catlo sitting that way in their long-ago match at Wimbledon to let the blood flow down into his legs.

19

THE ONE

NOW, AS THE BOY STOOD ON THE CLAY, I COULD SEE IT. THAT
rare thing that is the most moving moment in sport. *Is he the
one?* He stood there crouched and swaying on the baseline,
looking across the net at the greatest tennis player in the
world. There was no fear on the boy's face. There was no
longer even defiance. He was past defiance, past fear, past
doubt.

When had it happened? Surely it started with his decision
to continue play, that decision against all reason and common
sense, except that he made it be right. But it must have happened when that risk was taken, that ultimate risk of going
with the big serve on match point and getting away with it.
Not the point but the risk itself, a gambler's bet. A winner's
bet.

Now it came on like the sea in hurricane tide. A tide not
to be stemmed even when the champion held serve—barely,
taking three deuces to do it.

The boy took over. Blazing the ball across the net in a fury
of tennis shots. Owning the court. Holding his own serve and
then breaking the champion to go ahead at 2-1. Then on his
own serve coming quickly to 40-love.

The champion crouched to receive. No bouncing on the
toes now. All energy hoarded for the killer waves crashing
down on him from across the net. Jack Tillotston was tired.

Surely the boy ought to be tired too. Yet his supply of young energy seemed inexhaustible. The stamina of the champion was ebbing away, drained by sheer physical assault but also by pressure as the boy came at him with everything. How that last set must gnaw at Tillotston now. Not only for the losing of it but also for the way he lost.

The ball blew past him for a service ace. Three-1.

The champion to serve. Trying everything. Everything learned, mastered, refined in eight years of holding the throne of tennis against all comers. Forehand drives. Drop shots and lobs. Sidespins down the line. Touch placements. One had to admire the way he summoned all he knew about the game to repel the attack. But nothing worked. The boy was everywhere, all over the court, relentless—invincible. The champion was broken at 15. Billy Catlo at 4-1. Cross over.

The champion walked toward his folding chair beside the yellow refrigerator. When had his service last been broken twice in a row? Perhaps it was the racket. From his arsenal he selected a new one as though somehow a change of weapons might do it. He hesitated—then, slowly, laid it back down. It was beyond that.

He turned. He looked up at the flags waving from the Stadium rim as if there might be succor there. Indeed they were fluttering, as before. He looked up at the clouds. They were black and heavy. At the oak trees above our booth. Indeed their branches and leaves were rustling in the wind. He turned back, looked up again. This time at the umpire in the chair.

"It's too windy," he said. Our shotgun microphone picked it up. "How can you expect us to play decent tennis in this wind?"

The wind was about the same as when the match was resumed after that first interruption. When it was decided in council of players and officials that, though conditions were imperfect, tennis could still be played.

The boy was still in his chair, toweling off. Now the cross-over time was up. He stood and started for the opposite baseline, taking the two service balls from the ball boy. He was eager to play.

The champion did not move.

"Just a minute, Mr. Catlo," the umpire said.

The boy came back, still holding the service balls. The umpire descended from his perch. There were only the three of them now, standing there by the net post.

"Let me understand, Mr. Tillotston," the umpire said. "Are you asking for a postponement?"

"I'm saying it's too windy to play decent tennis." The champion was locked into that word.

The umpire raised his arm toward the Marquee. Presently a tall man was walking onto the court to join them.

"We've been through this," the referee Pat Hargraves said. "I thought we decided it was all right for tennis."

"That was then," Tillotston said. "It's worse now."

"Is it?" Hargraves looked up at the flags. He knew the wind had not changed. "Mr. Catlo, what do you think?"

No one ignored him like a ball boy now. No father was there. No girlfriend. The boy did not need anybody now.

He bounced a ball on the court, once, twice. He wasn't thinking about the playing conditions. He didn't care about them. Then he looked up, straight at the champion.

"It doesn't make any difference to me," he said. "I'm willing to let Mr. Tillotston decide."

It was almost exactly what the champion had said before. The knife was turned.

"Look, Jack," Hargraves said, "the *finals* are tomorrow—Sunday."

"Is there any law against playing the finals on Monday?" Tillotston said.

"You know what that means. The Sunday crowd, the Sunday television audience."

"That's too bad. Is that any reason we have to play in a windstorm?"

"Windstorm?"

Hargraves knew. He knew it was not the wind. If anything the wind was less now than before. What was bothering Jack Tillotston was beyond the elements and Hargraves knew it. But this man had been champion for eight years. For that he deserved something. Pat Hargraves could be a very tough man. But there was gentleness in his voice now, there was something very close to compassion.

"Come on, Jack," he said softly. "Let's play tennis."

Tillotston looked up from his racket. The two men looked straight into each other's eyes. Tillotston knew that Hargraves knew. The champion squared those big shoulders, then shrugged. Suddenly he laughed, that short, derisive laugh of his that seemed directed toward the world, or life, in general, as if everything in it was faintly ludicrous.

"All right, Pat. As a personal favor to you. And the Sunday television audience of course."

They went to their baselines. For one brief moment there was a resurgence in the champion. He fought Billy to a deuce on Billy's service before the boy took it at 5-1. Then Tillotston held his own service for 5-2. But that was it. Billy ran it out at 6-2.

"Game and fourth set to Catlo, six games to two," the umpire sang his litany. "Sets are two-all."

That fifth set. I had a spectral feeling watching that set. At one point I didn't know for a moment where I was. I seemed to be sitting not under black clouds coasting over the Stadium at Forest Hills but under sunny English skies. I was not watching a tennis match on something called Har-Tru but one on English grass. I was at Wimbledon.

But there was one difference from that match that defined the kind of champion this one would be. He did not humiliate the old champion. He did not put him on display, as that man had his father. His simply finished off the points as quickly as possible. Tillotston did not quit. He kept playing for it. But something had been taken out of him. On one crossover Chester Barney and I looked at each other, a long look. Saying nothing but saying everything. I saw it in his face, too, in his deep knowledge of tennis and of athletes. Jack Tillotston would win other sets, other matches, other tournaments. But he would never be the same. He had been beaten in the deepest way. By a will and a young daring stronger than his own. Beaten where it counts.

And how quick it was. Fourteen minutes only had gone by when Billy stood at 5-1, and waited, crouched, for Tillotston's serve. Four points to finish.

The crowd sat as silent as any I had ever seen. Jack Tillotston had not been a champion eight years out of weakness in extremis, out of any taste for surrender. Even now, serving that last game, he seemed to reach down into himself for some last reserve. He delivered three serves as big as anything he had sent across in that first set he had so dominated. All came raging back at him. He seemed baffled, uncomprehending. Love-40. Match point.

The champion toed the line in the ad court. He looked across the net at the boy crouched and swaying, his body low to the court. The champion rocked forward, rocked back. The ball rose, the racket came over. The ball came at the boy on its 130-mile-per-hour trajectory. It was a giant of a serve. It screamed over the net and split the intersection of the service and center lines, surely for an untouchable ace. From his down position the boy erupted out of his crouch, lunged and threw his body onto it. The ball exploded crosscourt. As he followed through, his body was straightened up, his cocked racket flung high across his body and over his head, a portrait of perfect tennis execution, a sculpture of grace, of beauty. The ball crossed the net with nothing to spare. Its angle to the net was no more than 20 degrees. Its speed was so great, its bounce so low, that it seemed hardly to rise from the line as it came off it and streaked toward the Marquee. The champion's racket did not move.

The crowd was on its feet, electrified. Its cheers and cries rocked the Stadium.

"Game, set and match to Catlo," the umpire sang his litany. "One-six, three-six, seven-six, six-two, six-one."

The boy and the man walked toward each other, met at the net. They shook hands across it. For one moment the old champion's hand touched the boy's shoulder, then fell away. They started toward the umpire's chair, the net between them.

Across the way I saw the young girl step down quickly from the box onto the mauled and mangled clay. Then she was running across it. I had never seen her run so fast. She went like a bullet, her white-blonde hair bouncing, slamming into his arms. I could see him holding her, her face smothered in his shoulder, his in her hair. They stood there for a moment. Then they turned. His arm around her shoulder, they started off the court.

The applause mounted. This crowd had seen tennis it would not forget. But in the applause there was something else too. A sense that the crowd had been present at something, present at the birth of a champion, of a name both old and new that the game would long know. And it had seen one thing more. It had seen a boy become a man.

Now from somewhere high in the stands a lone, clear cry rose into the afternoon grey.

"Ay, Catlo!"

The cry was picked up. Soon it was flooding down over the court in a cadenced, thousand-voiced chorus.

"Ay, Catlo! . . . Ay, Catlo! . . ."

As the cries swelled, the boy stopped and looked up. He looked all around the Stadium as the cries came down. Gravely he waved. Then, on his face I saw it. Seldom in my life had I seen that look. That look that enfolds one the moment he crosses over from what he was to what he has become. Not arrogance but confidence—and a certain loftiness. A sure knowledge of where he now stands, forever separated from us.

Then, borne on the cries, the boy continued across the court. As he reached the row of folding chairs he stopped.

He placed a hand on the girl's shoulder in a gesture to wait. Quickly he stepped out of his path, walked along the fake-geranium boxes to where his father was standing with the others. He embraced him. No words spoken. He stepped back, continued on to the Marquee.

But I was no longer watching the son. I was watching the father. I was watching Robert Catlo. There were tears on that proud man's face.

EPILOGUE

PIECES OF CAKE

THE CEREMONY WAS HELD IN THE LADY CHAPEL OF ST. Pat's. Robert Catlo was his son's best man and I gave the bride away. I never gave away anything so lovely. It was a small wedding, as they say on the society pages, the only others present being two fine ladies, Tish, as maid of honor, and Shelly. We stood bathed in the noon light shining through the tall, many-paneled stained glass windows, telling of the mysteries of the rosary, and it happened.

When we went outside there were three or four photographers from the sports pages. Billy and Lindy posed on the Cathedral terrace, the heaven-pointed spires behind them, an island of the spirit set down among the tall buildings for man's business. It was a grey and cloudy day, the first fragrance of autumn scenting the air.

At the Fifty-first Street curb, Edwards stood holding open the back door of the Silver Cloud, the original one that had made the gallant race against time in that tense twilight, now back, pristine as ever, from her brief scars. The saloon sparkled, its Spirit of Ecstasy figurehead silver-brilliant above the glistening radiator panels. Edwards handed Mrs. Billy Catlo into the back seat with the tender care of a man who might thus have installed a hundred brides off to new adventures. Then Shelly got in the back and then Billy, who sat between them, and then myself in front. Shelly had stayed over for the wedding and would be leaving for Washington shortly after Billy and Lindy left on honeymoon for the Tetons.

"La Guardia Airport, Edwards," Shelly said.

"The usual, madam?" Edwards said with a twinkle. "Or shall I see what she can do?"

"The usual this time, Edwards," Shelly said. "We don't have a match to make."

"I understand, madam," Edwards said. "There's just been a match."

We glided smooth as a dream crosstown, up the East River Drive and over the Triboro Bridge out of Manhattan. At the airport I walked the newlyweds into the terminal. We stood there waiting for the porter to bring the bags.

"Well, you did it," I said.

"What?" Billy said. "Oh. Yes." He looked gravely down at Lindy. "Yes. But only after I was in the money. It's clear she married me for the sixteen thousand five hundred," he said, speaking of the runner-up purse.

Billy had not won the finals. Ralph Graves beat him in five sets that lasted three hours and fifteen minutes. Billy was in there for every set and every game. When he finally walked off the court to receive the runner-up award, he got more applause than Graves. From the expressions on the faces of Catlo and Lindy, you might have thought he was already national champion. He wasn't, but as Chester Barney said into his microphone, "Wait till next year, fans. As they used to say in Brooklyn, wait till next year."

"It's true," Lindy said. "I married you entirely for the money. I didn't think I should tell you that until it was too late."

"When I said you did it," I said, "I was speaking of Tillotston. I was always sure about Lindy."

"Oh, Tillotston," Billy said, as if that had been a routine excursion. "What choice did I have? I had to save the family homestead. But he'll be back."

"So will you," I said.

"Yes, I'll be back." He had that confident air. Sure of himself and who he was. He was grown. Pretty much anyhow. "I'm going on the tour. Right after I attend to this one," he said, looking down at Lindy.

"Attend indeed. I'm going with you and we won't discuss it," she said firmly.

The porter was there with the bags. Billy went to the counter to get the tickets.

"Well," Lindy said brightly, looking up at me. "Well!"

She looked so perfect, radiant yet at peace, excited yet quiet, and absolutely sure about where she was headed and knowing she wanted to go there, knowing she could handle it. Serene. I wondered if that marvelous young love of theirs would survive the life that Billy was going to have to lead on the circuit as an obvious tennis superstar. I thought it would. She had such infallible instincts that I thought it would. She would keep him together. He would never be as grown as she.

"It couldn't have turned out better," I said. "Of course, Billy had some help. I think you really settled him down."

"Well, I did what I could," she said thoughtfully.

"Yes," I said. "I'm sure you did everything you could."

She looked up at me, her head cocked a little in that intent, concentrating way I had from the first found so funny, so charming.

"Everything?" she said. "What do you mean by that?"

"Why, I don't mean anything special."

"I'll just bet you don't."

For one moment I thought she might tell me. Then Billy was standing there with the tickets. I knew she would never tell even me. Really, I thought we had more freedom of the press in this country than that. I would never know whether you should or you shouldn't if you want to win in tennis. Sorry.

The airline public relations people had put her in a place

called the "V.I.P. Holding Room," of all things, where "Celebrities" could escape the common flesh while awaiting their planes. We sat across a tiny table and had Camparis. When the plane was called I took out of my pocket the exquisite little velvet case stamped "Cartier's" in subdued gold letters and handed it to her. She opened it and the pleasure on her face made the deed worth fortunes. It should have. I had never spent that much money on anything.

"You must have got this with your first television money."

"And my last. I'm only a print man, I discovered. But after all it was windfall money."

"I happen to know Fred made you an offer," she said. "Put it on me."

I stood up, walked behind her and put it around her neck and clasped it. I sat down and looked at her wearing it. It was perfectly smooth, apple-green jade, about 2 by 1½ inches, hand-carved long ago to an oval lump, set in 18-karat gold . . . $10,012 including tax. The twelve came out of my own pocket. I liked to think of it hanging there between her God-carved apple-white breasts.

"How lovely it is," she said, looking down at it. "I'll have to buy a lot of V-necks so you can see it on the show. I love the feel of it."

Her fingers moved over its surface. "Whenever you tune in and see me do this, you'll know I want you very much."

Then the fingers came across the table and into my hand.

"I wonder if I'll ever know if it was the right thing to do," she said.

"I think it is. It seems like having your cake and . . . well, you know."

"Maybe," she said. There was doubt in that word.

She had told them finally that she would take the new-job, new-network offer but on one condition. It had to be in Washington, not New York. Washington was what she knew.

"You have your cake. In Washington, one show a week,"

I said. "And you never again have to get up at five. You can date like other girls."

"Maybe," she said again. "The only thing is, I'm leaving the best piece of the cake behind in New York. Do you know what a nice piece of cake you are, Brinkley?"

"Well, you're a pretty good piece yourself."

"Speaking of other girls. You'll watch out for those young girls, won't you? I know those young girls in New York."

"Not a chance. I stopped picking green fruit when I grew up. I prefer my fruit ripe."

"I'm not *that* ripe."

Her fingers came around mine and squeezed them hard, holding tightly to them, as if for reassurance.

"Brinkley," she said, "I don't want to cry."

"Eastern shuttle flight," the p.a. was saying. "Departing for Washington, D.C. Last call."

Her fingers came away and lightly rubbed the jade pendant once more. "It'll be our talisman," she said. "It'll always bring me back to you."

She stood up. I walked her to the gate and we stood there a moment. Now and then a head turned and looked at her in recognition.

"I wonder who the smart ones really are," she said. "I almost wish we were Billy and Lindy. Doing what they did, going where they're going."

"I know."

Out the windows we could see a fine rain starting to come down.

"Why is it always raining when we say good-bye?" She came suddenly into my arms. "Hold me. That was always the best part."

I held her, tight, hard. I would never stop wanting her.

"Well, at least the second best," I said.

"Brinkley?"

"Yes?"

"I still may want to reassess my priorities."

She turned quickly and was gone through the gate. I started to go up to the observation deck to watch her plane taxi out and take off, as I always did. Then I decided I couldn't do that. She was always taxiing out of my life and I didn't want to watch it again. I would wait until some other plane brought her back to me, sometime. I walked away.

Edwards was standing at ease by the Silver Cloud. When he saw me coming he stepped up smartly and opened the back door.

"Do you mind if I ride in front with you?" I said. I felt too lonely to sit alone in a back seat. Especially that back seat.

"Certainly, sir."

He opened the front door and I got in. We moved out into the traffic toward the city. A September mist hung down from the New York sky.

"What will you do next?" I said.

"I never know, sir. The only thing I don't like about this job is that I have different clients and they vary. They're here today and gone tomorrow. I'd like to have just one all the time. You get used to one."

"Yes, I know," I said.

"In London I always worked for The Quality. Here sometimes I do and sometimes I don't. I'd like to have just one. Like Miss Blaine. She's The Quality. All the way through. You can always tell."

The rain began to pick up, slashing across the windshield. Edwards switched on the wipers. Through the half-circle clearing, I could see the skyscrapers coming into view, ranks of tall ghosts standing in the sky mists. We were crossing the bridge into Manhattan.

"Yes, she is," I said. "You can always tell."